PACIFIC HEIGHTS

PACIFIC HEIGHTS

S. R. WHITE

HEADLINE

First published in 2025 by
Headline Publishing Group Limited

1

Cataloguing in Publication Data is available from the British Library

Trade Paperback ISBN 9781035426546

Typeset in 12.29/16.68 pt Adobe Garamond Pro by Jouve (UK), Milton Keynes

Printed and bound in Great Britain by Clays Ltd, Elcograf S.p.A.

Headline's policy is to use papers that are natural, renewable and recyclable
products and made from wood grown in well-managed forests and other
controlled sources. The logging and manufacturing processes are expected
to conform to the environmental regulations of the country of origin.

Headline Publishing Group Limited
An Hachette UK Company
Carmelite House
50 Victoria Embankment
London EC4Y 0DZ

The authorised representative in the EEA is Hachette Ireland,
8 Castlecourt Centre, Dublin 15, D15 XTP3, Ireland (email: info@hbgi.ie)

www.headline.co.uk
www.hachette.co.uk

This book is dedicated to my father, Ray, who taught me the value of public service, and much else besides.

'I don't define the human eye as a camera. It's the starting gun for interpretation, error and prejudice. It can't be trusted.'

Chapter 1

Buildings are supposed to endure. They are built to withstand the vicissitudes of everyday life, the vagaries of heat and drenching rain, the basic carelessness of humans. If they're lucky they are cared for, as a mark of the symbiotic nature of the relationship – shelter in return for respect. They become cherished, appreciated. More often, they are seen by the occupants as simply a giant appliance; a generic set of boxes to be used and abused as people see fit. Those buildings look pained – you can see their anguish in the decay of wood and stone, the untreated blemishes of paint and plaster. You can tell, in fact, what people think of a building by the condition it's in. One glance would prove that the apartment block of Pacific Heights was in sad, mournful decline.

The district of Windoo was just scraping into upper-middle class; the coffee shops were independents or higher-end franchises, boutiques 'neglected' to carry price tags on their wares, courtesy electric chargers stood sentinel for locals to top up the Tesla. The trees were trimmed before delivery trucks and street-washing vehicles could give them a clout. People aspired to live here at *some point* in their lives, for a few years, but not for too long. It was a suburb that existed as a life phase for singles and couples; they who would later move on to districts with more greenery and less street art, gardens not courtyards, garages not bike racks. Many recalled it simply as a place that they *used to live in*; back then they were okay with shared houses, mattresses on milk crates, splitting the electric bill and not owning a car. Scuffles outside the Lebanese takeaway hadn't been a cause to dial triple-zero; they'd been a colourful and vivid part of urban life. Windoo had moved up but they'd moved on.

Human traffic tailed off here after midnight, when the last of the cafés and restaurants along Longman Street packed it in. Taxis didn't bother to forage and the council dimmed the streetlights to save the planet. Windoo looked in slumber because it was: too late to be kicked out of a bar, too early to be jogging. The only lights glowing on Longman were from the night baker, who stole a smoko every thirty minutes as a legitimate perk, and the Night Owl, where the cashier fell asleep over engineering textbooks. Occasional distant sirens from the nearby expressway crackled in small snaps of sound between the buildings. Possums scuttled across rooftops and bats flitted through the looping electric wires: thieves coursing through the district's exoskeleton.

It was not a night for murder. Some nights were – steaming, humid nights where the air fizzed with tension and expectation, when every minor dispute seemed to raise itself beyond threat and bluster. But not this night; it was calm, placid and safe.

Until it wasn't.

Chapter 2

City West Police Station. Thursday, 0351hrs

They sat on opposite sides of the office while the superintendent's assistant clacked the keyboard and tried not to smirk. If she was fed up with night shifts like this, she hid it behind a fastidiously elegant appearance. Lachie adjusted his collar yet again, feeling the fetid air; Bluey exhibited a Zen-like calm, tracing the patterns in the carpet. Jasmine had seen 'em come and go: lambs to the slaughter, human sacrifices. These offices were for the ritual disembowelling of careers, spilled blood to appease gods of media and *moving on*. At last a scratchy bark escaped from the superintendent's inner sanctum and Jasmine gave a quiet nod. Bluey smiled and politely let Lachie through the door first.

Superintendent Laxton sat ramrod-straight in his chair, a blotter in front of him. No one needed a blotter these days; it was somewhere to rest the coffee that wouldn't leave rings on the desk surface. He glared at each of them in turn.

'You're up for that murder on the west side. Windoo. Know why you're on the case?'

'Next cab off the rank?' Lachie had surreptitiously lip-read as the two detectives stood sentinel, awaiting official instruction. Now he offered a view that he knew would be strafed. He could smell furniture polish in the air. Cops who did military service first – everything spick and span; perpendicular corners, starchy collars and manners. Outside, it was still dark. Desk-lamp reflections in the black window caught his eye.

Laxton frowned.

'*Last* cab, more like it. We've had another drive-by overnight, up at Mission Plains this time. Two dead, including some poor bastard selling hot dogs, for Christ's sake. Plus a teenager who's on life support because he chose that exact half a second to pass a restaurant.'

He sighed, as though the two detectives were personally responsible for organised crime's recent dickhead-on-dickhead rampages. The new deaths made nine in three weeks – all gang-related in some way, adding another layer of feverish fear on to a population already wearying of it. Collateral damage – innocent people dead – was energising the media.

'Commissioner's screaming, papers are whinging, socials are off the charts. Everyone I rate highly is on those gangland killings because it's all out of control.'

Bluey swallowed, anticipating. It was never nice to know exactly how far down the pecking order you were.

Laxton gave a meaningful glare. 'So I don't have time to be fussy about who deals with this other homicide and I don't have time to be a bloody childminder, either. You, Bluey' – he pointed to Carl Blewson – 'are on this because you have twenty-five years as a detective and you can't have forgotten everything yet. You, Lachie' – he pointed to Lachlan Dyson – 'are on this because Bluey isn't allowed a gun. One brain and one pair of hands should be enough. I mean, there are eyewitnesses, boys. *More than one.* Don't screw it up and don't make me chase you.'

Laxton leaned in, as though he needed to shoulder-charge the message.

'I don't like the phrase "last-chance saloon" but, bugger me, if the cap fits, eh? Bluey, you know what grazing in pasture feels like. Expect to go back there if you're not an investigative asset. People tell me you're off the pace, mate. Prove 'em wrong. Prove me wrong. And as for you' – he glared at Lachie – 'well, you had to pay a prosecutor's laundry bill, didn't ya? Organisations don't like runaway horses or people who don't know how to shut up. HR knows how to deal with problems like you.'

Lachie gave a subtle nod.

Laxton sighed. 'Alrighty, you can bog off now.'

His fuming belligerence ushered them out of the door. They were in the corridor before they glanced at each other.

'Charm school should have given him a refund,' muttered Bluey.

Lachie smiled at the floor. 'Would it make you feel better to know he has a fine singing voice?'

'Not really. We should do the formals, I guess. Carl Blewson. Bluey.' They shook hands as they walked.

'Lachlan Dyson. Lachie. Good briefing that, eh? Chock-full of data.'

Bluey nodded. Lachlan Dyson. *Die-in-a-ditch Dyson.* Bluey had been told no one wanted to work with Lachie because the young detective had a high-and-mighty approach to ethics: no wiggle room and no common sense, recently suspended because he wouldn't back down. Oh, and he was deaf as a post, apparently. Wore a hearing aid. Correction; a cochlear implant. Which implied that he only got in the force because his dad is an assistant commissioner. Bluey had heard all that as soon as he mentioned he was paired up with Lachie. Brilliant. Bound to be a politics-free zone, then.

Bluey Blewson, thought Lachie. Fifty-something; apparently out in never-never land until his pension kicks in and he can officially take up golf. They took firearms off anyone over fifty-five these days: some uni in Melbourne did a study and it turned out the old mates' reflexes were too slow to be safe. Still, Lachie could have done worse. No one had actually slagged off Bluey – which was practically unheard of in City West – and he'd seemingly done well last month in a case for another district.

The tortoise and the harebrained. They made one good detective between them. Maybe.

'Apparently the body's still in situ,' offered Lachie. 'Medical examiner's stuck out at Mission Plains.'

The gangland killings were being laid squarely at the force's door. For years the public had heard little from the assorted gangs that once dominated the city – organised crime had been sufficiently disorganised.

Then the drive-by shootings began: a shopping mall, a KFC, a kids' footie game. Now everyone knew the names of the leaders, who held which neighbourhood, and how much those gangs made from drugs, vice, illicit gambling, tobacco and vaping. In truth, the state government had rolled back restrictions on gang members associating and this had driven their renaissance. But nuance, not truth, was the first casualty of war.

'Good,' replied Bluey, pressing the lift button. 'I prefer to see the scene as fresh as possible, don't you?'

Not really, thought Lachie, though he kept silent. He considered visiting the scene to be largely a waste of time, except to direct uniform so they didn't miss anything obvious. Most constables these days had enough forensic awareness not to actually screw up the scene. Witnesses could be made to come to them; in fact, that often intimated them into further information. He thought it was all a bit of an ego trip; the almighty detective showing up and bustling in, stopping everyone mid-tracks, then crouching by the victim and ostentatiously glancing about. The optics fed the ego, but also carried an implication that uniform needed to be in a crèche.

Bluey waved a desultory hand at Lachie's iPad. 'How's about you drive that and tell me what we have, and I'll drive the car?'

Lachie had heard that Bluey was a petrolhead and thought it a reasonable division of labour. Even so he had a pop, out of a sense of obligation. 'Technology a bit tricky for your generation, Gramps?'

Bluey eye-rolled. 'My generation built this country. Your generation just live in it.'

The crime scene lay a few clicks to the west of the station in the older suburb of Windoo. At four in the morning traffic was just starting up – the earliest of early tradies and the last of some night shifts. The tradies were gunning it in utes while the shifters were crawling home in battered sedans. Bluey took them past two servos where the cashier looked either completely asleep or a fentanyl victim, then past a crew just beginning to section off a road for some crane work. Normally Bluey liked driving this early in the day – it felt vaguely special, as though you were part of a small, select club who were up that early. But he already had a sinking feeling that this murder investigation wasn't easy. Though, he reflected, everyone clearly thought it was; they'd be on his hammer if it wasn't cleared quickly.

Lachie pecked and swiped until he was sure of his ground.

'So . . . yeah, okay. The victim is Tahlia Moore. Twenty-seven, waitress at What's Brewin', a coffee shop about two hundred metres from her unit. Discovered at 3.21 this morning in the courtyard of her apartment block on Reed Street. Early indications: no signs of a struggle, one stab wound to the chest, potential bruising on the skull, maybe hit her head on the way down. Tahlia lives alone – there's a sister, but apparently she's off doing a gap year.'

'Who found the body?'

There was an ominous pause. Then: 'Oh, Jesus.'

Bluey risked a glance across. 'He found it? How? Is he back again?'

'Haha. Yeah, it's just –' Lachie shuffled in his seat. 'Mate, it's Reuben Pearce.'

Bluey gave a quiet whistle. 'Please tell me it's another Reuben Pearce who's a totally nice bloke.'

Lachie shook his head. 'Nah. It's that one.'

Ah. Bluey swallowed and gave the revelation its due. Reuben Pearce. Undoubtedly more of an issue for Lachie than for him, but even so. Word would pinball around and the optics of how they played this would be reported – more or less accurately – in every police canteen and station in the state.

'Weren't you suspended for . . .' Bluey let the words hang.

'Yeah, yeah I was. We had a meeting with the prosecutors, going over evidence for discovery, that sort of thing. I might have expressed a strong opinion.'

'Which was?'

'That dear Reuben should go to prison for a long time for what he did. For the effect it has on others. I misread the room though, didn't I? All those people who agreed with me in private: they just shut up when the moment came and left me swingin'. Prosecution was preparing to soft-pedal the whole thing to make it go away – the minister was embarrassed by his first hot take and it's getting near election time. I was, uh, probably a bit strong with *how* I said it.'

Not to mention where, thought Bluey. Lachie was, so the rumour factory told it, about thirty centimetres from the prosecutor's face when he gave it all the hairdryer treatment. Spittle-on-the-suit close.

'I'm going to suggest that I deal with Reuben, when it comes to it,' said Bluey.

Lachie nodded. 'Fair enough. So yeah, Reuben found Tahlia in the courtyard. By the time he called it in we'd already had a triple-zero from someone else in the building. Lady by the name of Bryony Price. Then a couple more calls came in about the same thing, but uniform and paramedics were already up and about.'

Bluey shrugged. 'Our charming boss did mention witnesses.'

'Yeah, uniform started canvassing the locals soon after.'

Bluey negotiated a mini-roundabout before a burbling 70s Ford got there. 'You'd be lucky to get five people awake at three in the morning. How many live in the whole block?'

'Uh, fifty-six apartments, so I'm guessing a hundred-plus. Some of them would be kids, though.'

'Still, as Laxton said, *eyewitnesses*. How can we go wrong with that, Lachie?'

Lachie grunted. 'You've got some experience with Laxton, have you?'

'A bit. Back when I was part of the team.' Bluey stifled an urge to talk about his departure: it still felt wrong. 'Laxton was army first, for a while, then about fifteen years across the border before he transferred here, so he came from interstate. You know what Laxton's nickname was, when he first arrived? *Thrombo*. As in, a slow-moving clot.'

Lachie sniggered. 'Is he any faster now?'

'Not really. He's all right, I suppose, but media pressure gets him in a panic. That's why he's frothing now. Okay with any other sort of pressure, but he hates seeing his name associated with bad news. He's obsessed with socials like he's twelve years old. So it's probably best if we can keep this case off everyone's radar. Ah, here we go.'

Chapter 3

The apartment block – Pacific Heights – was a long way from the ocean and a long way past its best. Built in the 80s with a breezy aesthetic and a sense that three palm trees made anything 'tropical', its cladding panels had faded from dazzling orange to dust-flecked tan. A small orchard of satellite dishes on the flat roof were rusted and forlorn. The ground-floor windows were coated in various forms of powdery disdain – exhaust soot, construction dust, fallen slivers of plaster – and the ground strewn with fast-food wrappers and discarded bottles. The complex was all organised in a crude doughnut – *perhaps elliptical*, thought Bluey as they parked outside – around a large courtyard.

They entered the building into a hallway that ran through to the open space beyond. It needed painting and, Bluey observed, someone to care enough to scrape the spiderwebs off the ceiling. Scratched walls implied that deliveries bulldozed through, ricocheting off the plasterboard. A notice carried a smeared message about an upcoming fire drill. Pizza-delivery leaflets hung from the mailboxes like the tongues of thirsty dogs. A trolley for carrying large items to and fro sat, battered and bruised, below the stairs. The lighting was harsh and it flickered.

Into the courtyard and the view changed. The complex stretched up four or five storeys, the roofline framing the night sky. To the left was a small kidney-shaped swimming pool surrounded by black metal fencing of legal height; the sort of half-arsed pool that was there because the developer felt obliged. A couple of palm fronds and a cockroach shimmered on the surface in the breeze. Four bushy trees, around five metres tall, clung to each other near the shallow end. Next to that was a children's play area, seemingly underpinned by that spongy surface they made from recycled sports shoes. The sandpit held a lonesome Steeden someone had kicked there and a kid's plastic spade. Five concrete mushrooms, each the height of a decent dog, formed a circle. A swing, a slide, a small roundabout and a couple of metal structures that Bluey initially thought was a bike rack but then realised was an 'outdoor gym': not his area of expertise.

On the other side of the courtyard was a barbecue area with some white plastic furniture; some of the chairs were tipped on their side. The brick-work around the barbie was chipped, as if people were perennially striking it with a shovel. The palm trees looked as though someone had slapped them: unkempt fronds clung tenaciously. The key area was taped off and a white tent erected to shield the body. Lachie took a 360 and saw plenty of lights on; some residents were sitting on their balcony now, wrapped in a snuggly onesie or a blanket, sipping a coffee and pointing their phones. Someone's tragic death was everyone else's direct messaging.

Lachie called over a uniformed constable carrying a clipboard. The clasp glinted from an arc light to his left, creating a glare that was metal-lic and intrusive. The constable was short and slightly dumpy, a frizz of ginger hair over clumps of freckles and a frown.

'Are you the detectives?' he asked.

Lachie waved a badge. Bluey had drifted back towards the entrance.

The constable scribbled with a pen and then checked his watch. 'Formal handover to SIO, 4.09 a.m. Can you sign here, please, sir?'

Lachie signed, his left hand scrunching into a horrible crab position that made the constable wince. Lachie noted the name: Constable Tyson Richards.

'Someone on to the next of kin yet?'

Tyson nodded. 'Officer from City West informed the mother ten min-utes ago – she'll have to come in to do the full ID. Father's deceased, apparently.'

'Okay, Tyson, talk me through what I've missed.'

The wording was deliberate. Tyson could merely go through the motions, or he could prove he had a bit of spark and demonstrate some initiative. The choice would help Lachie to calibrate how much use the bloke was going to be.

'First call at 3.21 on the triple-zero. Bryony Price. Old lady lives on the top floor to the right, there.'

Lachie swivelled and saw a muted light from the centre of the top floor. The sky beyond remained jet black: it wasn't near enough to dawn to see a purple tinge in the east. 'That's . . . north, right?'

Tyson frowned. 'Not sure, sir. I'll get a map of where each apartment is, shall I?'

'Yeah, consider that job number one.' At first glance, Bryony Price's view of the dead body would be partly obscured by the roof of the barbie area, though she'd have a clear sight of each doorway on to the courtyard. 'Sorry, I interrupted you, mate.'

Tyson swallowed and resumed. 'Two minutes later, a second call about the dead body, from Reuben Pearce. He's . . .'

'Yeah, *that one*. I know. Where's he live?'

Tyson aimed his pen at a ground-floor apartment; a small terrace dominated by three large potted palms and a clothes line that was drying some beach towels. Two figures sat on metal chairs on the terrace.

'There. He rang from, well, the middle, here. Said the woman was in his arms and she wasn't breathing. They said he should try mouth-to-mouth.'

The two figures were too distant to make out in this light; Lachie felt Reuben's presence by instinct. He tried to suppress it, but his cynical side burst through. *Of course he'd do that, if he'd killed her. Make sure there was a legitimate reason for her blood all over him, for her fibres to be on his clothes. 'Course he would.*

'There's an officer with him, right?'

'Yes, sir. Constable Radcliffe. With him at all times.'

'Yeah, okay. Good. Who else called?'

'Jody Marks. Second floor, on the left, there, with the red lamp in the window.'

And those four bushy trees between him and the victim, thought Lachie, who was already trying to calculate logistics and angles.

'Oh, and last one: old mate on the ground floor behind you. Martyn Brooks. He wasn't sure what he'd seen.'

No; the swings, roundabout and half a mushroom saw to that, Lachie reflected.

'All right. Paramedics still around?'

'I asked them to wait. They're just outside on the parkland side, through there.' Tyson wielded the pen again, aiming at the other doorway to the courtyard. Lachie could see the blue pulses from the ambulance reflected on the stucco wall of the entrance. Tyson wasn't half bad, it seemed.

'Please tell me there's CCTV on this place.'

Tyson shook his head. 'Yes and no. There's a camera over each entrance, pointed in at the courtyard. One of those convex jobbies that takes in a complete 180. But the wiring's floatin' in the wind so maybe they're not recording. Was the first thing I asked. I've got a call in to Ivory Security, but nothing back yet.'

Their lack of response to an emergency situation probably reflected their brilliance in general maintenance. *Bloody hell*, thought Lachie: *those cameras would have seen everything*. Tyson tried to soften the blow.

'I've got the caretaker here; she might know about the cameras. Name's . . . ah, here, Sally Harris. Over there, on the mushroom.'

They both looked to one of the five psychedelically decorated mushrooms next to the playground. Sally Harris had a shock of coloured hair – maybe blue, hard to see in the half-light – and wore some kind of overall or jumpsuit. She sat, elbows on knees, wiping angrily at her eyes with a sleeve.

Lachie could see Bluey strolling towards them. He turned to Tyson.

'Okay. We're probably going to talk to the eyewitnesses first. Go and tell Sally she'll have to wait a bit longer. See if there's a scale plan of this place – would save us making our own. Then wait for us; we'll be needing you to navigate around a bit. Okay?'

'Sir.' Tyson was crisp, and Lachie was happy with him already.

Bluey took a deep breath as he joined Lachie. 'Thank God a sensible constable turned up and controlled the scene.' They were variable, he knew.

'Paramedics first?' offered Lachie.

'Just spoken to 'em. Thought I'd work outside-in, as it were. Nothing too amazing. They got a call of a woman collapsed and unconscious – nothing much more than that. They were updated en route that she wasn't breathing and had an injury. Had to wait to get through the outer door: no one likes intrusions into their apartment building in the dead of night. Eleven minutes from first call to touching the victim, so 3.32 when they got to her. Tahlia was on the ground, no pulse, no breathing. Reuben was standing next to her. Blood on him – front of his clothes, mainly. He'd tried mouth-to-mouth. Nothing worked on Tahlia, obviously. Reuben seemed shaken but aware; gave good details, offered to help.'

Lachie tried to picture the scene unravelling. 'Was Reuben ever out of their sight?'

Bluey nodded, liking Lachie's direction of travel and his speed.

'Yeah, I wanted to know that. Apparently, when the two paramedics were working on Tahlia, Reuben went and wedged the doors open between the courtyard and the ambulance. They can't swear it was only a minute; might have been longer.'

Both detectives were thinking about a man disposing of a bloody knife. Drains were popular, as was an almighty throw into the nearest set of bushes. They were thinking *search perimeter*; both calculated at least two hundred metres.

Bluey added fifty for luck. 'Two hundred and fifty metres, to be on the safe side?'

'Yeah,' replied Lachie. 'Although, he could have got rid of the weapon before anyone made a call. In which case, wherever.'

'Assuming Reuben's not just a good Samaritan who did the right thing.'

Lachie blinked twice. 'Yeah. Assuming that.'

Bluey was sure that Lachie was aware of the danger of leaping to conclusions: they hadn't even sighted the body yet, or talked to any witnesses. And yet . . . what Reuben Pearce had done – what he was notorious for – swept that caution away. Reuben was a proven liar. Famous for it. Known to be an unreliable narrator of anything that happened around him. It was hard to ignore that; Lachie wasn't trying.

Tyson came back from speaking to Sally Harris.

'She's got some scale plans in the switch room, she thinks; she can get us a copy once we've spoken to her.'

Bluey offered a hand. 'Carl Blewson. Call me Bluey, like the dog.'

Tyson shook hands and nodded. Bluey regarded the caretaker, whose foot tapped anxiously on the ground. 'Did Sally there know the victim?'

'I think so, si—Bluey. She's pretty shaken, anyway.'

Both detectives pondered for a second, whether to push Sally up the list. Bluey shook his head.

'Nah, let's give her a few minutes to compose herself, eh?'

Lachie turned to Tyson. 'I fancy meeting that bloke from the second floor over there.'

'Jody Marks?'

'That's the one. Lead on, mate.'

Chapter 4

Pacific Heights apartment block.
Apartment 32. Thursday, 0415hrs

They filed in through the door and caught the lift up to the second floor. Like all lifts, the lighting made them look like ninety-year-old zombies; even Tyson. The corridor stretched for maybe thirty metres before turning right. It smelled of settled, slightly brackish air, as though no one had passed through it recently. Lachie tried to get the geography of the building fixed in his brain – he could already sense that it would matter – and noticed that the apartment numbers held no logic.

Tyson knocked and they waited patiently, eventually hearing soft footsteps and the double-clack of the lock. Jody peeped out from behind the security chain. They all noticed that Jody looked like he would in the lift: pale, dishevelled, bloodless. Bluey waved his ID. Jody opened the door and stepped back.

Entering the apartment, Lachie swept a look around the place. He could see the edge of a mattress in the next room but Jody appeared to be sleeping on the sofa – a crushed pillow was wedged into the armrest and the doona was slopped on to the floor. Two large bottles of water rested on the coffee table; Jody held a smaller one in a cradled left arm, which he hugged close to himself. One table lamp had to illuminate the whole room; the red bulb by the window gave almost no light at all. The TV was on but paused; baseball from the USA. Tyson deposited himself right by the front door, hands clasped in front of him, and watched the three of them. Lachie kept one eye on Jody's left arm: there was enough space between elbow and stomach for a weapon.

Lachie wanted to cross straight away to the window. This apartment had no balcony: the large window was open, hinged at the top, and Lachie could hear the murmur of movement down in the courtyard. But instead of crossing the room he remained near the front door, intrigued and worried by Jody Marks. Sometimes body language hinted, rather than told. There was something off about Jody, but it wasn't certain if that was benign or dangerous.

The man wouldn't look at them. He shuffled his feet in barren, aimless movements, achieving nothing. That arm, seemingly welded to his flank: he switched on the ceiling light with his right, the movement unnecessarily awkward. His breathing – short, stuttering, needy snatches of air, as though he was either deeply exhausted or highly stressed. Or both. It was possible that he'd seen the whole incident, so Lachie didn't discount the shock of that. But, all the same, Jody felt evasive.

Jody swigged the water, careless of the spilled drops, and wiped his mouth; again, all with his right arm. His sweatshirt had damp patches under the arms and the moobs; the humidity in here was stifling. Bluey focused on the kitchen, where a loaf of bread had been opened up and several plates stacked in the sink. Next to the bread was a minor Manhattan of pill bottles. He glanced at Jody, who looked away, and went to the counter. He read the bottle labels while Lachie moved carefully to the main window; the two detectives had split and Jody couldn't watch both of them at once. Bluey liked that they'd each done that out of instinct.

Lachie began assessing what Jody Marks could have seen from this position, and whether that was making him behave this way.

'Can't you sleep tonight, Mr Marks?' Lachie opened the discussion.

Jody twitched. 'Can't . . . sleep . . . *atall*.' Three sparse stabs of words, punctuated by further grabby little breaths. Still he wouldn't move his left arm from his body, as though he held something trapped yet precious.

'No sleep? None at all? Not even a doze?'

Jody shook his head. Bluey turned and held up one of the bottles.

'Anti-inflammatories. Various attempts at toast. Compulsive water-guzzling. Painkillers.' He paused. 'Kidney stone, yeah?'

Relief flooded Jody's face, as though he didn't really have the problem until someone else spoke it out loud.

'Yeah. Hurts like a mother. You had one?'

'I did, couple of years back. When I was nineteen I fell off my motor-bike and fractured six ribs. That hurt less than a kidney stone.' He spoke more to Lachie and Tyson than to Jody. 'Just bloody constant, all day and all night, for nearly a week. Can't reduce it, can't reason with it; doesn't matter what you do. No painkiller gets within cooee; not unless they give you the green whistle, which they won't do if you're at home, eh?' He turned back to Jody.

'Bloody right.' Another quick swig. 'Just walk round and round the unit, drinking water. Trankies are bloody hopeless.'

Bluey waggled the bottle of anti-inflammatories in his hand. 'True, but you have to maintain these, mate. They're the *real* lifesavers. They keep the tubes open for the thing to pass, even if they do make you puke.'

'Exactly. Can't keep anything down' – Jody pointed to the kitchen – 'not even bloody toast. I'm losing two kilos a day here.'

'The good news is that passing the last couple of centimetres isn't as painful as you'd reckon. And then?' Bluey spread his hands like a preacher offering salvation. 'Miracle. Every bit of pain disappears instantly. You won't believe how quick.'

Jody grunted. 'Bloody hope so. It's been nearly four days.'

'Almost there, then. Stick with the anti-inflammatories, they're your best friend. How about you keep walking and drinking and we have a chat about what you can see from your window, yeah?'

Jody took a swig and began pacing out a small circle by the sofa. Tyson adjusted his stance by three millimetres and looked on. Bluey nodded to Lachie and the questions resumed.

'Had you actually fallen asleep, Mr Marks?'

'Didn't think so, but yeah, I must have done. I woke up 'cos I thought I heard a scream. You know, like you do – not sure if you're dreaming it and all? So, I waited. I dunno why I needed to, but until I heard the second one I just lay there.'

'The scream – male, female, short, long?'

'The first one? Quite short, I think. Sounded girlie but, you know, hard to tell. Like, sometimes people sit out there and get pissed, have a little party. The oldies around here hate that. You hear squeals and screams but you know it's just people buggering about, it's not serious. This one sounded serious from the get-go.'

'Any sounds in between the two screams?'

'Nah, I . . . I thought there was a siren, like fireys or something, but that seemed a distance away. I didn't get up until the second scream.'

'The second scream sounded serious to you?'

'Oh yeah, no mistaking that. Stumbled a bit getting to the window.'

'Was the window open, like it is now?'

'Yeah, always is when I sleep on the couch, eh? Yeah, so I looked through the blinds.'

Lachie pointed to the carpet.

'Standing exactly here?'

'To start with, but the trees got in the way a bit. I tried over to the right there, up against the bin, but it wasn't really any better.'

Lachie moved across to the edge of the window and looked again. Jody was right; the view barely improved. The foliage was thick and the shape of the trees – like a giant ball on a stick – impaired visibility. You could see someone's lower half, but their upper body would be obscured. He turned back again as Jody swallowed more water.

'What happened next?'

'There was someone holding up someone else, like they were drunk, or unconscious. They might have shouted after the scream. Can't say for sure. Anyways, they kinda lowered the person to the ground. For sure they needed paramedics at that point.'

'Could you make out the person on the ground?'

'The one crouching over them hid 'em a bit. Wearing jeans, I think. Weren't moving.'

'And the crouching person?'

'Yeah, not jeans. One-piece something; tracksuit, something like that? All dark colours, anyway. They were facing away from me and the light was crap. Couldn't see their head; they were bent over.'

Maddening fragments, thought Lachie. 'Next?'

'Oh, yeah, so then I turned away to find my phone. Bloody thing was caught up in the doona, took me a few seconds to find it. I came back to the window as I was dialling.'

'And?'

'And that other person was gone. Just . . . not there any more. Whoever it was, they were still on the ground, but the other one had disappeared. I looked at the two exits: the one on the left, the west one, the door was still swinging shut. So I guess they went that way, but I wouldn't know why. I started speaking to the operator. I could see a light up there, across the way. Top floor. She's a nosy old bugger, Bryony, so I wasn't that surprised. She's got binoculars; she might be worth a chat.'

'You weren't incapacitated by the pain at this point?'

'Yeah, nah, well, sort of. I mean, the adrenaline was going, wasn't it? Then the kidney stone kicked back in a bit. I had to come across here to get some water. When I got back, there was someone with the . . . the body again. Holding it up. Bloke this time, for sure. Yeah, he was on his phone and holding the body with one arm. Then he put the phone down and started mouth-to-mouth.'

'Can you describe the person?'

'The bloke? Yeah, it's him from across the way, isn't it? Reuben Pearce. We all know that bastard. Got that stupid perm last month because he *claims* he doesn't like being recognised. So I knew it was him. He must have come out of his apartment – he's ground floor, eh?'

'Did you actually see him come out of his apartment and cross the courtyard?'

'Well, nah. Okay, no, I didn't see that. But you know, it's obvious.'

'Did the person you're sure is Reuben look like the person who'd just left?'

'Oh. Oh, I hadn't thought – nah, yeah, a little bit. Similar clothes, maybe. But, to be fair, Reuben's looked more like a trackie and the other one was more . . . I dunno, *ninja*? I mean, the earlier person was facing away and bent down, so I didn't get a look at their hair or nothing. Uh, maybe the first person was skinnier? Hard to tell, really. Maybe skinnier.'

'All right. Then what?'

'So then people started arriving. Caretaker Sal, she was next out, just after the ambos got here. Reuben had to go and open the inner door, there. Paramedics went to work but, uh, you could tell pretty quick it wasn't flyin'. Sal sat down on a mushroom and then the cops turned up. One of them knocked on my door – big Pacific Islander, not your mate, here – and asked if I'd seen anything. I said yeah and he told me to sit tight and not to ring anyone until the detectives spoke to me.'

'And have you?'

'Nah. Wanna check? Nah, I don't know anyone well enough to ring 'em at four in the bloody morning. Even with this goin' on.' He glanced at the window. 'Is she okay?'

Lachie's eyes widened. 'Mate, you gotta know she's . . .'

'Sorry, I meant Sal. She's still down there, yeah?'

Lachie glanced down. Caretaker Sally was still sitting on the mushroom, now gnawing at a hangnail.

'Yup, still there.'

'Poor bugger. Bad luck seems to follow her. Happens that way, doesn't it? The nice ones get the crappy luck, the dickheads sail on through.'

Lachie glanced at Bluey, who leaned further on the counter and took over.

'Jody, what do you do for a living?'

'Work in a print shop. Posters, copies, that kind of thing.'

'Ah, yeah? Where's that?'

'Printability. Just across the park.'

'Walking to work? You're living the dream.'

Jody winced and touched his ribs. 'Yeah, about that: minimum wage, so just as well I don't need a car, isn't it? Why d'ya need to know?'

''Cos I'm a detective, mate. We're nosy. If we aren't, we get sacked. Been there long?'

'A few months. I used to work construction but I got a bit of white finger.'

'What, now?'

'Vibration white finger. Not enough protection when you use jack-hammers and such. Makes you crap at *fine motor skills*, they call it. Basically you start to act like you're wearing mittens; got all that coming to me down the track. Company screwed up and the union let it happen. I was lucky to get this job – had one of my calm days on the interview, didn't I? Compo's going through, but it takes forever. Bloody lawyers. Sal's been helping me with the paperwork.'

Bluey nodded sagely. 'I'm sorry about that, mate. I hope it works out for ya. How well do you know the other people in this building?'

Jody shrugged. He pointed at the pills. 'Can I get another painkiller? Bloody thing's kickin' on at the moment.'

Notwithstanding that the pain was actually constant, Bluey shook a pill into his hand and passed it across. Jody washed it down with the last of the water in that bottle. Bluey wandered towards the fridge and checked. Six small water bottles in two serried rows; he passed another to Jody.

He let the fridge door go and turned back to the room. Jody had side-stepped the question: Bluey's tone was harder second time around. 'Who you know, Jody?'

'Ah, yeah. Sorry. Not many. Only been here six months. Reuben Pearce – know him, of course. Couldn't believe it when I first saw him. You don't, do you? Expect to see people off the TV, I mean. Especially in a place like this. Anyway, I know him to flip the finger at, basically. Care-taker Sal? Sorted out the water pipes last month, saved me a few hundred bucks. Met Bryony – her with the binoculars – a few times. A couple of 'em to say hi to, but I wouldn't say we're big buddies.'

'You're not sitting by the pool on the weekend, checking out who might be, uh, interesting?'

'Nah, I've . . . I've got shingles scars. I look like crap without me shirt so, you know, I spare everyone that. Nah, except for the courtyard there, this place doesn't have anywhere people would meet, really. Parking's all on the street, so's the bins. We're all in our little boxes, looking out at that courtyard.'

Jody turned away to grab at another anti-inflammatory. Lachie gazed out at the space below, where the medical examiner had now arrived, looking harassed and overtired. There was a brief flurry of activity to accommodate him. Jody was right. Residents occupied the same space but didn't live as a community: it was a hive, without a hive mind.

Everyone was able to see into the centre of the complex. But they were each looking, Lachie reminded himself, at *parts* of that courtyard. And each other.

Jody assured them that he wasn't going anywhere except to sleep if he could, maybe the mini-mart at the end of the street and back home. Bluey wished him good luck with the kidney stone.

Tyson led them out into the corridor and they were twenty metres back towards the lift before he spoke.

'FYI, Detectives: a little bit of local knowledge. Printability is bang next door to What's Brewin'.'

'Ah,' said Lachie. 'So there's no way he doesn't know the victim?'

Tyson shook his head. 'Oh, he'd know her. I know her vaguely. She's, uh, memorable.'

'Really?'

'Yeah, great-looking. I'm not fussed, I'm paired up. But even so: you don't miss her. Very pretty, bubbly, that sort of thing.'

'Uh-huh. Would make a stalker, or someone who wouldn't let go, a major consideration.'

Tyson nodded. 'Yeah. I didn't mention that he'd know her because, well, the body hasn't been formally identified. And,' he added, 'I thought you might want to come back at him with that nugget in your back pocket.'

Lachie definitely liked Tyson now.

Chapter 5

Pacific Heights apartment block. Thursday, 0430hrs

Lachie watched his new partner move towards the terrace of Reuben Pearce's apartment. Two figures rose to meet Bluey, one puffing his chest as if Bluey was a style guru he needed to impress. Of course, Bluey was right: the history would have made it absurd for Lachie to interview Reuben. All the same, a sliver of his detective mind wanted another shot at Reuben: he hadn't just embarrassed the detectives who'd interviewed him but had also disgraced various entities in victim support, prosecution, politics and elsewhere. Lachie could think of a number of people in his local café who'd been vocal – not to say antagonistically positive – about Reuben Pearce and his supposed plight, only to have to walk back that support later on. *Anger is an energy*, as John Lydon sang; so is public humiliation.

He turned, to save himself from the view of a grinning Reuben Pearce once again shaking hands with a detective, and focused on Sally Harris. A female caretaker for an apartment complex was not unknown, but it wasn't commonplace. Jody Marks had said that she'd saved him plenty of cash by fixing his hot water; she presumably knew her stuff and probably heard plenty of gossip as she worked around the place. She'd lived here for some time, according to some initial digging by Tyson's iPad, but took on the caretaker job last year. If anyone knew how the local dynamics really operated, it would be her. Besides, Jody had semi-identified her as someone near the scene when Tahlia died: Lachie wanted to see how she played that.

Dawn was starting to shift westwards and his eyes were adapting to the light. Sally was still perched on the same mushroom as earlier: they all had lurid kiddie-colours and this one was a bright blue with yellow spots. Leaned forward, hands pushed hard against her kneecaps, she was wearing a dark-blue boiler suit and had her hair tied up in a loose scrunchie. He noted her short fingernails with no varnish and no rings; in the harsh light from the arc lamps a scar on the back of one hand glimmered. Her face was freckly and had a slight bloom to it, as if she'd stood out in a strong wind. She was short and fairly stocky, but in a way that suggested no-nonsense strength rather than office-imposed sloth.

'Sally?'

'Yeah? Oh, sorry. Yeah, Sally Harris. You're a detective?'

Lachie angled the badge towards her and she gave a vague grunt. He sat opposite – purple with pink spots for him.

'Rough night, eh?'

'Bloody oath.' She puffed her cheeks. 'I guess this is normal for you, but it isn't for the rest of us. I'm supposed to take old Martyn over there shopping today. All we'll bloody talk about is someone dying.'

Lachie nodded. Sometimes he forgot that his daily doses of trauma were another person's nightmare of the year, of their life. It wasn't that he was oblivious to how it affected them; more that he often chose to focus on the processes, the parts within his control, letting some of the emotional impact slide by.

'I'd like you to take me through your day, please, Sally. Start at lunchtime, mate: people find it easier to remember recent stuff if they have a bit of a run-up. Take your time, eh.'

Sally swallowed hard and blinked back a tear.

'Okay. I'm the caretaker here, you know tha—Okay. So, today I was keeping weird hours. The hot water in this building is a bit odd. We have eight different hot-water systems around the place. Each one serves seven apartments but they're all separate. Anyway, I had to service this one' – she pointed to her left – 'and you have to see how it operates on the changeover. Which is three in the morning, so it doesn't disturb people's routines. Does that make sense? Anyway. I was over there from 2 a.m. and . . . well, I saw the paramedics arrive.'

She'd been closer to the action than he'd thought. The switch-room door was flexed back, nudging against its hinges. It opened out directly on to the courtyard, next to the western entrance. He could see inside to the water tank, the pipework, her tool bag resting against a tall stool. She would have been barely twenty metres from the place where Tahlia died.

'Did you have the door open or closed?'

She squeezed her hands together and blinked at the sky.

'Urgh, I have strict orders to keep it closed. *Closed*. I know, *I know*. If I'd . . . then maybe . . . maybe. It's a safety requirement. But also, I wanted to play some music while I worked and I didn't want any of these bastards moaning that I kept them awake. I was in my pathetic bubble and, all the time . . . it's Tahlia, isn't it? Tahlia was killed?'

'I can't say. There's been no formal identification and –'

'No, no, of course. It's just . . . it's just that, sitting here, I can see into that tent thingie when the wind blows. Her boots. I recognise her boots. Italian, special import. That gold flash near the heel. We talked about 'em last week. I can't think of anyone else who wears them, could afford them; not around here.'

'Italian usually means pricey, seems to me. How *could* Tahlia afford it?'

'Yeah, that's the obvious question, isn't it? I mean, they have tipping at that café of hers and she was always a big hit with the customers, especially the guys, but even so. She said her sister sent her some money from New York. Got some gig in social media, vaguely related to some minor Kardashian or something. They're like that, aren't they?'

'Who?'

'The Kardashians. Well, those kind of people: famous for being famous, that kind of thing. Money just drips off them and lots of people crawl around underneath with their tongue out, hoping for a drop or two. She said her sister lucked into something like that. Anyway, that's how I know it's Tahls.'

The more he saw of social media, the more Lachie was determined to stay away from it. The impact, it seemed to him, was the same as drugs or heavy drinking: people got stupid, people made crappy decisions, people caused each other harm, people got careless of the emotions of others. It had the same deadening effect on conscience, and that always bit deep with Lachie.

'You were going to start at lunchtime for me, Sally.'

'Oh, crap, so I was. Yeah. So your lunchtime probably wasn't mine. I was asleep until about seven this evening. These places are surprisingly quiet. The building was thrown up in double-quick time, apparently. One of those developers who goes bust every couple of years, avoids all the creditors, then reappears with a new company name. Gutted-dog behaviour, really: but if they can, they will, eh? So a lot of my work is making up for the corners they cut, the shonky crap they installed, the things they just plain missed. But the sound insulation, the party walls? Decent job. Anyway, I can sleep through till seven, easy as. Then some food, watched some news. Went to the gym – it's really quiet then – and back about ten.'

'Did you speak to anyone during this time? Anyone else at home, or while you were out and about?'

'Nah, just me at home now. My son . . . he died a while ago. Just me now. I nodded to a couple of people at the gym, but I don't really like chatting: just put the pods in and get on with it. But they have cameras – they can show me going in and out, if that's what you mean. You do mean that, don't you? Alibis and such, everyone's a suspect?'

'I do. So you're back at home at ten last night. Go on.'

'Yeah, so then I check the outdoor pump. We don't have a cellar or an underground car park, but we have a little space on the north side that has a pump. In case of flood in the shared areas, we can operate the pump and get the water away without calling out the fireys. So that needs checking, and it was playing up. Bloody thing needs coaxing, which you don't want to do in an emergency. So I had my head down a hole for a couple of hours.'

'Did anyone see you, speak to you?'

'Nah, no chance of that. It's screened off by a wall on three sides – protection in case some moron slides off the road. So no, I don't think anyone saw me. But then, if I had my head down a hole in the ground, I wouldn't know either way.'

'All right. When did you finish at the pump?'

'Just after midnight. I checked my watch because it's easy to lose track of time with something like that and I knew I had to be in the switch room by 2 a.m. So I went back to the apartment and did some really boring admin – time sheets, a couple of quotes for something that has to go to tender.'

'See anyone, notice anything?'

'I saw it rain. I was thinking how lucky I was to get the pump done before it chucked it down. So, no; my desk overlooks the courtyard, but no one was out there. There's not much point when it's pissing it down, eh? I could see the light was on in Jody's, if that's any help. He's off to the left of me so I can't see *into* his place, but I could tell that he was up. Had his TV on, too; light kept flickering and changing colour. Maybe worth talking to him? Yeah, so, went down to the switch room at two on the dot.'

Lachie reflected that a surprising number of people were about, or awake, in the middle of the night. It seemed unusual, but maybe he underestimated how many people found sleep to be elusive. It did mean that, apparently, they had plenty of witness information. But not necessarily anything that helped.

'Why do you need to be in the switch room an hour before this changeover thing?'

It was a question he figured Bluey might ask, so he needed to have the answer himself.

'Ah, right. I won't bore you with the tech, but basically you have a lot to set up before you can monitor. Pressure, temp, flow, water quality, that kind of stuff. Takes about forty-five minutes to get everything ready. Then the changeover happens in around twenty minutes; you monitor how that goes, make the adjustments, then pack up. Near two-hour job,

each time I do it. Since it's the middle of the night, I take some music and
snacks and stuff.'

Sally had recovered some balance, talking about technical detail she
knew in her sleep. He'd guessed right: it had calmed her down and got
her on to an even keel.

'Did you see or hear anything, while you were setting up?'

'Nothing. That wouldn't be unusual. I've done five of the eight water
systems since ANZAC Day and I'd never seen anyone those times, neither:
it's the middle of the night. There's a few here that work night shifts, but nah.
Got into the switch room, got myself set, waited for the changeover, which
came at . . . 3.02. The timer in there is slightly out. A few minutes on observations and then there was a bit of screwdriver work. It was stifling in that
room. I . . . I saw . . . Tahls. Looked like Tahls.'

'Where was she?'

'Just lyin' there by that point. By the playground. On her back. Reuben
was standing next to her; before I could move towards him or call out,
two paramedics came past me. I don't think they even knew I was there.
They rushed to her and started . . . well, started their stuff.'

*Hmm. She's placed at the scene but, like Jody, only saw dribs and drabs.
Not an eyewitness to the whole thing*, thought Lachie. He'd been told that
he was overly suspicious of everything – beyond the scepticism the job
required – so he'd run that by Bluey later.

Lachie glanced around the courtyard, then across to the white tent.
'You stayed by the switch-room door while the ambos worked?'

'To begin with, yeah. The paramedics started with the shock pads and
the adrenaline and whatnot. I came outside to see if I could help but . . .'

'But what?'

'Reuben saw me and shook his head. He was covered in – well, he was
covered. I could tell anyway, from his expression. You know; you must
know, your line of work? People have that look that says it's over. So I
knew.'

'How much of the body could you see, from where you were standing?'

'She was on the floor and the ambo's bag was blocking her feet. I could see jeans and a bit of a white blouse. The rest of her was blocked by the two of them while they worked. I'd seen her top and her hair, before the ambos got going.'

'What did you do then?'

'I didn't know what to do. Shock. Total shock. Nothing to indicate *crime* at that point, from where I was standing. You wouldn't immediately think it, would you? Maybe *you* would, I suppose. She might have fallen and hit her head, or had some kind of stroke, or whatever. Jesus.'

She rubbed her face vigorously, then continued. 'A couple of cops arrived and I guess they wanted everyone to stay where they were, stick around for you guys. They told me to sit on a mushroom until a detective spoke to me. Then they whacked up the white tent double-quick. Everyone was really fast, you know? Really smooth. Maybe, when I think back on it, I'll be grateful they were so professional and all. We can all see this courtyard, so I suppose it gave Tahlia a bit of dignity. But at the time it seemed a bit callous – like she was a problem to be managed, not a person. I'm probably a bit harsh, sorry.'

She's definitely recovered her balance if she's up to critiquing the emergency response, thought Lachie.

'Nah, nah. We get that all the time. The best way we can honour the victim is to find out who did it. That means moving quickly to preserve the scene and start the investigation. Sometimes it comes off as heartless, but it isn't.'

Sally nodded and gulped. The medical examiner emerged from the tent, tucking glasses into his top pocket. The body would be moved soon and Lachie decided that he wanted to spare Sally that image if he could.

'We'll be trying to get a fix on Tahlia and her life, obviously. You knew her quite well?'

'Ah, yeah, sort of. She and my son, Josh, had a bit of a . . . I don't even know what they call it these days. A thing. An on–off thing. Friends with benefits, then just mates, then more into it: the whole thing kinda came and went a lot, you know? Hard to keep score. There was a gap – she's twenty-seven and Joshie was twenty – it's significant at that age, isn't it?

He was besotted, but I think it was a bit less for Tahls. So, you know, sorta knew her from that.'

'What kind of person was she?'

Sally puffed her cheeks before replying. 'Beautiful. She was very beautiful. That was the first thing people noticed, often the last thing as well. She was that kind of look where you wonder why she isn't on a magazine cover – not just cute, but symmetrical and wild green eyes and cheekbones and all that.'

Lachie was half certain there was some kind of hinterland here, somehow. But he didn't have enough background: he was overly reliant on whatever she said.

'Beautiful people aren't automatically nice, are they?' he ventured.

'Oh, she was pleasant enough in some ways. Not quite as smart as she thought she was, sometimes, and she was a bit careless of Joshie.' Sally smiled as she shook her head. 'Probably an overbearing mum saying that, eh? Josh was . . . inclined to go all in. He always thought the best of people, thought they wanted the best for him. Ah, maybe she wised him up a bit. They were on–off, like I said, and of course I always took Joshie's side.'

'Aside from Josh, who was in her life, do you think?'

'Her sister, Reagan, lived with her until a few months ago. She went off for the gap year – Europe and the USA, I think. Apart from that, I reckon Tahlia was a bit of a freewheeler – lots of people dipping in and out but no one consistent. Maybe she was mates with people at work? I dunno; I never go there.' She paused and gathered. 'Coffee every day is a luxury really, isn't it? I mean, five bucks a day is two grand a year: I don't have that lyin' around. Everything's got more expensive, like, overnight. I'll settle for paying the bills and skipping the luxuries. Anyways, maybe they have some idea at What's Brewin'?'

Lachie nodded. 'We'll follow up at the café once they open. Can you think of anyone who'd want to harm Tahlia? Anyone you've seen arguing with her, threatening, even just hanging around?'

Sally sat back for a moment and picked at her lip.

'Hard to say. I haven't really talked to her much since Josh died. Been a bit wrapped up. Uh, let me think. No one here, at Pacific Heights, that I can recall. Most of us just nod and say hi; we're not in each other's pockets. I mean, why kill a waitress? She serves coffee and cake, she goes home; what would be the problem with that? I don't know much about her private life, outside of Joshie. No. Sorry, that was no help, was it?'

No, it wasn't, thought Lachie. Though he'd found that apartment blocks were less inclined to be friendly, and less able to be nosy, than houses. People could come and go without neighbours knowing; lives could blossom or wither and it would all look the same to everyone around them. He preferred housing that had been there a while – people took an interest, to say the least, and they had a collective folk memory of the area that could be useful. Rabbit hutches – even when they all faced the same deadly space – didn't have that.

'CCTV cameras?'

'Urgh. Gave out a few weeks ago. We only have two; over the doorways, there. I know – it was the first thing I considered. If only, eh? Nah, they aren't even producing bad pictures: totally buggered. I've emailed the company three times. They told me to unplug, insulate the wiring and leave it to them. They're bloody hopeless.'

Crap, thought Lachie. 'While I have you here; as caretaker, do you have a master key? We'll need to sort Tahlia's apartment.'

Sally grunted and reached into a pocket. There were about ten keys on the same loop. She twisted and snapped and one key, marked with red electrical tape, came free. She held it, rather than handing it over.

'Don't bloody lose this, mate. Comes out of my salary if you do – about five hundred bucks to get a new one, plus all the paperwork and a bollocking from the body corporate. Guard it with your life and, when you're done, I need it placed in my hot sticky hand. Not chucked in my mailbox and hope I spot it. Deal?'

Lachie felt suitably warned as it fell into his palm. 'Deal.'

He wandered away to check his phone for messages, taking a breath. He'd hoped, as he always did, for some huge game-changer early on. It wasn't laziness – it was recognition that each hour they weren't focusing in on the killer, that individual had the chance to run. Or create a smokescreen. Or destroy evidence. Or gain a false alibi. Or intimidate a witness.

Time mattered.

They'd spoken to three witnesses in the first forty minutes on-scene. Jody might have misled them about the victim, Sally was there-but-not-there, Reuben was already a proven liar.

Great start.

Chapter 6

Pacific Heights apartment block.
Apartment 6. Thursday, 0430hrs

Bluey took a deep breath before walking towards Reuben Pearce. He understood that it would be a stupid error to attempt, in this incident, a *get even* for another horrendous incident. Especially because this was a murder investigation and he needed the cooperation of the man in question. He had to park what Reuben had done because, like it or not, Bluey needed whatever information Reuben had. But it left two problems.

Firstly, he hated the bloke and wanted to blow up *deluxe* for what Reuben had deliberately perpetrated and tried to excuse. Most police officers did: half the country did. He had a theoretical opportunity here to launch into exactly that; but he couldn't, and he suspected that Reuben knew that. Secondly, Bluey also understood that he couldn't rely on anything that Reuben told him. While the information might be invaluable, it could also be bullshit. It would need checking far more closely than any other eyewitness account. Reuben had a credibility gap wider than the Nullarbor.

Reuben was strangely relaxed for someone whose black tracksuit was caked in the blood of a dead woman. He slouched on his seat, watching the comings and goings with a detached amusement, as though it was a series of badly played recorders at a school concert. He evinced no respect for the dead, no semblance of solemnity for the work the police had to do here. Instead, he proudly displayed exactly the kind of selfish insouciance that Bluey expected.

Reuben's hands had been bagged by the uniform officer next to him – Radcliffe, the name badge said – so that Reuben resembled a bizarre combo of failed pop star and Gladwrap. Reuben was gesturing with his eyebrow for the officer to help him swig some water, but Radcliffe was too busy standing in Bluey's presence. They shook hands.

'Good job, mate,' said Bluey. 'Can you go over to the tent people and ask a forensic officer to come over when I'm done? We'll try to process Mr Pearce here as early as possible.'

Radcliffe nodded and departed; Bluey sat on the other cheapo plastic chair on Reuben's terrace and set his phone to record. He had a view into the lit interior of Reuben's apartment – the tiger-skin rug and the possibly fake Lebron singlet in a frame were both tiresomely predictable. Reuben's public persona was a boorish, loudmouth, unlovable larrikin-wannabe who'd long outstayed his welcome with the public, even before his bizarre legal shenanigans. In real life, he could easily be the same.

Bluey's view across the courtyard was split into five sections: one of the entrance doorways and a few metres of courtyard, then the back of the barbie, a sight line towards the dead body and the playground equipment, a semi-view below the foliage of the four trees, then more flat concrete and the second entrance doorway. Oh, and some sort of other door next to that, which was currently tilting gently in the breeze. He'd have to ask Lachie about that door. All in all, a better set of images than Jody Marks would have had, despite being on the ground floor.

In view of the circumstances, Reuben's manic energy was inappropriate. 'Bloody wild, eh?' he offered. 'Probably routine for you blokes, but for us punters it's . . . well, cray-cray. Stuff like this just keeps happenin' to me, somehow.'

His eyes were shining slightly and a smile held around the lips. Not surprising, thought Bluey, that he was relishing the proximity to something dramatic; a setting where he could pretend to be the focal point. Right now the most important person in this entire complex was clearly

Tahlia Moore, but Reuben would naturally make it all about himself. He seemed physically incapable of any other attitude, judging by his recent history, and Bluey found himself wondering how such a stupendous level of self-referential onanism could become so ingrained. Basic etiquette, good manners or a respect for what had happened? All absent, it seemed. *Beyond* absent: never in the same postcode. As though any trimming or pruning of his stupidity – by society or everyday life – had never happened.

'Did you know her?'

Reuben nodded. 'Yeah, a bit. Once seen, never forgotten, that one. Knew it, too. Knew how to . . . what can I say, present herself? Never saw her without make-up. Lots of crop-tops, sports gear. Good-looker, canny; you know?'

Bluey did know the type, although it was perfectly possible that Tahlia was not like that at all. In some respects, getting evidence from Reuben was simply muddying the waters. He was not only unreliable himself; he also held the capacity to undermine the credibility of others. Plus, Bluey regarded him as a murder suspect. People covered in someone else's blood often suffered that stigma.

'Did you see her outside of this building, or just around and about the apartments?'

Reuben half bounced back in his chair; skittish, fizzing with nervous energy that refused to dissipate. It might have been adrenaline fading, but it didn't look like shock.

'Yeah, I'm a regular at the coffee shop now. They all know me down there. Large ristretto, every morning, all the extras. Apparently I'm the only customer ever orders one. Ten bucks a go but, you know, you only live once, probably. Yeah. Anyway, they kinda like having someone famous in their poxy shop, eh?'

Bluey swallowed down a mouthful of disgust, keeping his opinion to himself. *Well, you weren't famous, champ. You once came seventh in Australian Idol, butchering a Cold Chisel classic and looking comically perplexed when we all voted for you to bugger off.* Australia loved the winner; *she* had several hits, a couple of Arias and gave it her all at the Christmas carol blubfest from Sydney Harbour. *You* voiced a tacky commercial for a now-defunct broadband company. Even regional RSLs don't book you. When you can't get a gig in some place that makes all its money from schnitzels and pokies, you can't get a gig at all. Hence your little stunt last year.

'Before now, when was the last time you saw her?'

Reuben shrugged. 'I don't keep score, mate. People remember me, not the other way around.'

Bluey gave him the hard stare, but Reuben's shellac of self-regard was bulletproof.

'Try harder. *Mate.*'

Reuben sighed. 'Whatevs. Ah, wasn't Monday because she wasn't workin'. She splits her shifts some days with Cassie. Cassie with the DM boots and the baggy clothes. Chalk and cheese, that's all I'm sayin'. So it would be . . . yesterday, I reckon.'

'And how did she seem?'

Reuben leaned forward and the hand-bags crackled as he tried to squeeze his ring finger.

'Now then. It was a bit unusual, now I think on it. See, normally Tahlia's a bit of a flirt. She's a babe, like I say, and she likes the tips. Minimum wage, I guess, but anyway. She's usually all perky and full of herself. But yesterday? A bit . . . *chastened*. Yeah, that's the word – hey, I even impressed myself with that one. Yeah, like she'd been told off, or told her fortune. Or maybe, someone said she was a six when she thought she was a ten. You know – that look when you've been taken down a peg or two? I assumed it was something at work. Get a bunch of girls together, it always goes bitchy in the end, doesn't it?'

It was depressingly unsurprising that Reuben created more ammunition for hating him the longer he spoke.

'And you,' Bluey sat forward, 'you didn't argue with her, or anything?'

Reuben stopped, the slightly leery grin receded. 'Ah, come on. Nah, seriously? You can't think that I –'

'I'd ask that question of anyone who had the victim's blood on them, eh? Would be remiss of me to avoid it.'

Reuben chewed on that for a moment.

'Yeah, okay. But nah, no cross words goin' on. Look, she was a cute chick who brought me a coffee. Bit of chitchat, that's all. Never thought I was in with a chance or nothing, never tried it on. Believe it or not, I know my limits.'

Bluey doubted Reuben had that level of self-awareness: he'd demonstrated the opposite for several years. All the same, he could see a beautiful woman making it so clear that even Reuben couldn't miss it: something ending in *off.*

'What were you doing this evening, Reuben?'

'Chillaxing. Bit of gaming, pissed about on Tinder. Nothin' major.'

Bluey reflexed a glance into the apartment: a tequila bottle on the kitchen table was three quarters empty. No telling how much of that was tonight.

'When did you first become aware that something was going on in the courtyard?'

'Ah, they woke me up, didn't they? No idea what time. In fact, don't know what time it is now. But it woke me up. I'd left the patio doors open, stupid me. Just sounded like two people messing about. I could hear that they were talking, but not what they said. It got a bit heated, by the sound of it. Raised voices, then it went quiet. I was still lying on the lounge at this point. Thought, *Thank God, stupid drama's over.* I was going back to sleep when I heard a scream. Real loud.'

'Just one?'

'Yeah, mate, I can count to one.'

'Those voices – male, female?'

'Hard to say. At least one was a woman, but they were talking over each other. I guess that means they're both women, hey?'

Another one that Bluey had to let slide, for the good of the justice system.

'What happened then?'

'Well, the scream got me off the couch. When I got to the terrace here I could see the door there' – he pointed to the west – 'swinging shut. Tahlia, she was lying on the ground. Funny angle, though, sorta twisted. Didn't look right. So I went out to see what's what.'

Bluey was trying, on the fly, to line up this evidence with Jody Marks' effort, even though he knew Reuben and Jody were both potentially unreliable. He could sense, rather than fully define, that they didn't quite meet in the middle. Some aspects gelled, but others diverged. It was hard to say whether that made Reuben's version more or less authentic.

'Did you see or hear anyone else at that point? Anyone looking down from a window?'

'Dunno, mate. Was focused on her; I was startin' to really worry, eh? At that point I thought she'd fallen over pissed, or passed out or something. Maybe cracked her head on the way down, you know? Was gonna put her in the recovery position and that's about it. Got up closer and saw it wasn't so good.'

Bluey remained cautious of Reuben's take on things. He should track down or confirm when that tequila was bought. Sometimes, it paid to slow the interviewee down; especially on the first take, their adrenaline made them rush through and miss something useful.

'Think carefully now, Reuben, take your time. This bit really matters. Did you see anything on the ground, or near Tahlia, as you approached?'

Reuben squeezed his eyes shut, as though he was really trying.

'Her bag. Handbag. On the floor by her . . . left hand. Not open or nothin', just lying there. Ah, some leaves from the tree overhead, just scattered about. Other than that, nah.'

'Any sense of someone else around – noises, anything moving, smells, anything?'

'Nah. Just what I've already told you. Nothing else.'

'Okay. So what happened when you approached her?'

'I called her name, thinking she might wake up if she was just pissed. Then I saw the blood.'

'Where? Precisely.'

'Ah, here' – he waved vaguely at the left side of his chest – 'running down to her belt, then dripping on to the concrete. Kinda knew, then.'

'Knew what?'

'That she was dead, mate. Hard to see her coming back from that.'

'What did you do?'

'Looked around the courtyard, hoping someone was going to deal with it, or at least call the paramedics. Couldn't see anyone come runnin'.'

'*Couldn't see anyone come runnin'*. Interesting phrase. I'll ask again: could you see anyone *looking*?'

A flash of annoyance from Reuben, which he tried to hide with a stifled cough.

'Oh, Bryony up the top, there. No surprise. If you lived up there and you could see everyone else, you'd be a sticky-beak, wouldn't you? And ol' Martyn, there, across the way. Not that he'd be coming out.'

He winked at Bluey as if they were mates. Bluey gave it a blank two seconds.

'Okay. But no one making a move to help?'

'Had to do it all meself. Rang triple-zero and sorta scooped her up, hoping she might still be conscious, I suppose. Guess I wasn't supposed to touch her, hey?'

'Never mind. You were trying to save her life, we get that. Triple-zero answered?'

'Yeah. I said she was bleeding out, confirmed the address. I tried to feel for a pulse, but they said nah, most people don't do that right, so leave it. See if she's breathing. I had to locate the wound.'

Even in the half-light, Bluey could see the colour drain from Reuben's face at the recollection. He did have a conscience, after all.

'You did that?'

'Yeah, as much as I could. It was kinda pouring out, you know? Stuffed my scarf thing against it – only thing the right size. Didn't make a difference.'

Despite his dislike for Reuben, Bluey found some compassion. What a godawful thing to experience: trying to do something that might buy

Tahlia a couple of minutes of life. The blood, the sagging, fading body; the brutal certainty that what he was doing was, in fact, next to useless. It reminded Bluey not to dismiss what Reuben said, just because he'd been a colossal tool in the past.

'They asked if she was breathing and when I said no, they said I should give it a try if I knew how to do it. Mouth-to-mouth.'

'And did you know how?'

'Yeah, sure. I was a nipper on the Central Coast: you don't forget the basics. I gave it a try for, I dunno how long, few minutes or so? It was useless. She was already gone. By the time I stood up there were a few lights on round here. Then the ambos arrived and I told them what I'd done. I told them she was probably dead but, you know, they had to do their stuff, didn't they?'

'Who came out to see if they could help?' Bluey asked.

'No one. I mean, what a sad bloody state of affairs, eh?'

These things varied, thought Bluey. He'd seen minor road accidents when fifteen or twenty people had immediately run over to assist. He'd seen footage of women thumped on public transport and everyone just drawing away, feigning complete ignorance. There seemed no rhyme or reason to public intervention. Reuben, however, had a definite opinion.

He paused, chewed his lip for a second, then pointed angrily at the ground. 'I know what people say about me, mate. I've got a phone. I *know*. They think I'm a waste of space, a pain in the arse. Well, push came to bloody shove tonight, didn't it? Someone was dying and every single person here either slept right through it, or just watched. I was the only one that . . . *actually bloody stepped up*. Next time they wanna slag me off on some website, think they'll remember all this? Will they buggery.'

All that was almost certainly true, thought Bluey. Especially the last bit.

'No one came out at all? At any time?'

'Uh, only Sal. Caretaker chick. She just sat on a bloody mushroom. Shock, eh? To be fair, by the time she was sat down the ambos were almost done, I was definitely done, and I gave her the head shake. Not much she could do. But nah, none of these other geniuses could be bothered to put their shoes on.'

He had a point, Bluey reflected. People were always quick to offer judgement – Bluey and Lachie had both done so before the car came to a halt – but Reuben *had* stepped up, *had* tried to save Tahlia. He'd definitely been a good citizen for a minute or two, even if the rest of his life was a slow circling of the drain.

'Can you think of any reason why someone would want to hurt Tahlia?'

Reuben shook his head. 'Nah. Was thinkin' on that when your mate sent me over here with plastic bags on my hands. Nah. She was a flirty, cute chick who made people smile. Liked a party, liked her clothes, I think – fashion and stuff. Nothing complicated about her, I reckon. I mean, if I'm pushed for a reason . . .'

'Yes?'

'I guess there's blokes don't take no for an answer, don't like being dumped. I mean, no one *likes* being dumped, but, you know, blokes who *really* don't like it. There's a few of them knocking around, so maybe she got on the wrong side of that. Haven't ever seen it, or seen anyone hanging about. Tahlia's normally with girlfriends whenever I see her away from the café. But that's the only thing I can see that might get her into trouble.'

That suggestion fitted, Bluey was forced to admit. But, perhaps inevitably with Reuben, he couldn't help feeling that there was more going on, that there was more story to tell. He didn't want to dig into that until he had more information about the crime scene, about Tahlia, and about Reuben.

Bluey nodded as he thought. 'Okay, Reuben, thank you for that.' He beckoned a crime-scene tech, who picked up a black case and began to make his way over. 'Vinny here will sort out your clothes, deal with your fingers and hands, all the rest of it. Oh, one last question. When did you buy the tequila?'

They both glanced across to the bottle.

'Ah, am I pissed right now, you mean? That bottle was fresh yesterday lunchtime, got into its work in the afternoon. But I know what I'm about.'

'Fair enough. We might have other questions later in the day, so be available for that. But thank you for now, Reuben.'

Chapter 7

Three interviews should be enough, Bluey reasoned, to begin forming a view. If not a firm image of what had taken place, then at least a context, an overview. This one was defying the logic. In some ways, he felt he knew less than when he'd arrived. Just an hour ago he could see fixed points in proceedings – the phone calls to emergency services, someone giving first aid, the paramedics arriving – and which parts of the information he'd felt were authoritative. But now each witness had given different vibes, had seen from different angles, had taken a different interpretation, had offered a different perspective, had radiated a different attitude. He and Lachie weren't merely trying to square a circle, here: they were trying to fit spheres into cubes. A Gordian knot, but with no sword in sight.

For two people who'd never worked together – or even met before – Lachie and Bluey had remarkable synchronicity: each exited their interview at the same time and they met near the white tent. Activity around the courtyard had slowed to a steady pulse; Forensics were preparing to remove the body and a tech began clearing the path to the ME's vehicle. The ME himself was scratching at a clipboard. It seemed natural for Bluey to take the lead here.

'Doc? I'm Detective Carl Blewson, this is Detective Lachie Dyson. We've been assigned to this case.'

Dr Lawson peered over frameless glasses, as though Bluey was an impertinent child at an upmarket private school. Well known for his lofty dismissal of anyone who couldn't keep up, he hadn't softened as he matured. Quite the opposite: a slight sneer was his default facial expression. A tall, angular man with a smoothly shaved head, he had a habit of resembling an eagle with something putrid caught in its talons.

'As I'm sure you know, Detective, I won't commit myself to anything at all until the examination is complete and I've written the full – Dyson, you say?'

Lachie nodded, ready for what came next.

'I hear you handed Prosecutor Fuller his arse over that Reuben Pearce case. And then the commissioner handed you yours. That true?'

Lachie shuffled his feet. 'Yeah, that's a fair summary.'

Lawson grunted. 'Well, off the record, good on ya. Bloke's a dick.'

'Pearce or Fuller? Or the commissioner?'

'Yes. Anyway,' – he turned back to Bluey – 'cause of death is likely stabbing. One incision that I can see, under the heart. She'd have been gone in seconds, if that. No obvious sign of defensive wounds, but we'll check in detail. Time of death you already have, within a few minutes, from the paramedics – I won't be contradicting that, I wouldn't think.'

'Any idea about the weapon?'

'A sharp, thin blade. Might have been tugged out, rather than pulled out smoothly. We'll look at the trauma inside the wound, but that exit might make it difficult to be certain of the precise shape or length.'

'Any ideas about the nature of the attacker?'

'Probably right-handed, judging by the angle. The victim could well have been standing up when attacked. The attacker might be anyone, I'm afraid; the blade could be so sharp that it didn't need a lot of strength, just accuracy and the willingness to do it.'

All three understood that this didn't narrow down anything at all.

The rustle of white suits announced the moving of the body. Tahlia had been placed inside a body bag and was now on the gurney at the entrance to the tent. The techs paused, waiting for Lawson's terse nod before they wheeled it out. Bluey clasped his hands in front of him and looked silently at his shoes. Lachie noticed and followed suit. They both reflected silently as Tahlia Moore was wheeled away. By the time they looked up, Lawson was using disconcertingly springy strides to head for a slate-grey Mercedes out on the street.

'He's chatty,' said Lachie.

'Yeah. He's not the worst, mind. Nor the best. We won't get a report from him before mid-evening at the earliest; the autopsies for the two victims in that drive-by will take precedence. I can't remember an ME doing three examinations in a day. Thinking about it, maybe we shouldn't count on anything significant from that source until tomorrow.'

'Crap.'

'Eloquently put, Lachie. Positively Shakespearean, mate. Yeah, it'll be hard to move forward with some things until we know, for example, what the weapon looks like.'

'Or whether Tahlia had some DNA under her fingernails from fighting back.'

'Exactly.'

'On a better note,' offered Lachie, 'I have the master key to access her apartment.'

'Oh, cool.'

Bluey drifted over to a tech to tell them that the detectives were going to have an initial look at the apartment. Collecting booties and suits from a pile by the tent, he joined Lachie and they crossed the courtyard to the south entrance, where Tyson stood ready to guide them.

'I got a blueprint of the apartment building, sir, from Caretaker Sally.' He waved a folded A3 replete with smears. 'It's a bit smudgy; it's the one she keeps in the switch room. It'll do for now, I think.'

Lachie nodded and took a photo of the map as Tyson held it open. 'Good stuff. Okay, her apartment. Number 41.'

Tyson gazed at the map for a moment, tapped it in confirmation, and set off down the corridor.

Pacific Heights apartment block.
Apartment 41. Thursday, 0459hrs

The corridor to Tahlia's unit was as anodyne as the one outside Jody's place: a mild dose of anaglypta and the sort of vague grey that was inexplicably the colour *du jour* for new apartment blocks throughout the city. No one wanted to use vibrant colours any more, in case one or two people were put off: apparently, it was better that everyone was mildly disappointed. Tyson came to a halt outside number 41 and stood to one side. There was a long two minutes of huffing and puffing while Bluey struggled into the one-size-doesn't-quite-fit-all forensic suit; his new partner took twenty seconds. Lachie gave Tyson an arched eyebrow and got a controlled smirk in response. Bluey felt his age as he leaned against the wall to put on the plastic shoes.

'Right, Tyson,' he said, 'we're going to have a little lookie in here, before the techs get to grips with it. We promise to play nice, so they don't need to worry. Meantime, can you hook up a time for Tahlia's mother? We can meet her at the morgue if she wants to do the ID now, but it would be ideal if we met at her home. Okay?'

Lachie had to wiggle the key before it clicked. The door swung open on its own weight, tapping eventually against the wall. The apartment was in darkness, even though sunrise was imminent: perpendicular washes of light bled in around the edges of the blinds. They entered and closed the door behind them as Tyson started dialling Tahlia's mother from the corridor. The ceiling light jarred the senses when they switched it on; it all felt stark and artificial.

They were aware of the timing: Tahlia's body hadn't yet reached the morgue and here they were, pilfering through her private life. It always felt slightly seedy, slightly wrong, to walk into the home of someone who'd just died. Despite the investigative urgency and necessity, it struck Bluey as an intrinsic lack of reverence, a deliberate blundering. He paused and looked around.

The homes of the immediately deceased varied, in his experience. Some of them looked hollowed out, as though they were instantly bereaved. The detritus that assumed life was ongoing – a frozen chicken set out to thaw, a note about a school pick-up that day – screamed that the place was already grieving. Other homes appeared to silently go about their business whether the person was there or not, autonomous and inert. Tahlia's unit felt as though she'd merely popped out to fetch the mail.

Look, he thought, *look what a life she'd built.* A life didn't have to be crammed with riotous experience, make a huge dent on the world, or be vivid and dazzling to be one that was missed. People made the mistake of thinking that their life had to be memorable, breathtaking or glamorous, to count. It didn't. Regular lives hurt just as much when they were snuffed out, left an identical hole when they ended, mattered just the same.

The kitchen was a disaster zone – one drawer front was missing and one cupboard door lacked a hinge. Plates were piled up in the sink while the maw of the dishwasher lay empty, a tea-towel slopped on to the rings of the hob, an opened carton of milk festered to one side. Serried ranks from shot glasses to tumblers littered the draining board. Bluey looked for signs of a partner, lodger, or even a pet, but it seemed clear that Tahlia lived alone and, he conjectured, on a downward slope. Things that needed doing were being left fallow: either Tahlia had become super-busy, or something in her life was pulling her down.

On the counter by the kettle was a small pad: one of those freebie notepads you got from a dentist or physio clinic. He checked the top sheet for indentations, but this seemed to be the first sheet to be used. Her writing was large and almost childish – big loops and a heart-shape for the full stop. She'd written Reuben, Scotty, Anthony, Martyn down the paper. Only Scotty had a tick: the others had question marks.

He went towards the calendar on the kitchen wall as Lachie headed for the bedroom. Dates and notes centred around Tahlia's café roster – leave days had a red triangle in one corner – and a reminder next week to pay 'rest of holiday money' to whoever. He flicked back through previous months, but Tahlia had used the calendar sparingly. No mention, for example, of anyone's birthday but her own. Presumably, her mobile phone held more information. He was about to open the fridge when Lachie called.

'Bluey. In here.'

Lachie was standing by the bed. The doona was splayed to one side, as if Tahlia had just got up. It added to the sense of intrusion. The room reeked of snuffed joss sticks and the sickly aroma of some perfume or other: both men were itching to open a window. Bluey took a photo of the dressing table with his phone. At least six pairs of shoes sprawled on the carpet, pleading for attention. Clothes poured from a giant twelve-drawer unit along one wall; lots of Asian prints and bright colours, it seemed to Bluey.

Lachie pointed to a bedside table. He'd tugged open the drawer with a gloved hand and then opened an ornate wooden box – maybe Indonesian – to reveal the contents. Two small baggies of white powder and a miniature silver spoon. Lachie sighed.

'I've gotta say, this seems almost inevitable now. I reckon half the rooms I toss – when it's young people – have something in it. I'm beyond surprised.'

Bluey nodded. 'Yeah, I know. No disincentive, is there? We're pretty much decriminalised for personal use in this state, so why fret? They used to worry about not being allowed into the USA with a drug conviction, but these days they don't want to go there anyway because it's still the home of the Bad Orange Man.'

Lachie gave a sidelong glance and an ironically raised eyebrow. 'You from MAGA country, mate?'

Bluey chuckled. 'Hardly. I'm from Bluey country. A small, dusty place where everyone's slightly bemused, population: me. Any signs of where she got that stuff?'

Lachie was snapping a clear evidence bag to attention. 'Nothing yet, but her phone might be a good start. I doubt it's in contacts under "dealer", but some people aren't far off that stupid.'

Bluey glanced at the bookshelves above the bed. Not that he automatically equated reading with brains, let alone common sense, but he felt that the shelves indicated Tahlia was quite bright. Plenty of weighty classics between easier reads; they were creased along the spine and some were dog-eared. Even if she'd bought them second hand, she'd still made use of them.

The sliding doors to the wardrobe stuck along the track and needed a hefty shove. The clothes rack was jammed tight. Beyond tight, in fact; Bluey doubted he could fit an envelope in there. Blouses by the dozen, many with the shop tags still attached. He wondered if Tahlia had simply lifted these, rather than buying them; to his untrained eye the quality of the stitching and the rich softness of the fabric suggested they were pricey. He took several photos in detail, to show to someone who actually had a fashion sense.

Back in the living room now, having bagged and tagged the cocaine and spoon, Lachie stood by the couch. A bowl of half-finished Weetbix was crusting up on the coffee table, next to the TV remote and a spray of Polaroid snaps. Sometimes people just had a throwaway camera like this for a party. They all featured Tahlia with a couple of buddies. He picked them up by the edges for a closer look. One was a flop-haired doe of a boy with large eyes and androgynously luxurious skin, a few years younger than her, smiling shyly and clutching her arm. The other, a few years older, was more confident; he was standing taller, looking straight at the camera. Tahlia, in most of the shots, had her head back in laughter. She was, as others had said, luminously beautiful. The trio glowed like pre-packaged images from commercials: not a spot or a blemish in sight, just the unspoken narrative of gorgeous people who firmly believed that they would never come to harm.

'You know what's ironic?' Lachie called to Bluey.

'Nah, Alanis, what?'

'If Tahlia stood in her own living room, she'd have a great view of where she died. Better than Jody, any rate.'

Life turned up grim coincidences, Bluey thought to himself. Someone who would have been the ideal witness to their own murder. Lachie was tuned in to lines of sight, while Bluey was more interested in lines of reasoning – what made someone flick from angry to killer?

No laptop, Lachie suddenly realised. The apartment was a mess, but not the havoc of a break-in; more that Tahlia lived this way. Maybe she didn't have a laptop and just did everything on her phone. He looked around for that, but all he could see was a phone charger in one corner, fighting for space with a table lamp, two boxes of tissues and a collapsed stack of magazines. Probably Tahlia still had the phone in her pocket or handbag; he'd ring Forensics later for an inventory from the body.

He could see Bluey in the bathroom now, scouring the medicine cabinet above the sink. Bluey took an initial photo of the cabinet, then turned each bottle to assess the label. He felt himself being watched and came back into the living room, shaking his head as he emerged.

'Bog standard. Stuff for girls and cures for headaches. Some antidepressants, but the lid was dusty.'

'Whaddya reckon overall?' asked Lachie.

Bluey looked around again. It was better to leave the blinds down until the techs were clear: no sense in giving the neighbours a free *CSI* episode.

'The usual sort of chaos from a twenty-something living on their own. Nothing much that I wouldn't expect. Lots of clothes, though I wonder if some of those were acquired with light fingers. No indication of a partner or regular stopover. Nothing much out of step with her income bracket if those clothes are knock-offs or stolen, for example. The coke isn't a big surprise, either. I'm struggling to see something here that would raise hackles, evidence a feud or stalking, or give any indication as to why she was attacked.'

While he was talking, Lachie was nodding but flicking through his phone. He held it up, screen showing, as he replied.

'Rent in this building is pretty high: location's good, the building isn't. No wonder she had her sister living here, sharing the expenses.'

'Ah yeah, the sister. Only one bedroom; that would have been a squeeze. Lounge probably pulls out into a bed, but all the same, yeah. All too expensive for one waitress wage?'

'Borderline, at best. Like you say, the sister would have helped for a while, but Caretaker Sally seemed to think she'd been gone for months. I'm no expert on women's clothes . . .'

Bluey smiled. 'Are you sure? You can tell me if you are. We welcome diversity, mate. It makes us stronger, you know.'

'. . . but I reckon there's some very pricey gear in here. Assuming it's not knock-off copies, as you say, a lot of it seems to be high-end American labels and some Euro imports.'

'How d'you acquire that level of insight, Lachie?'

'Those glossy mags they have in the weekend papers? You chuck 'em, I read 'em. Usually to astonish myself about the junk people buy and what they pay. But even so, some of the brand names stick.'

'How do we think she's managing that expense?'

Yes, that was a worthwhile question. They'd have all the financials shortly, back at station. Lachie shrugged.

'Indulgent parentals? Second job? Inheritance? Sugar-daddy? Only Fans? Could be anything. I reckon we need a handle on her online life, anyway.'

Bluey nodded as he took a final look around. They always felt these days that the online life was the key: particularly for younger people, it could be where the *real them* lurked, where the important moments played out. Besides the obvious infrastructure of appointments, photos, searches for jobs or cars or unit rental or holiday flights, online was where they expressed themselves.

But often, in Bluey's experience, the online stuff was a busted flush. It simply demonstrated that they followed a crowd, that they had little hinterland or natural curiosity, that they stayed in their lane, that they led dull lives. If online wasn't the life panacea for the victim, it was unlikely to be the breakthrough for the detectives, either.

Chapter 8

Pacific Heights apartment block. Thursday, 0528hrs

Tyson was waiting outside the door, like a patient dog left in the car. Lachie shucked the forensic suit as Tyson brought him up to speed.

'Just spoke to Tahlia's mother, Vanessa. Single parent, no current partner. She's obviously still in shock but she has a next-door neighbour with her for now. Vanessa's sister, Ruth, is flying in from interstate; her plane takes off in half an hour. We agreed that Vanessa would come to City West at 1100: she'll have her sister for moral support by then and they can go on to the formal ID after that. I didn't think the medical examiner would be starting on . . . *starting*. Besides, Tahlia looks okay if you're just doing identification.'

Lachie nodded. Tyson had thought it through: the detectives would have enough time to sift through some of the evidence, especially financial and online, before sitting down with the victim's mother. That might make the interview more focused and useful. Since Tahlia had been stabbed, her face had not been noticeably damaged: Vanessa could see enough for an ID without becoming retraumatised by visual injuries. Lachie checked his watch.

'Five thirty. We've got the two elderly people still to see, is that right, Tyson?'

'Yes, sir.' He juggled the phone and the clipboard. 'That would be Bryony Price and Martyn Brooks. Both on the far side of the complex from here. Martyn's on the ground floor, Bryony's on the top floor.'

Lachie deferred to Bluey, who had finally fought his way out of the Babygro and had a furrowed brow as he pondered how, and whether, to fold it.

'Yeah,' said Bluey. 'Let's try the top floor first: I feel like we need a bird's-eye view of things. So far it's all too close up, low down, half there and half missing. Maybe this lady's got the bigger picture.'

Lachie doubted it, but Tyson was already on the go.

Recrossing the courtyard, they almost felt like newcomers. Gathering light had altered shadows, angles, the feel of the whole courtyard. The forensics team was now working the area within, and around, the tent. They were looking for fibres, blood droplets, nicks and scratches; anything to give a semblance of who, how and why. Another pair were dusting the two entrances for fingerprints, while a further tech was in one corner of the courtyard, taking general photos and measurements. The latter was needed to put together a 3-D software visual of the courtyard: it would enable them to run scenarios to see where people may have stood, and lines of visibility to cross-check witness statements. Constable Radcliffe was coordinating the effort and gave Bluey a slight nod as they passed.

Through the western entrance again – careful once more not to touch a surface – and up the stairs to the fifth floor: the lift was now unavailable until Forensics were done. Bluey was trying not to wheeze heftily and the two younger men diplomatically stopped halfway to 'switch off my phone' and 'recheck the map, sir'. When they reached the top, he puffed a weary *thanks, boys.*

Lachie turned back to Tyson. 'Did you say you knew her? Tahlia?'

'Yeah, little bit. She goes to the same gym as me, down on Lucknor Street. I do shifts so I'm not always there at the same time each day, but yeah, see her a couple of times a week.'

'And?'

Tyson shrugged. 'Cute, in good shape. If I'm pushed: more of a blokes' girl than a girls' girl, if you know what I mean. The gym runs classes and most of 'em in there are women: they come out all gabby after the class and she's standing a bit apart, seems to me. But she doesn't strike me as the shy type, so it isn't that. More likely that blokes are talking to her.'

Lachie raised an eyebrow.

'Anyone in particular that you –'

'Ah, no, not like that. Not that sort of vibe in my gym; it's one of the reasons I like it. Nah, old fellas, young guys, whoever – it's chatty, not chat-up. But more of them than women around Tahlia, if you're keeping count.'

'How does she work out?' asked Bluey.

Tyson frowned. 'How do you mean? What machines does she use?'

'No, I mean how does she go about it? Focused, organised? Always checking her phone? Posing for selfies? Careless?'

'Ah, right. Yeah, she does a few selfies in the mirror on the free weights – *livin' my best life* kind of crap. But once she's on an exercise, she's pretty precise. Good balance, good posture, controlled; takes it serious. Is that what you meant?'

Bluey nodded.

Pacific Heights apartment block.
Apartment 50. Thursday, 0530hrs

They'd arrived at Bryony Price's door. She had a welcome mat that said *Welcome* and a door chime when her neighbours relied on knocking. *She might be a bit deaf*, thought Bluey, and then realised how well Lachie seemed to cope with the cochlear implant. Bluey had made no allowances whatsoever for that since he'd been told.

The door was opened by a woman in her early seventies with elfin features, sparkling eyes and a shortish haircut that managed to look pricey. She was dressed in jeans, an orange T-shirt and moccasins. Lachie got an immediate impression that she was on the ball and likely to be a credible witness.

'Ah, the detectives. Come on in.'

She stood back and they entered an apartment at least twice the size of

Tahlia's, although it gave an impression of space partly by being show-home tidy. Cream carpet and white walls bounced the emerging daylight, aided by beige sofas and white 2-pac furniture. Artificial flowers sprayed from three black-and-gold floor vases, framing two sets of patio doors leading to the balcony. Up this high, they could see the crowns and blinking lights of CBD towers. A subtle aroma from the pot pourri had taken root. Settled and prosperous was the tone.

'Do you prefer Bryony, Ms Price . . .' asked Bluey.

'Oh, good grief, yes, Bryony is fine.' Her voice had a slight throaty catch, giving it some refined and pleasing texture.

'You'll understand that we're here about the incident down in the courtyard. Could you talk us through your own time from midnight, please?'

They sat facing each other across a tabletop that looked like onyx and probably was. It was bisected by two hefty books about South America. The sofa was squidgy but immaculate. Tyson took up his now-familiar sentry pose, this time by the breakfast bar, as Lachie showed Bryony that his phone was recording. She nodded.

'Okay,' she began, 'so I woke up around two thirty in the morning. The reason being that I call my grandchildren each week around then. They're in Spain; Girona, to be precise. My daughter married a Spaniard and, after they divorced, he gets the kids for a couple of months a year.'

She pointed to a photo of two munchkins with oddly 70s hair, both offering a gap-toothed grin at the camera as they waved kayak paddles in the air. The mountains beyond were steep, craggy and dotted with cling-ing pines. The father was, ironically, not in the picture.

'He takes them up into the Pyrenees a lot – hiking, canoeing – so I have to ring them at precise times. Anyway, I had to be online before 3 a.m. I'd made myself a tea and set up the computer and everything. It was still dark outside, of course, but I don't remember hearing or seeing anyone.'

Bluey glanced at the laptop sitting on a sideboard.

'Where were you sitting?'

'Oh, here. On the sofa. The lighting is awful in the study. This is, uh, kinder. When you get older' – she glanced at Lachie – 'you pay attention to that sort of thing. I don't want to look like the Wicked Witch of the West: frightens the kiddies, doesn't it?'

Lachie doubted that she did: Bryony gave the impression that she'd always been attractive and possessed good genes.

'They came on just before three and we chatted for about fifteen minutes, at a guess. They're eight and ten – they have short attention spans and get too much sugar. I love them to bits, but they lose concentration quite quickly.

'I'd said goodbye to them when I heard some sort of noise outside. I couldn't swear what it was, but it sounded like an argument. Then I had a quick word with their father, Antonio, to be polite. By the time I'd shut it all down and walked across to the windows, the noise outside had stopped. My eyes took a few seconds to adjust from the light in here to the dark outside. I might have seen the western door open but I couldn't swear: I got that blotchy thing, you know? The green blotches? As soon as my eyes cleared, I grabbed the binoculars.'

She paused and drank some carbonated water.

'Yes, so then I could see much better. She was on the ground – poor Tahlia. Such a beautiful girl but she always looked like trouble, either for her or for someone else. Just something in her eyes; the kind of person who didn't avoid trouble because she thought it was part of life. In and out of scrapes, I would think. But poor girl, she's lying on the ground, there, where you have the tent. He was leaning over her.'

'Who was?'

'Well, Reuben. Reuben Pearce, of course.' She looked at Bluey sharply. 'Hasn't anyone else identified him? Lord, I can't be the only one who saw it.'

She seemed momentarily annoyed, then alarmed, but reset her position on the sofa.

'He was standing and leaning over her. I was ringing triple-zero by then, but I kept watching while I was giving the address. He crouched down. She wasn't moving. From up here I'm looking down and from the side, so I couldn't quite see his right hand. But suddenly he thrust it at her, at her ribs. Pushed a couple of times and withdrew it. Then he looked around to see if anyone was watching. I ducked back, hoped he hadn't seen me. I know my table lamps were on, but I don't really want to – I mean, I'll make a statement but, you know, I have to live here. If he gets bail. You know.'

It was always a problem when the neighbours were the main witnesses to violence: the alleged attacker frequently got bail and it was reasonable for them to live at home – close enough to intimidate the witnesses and collapse the case. Bluey made a note to consider that issue if it looked like Tahlia's killer lived in the complex.

'You didn't see what was in his hand?' he asked.

'I didn't need to. He pushed at her ribs a couple of times and then I could see the blood. There wasn't any before . . . before he touched her. A little pool of it, under her back. Then he knelt down and half picked her up. He was talking to her, but I couldn't hear what he said: the window was closed and I wasn't going to draw attention by opening it. He put her back down – quite gently, to be fair – and got his phone out. I'd like to think it was the ambulance he was calling, but who knows? Anyway, shortly after that he started mouth-to-mouth.'

Both detectives were trying to marry this to the evidence they'd already heard from others, before giving up and accepting that they'd have to knit it together back at the station.

'How long did he do that for?' asked Lachie.

'Not long. A minute, perhaps? I know they say resuscitation is tiring, don't they? But that's mainly when you're trying to start the heart, I think. It went on for two minutes, at the most. He seemed to give up and ran back towards his unit. It's right underneath here, so he disappeared. He came back out and I saw the blue lights outside: you could see their reflection in the entranceway over there. Reuben went over and let them in.'

That was already a bone of contention, then, thought Lachie; Jody had said different. Lachie was pleased to have noticed an anomaly: so far, all the evidence was nebulous and probably contradictory, but hard to calibrate with any accuracy.

Lachie risked another interruption. 'As the paramedics came into the courtyard, who was where, exactly?'

She thought for a moment and closed her eyes. *A serious witness*, thought Bluey.

'The first paramedic came through the door on the western side. A man. Then Reuben, then the female paramedic. The two paramedics knelt down and started working. Reuben stood around like a spare part.'

She stopped, regathered. 'Oh, he shook his head at someone. Someone off to his left. At first I thought he was just shaking his head at the whole scene, at how sad it all was; but no, it was at *someone*. But when I looked to his left, I couldn't make out anyone. They were still working on poor Tahlia when Reuben wandered off and wedged open the entrance doors. I suppose the paramedics would need to go back and forth to the ambulance, I don't know. When he came back in I noticed Caretaker Sally standing by the door. I don't know when she arrived. He said something to her on the way past and she nodded.

'The paramedics kept at it, until the first police officer arrived. Then they stood up and everyone gave a minute's grace. Stood quietly, honouring that she was gone. It was quite moving, really, that they took the time for that. A minute later another officer brought in that tent thingie, in a big bag. After that, I couldn't see much. An officer took Reuben back towards his apartment. He did something with Reuben's hands, but I couldn't see because they passed below me then. About five minutes later, this constable here knocked on my door.' She glanced to Tyson. 'I assume you'd seen that my lights were on. He told me to stay put until a detective had interviewed me.'

It was coherent, it was well observed. Bryony hadn't offered much in the way of conjecture; she'd done what was asked and simply reported what she'd seen, in the sequence that she'd seen it. Lachie liked this kind of witness – the type that didn't embellish or overreach. Juries liked them, too, if it came to that.

'You talked about Tahlia earlier: I assume you've met her?'

'Yes. Well, in passing. We're very different generations, but we all have to put the garbage out, don't we? She doesn't have a car, as far as I know, but sometimes she'd be getting out of a friend's car as I parked. Besides, Sally talked about her a bit; we're in the same book club and Sally's done a bundle of electrical work in here – it was a disaster zone for a while. Her son and Tahlia were . . . oh, God, I sound so old when I don't know what they call it these days.'

Bluey agreed ruefully. 'You and me both.'

Bryony smiled. 'Anyway, whatever *that* is, they were, apparently. For a while and a bit up and down, I think. I'm not sure Sally was overjoyed about it: Tahlia was beautiful to look at but, as I say, she seemed like the type who'd be drawn into something, sooner or later. I'm not entirely certain why I think that, but I suspect Sally thought the same. Something about Tahlia's . . . flightiness, butterfly mind, whatever you'd call it. When she made the effort, she'd be beautifully dressed. Tahlia had the figure for it and a nice taste when she wasn't slopping around. Teens and twenties; they take their skin and their muscles and their energy all for granted, don't they? Sometimes I want to scream at them to take better care of it all, but I'm sure they'd think I'm a crazy old lady if I did that. Tahlia's carelessness was a little more than the usual young-person carelessness. Sorry, I'm not sure that's very useful.'

'No, no, it is. When was the last time you saw Tahlia?'

'Oh, at Crescendo. Looking in the window.'

Bluey was bemused, but Lachie knew the place: a musical-instrument store in a *very* upmarket arcade in Mission Plains. 'At anything in particular?' he asked.

'I asked her about that. She pointed at the saxophone and said she'd always wanted to learn. I was about to offer the details of a tutor I know, but she wandered off. Swaying a bit: I wasn't sure if it was drink or drugs, but she was definitely struggling with a straight line. She was a very pretty, floaty kind of drunk, though.'

'When was that?'

'About three, yesterday afternoon. I was on my way home to go to bed, since I'd be up in the middle of the night.'

'You don't go into her café, What's Brewin'?'

'No, not a fan. I prefer tea and theirs tastes like dishwater. Besides, Reuben goes there now, apparently, and I wouldn't want to bump into him.'

'Because?'

'Have you met him? Well, then, you know *because*. Frankly, I don't trust myself; I might want to explain to him again why his actions last year were appalling and how much damage he's done without being remotely aware of it. As I understand it, he doesn't always take kindly to people pointing out his many inadequacies.'

'Has he ever threatened you; given you cause for concern?'

'No . . . not me, no. But I think he's inclined to, how can I say it, go from zero to angry pretty quickly. Not so much a short fuse as an on/off switch. There aren't many people in this complex who'll give him the time of day.'

Bluey gave that the short pause that it merited.

'And Tahlia, have you ever seen or heard of someone wishing to do her harm?'

'No . . . no, I don't think so. I only bumped into her occasionally. As I say, a bit flighty and ephemeral, but I daresay that isn't unusual, not these days. I'm sure I wasn't much different at their age, but it certainly feels like it, doesn't it? Her generation appears stuck either way: simultaneously poorly anchored to real life but weighed down by the cares of the world.'

True, thought Bluey. But he was troubled that a motive wasn't swimming into view. She seemed a young, pretty, butterfly of a woman, with no apparent enemies and little in her life that might prompt someone to end it.

Tahlia Moore should still be alive.

Chapter 9

What's Brewin', Boundary Street, Windoo. Thursday, 0554hrs

In this part of the city, the pale sunlight sliced through well-watered trees and on to intricate block paving. It didn't have to slide between industrial units or barrel over a burned-out joyride. Westies got their bins emptied at night; Easties during the day. That reflected the priorities since the city's early days, and it told a tale. West of the river was where the money settled, like sand in a jar. No matter where it was generated, it came west to stay. From the Pacific Heights units it was a two-hundred-metre stroll through a long, slim parkette; overhanging figs, curved topiary, outdoor chess and irritable corellas. At the other end, just past the ornate cycle racks, was the café where Tahlia had worked.

It was six minutes to opening time at What's Brewin'. Cassie Stewart was pushing the A-frame sign up against the lamppost. She unfurled herself slowly against aching hammies from last night's Pilates class, and watched a pair of utes squeal their tyres as they turned left.

As she lugged the second table out on to the terrace, two men approached. Not regulars; she sussed that straight away. Collars and ties weren't frequent around here – too many students, laptop heroes and supered-up retirees for that – so she guessed at real estate. It was really only real estate, pollies and undertakers wearing ties these days. Or, she thought as they neared the tables, maybe it was a father and son. When they reached the door she held up a hand.

'Sorry, guys, we're not officially open yet. You can come in, but we can't actually serve until six. Blame the premier; we all do.'

The younger one winced slightly and showed police ID.

'You'll probably want to stay closed a bit longer, actually. Is the manager inside?'

Cassie swallowed and managed a nonplussed nod. 'Scott. Scott Villiers. Yeah. Behind the counter.'

'Jesus Christ. Are you sure . . . are you sure it's Tahlia?'

Bluey scooted his chair closer to the metal table.

'We're still waiting on the formal ID, but several people who knew Tahlia were at the scene; so, yes.'

'Bloody hell.' Scott stared at the table, then looked across at Cassie, who was organising the outdoor chairs. 'Cass, lock the door and turn the sign to *closed*, thanks.'

Cassie frowned. 'But it's nearly –'

'Now, Cass. I'll explain soon enough.'

Cassie flipped the sign and shook her head at an elderly man emerging from a badly parked Kia. She shrugged at him, as if this provided more information, then pretended to check the milk jugs so that she could eavesdrop.

Scott sat back and puffed his cheeks.

'God, her sis. She won't know, will she?'

Lachie raised a placatory hand. 'Tahlia's mother knows and she's contacting the rest of the family. You knew her sister?'

'Reagan? Yeah, of course. She worked here before she went on the gap year. Cass was her replacement. Yeah. Oh, man, this is crap.'

Lachie leaned on his elbows. 'When was the last time you saw Tahlia?'

'Oh, she did a shift yesterday with Cass. She was originally supposed to be doing today, but her and Cass swapped over. I was expecting her in tomorrow morning. Bloody hell.'

'We never met her, mate. What sort of person was she?'

'Oh, customers bloody loved her, you know? See the jars?' He pointed to a series of narrow-mouthed glass jars anchored on the side counter, next to the sugars and stirrers. 'She's the middle one, there.'

Jeez, they're tip jars, thought Bluey, shocked. You could slide coins or the occasional note into whichever jar you chose. On the one hand, it meant you could reward the person who'd served you, rather than have it slip into some generic account or Scott's pocket. On the other hand, it was a very public measure of who wasn't popular – an audit of extrovert charm for all to see. He thought it was cruel and mocking if you weren't the apparently popular Tahlia Moore. The middle jar had more money than the others combined.

'She was, uh, occasionally challenging to manage, I've got to be honest. Not feisty, as such, but sometimes she wasn't really a team player, and lately . . .'

'Lately?'

'Ah, last year or so, a bit unreliable. Timekeeping, shifts, that sort of thing: fine when she was here, but. A friend of hers died not so long ago and, well, she's been a bit rocky. We made allowances.'

Lachie glanced over at Cassie and therefore caught the inaudible sigh.

'Was there anyone here who was hassling her? Customer wanted to date her, maybe?'

Scott gave a sardonic smile. 'I'm sure there were plenty, yeah. Look at the jar. But nah, no one who made any real noise; no one she was worried about, that I know. I think she'd have said. She didn't stand on ceremony.'

'And outside of work? What did you know about that side of things?'

'Ah, not much. She lived in Pacific Heights, through the park, there. Ah, crap, you already know that, 'course you do. Sorry. Still, you know, bit shocked. Yeah, shared the unit with her sister until Reagan went travelling. Plenty of people picked her up after work: lots of different people, but no one that regular. I know Tahlia hung out with that Josh kid, Josh Harris, for a while. From the same units. That was a bit on and off, I think. Cass might know better than me. I'm considered the oldie around here.'

Bluey tapped the table. 'Okay, mate. We'll need to speak to Cassie. After that it's up to you if you open the place, or when. You need to

organise the data for Tahlia's shifts, wages, employment details, super
payments, all that. We'll come back for that later, but it'll save you a heap
of time to start on it now. Oh, and we'll need to see the CCTV from her
last few shifts as well.'

Scott nodded, although it didn't seem clear that he'd heard all that, or
that he'd remember it later. Lachie noticed that Cassie had heard it all
and assumed she'd remind Scott.

'I can set up the CCTV now, if you'd like,' mumbled Scott.

Ideal.

'I'll sit in on that with you,' offered Bluey, 'while Lachie talks to
Cassie. Saves a bit of time, eh?'

And enables two shuttered conversations.

The pair wandered off to the office at the back of the café, while Lachie
beckoned Cassie. She sat uncertainly and flicked glances back to the front
door, as though she could flip the sign and all would be magically well.

'You heard all that, right, Cassie?'

She bit her lip. 'Most of it, yeah.'

'Those jars: that's a bit brutal, eh? Why do you put up with it?'

Cassie shrugged. 'Was like that when I started. Reagan did pretty well
from it: paid her airfare to Europe off her tips, she said. I guess it's tax free
at least, so we'd be stupid to complain.'

'Yeah, point taken. All the same, if you're not Tahlia Moore it's inher-
ently unhealthy to look across at that three-dimensional league table,
isn't it?'

Cassie looked skyward for a second. 'Yeah. Yeah, it is.'

Lachie leaned forward and skewered her with a serious glare. 'We're
looking for someone who meant to hurt Tahlia. It's not an accident, or
something getting out of hand. It's deliberate. So, cards on the table,
mate. What was Tahlia really like?'

Cassie tapped the café keys on the edge of the table.

'Just like Scott said, but a lot more so. He sees what he wants to see; he
likes a quiet life, that one. She was really appealing to the punters; you could
see it all get switched on when she turned their way. If I just came in here to

buy coffee, I'd think she was adorable. Pretty as hell, charming. If you worked with her? She was unreliable, catty; a bit of a bitch, really. Oh, and –'

'Yeah?'

'Look, not my place, and I'm not an expert. But she'd really gone downhill the last few months. Not just the unreliable thing, neither. I mean, you could see it in her skin, around the eyes. She was a bit jittery, a bit . . . *off*. I don't really buy that she was upset about her friend dying. She spun that to con Scott: he's a bit of a soft touch, terrified someone will call him a bully, so he's easy to get around. She played it for all it was worth, but the friend – Josh, I think his name was – I don't think she was fussed. She never acted upset about it until she wanted a day off, or a shift swap, or something. Then the simpering came on, the waterworks, the cat-from-*Shrek* face.'

'You didn't like her.'

'No, I didn't. To be fair, we were probably just very different, so maybe we were never likely to be besties. Reagan was lovely, genuinely lovely. Tahlia was two-faced but smart about it. Hard to like that, isn't it?'

'And *was* anyone hassling her? Looking for a date, or whatever?'

'Nah. She knew how to shoot them down without them feeling the bullet. I'm a bit jealous of that talent, really. Not that I, not that everyone's – Anyway. Nah, she said she had a type and they never came in here.'

'What was her type?'

'*Six feet, seven figures and eight inches*, she always said. I believed her: you don't look like that and go out with an average guy, do you? She struck me as high maintenance if you were the bloke. She sure wasn't going to pay for anything; but she'd look great on your arm, eh?'

'So, no boyfriend that you know of?'

'Not that she mentioned. She sort of tumbled through mates at a rate of knots. Found them easy, moved on easy. She had *contacts* that got her into nightclubs, into gigs. She thought she was a VIP and in demand. That stuff bores me witless so I tuned her out.'

'Did anyone else work regularly with her?'

'Scott and me, mainly. Brianna did quite a few shifts with her – she's in Bali this week, though. Yeah, mainly us three.'

'Okay. We might have some follow-up questions later on. Oh, for the record, where were you between midnight and five thirty this morning?'

'That's a weird –'

'It's for completeness. Everyone associated with her, no exceptions.'

'Ah, okay. Well, I need my sleep: I get up at four thirty for this so I'm in bed at stupid o'clock. Alarm would be at half four, shower, here by half five; I was opening up today so I was here before Scott.'

Yeah, thought Lachie, *you totally didn't answer the question and you don't appear to have an alibi.* Vague terms, generalities: nothing specific about this morning, just her average routine. He made a note that she might need to be backgrounded later.

'All right. Well, I'm sorry to bring you all such bad news. We'll try to be discreet if we need to come back later, okay?'

Cassie nodded, but none of this looked to be *okay*.

The office at the back of the café was crowded, to say the least. It was a natural overspill for the dishwasher just outside the door – the filing cabinet was topped off by crockery bearing the name of the coffee-bean supplier. Bluey remembered that cafés often made themselves basically indentured staff for the coffee supplier. It was the supplier that provided the beans themselves, the crockery, the coffee machine with maintenance thrown in and just about everything else a start-up needed, in return for absolute fidelity. Scott looked like an entrepreneur under pressure. Until he could replace Tahlia he'd be one staff member down in a tight job market, and Tahlia, judging by the tip jars, had been a star attraction. Strip out a few weeks of pity-purchases to come and he'd be struggling.

Eventually, sliding piles of paperwork and half-opened cardboard cartons were rearranged and Bluey could watch the CCTV being cued up. Much of it, as they ran it at x12 speed, was dull and predictable. Halfway through yesterday's shift, however, something caught Bluey's eye.

'Whoa, back up. About ten minutes back. She had a bit of a row with someone there.'

Scott rewound and stuttered through until Bluey's raised hand made him play at normal speed. There was no sound, but the picture quality was good.

'I see Tahlia, but I don't see you guys.'

'Ten forty? Would probably be Cass's break, then. She'd be taking a smoko out the back. I have told her to give it up. I would be . . . yeah, I went out the back a minute or so before this. Probably the dishwasher – we've got to the stage where the customers tell me when it's beeped.'

Tahlia had just delivered two coffees to a table, pawing slightly at a customer's arm as she laughed. A young man, maybe nineteen, had entered the café with a stilted, awkward gait. Seemingly uncomfortable in both his clothing and the location, he held his arms across him as if in pain, or fearing a strike. The uncertainty reminded Bluey of a baby bird, in limbo between staying in the nest and attempting its first real flight. He had the kind of haircut that he might have done himself, graceless squared-off features, and he walked with splayed feet.

He stood so close to Tahlia that she practically thumped him as she turned. She took a step back in surprise; he, however, was not for moving. He merely opened his hand to reveal his phone. She paused, not sure what was coming but, when he didn't speak, she leaned closer to the phone's images.

Bluey and Scott saw the shudder: it was that visible. She recoiled slightly, leaned in again, then reared back. The body language said fear, anger, revulsion. She moved a little closer and it seemed that what she said was whispered, or at least hissed. She jabbed a finger on to his shoulder, but he still didn't move. The phone remained over his sternum, still playing whatever-it-was. She made a sharp play for the phone, but he was disconcertingly quick. She pointed and seemingly hissed again. He didn't appear to back down, but the phone dipped from sight and he moved robotically, headed for the door.

Tahlia turned, unwittingly facing the camera. *Yes*, thought Bluey, *it was revulsion tinged with anger and a sense of desperation.* She ran her hand across her face. Then, presumably in response to a customer, she regained her game face, gave a dazzling smile and a nod that she was okay, and went back to the counter.

'Who's that kid?' asked Bluey.

Scott was bemused. 'Dunno. Never seen him before, he's not a regular. Cass might know. I wasn't working the day before that one. Maybe he'd come in then? Looked like he was complaining about something.'

No, thought Bluey, *that wasn't it*. That wasn't a tantrum because yesterday's cappuccino wasn't frothy enough. The young man had simple actions, clear-cut, and what he was concerned about was the images on the phone. It didn't strike Bluey as work-related at all. The reaction and the look on Tahlia's face said that it cut deeper.

They needed to know who that was, and why he'd terrified and enraged Tahlia Moore.

Chapter 10

Boundary Street, Windoo. Thursday, 0615hrs

Printability was indeed next to the café, as Tyson had said. It would be almost impossible for Jody to work there and not notice Tahlia Moore. Especially as she seemed to be the noticeable type. Having emailed the CCTV footage and Scott's details to Tyson for the follow-up, they strolled back through the parkette towards Pacific Heights.

'Thoughts?' prompted Bluey.

Lachie pointed to the outdoor chess set dozing in the morning sun. 'Black's bishop is vulnerable. Oh, and he should castle.'

'Grand master crap aside, thoughts?'

'I have too many right now,' Lachie replied. 'They're all cutting across each other. I mean, we have something from each eyewitness and some details from the café there. But really, it's all a mish-mash, isn't it? I'm not convinced anyone got a completely clear view or a long enough run at it to see the whole thing: everyone's arrived late, arrived early, saw some of it but not the rest, or missed a crucial bit somehow.' He swatted at a stray grass that had drooped into harm's way. 'I can't believe someone didn't have a perfectly good angle to witness everything we need. Doesn't seem possible. It's like they all conspired to have a couple of jigsaw pieces each, but everyone agreed to throw away the rest.'

Bluey found it hard to disagree. Back in station, Laxton would be assuming that this many witnesses meant an easy solve. He'd tell his own bosses that at morning prayers – *yeah, a slam dunk even with those two on it, trust me.* But the reality, as Lachie said, was a partial mosaic. They would need to gather all the information together and go through it piece by piece, looking at which evidence backed up a claim and which evidence countered a claim. They might be left, after that process, with the thick end of nothing.

Tyson was waiting for them at the western entrance to Pacific Heights. *He has enviable posture*, thought Lachie, who battled periodic sciatica and treated every twist and bend as a potential disaster. The sun was stronger and the traffic was beginning to pick up. Now was peak tradie time; in another half an hour it would be peak office time, then peak school-run time. The 'rush hour' was two and a half hours: successive waves of people too busy to wonder why they were so busy.

'Just so's you know,' said Tyson, holding the door open for them, 'the media are on to this now. There's a journo from the *Herald-Chronicle* knocking on apartment doors as we speak.'

'Bugger,' said Bluey. 'You just know that some neighbour's going to say something we haven't picked up on yet, or some crap that isn't true, and that's all we'll be asked about in the press conference.'

Lachie shrugged. 'Don't do one, then.'

Bluey raised an eyebrow. 'Seriously?'

'Yeah, seriously. I don't do 'em. Waste of time. We put out a holding-pattern press release where we refuse to comment on an ongoing investigation at such an important time, remind them to respect the family of the deceased, and get on with our actual job.'

The notion was oh, so inviting. When he did pressers, Bluey had an amiably avuncular style that generally went down well with the media; he seemed like he wasn't trying to hide something significant. It was tempting for now to ignore the media: they'd be obsessed with the gangland drive-by killings and this would be a low priority for them. But that delaying tactic would only stretch so far.

'Let's try that for twenty-four hours. I doubt Laxton will let us get away with it for longer than that.'

Tyson left them so that he could push the door-to-door inquiries, in the hope that they could beat the journo to whatever investigative gem was out there. The detectives crossed the courtyard for the umpteenth time. In full daylight it looked benign, although the dark stain to the concrete told its tale. There would be a specialist crew in an hour or two to clean that away. The tent had been completely removed now, though the area it had contained was still taped off. People would be ignoring that tape shortly, their morbid curiosity too much to resist. Forensics knew that; they made sure they had everything before they left it to the public. A tech had hitched a temporary camera above the eastern entrance to watch the crime scene. That was primarily because offenders often revisited the crime scene; it helped to know who was doing so. It would also be a minor disincentive to ignore the tape but, once the first person disregarded it, everyone would.

Fig leaves; sometimes Bluey felt like he just organised fig leaves.

Pacific Heights apartment block. Apartment 7. Thursday, 0620hrs

Ground floor west was the location for the last of the eyewitnesses – that they knew of – Martyn Brooks. He was sitting out on his terrace, a large flask of coffee and a stack of paper cups next to him. There was also half a fruit cake, some plastic barbecue plates and a black bag for the garbage. Martyn had clearly appointed himself free caterer to the investigation team.

'Ah, getting some cake while it lasts?' he chuckled. He was tall and sinewy, tending to lean forward like a mantis when he stood. There was nothing forbidding or threatening about it, just the best way to semi-fold a large frame into an acceptable space.

'That's very kind, Mr Brooks,' said Bluey, extending a hand. The shake was predicably robust. 'The boys and girls are waxing lyrical about your little corner shop, here.' It wasn't true – none of the ungrateful buggers had even mentioned it. 'We're Bluey and Lachie, the detectives. We need to ask you about what you've seen during the night. Can we sit?'

Martyn gave a silent *ah* and waved them to two squeaky and disconcertingly wobbly cane conservatory chairs. He sat and fussed about the
paper cups as a gust of wind threatened to derail them.

'So, Mr Brooks –'

'Martyn, please.'

'Martyn. Can you take us through things from your perspective,
starting yesterday evening, please?'

'Of course. I had dinner at seven – watched the news, as usual, even
though I find it all quite depressing. Then there was an old episode of *Lewis*
on. I love *Lewis*. More than *Morse* – I think it'll stand the test of time better.
Oh, sorry, you aren't interested in that, are you? I used to watch *Lateline*
before I went to bed, but of course they dropped that, didn't they? So now,
I'm in bed by ten. I say that, but I don't fall asleep very easily these days. So I
listened to the radio for a while and then fell asleep.'

It was always worth letting witnesses like this ease into the space. 'You
slept right through?'

'Oh, God no. I can't remember the last time I did that. No. I get up a
few times for the, uh, call of nature.'

'How often?'

'Five or six, on a good night.'

Lachie spluttered inadvertently.

'Don't smirk, young man, you have this in your future. I don't drink
anything after 6 p.m., but it doesn't matter: my system just prefers it that
way. I remember it was raining hard on one trip to the bathroom. I don't
look at the clock, sorry. If I clock-watch I just worry about how much
sleep I'm missing.'

'Apart from the rain, all quiet on the Western Front?' asked Bluey.

'Yes, yes. It was very peaceful. Next door have two teenagers and,
while I do like them, the quiet is a rare and miraculous thing.'

'I haven't seen that family around.'

'Oh, they're on the Goldie. They're back next week.'

Bluey smiled slightly and nodded. Martyn drifted for a moment.

'Hmm? Oh, sorry. Yes. So, at the fifth or sixth hurdle I heard a noise as

I returned to the bedroom. I peeped out through the curtains. I think the western exit was open, which was unusual. But mainly, I saw him.'

Lachie surreptitiously half turned in his chair. The view to the deceased would have been blocked by the swings, the roundabout and two mushrooms.

'Who?' asked Bluey.

'Reuben Pearce. The strange bloke from across the way.'

'Strange in what way?'

'Oh, most ways, I think. I mean, that thing you caught him for: doesn't get much stranger than that, does it? And besides, he creeps around here quite a lot. He was out here sitting on one of my chairs the other night. I only realised because of the cigar smoke. Told him to bugger off, I did. He just laughed as he left. Anyway, he was out there, where you had your tent earlier.'

Reuben kept reappearing front and centre: first Bryony, now Martyn. It could be an accident of timing – that's when they each happened to look at the courtyard – or it could be that he was the primary person involved.

'What was he doing?'

'Holding her up. The poor girl. Tahlia, wasn't it? That's what Bryony said.'

Urgh, Jeez, thought Lachie. *Bryony Price has spoken to him already. Witness tainted.*

'Bryony Price spoke to you?' asked Bluey.

'Oh yes, just after the ambulance arrived. I rang her, to find out what's what. She's on the top floor and she has binoculars,' he said proudly.

'Yes, she does. Back to Reuben. What was he doing?'

'As I say, holding her up. I thought she was just drunk. I've seen her, you know, half cut out there, sitting on the swings, or whatever. Quite a benign drunk, I've always thought: she seemed soft and dreamy. I was in the army and I've seen every kind of smashed you can imagine. But she wasn't drunk, was she? He put her down on the ground, spoke into his phone, and then tried mouth-to-mouth. Well, I called triple-zero straight away. You should, shouldn't you?'

'Absolutely. You did the right thing, there. How long did he try?'

'Well, when I got back from the phone he was gone. So not very long. Maybe a minute?'

Got back from the phone. Lachie glanced and saw the handset on the kitchen wall. Presumably, no mobile; or, not one in easy reach. It was a generational thing.

'Yes, couldn't have been long. I kept it short and sweet with the operator. They'd already dispatched someone, apparently. When I got back, I could see she was on the ground and . . . well, I saw blood. Plenty of it.'

There was an obvious question – *why not help her?* – but Bluey deliberately withheld that card.

'What next?'

Martyn had been quite forthcoming in his way, but now he looked away for solace, back into his own apartment.

'I, uh, dithered. To my shame. I should have gone out there and helped. But . . . it struck me that if someone had done that to her – possibly Reuben, possibly someone else – then they might be still out there. I'd done the decent thing and rung the ambulance, after all.'

His voice tailed off. Lachie could understand the lingering indignity: a grown man, an ex-soldier, staying in his apartment because he feared for his personal safety. It must be so very hard to swallow.

Bluey kept his voice soft and judgement-free. 'What made you think she hadn't collapsed, or had an aneurism? Why the sense of foreboding?'

Martyn flexed his ring finger as he thought. 'I'm not sure. Even with the blood, I couldn't see where it was coming from. You're right, of course, I had no way of knowing. Just a feeling that came over me and seemed . . . correct.'

Not the first person to think that, mused Bluey. Presumably there had been something about the circumstance, the arrangement of the people, the body language, the urgency or lack of, the atmosphere: *something* convinced everyone, sooner or later, that the scene had a dark cause and a darker outcome.

'I'd actually almost talked myself into going outside when Reuben came back. He stood over her again, then he nodded. To himself, I suppose, because I couldn't see anyone around. No one was rushing to the scene. Then I saw the ambulance lights outside; their reflection, I mean. Eventually Reuben went over and let them in. Hmm. That's it, really.'

'The initial noise that made you go to the window, what was that?'

'It's . . . hard to describe. Not a scream, exactly. Not a squawk. A bit half and half.'

'Half a scream and half a squawk?'

'I said it wasn't easy to describe. Maybe a scream that was stifled, or shortened, or prevented? Yes, more like that.'

Both detectives got the sense that Martyn was talking himself into his testimony as he gave it; that everything was contestable and malleable until it was said out loud. Lachie flicked his arm; a gesture that said he wanted to take over. Bluey sat back and yielded.

'Martyn, how tall are you?'

'Six foot five. Sorry, that's in old money.'

'No problem. When you were watching events out there, were there any lights on in your apartment?'

'No. Oh, wait, there was one. There's a nightlight between the bath-room and the bedroom. Stops me going arse over apex when I need to pee. It's not very bright, if that's what you're worried about.'

It was. Lachie smiled slightly and continued.

'Thanks, mate. Was your view obscured, or do you think you could see the whole thing?'

'Ah. Good point. Okay.' He stared out towards the middle of the courtyard. 'When Reuben was standing over . . . over Tahlia, I could only see the bottom half of him. That end tree, you see. When he was standing around while the paramedics worked, I couldn't see his bottom half: the roundabout and those stupid mushroom things.'

Martyn had a partial view, just like every other concerned citizen who'd looked out of their window, thought Lachie. It still seemed impossible: to be fifteen metres from a killing yet unable to see it properly. Checking all this on the 3-D software couldn't happen quickly enough.

'Tahlia Moore: did you know her?'

'No, not really. I'd seen her round and about a few times. She liked sitting on the swings when it was dark and next-door's kids were inside. She had a ciggie there quite often. I'd see her drop the stubs. The kids like to pick them up and light them, in my experience, so she was a bit careless, certainly about litter. Very pretty girl, but there was something . . . hmm, something wrong with the light.'

Lachie waited patiently for the coda. Martyn reached for exactly the words he wanted and found them.

'I mean, she could produce this dazzling smile and turn on the charm. But if you saw her alone, like when she was on the swings? Very melancholic. The light went missing.'

Chapter 11

Lachie and Bluey selected a mushroom each. Tyson had rejoined them and automatically stood to one side, feet at shoulder width, awaiting instructions.

Lachie frowned. 'Why would he go for a piss five times in a night? Prostate problems, or something?'

Bluey shrugged. 'Could be. But nah, it's most likely precautionary: he doesn't necessarily need to go. When you get to his age, you'll go to the bathroom at any time purely for the *reassurance trifecta*. Which is' – he counted off with his fingers – 'that you're definitely upright when you go, definitely aiming and definitely mean to do it.'

While Lachie smirked, Bluey turned to the constable.

'That's all the eyewitnesses, Tyson?'

'That we know of, si—Bluey. They've just finished door-to-door, so once I've collated those reports we should know if anyone else saw something.'

And what exactly was the *something* that everyone had seen? Lachie hadn't really been able to piece it together on the run, which was unusual for him. He was normally capable of assembling and contrasting what people were saying – picking the incongruence while he was hearing it. But his sixth sense of what jarred, or was omitted, had gone astray.

'Do all these pieces fit?' asked Bluey.

'Nah. Not for me. Not yet.' Lachie lined up the reasons. 'What happened before anyone even heard a scream? What was the conversation before the scream? Who was talking to Tahlia? One scream, or two? Anyone there before Reuben? Who was bending over her? One minute for the mouth-to-mouth, or two, or five? What was Reuben's right hand doing? Was he nodding to anyone before the ambos were here? How did the killer get out of the courtyard? Or, did they? Maybe Reuben relied on his bloody clothing being explained by the first aid? Where's the weapon? How did the killer get rid of it? What was the motive in the first place?'

'That's a lot of questions, mate.'

'I know. It's as many questions – and most of the same questions – as we had when we parked the car.'

That was true. The eyewitnesses had barely corroborated anything: there seemed little that several saw and agreed upon.

'That's the trouble with eyewitnesses, Lachie: the eyes. We think, because they've seen something, that either it's true or we can prove that it isn't. But it doesn't work like that. The eyes take in the light, but the brain processes the data. That's the tricky bit. I don't define the human eye as a camera. It's the starting gun for interpretation, error and prejudice. It can't be trusted.'

'Now you tell me,' muttered Lachie, offering an eye-roll to Tyson, who gave a Sphynx of a smile. 'So what do we do now?'

'We gather context. We get all the fundamentals of Tahlia's life – the financials, the phone records, the online history – and we talk to her mother. Then we start assessing the witnesses, and their statements, in the light of that.'

He turned to Tyson. 'Will your sergeant be okay with us borrowing you for a day or two? Only, you know the local area and we don't.'

Tyson nodded. 'Already checked that, si—Bluey. I'm available for today and tomorrow.'

'Awesome.' Bluey glanced at Lachie, in case there was anything he wanted to add. A slight shake of the head. 'Okay, then. Back to base to see what we've got on Tahlia's life.'

Chapter 12

Tyson sat in the patrol car and looked at the sheaf of door-to-door reports in his hand. He'd been given four uniforms to conduct the task, seeing as this was a murder. On a regular case he'd be splitting the effort between himself and anyone he could cajole, emotionally blackmail or otherwise dragoon. While he'd enjoyed following the two detectives around and watching how they operated, there was a downside. It meant he'd had to fully delegate the door-to-door, and now, looking at the reports, he had a feeling he might regret that. You couldn't really redo those interviews: they worked primarily because they were an unexpected one-off for the apartment-dweller, caught in the moment and perhaps buoyed by the excitement of flashing lights and detectives. Good intel often came when you keyed into the interviewees' adrenaline and willingness to be part of the investigation they were watching. But if you went back later, the novelty of the drama had worn off and you were just some bastard keeping them from their lunch.

He wished he'd kept the map he'd been given by Caretaker Sally, even though it was a bit grungy and used. The detectives were glad to have it, stains and smudges and all. But now Tyson needed it because this apartment complex was weird. His girlfriend was a nurse and, when she'd started at City West Hospital, she'd carried a map of the layout on her phone for about three months. Eventually she got used to the place, but it took a while. Pacific Heights' ostensibly easy doughnut shape belied the trickery within: Tyson had no idea how to get from number 12 to number 26, or 49 to 17.

He put the forms into the numerical order of the apartments, although he'd already realised that wasn't the same order as the apartments. Bryony Price, up on the top floor, was number 50. But her next-door neighbour, he'd noticed when they'd walked the corridor, was 42, not 49 or 51. Likewise with Martyn, on the ground floor: he was number 7, next door to number 11. Reuben was number 6 but not near Martyn. Some genius had split the complex into arbitrary groupings that bore no relation to the building itself. Being in numerical order made it quick to find any particular paperwork but meant bugger-all in any other terms.

Watching the detectives had been an education. Bluey had seemed like an old hand sauntering through it all, hands in pockets and an easy informality. But, Tyson sensed, he hadn't missed a trick. Bluey had discerned Jody's kidney stone while Tyson and Lachie were thinking *agitated, sweating, keeps his arm next to his body . . . hidden weapon*. It was good to watch Bluey's unflashy, apparently undemanding way of going about it.

Lachie, on the other hand, was a bit less gung-ho than he'd expected. When the detectives arrived he'd vaguely recognised the name and had fired a text to a colleague. The message came back – *that bloke who got suspended over Reuben Pearce*. Tyson had expected to be treading on eggshells if Lachie and Reuben came into the same space, but Bluey had headed off that problem as well. All the same, Tyson had been expecting Lachie to be a hothead, a large and fragile ego, a loose cannon. But Lachie was more measured and more willing to admit that he didn't know something than Tyson had anticipated. Maybe he was just that way when Bluey was around.

With the forms in some kind of order, Tyson began flicking through. Handwriting was always a challenge, since these forms hadn't yet been added to the force's e-form system, despite everyone agreeing that they were a priority. He quickly found who was going through the motions and who was doing a good job. Constable Willie Ofusa – an officer who combined a subdued frizzy hairstyle, dimpled smile, laid-back Samoan vibe and the ability to physically subdue any prisoner – was the standout.

Diligent, comprehensive, he'd clearly asked smart questions around the standard ones, and Tyson looked through his contributions first. One of them stood out.

Apartment 16. First floor, east side. Home to Stella Peters, son Anthony about eighteen. Both at home all night. Did not hear any activity in the courtyard until the arrival of paramedics. Did not know the deceased. Anthony's behaviour awkward. Stella Peters says that her son is autistic. Noticed Anthony had a drone on the floor and chatted to him about the features. Anthony became agitated. Stella demanded that I leave.

I do not believe Anthony became agitated because I was asking about the drone's power pack and flight time. I believe he may have some footage relating to the deceased – it was when I asked about recording and wanted to see what the picture quality was like that he became concerned.

I suggest a follow-up visit from detectives.

This, thought Tyson, is what good policing can do. Observation – a drone sitting on a desk or, as here, half underneath a bed. Context – detectives were speaking to eyewitnesses and so visual evidence was important. Hunch – that a chat might yield something useful. Instincts – that the chat is getting a little close to the bone. Assessment – that the agitation wasn't related to Anthony's condition but the prospect of others viewing the footage. Recommendation.

Tyson texted Ofusa to congratulate him on the excellent work. Then he rang Lachie.

'Tyson, what's up?'

'Well, it's a long shot, but I may have found another eyewitness. If not to the incident itself, someone who can tell us more about Tahlia.'

'Please tell me it's someone who can see the top half *and* bottom half of people running around?'

'This witness, sir, might just see all the courtyard, all the time.'

*

Lachie looked at his watch. He was pulled over on the side of the road and at the mercy of a phalanx of utes if he needed to move out again. Nearly 7 a.m. He'd wanted to get back to the office because the financial and electronic data for Tahlia was starting to come in. Paradoxically, he'd found that it was easier to get financial information out of office hours: the night shifts at these call centres seemed more amenable and less inclined to *escalate this as a priority, sir.* The law said they had to hand it over *pronto*, but they didn't always do that. Lachie certainly wanted a run through that information before meeting Tahlia's mother, but the chance of another eyewitness – who apparently wasn't looking through some sort of obstacle filter – was too good to miss. He texted Bluey that he'd catch him up afterwards and started looking for that rarest of Australian fauna: a tradie who'd let him out of a parking spot. More chance of running over a thylacine.

Pacific Heights apartment block. Apartment 16. Thursday 0710hrs

Tyson met Lachie at the eastern entrance this time. It didn't seem to make much difference: the same neglected air, the same scrapes on the walls. Only the lack of mailboxes seemed to tell east from west. Combined with the anodyne identikit corridors, Lachie wondered how people didn't get lost in their own apartment complex. Especially when they were pissed.

Tyson handed him the door-to-door report.

'Ofusa's steady as, sir; if he says there was a vibe, then there was. I get the sense there might be some footage of Tahlia, even if it's not from last night. Thought it was worth a shake.'

Lachie considered as he skim-read. 'Yeah, good job. You've thanked this Ofusa guy?'

'Already done, sir. It's up these stairs.'

Lachie trailed Tyson up the stairs to the first floor. As they made their way down the corridor Tyson pointed to the nearest door.

'Number 23, which is next to number 16. This place is like a psychology experiment.'

Lachie nodded and thought of the film version of *The Shining*: the corridors that didn't match up, little Danny on his trike, those identical twins, *here's Johnny*. If this building had an apartment 237, Lachie would start running.

The door opened and Lachie got his first look at Stella Peters. She was older than he'd expected, given that Ofusa had suggested that Anthony was around eighteen. She was perhaps late fifties, with curly brown hair that needed a re-perm and the highlights rescued. She had a pinched face that the unkind would suggest was mousy, pursed lips and a habit of touching her nose. She clutched a blue cardigan closed and pushed one slippered foot on top of the other. It made her posture curl around the edge of the door.

'Stella Peters?' Lachie showed the ID. 'One of my officers visited you about half an hour ago. We'd like a further chat, please. Can we come in?'

He took a pace forward to imply that he could. Stella instinctively stepped back and the door opened wider. The gap was just about shoulder-width and Lachie took it as an affirmative. It was only when he was inside that Stella opened the door properly to allow Tyson to follow.

The hallway was painted a dusky pink that was too faded to be Barbie-esque, but too lurid to be an understated tone. The ceiling lamp was frills and rustic imagery, a draught excluder in the shape of a sausage dog slunk along one skirting board. Lachie was already picturing knitted ballerinas to hide the toilet rolls, a long shelf full of assorted knick-knacks, or those horrendous cutesy models of non-existent cottages. This was definitely Stella's home and Anthony merely lived here: he might have a bedroom that was very different, but it would be the only signal of his existence in the whole unit.

The living room was a continuation of the slightly off aesthetic, which somehow pitched between insipid hues and little nods to bygone eras. The wallpaper was striped pastel shades of yellow, pink, green and blue;

they repeated like candy prison bars across an entire wall. The chairs had needlessly plump and round cushions, as though they were inflated. They looked so marshmallow that they were a freeway to sciatica and he decided he'd stand like Tyson. There were owls of all kinds on shelves above the sofa – plush, carved, photographed. A tea trolley with curlicued side bars and gold wheels sat in the corner, hosting sherry, gin and Kahlua; the kind of thing you might have won on a game show in 1973. The whole room was Willie Wonka meets *Whatever Happened to Baby Jane?* Lachie glanced at Tyson, who raised a Spock eyebrow.

Stella hovered, unsure of the etiquette.

'Please, Ms Peters.' Lachie indicated a chair in her own home and she complied.

'Is this about the girl down there?' Her voice was uncertain and sought permission.

'Tahlia Moore, yes. Did you know her?'

'Only a – no, not really.'

'Only a what, Ms Peters?'

'Stella. Only to speak to, occasionally. We didn't cross paths, really.'

'Hmm. When did you last cross paths?'

'Uh, yesterday afternoon.'

Now Lachie raised an eyebrow. 'Oh? Please tell me about that.'

'We were just fetching the food from the car. We go to Aldi,' she said proudly, as though an Order of Australia was dependent on it. 'We were bringing in the food and she . . . she accosted Anthony.'

'She *accosted* him? What did that look like?' Lachie lowered himself carefully on to the arm of a chair.

Stella twisted her hands together.

'She was horrible. Horrible. So angry. She came up to Anthony while I was closing the boot. I didn't see her at first. Then she shoved Anthony hard, very hard. With her hand. On his shoulder. He bruises easily.'

'Could you hear what she said?'

'She . . . I didn't catch all of it. The tone, you know, I caught that. Hateful young woman – I've never liked her. She'd eff him up, she said.'

'I'm sorry. That sounds very unpleasant for you. What did Anthony do?'

'Well, nothing. He never does. Anthony is autistic.' She visibly rose and her posture straightened. 'He doesn't understand things like that, does he?'

Lachie could feel the eggshells under his feet. He hated vulnerable witnesses – it always seemed like a human resources review waiting to happen. Few officers could pitch head-first into a career sinkhole like Lachie.

'Wasn't he upset?'

'No, no. He doesn't understand when people are angry. Or *why* they're angry. It's a symptom, isn't it? I came around the car and told her to go away. I was polite.'

'I imagine so. And did she go away?'

'No. Oh, no. She came at *me*, then. Pointing her finger. She called me names. Called me a stupid old trout. But she did start leaving then. When she got a bit further away, she pointed at Anthony and called him . . .'

'We're used to bad language, Stella. It's okay to tell us.'

'She called him a retard. An effing retard.'

Lachie hid his lack of surprise with an appalled look. 'That sounds awful. How was Anthony?'

'Well, I looked for signs that he was shocked, or hurt. But of course, he doesn't do that. He just started carrying the shopping bags to the door, waiting for me to unlock.'

'And has he mentioned it since?'

'No, no, he never would. Least said, soonest mended: we both believe that.'

'And what time was this, yesterday?'

'Oh, about four.'

'Where, exactly?'

'Out there, by the east entrance. We own the Nissan.'

'Hmm. Did anyone else witness this, or come to help you at all?'

'I don't think so, no.'

Bugger, thought Lachie. He wanted a second opinion, but yet again there may not be one; no CCTV cameras from this building, and the run of trees between the parking slots and the main road would obscure any view from across the street. He'd never thought of this city as being replete with restricted views; today was teaching him the folly of that.

'Anthony didn't say what it was about?'

'No, he just shrugged. Anthony doesn't bear grudges. Once something's happened, he just gets on with it.'

Lachie glanced around. Sure enough, there was zero in these rooms to indicate that Stella didn't live alone.

'Is Anthony here?'

'Oh, yes, of course. But he's in his bedroom.'

Stella sat back slightly and put her hands in her lap as if nothing more could, or should, be said. Or done. As though Anthony was in one of those bank safes that couldn't be opened until the clock struck nine.

Lachie waited a beat and then said, 'We'll need to speak to him, Stella. Now, in fact.'

She frowned, then considered a moment, as if she had to strategise calling out or opening a bedroom door.

'Well, I could try.'

'We'd appreciate that, thank you.'

He shouldn't unintentionally mimic the reluctant cadence and apologetic air of Stella's speech; it felt almost malicious but was hard to avoid. She shuffled out of the living room and they could hear her padding down the hallway. Lachie glanced at Tyson, who mouthed *careful, sir* in an exaggerated way, presumably unaware that Lachie was a lip-reader. *He was right*, thought Lachie; there would be limits to how this conversation could be conducted. It might be a preliminary to a longer discussion elsewhere and Lachie couldn't afford to blow goodwill here if he could avoid it.

Stella emerged back into the room and Anthony traipsed behind her. Lachie's heart boomed as the teenager entered. The same kid from the café footage earlier: Tahlia's apparent tormentor. Bluey had shown him the images when they walked back from the café. In exactly the same clothing, with the same awkward gait, the same hemmed-in body language. *The same kid.*

Lachie again indicated a chair that the unit's resident might like to sit in. Stella stood by Anthony's side, her hand attempting reassuring contact on his shoulder. He shuddered and she withdrew.

'Thank you for joining us, Anthony. I'm Lachie and this is Tyson. We're looking into the incident involving Tahlia Moore during the night.'

Anthony had a disengaged expression: he appeared to be looking straight ahead but was staring at a point through Lachie and beyond. He seemed indifferent to Lachie's movements, or what was said.

'She's dead.' The voice was flat, devoid of intonation.

'Yes, she is. Did someone tell you that?'

A shake of the head.

Lachie leaned in. 'Then how do you know she's dead, Anthony?'

A long pause. Possibly slow cogs in Anthony's brain, almost perceptible – a reckoning of some kind.

'Anthony? How do you know that Tahlia's dead?'

'Dr Lawson. He only comes when people are dead. He's a dead doctor.'

'How do you know Dr Lawson?'

'He's on news reports. I watch news reports. He's on when people are dead. He's a dead doctor.'

Simple logic: it was hard to contest. It sounded heartless and slightly weird, but not in a way that Lachie could parry straight away.

'Did you know Tahlia?'

A silent nod. Lachie's question hadn't been sufficiently accurate. He learned.

'How do you know Tahlia?'

'She lives across there. Number 41.'

'Can you see Tahlia's apartment from your bedroom, Anthony?'

Another nod.

'Did you go to What's Brewin' yesterday?'

Stella frowned and made to intervene. Lachie's raised hand stayed her.

'Anthony? Did you go to What's Brewin'?'

'Yes.'

'Why did you go there?'

'To see Tahlia.'

Stella physically cut across in front of Anthony.

'That's enough. You're bullying him. He's autistic. I told you.'

Is he? thought Lachie. He wasn't entitled to disbelieve her – not without evidence – but he was entitled to clarify.

'Autistic? Is that a confirmed diagnosis from an expert consultant, Ms Peters? Who's his GP, please?'

Stella slipped to fuming, impotent frustration.

'We don't trust doctors any more. He's autistic.'

Lachie dredged some half-knowledge from his memory. *What's his score on the ADI-R? Or the other one . . . the ADOS? Where does he place on the spectrum?* He fought the temptation to fire those salvoes.

Stella let a tear slide from her eye. She made very sure that Lachie saw her wipe it. She gave her voice a gauche vibrato.

'You're . . . this is very upsetting. I'm sorry the girl's dead, but bullying my son won't bring her back.'

Lachie glanced at Anthony.

'I'm not bullying Anthony. I'm treating him politely and respectfully, though I still need answers from him. A serious crime was committed, Ms Peters.'

Stella shook her head, more at her own failure to head him off than anything else.

'So, Anthony. Why did you go to What's Brewin'?'

Anthony resumed the through-you stare. 'To speak to Tahlia Moore.'

'You showed her some footage on your phone. That's right, isn't it?'

'Yes.'

'What was on that footage?'

'It's private.'

'Private to you, or to Tahlia?'

'Tahlia.'

'What did it show?'

'Dirty. Dirty Tahlia. Not right.' He shook his head.

'Can I see that footage, please, Anthony?'

'No. It's private. Tahlia wouldn't like it.'

'You know that, because I'm a police officer investigating a crime, I can insist that you show the footage to me?'

'Don't care. Private.'

A sixth sense told Lachie to back off, but he didn't want to end the conversation quite yet. He signalled to Tyson to take over. Tyson crouched down on his haunches before speaking.

'Anthony, do you remember when the other policeman was here earlier? The big guy?'

'Samoa.'

'That's right, he's Samoan. Willie, he's called. He asked you about your drone?'

Anthony nodded, still staring through Lachie.

'Which model of drone do you have?'

'Lockstar 546.'

'Does anyone else fly it? Like, your mum, maybe?'

'No. She'd break it. She doesn't understand stuff like that.'

Lachie's eyes flew quickly enough to see Stella's face crumble, then stoically recover. Tyson took a breath and continued.

'Does the drone camera record on to a memory card?'

'No.'

'Direct upload to the Cloud?'

A nod.

'Would you give us the access details to the cloud account, if we asked you?'

'No. Private.'

Stella gathered herself.

'That's quite enough. Quite enough. This is our home. You're no longer welcome here. You need to leave. Leave us alone.'

Lachie suppressed a sigh and rose slowly.

'We'll be taking the drone with us, Ms Peters. We have the right to examine it for potential evidence relating to the death of Tahlia Moore. Tyson will give you a receipt.'

Uniform officers were miraculous for housing every conceivable need within three or four pockets, like a cricket umpire. Tyson had a plastic evidence bag large enough for a drone. There was a short pause while he rescued the drone from under Anthony's bed, then wrote out the receipt. All the while Anthony stared at the wallpaper behind Lachie; Stella glared directly at the detective, her angry breathing audible.

'So, Ms Peters. I'm happy that Anthony has more information to offer us. I don't want to arrest him, but we must speak to him later today. He should be at City West station at twelve o'clock. You can sit in on the interview as his mother, or you can ask a lawyer of your choice to sit with him; or he can sit on his own. I'll leave it to you and Anthony to decide. Twelve o'clock: we expect Anthony's cooperation.'

Just before they closed the front door, they heard a strangled sob emanate from Stella Peters.

Chapter 13

'Thoughts, Tyson?'

They were back downstairs, holding the door for a harassed young mum cursed with a double buggy and two wide-eyed but slightly dribbling babies. She muttered *thanks* as she manoeuvred, a misty sheen across her forehead, and bumbled the three of them towards a battered Mazda.

'My nephew's on the spectrum. They're tricky to communicate with, but if you ask right, they don't lie often. Anthony was more . . .'

'Yeah? Say what you think, mate, there's no one recording.'

'My nephew is definitely autistic – quite a handful. Anthony was . . . an ignorant person's idea of what an autistic person would be like. Seemed that way, anyway.'

'Thank God, I thought I'd be the only one seeing that. I was getting vibes like that *Good Doctor* show. You know: speak in a monotone and stare into space. He needs checking out, that's for sure.' Lachie smirked. 'Yeah, like a walking cliché, wasn't he? I know there's specific tests around autism, but I wasn't totally sure of my ground. I assume Anthony's seen a proper doctor about his condition.'

'Maybe. What if we're overstepping, though?'

'Yeah, I was careful. Well, he had his mum with him the whole time, he was at home where he's most comfortable and we only spoke for a few minutes. Got it all on tape, but I think we're okay for now. What did you make of how they're living?'

They stepped outside, where the traffic hadn't abated and swept past them in a haze of exhaust fumes, subliminal flashes of talk radio and a whine of Nickelback.

'I don't reckon he's going to school. He should be year eleven or twelve – I'll check the exact age. Had a swift look while I was rescuing the drone; no schoolbooks I could see. You usually get something in a kid's room – class photo, some form they need the parentals to sign, uniform in the wardrobe, that kind of thing. Nothing in Anthony's.'

Tyson hadn't had long – any longer would have aroused suspicion – but Lachie was glad he'd taken the opportunity.

'Yeah. Yeah, good shout. He definitely has something on Tahlia, there. Bluey forwarded you the footage from the café CCTV – it might be worth seeing if any customers saw it or overheard that incident: maybe get Cassie to identify the customers in the background. Anthony showed that phone footage to Tahlia in the café less than twenty-four hours ago. She went ballistic, he left. They argued later that day. Now she's dead and he won't let us have any footage. What did he call her?'

'Dirty. Dirty Tahlia.'

'Hmm. Something sexual, maybe? Not sure what fits his definition of *dirty*; might be different to yours or mine.' Lachie tapped the bagged drone. 'What do you think we can get off this?'

Tyson shrugged. 'My nephew has the version before this. Anthony's lucky – this one is seriously pricey and they don't look loaded. Spend most of it on owls, eh?' They both sniggered. 'If we're lucky this'll have some kind of rolling short-term memory, like a dashcam does, and we might get the last minute of footage. More likely there'll be no footage as such, but at least we could see the coordinate metadata and know where it's been flown and when.'

That, thought Lachie, *would be a good starting point for interview.*

'Okay. I'll take the drone to Tech, see if they can run some quick analysis to tell what we've got here. I'd like you to finish up the other tasks. The cleaners will be here soon to tidy up the crime scene, then we can give the courtyard back to the residents. Hang around while they do it – the rubberneckers will want a squint and they might give some hidden gem in amongst the bull. Then, go back to What's Brewin' and see if you can tag any of the customers from Tahlia's shirtfronting of Anthony. I'll be back at City West going through Tahlia's stuff before we speak to her mum. Once we've done that, we'll put together a strategy for tackling Anthony again.'

'Sir. I'll give Ms Peters a ring about eleven, make sure she can't claim that she forgot.'

'Good idea. You want in on the Anthony interview? We'd appreciate a third perspective.'

Tyson tried not to light up. 'Definitely, sir.'

City West station. Thursday 0720hrs

It probably wasn't appropriate to swing your car keys jovially as you walked into a murder investigation office, but Bluey couldn't help it. A few weeks ago he'd been on the scrapheap – another late-fifties zombie hanging on for the superannuation, being treated like an organisational chicane. Then, a chance phone call asking him to do the city-based investigation bits and pieces for a regional murder: he'd done okay, felt good about doing it. A few months later the drive-by brutality and the front-page headlines had ramped up, taking the brightest and best talents of the detective squad; he'd been added to the back-up roster. Very much the eighteenth man praying for someone to get injured or concussed, he'd been silently thrilled to get the call on this one. Even if Laxton still thought he was bloody useless.

That earlier period of stasis – ignored by colleagues and beset by a sense of strolling on a treadmill – had made him rethink retirement. He'd have to find something useful, something that actually *felt* useful, when he finally quit. He'd been dabbling with the idea of becoming a counsellor – for someone, about something or other – and resolved to look into that when he got a spare moment. For now, he was enjoying the gentle flow of low-level adrenaline.

Bluey was the first detective to the new investigation office – a slice off a large open space that had recently been almost-reno'ed but was full of wires hanging from gyprock, spare computer equipment still in boxes and a stack of microwave ovens that had no apparent reason for being there. The windows were heavily tinted and faced the back of an insurance company's headquarters; a blissful view of whirling aircon units and the emergency stairs. The proper space for criminal investigation – floors five and six – was taken up by the drive-by shootings. That team had already blown out their budget and wasn't allowed to slow down, therefore everyone else had to run dollar-shop investigations.

The cut-price 'office' was one corner, where four desks had been slung together and sectioned off from the empty remainder by high dividers. The photocopier was down a long corridor and coffee was several minutes away. Bluey tried to con himself that this was a careful piece of ergonomic strategy aimed at achieving maximum focus, but he couldn't help feeling that he and Lachie were as incongruous and superfluous in this space as the microwaves.

Their admin officer was Kat Ross, an experienced pro who'd got bored in one department and now operated as a floating needs-must support to hapless and politically isolated refugees like Bluey. She frequently turned up on homicides because she could switch roles at short notice, so went by the moniker of Killer Kat. It really helped that she knew the ropes: when Bluey arrived she'd already put up the whiteboards and added transcripts of all the interviews to the shared drive. She also had a number of photos of the courtyard, taken from different angles, pinned to the back of one of the dividers: a preview of the computer modelling of sight lines that would apparently arrive later. An interview room on the floor below was booked out in their name for snippets of the next seventy-two hours, nestled among some drug cases.

Bluey had worked with Killer Kat several times before and had always admired the fact that he still knew absolutely nothing about her life outside the office. She seemed to walk to work, so no one even knew what car she drove. No one could recall bumping into her anywhere, either. She never mentioned partners, family, friends or pets; had no anecdotes from the past; told no tales about weekends or holidays. Her phone never seemed to be on, yielding inadvertent details or context. It took, Bluey figured, considerable care not to accidentally divulge a star sign or medical appointment, political view or favourite TV show. He liked her commitment.

'Whaddya reckon, Kat?'

They both leaned against the same desk, arms folded, and regarded the completely empty whiteboards.

'I reckon you've got me working with die-in-a-ditch Dyson.'

'Yeah. Sorry, and all that. If it's any consolation and speaking as I find, he's been fine so far. As long as we keep him from any prosecutors or important ethical decisions, we might be okay.'

Kat's *hmmm* was universally understood to mean *totally unconvinced*.

Bluey continued. 'I think we'll need to pull the meat from those transcripts first. We had a barrage of stuff from all the eyewitnesses and I don't think Lachie or I really had time to step back and put the pieces in order.'

'That's your diplomatic way of saying you don't have a clue.'

'I have clues, but no clue how to put them together, yes.'

'Fair enough.'

The next hour was spent painstakingly covering each witness interview. Colour-coding of arrows and names – Kat's own system that Bluey caught and liked – helped to keep all the data in one place without being confusing. At various times, Bluey had Kat attach a red flag next to an individual line – this meant that he wanted to come back to it, but it wasn't linked to who could see what and when. Those red flags included, Kat noticed, things that were omitted or unsaid, as well as overt anomalies. At last, as they ate some chocolate-chip cookies that Kat had brought in, they could see the whole panorama across three of the four whiteboards.

'What a clusterfudge,' muttered Bluey.

'Looks like thirty-six Huntsmans got into a paint factory,' responded Kat. She pointed to the multicoloured swirls of arrows, question marks, crosses and ticks. 'You don't know anything at all, do you?'

Bluey choked briefly on some crumbs. 'Not really, no. I'll have a crack at it with Lachie when he gets here. Meanwhile, can you put together Tahlia's financials, please?'

City West station. Thursday, 0815hrs

By the time the financials were in order, Lachie had arrived. He'd dropped Anthony's drone off to Tech. They'd take an initial dive and at least tell him if there was any cache memory, or if he'd absolutely need the account in the cloud.

He shook hands with a desultory and suspicious Kat and confirmed the existence of the sound file with Anthony's interview for transcribing, before taking note of the whiteboards.

'Holy crap. Look how much they told us without telling us anything.'

Bluey smiled. 'Yeah, I know. Frustrating, eh? Wanna take a run at it?'

'Why not?'

They sat face to face, at right angles to the boards, each poised over a notebook. *Star chamber*, Bluey called it. Facing each other meant that they weren't scanning the data continuously, becoming fixated or distracted. Instead, they'd have to home in purely on each piece of data they were after, when they were asked for it. They were to ask direct questions with a clear-cut answer.

'Me first,' decided Bluey. 'How many witnesses heard two screams?'

Lachie found his rhythm easily and the way Bluey had laid out the information now made sense. He could flick from witness to witness and find the answer easily.

'Jody. Only Jody. He seemed quite certain the first one woke him, he was definite about the second. Reuben was adamant there was one scream. Bryony didn't mention a scream at all – just some noise – but she had the windows closed when Jody and Reuben didn't. Martyn, likewise, didn't mention any scream as such, just *noise*. Caretaker Sally says she heard nothing; she said her door was closed as well.'

Bluey checked himself as he wrote. 'Just to remind ourselves: Martyn rang Bryony before we got there and got the tea from her. I'd expect those two to line up more than the others. Okay, your turn.'

Lachie tapped his pen for a second before deciding. 'Who saw Reuben's hand move towards the flank of Tahlia Moore?'

Bluey scanned down the columns quickly. 'Bryony said that Reuben pushed at Tahlia's ribs. She implied that there was no blood until he did that. Reuben outed himself and said he tried to plug the bleeding from the stab wound with some kind of scarf. Martyn and Jody both mentioned blood and how much there was, but not Reuben's hand going towards Tahlia. Caretaker Sally saw nothing.'

Bluey checked his earlier notes. 'Paramedics say they found a scarf by Tahlia, saturated in blood; it's with Forensics. Backs up Reuben, but doesn't prove Bryony wrong.'

This was working: clarifying, crystallising. Bluey went next.

'How long was Reuben conducting mouth-to-mouth?'

Blue stars next to the data were the visual code that Lachie followed here. 'Jody didn't give a time. He implied that once it started Reuben kept going until the paramedics arrived. Which would be around seven minutes, if we take the ambo data at face value. Caretaker Sally didn't see any mouth-to-mouth: her visuals start with the paramedics. Bryony said it was one to two minutes, then Reuben went to his apartment until the paramedics arrived. Martyn saw the mouth-to-mouth but not when it stopped. Reuben claims five minutes and he only stopped because of the blue lights.'

Lachie's question followed on.

'How long was Reuben absent after giving mouth-to-mouth?'

'Jody and Reuben suggest no time at all – that he stopped when the paramedics got there. But Jody is less definite about that. Bryony says that Reuben was gone for three to four minutes after attempting resuscitation. Martyn said that Reuben was gone and came back, but had no timings. Caretaker Sally didn't know about this bit.'

Bluey's next question focused on the moments when Reuben was known to be standing alongside the body, watching.

'Who saw Reuben nod or shake his head while the paramedics were working?'

The words *nod* and *shake* were easily spotted: they were green.

'Caretaker Sally says it was a shake of the head to her, once the paramedics started their effort, to say Tahlia wouldn't make it. Jody didn't mention a nod or a shake. Reuben backs Sally: a head shake to her while the medics were on the tools. Bryony says the same, but didn't see who it was aimed at. Martyn says that Reuben nodded – maybe to himself – but that was *before* the ambos got there.'

So far, so good, thought Bluey. It wasn't as though they'd found a golden thread already; more that they were starting to separate the wheat from the chaff. Something could be true even if only one witness saw it; or false, even though two said it happened. But it was all beginning to come into focus. Bluey could sense that Kat was listening in, even as she typed.

'All right,' he said. 'Lies, omissions and observations. One by one. Jody?'

'He knows Tahlia – works next door – but lied about that. He heard two screams when no one else heard more than one. He said he saw the western entrance swing shut, which others saw. But don't forget he was dosed up on trankies and hasn't slept properly in three nights.'

Though, Bluey reminded himself, Jody wasn't too frazzled or discombobulated: he knew where he was and which way was up.

'Bryony?' he asked.

'Credible witness, in my view.' Lachie leaned back until the chair creaked. 'Good observation overall. Her timings from international calls and so on look viable and checkable. She had blotchy vision at first. She used binoculars, so probably better vision than the others, plus she's higher up. She didn't embellish.'

'On the other hand,' Bluey pointed out, 'she was very fixated on

Reuben; apparently doesn't like him, fears him. She said Reuben *spoke* to Sally, rather than just a head shake, which no one else said.'

Lachie agreed. 'Yeah, fair enough. Since I interviewed her, you can take Caretaker Sally.'

'She had the door closed and music on, so very little on the visuals or audio. She also has accurate timings, assuming we believe them. But she didn't witness the build-up like the others did. She did admit to knowing Tahlia better than the others did.'

Yes, thought Lachie, *Sally's focus was on Tahlia. Whereas the others' reference point was always Reuben.*

'Reuben Pearce?' asked Bluey.

'Proven bloody liar. Just sayin'.' Lachie gathered himself. 'He also saw the western door swing shut. He's the most closely involved: attempted mouth-to-mouth. He was one of the triple-zero callers with Jody and Bryony and Martyn: we can verify that. He was covered in Tahlia's blood. But . . . he may or may not have gone back into his apartment between the mouth-to-mouth and the ambo arrival. Oh, and he was at least half-pissed, you said?'

'At least half, yeah. Maybe more. Depends on his capacity, I suppose.'

Bluey made a mental note to himself *not* to allow Reuben's past excesses and indiscretions to intrude here. He had to regard Reuben as a blank-slate witness. For now.

His next question. 'What about Martyn?'

'Yeah, the idiot rang Bryony, didn't he? So we don't know for sure what's his view and what's gone into his head from Bryony. He got up and down from bed six times so maybe he's a bit disoriented, at least with timings. He was scared to go out there, so might be holding back a bit out of embarrassment.'

They stopped and Bluey passed a cookie to Lachie, who raised it in thanks to an oblivious Kat. Bluey checked his notes.

'Jesus, it's not much is it? Okay. Anything else?'

Lachie stared at the notes. 'Oh, yeah, what's stated by more than one witness?'

Bluey ran his pen down the page.

'Not a lot. One scream, or other noise. Tahlia on the ground. Western door swinging shut. Blood. Reuben's hand moving towards her ribs for some reason. Reuben doing mouth-to-mouth. Reuben letting the paramedics in. Reuben nodding or head-shaking. Sally arrives. Tahlia dead. Cops arrive and set up the scene. And that's all they wrote.'

There was a pregnant pause, broken only by the snap of Lachie biting the cookie in two. *Four hours in*, thought Bluey, *we're only four hours in*. No autopsy yet, no idea of a weapon, just getting the background through on the victim. *Four hours.*

'I have a question.'

They both turned to Kat, Lachie surprised because he'd assumed she was busy. She'd removed her headset and was staring at the whiteboards.

'Yeah, fire away, mate.'

'This Reuben bloke, who I assume is that dickhead from last year?' Nods all round. 'Okay. He tries mouth-to-mouth, presumably gets blood all over him. Can't you trace where he goes from the blood? I mean bloody footprints, drips, that sort of thing?'

'Very good point.' Lachie rocked his chair back to four legs and reached for the mouse. 'We've just had some more forensics through. They were supposed to be covering this first.' He clicked twice and then pointed at the screen.

'So, they did track bloody footprints, which seem to match the crocs he was wearing.'

'Crocs,' murmured Kat, unimpressed. 'Be still my beating heart.'

Lachie smirked and carried on. 'I'm not sure Tahlia was bleeding much initially. The footprints went to a drain just in front of his terrace, but the blood's getting fainter with each step. In fact, there's no bloody prints going *back* to Tahlia, even though we know he did that. They're testing the soles of his shoes now to make sure it all matches up.'

'Tell me they looked down the drain,' said Bluey.

'Oh yeah, they did. Puke. Dried puke. Seems like, when he realised

Tahlia wasn't going to make it despite his first-responder effort, Reuben chucked his guts into the drain.'

Understandable, thought Bluey, *not least because the bloke was half cut.* While he regarded Reuben as a suspect and an idiot, he thought back to his discussion on the terrace. After his initial crap, Reuben had shown surprising self-awareness and seemed genuinely moved by the emotion of what had happened. Under the bluster and bravado, he did understand the magnitude of it and he did care.

'He'd have been out of Bryony's sight: right under her balcony. That's why she assumed he'd gone back indoors. She wouldn't have heard him heaving with her window closed. So that bit still tracks with her statement.' Bluey considered for a second. 'But of course if he killed Tahlia he could have dropped the weapon into the drain, then made himself vomit to cover the weapon. We'd probably take a sample of the puke to check that it's his, because that would rule out someone else being present at the scene. But would we check *under* the vomit?'

'Hmm. It's a good cover. He can legitimately argue that the whole drama made him want to hurl; we can't really argue against that. But it provides a handy blanket over any weapon, yeah.' Lachie raised an eyebrow. 'We know he likes to cover up with fake forensic material, don't we? Also, he might be hoping for more rain to wash the weapon away before we go digging too deep.'

Bluey was already texting. 'Right, Tyson can call back a tech and get them to lift the drain and check under the vomit. Someone's going to love doing that.' He turned. 'Great shout, Kat, thank you.'

Kat nodded. 'Detective work. Piece of piss. Don't know what takes you so long.'

They both grinned, then turned back to the whiteboards. Despite clarifying some of the details – and it certainly felt more cohesive now, if only in their minds – they seemed no nearer to a suspect unless the vomit inspection went well. Everything still lacked motive.

'Want me to cheer you up, Bluey?' asked Lachie.

Bluey glanced up. 'This *is* my cheery look. Don't discriminate against people with bitchy resting face. We're an oppressed minority. That's a microaggression and I'm telling HR.'

'Fair enough. Do you want me to tell you something which is advantageous to the investigation of this crime, esteemed colleague?'

'That's more like it.'

'First, the bad news: the search team is now a hundred metres out from the apartment complex, and they've found nothing.'

'Nothing?'

'No weapon, or anything like. Apparently locals there drink a lot of protein shakes and don't recycle much, if that's worth knowing. On a brighter note, we identified the kid in those images from the café – the kid upsetting Tahlia yesterday.'

Bluey sparked up. 'Oh?'

'Yeah. One of the house-to-house guys noticed that there was a drone in a kid's bedroom. When he asked some chatty questions about it, the kid got ratty and clamped up. He thought it was worth a second tug, so Tyson and I visited. Kid's name is Anthony Peters. His mother told us he's autistic. Kid won't let us see the footage; Tech are looking at the rig now to see if it has any memory on board, or whether we need Anthony to lend us his cloud password. It all seemed a bit *bobbing and weaving* to me; so Anthony and his mum are coming in at midday.'

Bluey tapped his pen against a roll of Sellotape. 'You think the drone footage might cover . . .'

'Oh, it might not. Nah, I don't know if he was flying it in the wee small hours. But he has flown it in the courtyard before, I'd bet my life on it. He admits that the footage he has is embarrassing for Tahlia and makes her look "dirty" – his word – but he won't say why. Put it this way: he's a teenager who has a hot woman living across the way and he has a drone. I'm choosing to join the dots in that direction, yeah.'

It fitted the reaction from Tahlia when the kid showed her the video on his phone, thought Bluey. Just a few hours before she was killed.

'Did you ask this Anthony about confronting Tahlia at What's Brewin'?'

'Yeah, I did. He was evasive. Correction. I say evasive; he's not giving off the usual signals, understandably. But he didn't give a straight answer. Another reason to insist he comes here for a chat.'

'Okay. Well, that's good. That's progress. I like it. Kat, can you look further into Anthony Peters for us? He's in apartment . . .'

'Sixteen,' offered Lachie.

'Sixteen, Pacific Heights. See if he has any online presence, as well. Plus, any reference about autism or the spectrum that we should know about before we interview.'

He turned back to Lachie. 'How old is he? Do we need an adult?'

Lachie shrugged. 'Not sure. Pretty sure he's home-schooled, though I wouldn't swear his mum could get him through the HSC. Might be eighteen. Tyson said he'd check: I'll give him a buzz.'

'Financials for Tahlia Moore are up.' Kat swung her handbag on to one shoulder. 'And I need coffee.'

She simply upped and left.

Lachie smiled as the lift door closed sharply. 'Do we need coffee?'

Bluey shook his head. 'I think we're the base of the pyramid here, aren't we, mate? Don't fight it. Hey, Tahlia here has a lot of outgoings.'

They scanned the statements. Regular payments for rent were obvious. There was no car, so no insurance or rego to worry about. Most bills were the usual – mobile phone, electric, water, body corporate, broadband and Netflix. But the cash withdrawals were significant. *Much larger*, thought Bluey, *than you'd need for food and a bit of entertainment.* He thought back to the car wreck of a bedroom, seemingly festooned with designer gear.

'That spending strike you as a bit rich?' he asked.

'Yeah, it does,' replied Lachie. 'I'm looking back to twelve months ago, when her sister began staying with her. I don't see much difference in spending between then and now.'

Bluey shrugged. 'The sister's there, so they went out more but split the cost. Now she's solo, she goes out less but the cost is all on her?'

'Possible. But all the same, Reagan was helping with the bills, wasn't she? Presumably part of the rent and deffo the utilities. And also paying her whack at the pub, the nightclub, the movies, whatever. I don't see that here.'

'I'm guessing that Reagan handed it over in cash each time she got paid. Maybe it just stayed in the purse and got spent.'

'Okay.' Lachie frowned. 'But there should still be a noticeable difference in spending between then and now: Tahlia's got less income coming in now, hasn't she?'

'Mate, some people have a spending rate that bears no relation whatsoever to the income. If the income is high, it's affordable. If the income is low, it's stacking up debt. The income changes, but the spending doesn't.'

Lachie took a chance. 'Is that based on wife number one, or number two?'

Bluey had to give some grudging respect for Lachie's detective work, there: he didn't normally discuss domestics. 'Oh, number two, no doubt about that. We'd have hard yakka getting a warrant for Reagan's bank statements, though, so it's tricky to verify.'

That was true. It would be tough to claim close involvement for a sister who was thousands of kilometres away when the murder happened. That struck a nerve with Lachie.

'How do we know for sure where Reagan is?'

'What do you mean?'

'Well, all we know is that Reagan stopped working at What's Brewin' a few months ago. Tahlia apparently said she was in Europe and that's what Caretaker Sally initially thought. But then, maybe she was actually in the USA at that point. Or not. What's to say she hasn't already come back?'

'We can ask her mother in an hour or two. But yeah, probably best to get Kat to check that Reagan's where everyone thinks she is.' Bluey frowned. 'Hey, how much does someone make schlepping coffee, d'you think?'

'Award rates, but exactly how much depends on the shifts. Weekends and holidays pay more. Plus, Tahlia might not have been working forty hours. I don't think she was a casual, but maybe we took for granted that she was full time. Why?'

'I'm guessing around forty a year is minimum wage, right? Let's say it is. Add in a bit for some weekends, like you say. Between forty and fifty a year if you're full time, so closing on four thou every four weeks, yeah? But I'm looking at her account and there's double that going in. I mean it literally – double. She's getting paid a four-week wage every two weeks. What's that about?'

Lachie scanned the same figures. Every four weeks was a set amount: it didn't vary throughout the year. The other payments – two weeks later each time – went up and down a little. The latter looked like genuine wages, reflecting shift patterns and penalty rates. The former looked like . . .

'Tragic clerical error? Or blackmail payment?' offered Lachie.

What's Brewin' was a chain, but Bluey knew it was a franchise thing: he'd read an article about it. Scott Villiers would be an entrepreneur who sweated on every dollar; he wouldn't be accidentally paying someone who'd left months ago. Especially, concluded Bluey, to the bank account of that person's sister.

'The second one: blackmail,' replied Bluey, visibly annoyed. 'World's full of bloody liars. Get Tyson to bring *Scotty from Coffee Pouring* in here. We'll chat to him after we've seen Tahlia's family. He has a lot of explaining to do.'

Chapter 14

Vanessa Moore was already partially in black. Expensively tailored pants offset a peach blouse. Her hair was pinned up, tendrils touching each cheek. Her skin might have been blotchy half an hour ago, but she'd clearly looked to present her best now. It struck Lachie that this was the type of family that responded to tragedy and difficulty by attending to the visuals first, as if beauty would automatically rescue the situation. Her sister, Ruth, showcased the family cheekbones below highlights and hazel eyes. They were both elegant even in grief, but it was clear how the hierarchy lay: Ruth stood off Vanessa's shoulder.

They'd been placed in one of the ten interview rooms off the main reception in City West. The rooms catered to a revolving sequence of various family members, witnesses and their support, rarely needing more than ten minutes of business before they were free again. It always felt to Bluey like a bit of a zoo; despite best efforts, people milled around in the large foyer, yammering into mobile phones and occasionally spilling over into slanging matches, threats and raised fists. He'd hoped to steer Vanessa Moore into something more secluded and serene, but of course the drive-by shootings were taking up all the building's civilised visitor space. His carefully booked interview room on floor 10 had been commandeered by drugs officers – another front in the phoney war they'd kickstart with just about anyone. It was all a reminder of this case's lowly status and, by implication, that of the detectives.

Bluey and Lachy shook hands with suitable solemnity and invited the women to sit.

'Ms Moore. My name is Carl Blewson – feel free to call me Bluey if that helps – and this is Lachlan Dyson. We're the detectives working on the death of Tahlia. I'm very sorry for your loss, and I apologise for these surroundings – they weren't our choice.'

Vanessa swallowed and blinked back a tear. 'What can you tell me, Bluey?'

The rules here were simple: be sympathetic, promise nothing definite, say things you can prove, *and listen.*

'Tahlia died just after three o'clock this morning in the courtyard of her apartment complex. Four people rang triple-zero trying to save her and a member of the public performed mouth-to-mouth. Paramedics reached her very quickly, but sadly not in time. Your daughter was not alone when she passed away: at least three people did everything they could to resuscitate her.

'We're treating the death as suspicious. A post-mortem will be conducted soon and it should tell us more about how Tahlia died. We've already begun our investigations and spoken to a number of witnesses: they're helping us to build a picture of what happened. We'll continue those investigations and the post-mortem should help us to decide our next priorities.'

Ruth lightly touched Vanessa's shoulder, but it didn't seem to help. Vanessa closed in on herself, as if she was being squeezed around the core and the oxygen was gradually leaving. She pushed a handkerchief into one eye and took a deep breath.

'When you say *suspicious?*'

'Obviously we've been to the courtyard, we've spoken to people who were there in the moment. We have some leads and some ideas. In my experience, it's not helpful in the long run if detectives give out early theories in an effort to console. We can't console you. We can't make this terrible thing better. What we can do is solve the crime and make sure that whoever is responsible is identified. I can promise you that Lachlan and I will do everything in our power to make that happen.'

Vanessa nodded, blinked hard and looked at her knees. Bluey leaned forward slightly.

'May I ask you some questions about Tahlia?'

Another swallow, another nod. She was barely holding it together.

'We're trying to build a picture of Tahlia and what she'd been doing recently, how she was feeling. What can you tell us about your daughter?'

'She was . . . she was beautiful. Always was. Even in the pram, people would notice. Could have been a model, if that was what she wanted. But she never really worked out what she wanted. It was a problem for her. She drifted. She could charm her way into starting almost anything, but nothing seemed to suit her in the longer term. She couldn't settle. Reagan? Her sister? Reagan wants to be a vet, always has. Knew it from early on, and it gave her a . . . stability, a certainty. Tahlia never had that. It was always brief tries at things, brief relationships. Skating, not diving, you know?'

'How often did you meet up, or speak?'

'Oh, we had lunch every month. Tahls wasn't big on family get-togethers: she'd send Reagan as an ambassador. But we kept to the lunch thing. It was . . . it was enough. She'd text me with stupid memes from the internet, but the lunches were the real communication. She didn't like questions about her private life, who she was seeing; kept it breezy all the time. So if you're asking about boyfriends or girlfriends, or anyone hassling her, we wouldn't know. She didn't share that; she just dealt with it herself.'

'Would she have shared that with Reagan, do you think?'

A hint of a smile; a phantom emotion amid the stupefying grief.

'No, no, she wouldn't. Reagan was an open book and Tahls used to take the pi—the mickey. No; they lived together for six months but the only things Reagan would know is what she saw, what she took in. Not anything that Tahlia shared; she wasn't like that. Reagan's clever, though. Clever.'

'Where is Reagan currently?'

'She's flying from Boston, I believe. I rang her and she said she'd get the first flight she could. I don't know how she's getting here. Los Angeles first, I suppose. I didn't ask and she didn't say.'

'I see. It would be helpful for us to speak to her, as soon as she's able. Did Tahlia mention how work was going at What's Brewin'? We're trying to get as comprehensive a view as we can.'

Vanessa glanced at Ruth, then back again.

'Not really. I mean, she was bored at the café, I knew that much. She moaned about that and about her boss, but she said the tips were great. I think the apartment was okay, just about affordable, you know? I offered to help with the rent – she's on minimum wage and it's all crazy prices these days – but she said it was fine. In fact, she said she was doing better financially than she'd expected; I guess Reagan helping with the rent was a boost. I don't think she had much to do with the neighbours, though. Oh, one of them was that Reuben guy.'

'Yes, we've spoken to him, along with a number of other neighbours.'

Vanessa's eyes widened, as though Bluey had offered a path to the root of her pain. People desperately wanted to believe in something; yet they also lived in an era when they actively refused to believe much. But when they were distraught or scared, or grieving, they clutched at anything vaguely plausible as though it could winch them to safety.

'Yeah, yeah, she mentioned him a few times. That thing last year that Reuben started? Tahls didn't mention newsy things much, but she went on about that. Shocked when he moved into the same block of units. I think they . . .'

'Yes?'

'I think they had a few arguments. Tahls would have said something, if their paths had crossed. You know, about last year. I think she did that a couple of times and Reuben kinda reacted. Then he started coming into her café, too. Oh, God, you don't think –'

Bluey stopped the runaway locomotive before it could crash.

'We don't leap to conclusions. We'll take all that on board, though. Thank you.' He turned to the aunt, who was looking at her sister with a strange mix of compassion and incredulity. 'Ruth, did you spend much time with Tahlia?'

'No. I'm interstate, but even so we – look, to be honest, Tahlia and I didn't get on that well; I'm closer to Reagan. I'm a florist: Tahls thought that was a crappy job and a crappy business and she said so. I love my sister and I love Tahlia, but there's no point spending too much time if people don't respect what you do. Sorry, 'Ness, they need us to be honest.'

Vanessa flicked a hand without turning around; it might have meant *no worries* or it might have meant *you're dead to me*. They radiated awkward silence.

Lachie rescued them. 'Do you have contact details for her friends? We're password-blocked on her phone and her socials at the moment, so anything you can give us would help.'

Vanessa bit her lip as she thought.

'Not really. Like I say, she . . . she really kept us apart from all that. There was one guy, though. What was his – oh, the guy that died. Warren. Warren something. Warren Bartlett, that was it. She called him Wasbar. They seemed like a thing, although she rolled her eyes when I said that. Apparently those kind of labels are so uncool. Anyway, he died, oh, a while ago. She had plenty of photos with him and, in Tahlia's world, the more photos you had alongside her, the cooler she thought you were. It was like a league table. Get into her Insta – that was where she lived. Clothes, fashion, photos she was in. Not that she shared her password. Sorry.'

'Hmm. Anyone else? We're not finding a pattern of people she regularly hung out with, to be honest.'

'But that was what she was like, Detective. A gorgeous butterfly with a butterfly mind. She'd go out in the evening with no idea where she was headed. Something would catch her eye in the rideshare, then she'd get out and take a look. Party, gallery, nightclub, whatever. Like I said, she could charm her way into anything, but not necessarily out of it. Lots of brief experiences.'

'Shallow.'

It was Ruth. Vanessa glared at her.

'Oh, come on, 'Ness. We need to help, here – they're trying to find who killed Tahls. There's bugger-all sense in sugarcoating it. Tahlia was, in my view, quite shallow, Detectives. Not that she wasn't smart – she could be – but she had zero application. Her apartment will be full of started projects she never completed. I bet her books are all marked in the first third. You'll see. I'm sorry, 'Ness, but really. The reason you can't find any lifelong friends or enduring passions? She didn't have them. She flitted from one thing to another and never stuck around.'

Ruth stepped forward, now face to face with her sister. 'Prove me wrong.'

Vanessa's voice faded to a whisper.

'Jesus, you're a poisonous little bitch. Not here and not now. But *soon*.'

The last word was almost spat. Bluey decided they'd be better interviewed apart, and later.

'Right. Well, I think that's enough to get us started, at any rate. Cases like this tend to move more slowly than you expect at first: we do a lot of information-gathering and cross-checking. But we will need to speak to you both again. We have your contact details, so we'll follow up soon. Thank you.'

They stepped from the frigid air of the room to the musty atmosphere of Reception.

'We could accompany you, if you like,' said Bluey. 'The ME's department is the white building, across the street, there. One of us could be with you, if that would help.'

Vanessa flicked a glance at her sister, then shook her head silently. Bluey took a step back.

'Okay, then. We'll talk again, later today.'

Vanessa nodded curtly and swept out like an ice princess, Ruth trailing in her wake but apparently unrepentant. Lachie could only imagine the temperature of the trip home.

Chapter 15

They returned to the office via the lift.

Meeting the bereaved was always a mixture of emotions. It was hard not to be affected by people who'd had part of their life ripped from them. On the other hand, the best assistance to those same people was to remain professional, inquisitive and focused: they might hold vital information, or potentially be involved. It served no one to shut down those pathways because you wanted to seem like a new best mate.

In Bluey's judgement, far too many people these days thought with their emotions. There was a reason that, down the ages, humans had believed that their thoughts were in their brain and their feelings were in their heart: they were two separate things. People now assumed they must be right simply because they were more demonstrative than someone else. Emotions, Bluey would contend, were not an intrinsic badge of superior argument.

'Talk to me, Lachie.'

Lachie was struggling with the notion that he didn't like Tahlia, or what he knew of Tahlia. It happened sometimes; often, when criminals were murdered – the lack of empathy made it harder to see through the victim's eyes. It was probably the case right now on the drive-by murders: the crew on the fifth floor would hold an element of *who cares if hardened crims kill each other* no matter how much they tried. The investigation would remain professional, coherent and orderly, but never prompt the insights and ideas that come from genuine involvement.

'Tahlia sectioned off her life, didn't she? Chinese walls, basically. She didn't socialise with work colleagues, she didn't spend time with half her family, she didn't tell her family about her friends. Separate compartments; worlds that could never collide.'

'You reckon they never did?' asked Bluey, slapping the button to go up. 'It wouldn't be the first time someone tried to keep their life discrete but it backfired. If you shutter people off from each other and then they bang together, you get sparks. For example: unsuitable boyfriend prompting family friction, or work relationships that spill over – that sort of stuff doesn't become impossible just because you try to avoid it.'

'I dunno. She didn't see her family enough for a motive to build, as far as I can see. If she's the butterfly they said she was, how does she spend long enough with someone to prompt a motive for murder? It would have to be a seed from something long ago, something buried that suddenly rose up. Or someone she's around constantly – work or close neighbour. No one waits that long for an opportunity without trying to create one; it's hard to see that anyone in the family did that.'

Bluey nodded – that was fair comment. Families who'd been recently bereaved often got out the airbrush, both for themselves and the departed. Comments about their loved one being *an angel*, about *lighting up a room*, about *giving you the shirt off their back*. Sometimes these things were true; just as often they were unevidenced and empty word salads that got the bereaved through the days and, especially, the nights. But neither Vanessa nor Ruth had reached for that. It appeared that Tahlia had been a beautiful but drifting young woman, attractive but not central to the lives of others, uncertain where her future lay and busking it in the meantime. She'd skated by on looks and an apparent ability to dazzle with a smile, but deep down she didn't seem to impress anyone. Except, perhaps, Josh Harris and this other young man, Warren Bartlett.

'What about your theory that Reagan never went away?' asked Bluey. 'Vanessa Moore said Boston, mate.'

Lachie's idea was based on the notion that Reagan was the person who'd spent most time with Tahlia in the past year and was therefore most likely to have developed a motive for attacking her, or to know who did. Reagan's apparent location in the USA was only dampening the idea, not crushing it.

'Don't knock it. Until Kat can prove that Reagan went overseas, she remains an *alleged* traveller.'

They reached the office to find that Kat had provided herself with a full tea service. White porcelain with a classy little green-and-gold motif around the edges, on a tray with mahogany handles. It all sat on a pile of files from who knew where: teapot, cup, saucer, side plate with several Kingstons.

Bluey pointed. 'The emperor of biscuits.'

Kat nodded, as if everyone knew that.

'I prefer Monte Carlos myself,' offered Lachie as he passed.

Kat's expression was on a par with Lachie confessing to strangling kittens for a laugh.

'Rookie error,' countered Bluey, fearing for Lachie's safety at this point. 'You've been conned by the name. You see *Monte Carlo* and you think millionaires and glamour. You expect luxury, but you don't get that. Instead it's just wallpaper-paste cream, low biscuit quality and too crumbly; it's marketing hype with nothing behind it. Kingstons are the real deal.'

Bluey would swear that Kat looked at him with genuine gratitude.

'Kat, what can you tell me about Anthony Peters?'

'Drugs have gone off for a long lunch, so lucky us, we can use a proper interview room. Anthony's in Interview Q, downstairs on 10, with his mummy. You won't like either of them when you meet them. I didn't. Anthony was eighteen a fortnight ago. They whinged about having to come in and Anthony wants to know when he can have his toy back. Oh, and his actual medical records are there on the first page. Interesting.'

She passed Bluey a thin file, adding, 'He also has an online presence. Page three.'

Lachie read over Bluey's shoulder until Bluey gave him a glare. Returning to his seat, Lachie was rewarded with the first page of details. They both read in silence while Kat took her tea service down the corridor to the kitchen.

Bluey clicked the mouse on Anthony's online efforts and this time he beckoned Lachie to take a look over his shoulder. They flicked rapidly through pages, images, some snide online commentary on a near-daily basis.

'Oh, yeah,' muttered Lachie. 'I want another go at this one.'

Chapter 16

City West station. Thursday, 1205hrs

Stella Peters paced up and down. The room was only three metres wide; her shadow constantly flitted across Anthony's line of sight. The slow-motion blip of disturbed light nauseated Anthony, who eventually put his head down on his arms and feigned sleep. It didn't disrupt Stella's rhythm.

Lachie watched through the glass from a side room: because he'd already interviewed Anthony, they'd decided to go with Bluey this time. The conclusion was partly based on who might form a connection. Bluey had pointed out that Anthony might respond to a father figure more than an older brother. In addition, Anthony was eighteen by only a couple of weeks and was potentially somewhere on the spectrum. It was less likely that Stella could claim any form of bullying or coercion if the older, more experienced detective was in the room this time: Lachie interviewing twice in a few hours might look intimidating to a judge. Or an appeal court.

Because Anthony, no matter what he currently thought, was in a heap of trouble.

Tyson slid into the side room.

'Cool, you made it,' said Lachie. 'Sorry we loaded you up when we shoved off.'

'No problem, sir. I tried Cassie about the customers behind Anthony in the café – got a few to chase up later today. Forensics are back doing a deep dive on the puke drain. Scott from What's Brewin' will be here in . . . forty-five minutes.'

'Good. Bluey's just about to launch.'

Bluey entered the interview room and held out his hand.

'I'm Detective Carl Blewson, Ms Peters.'

Her handshake was wet and feeble. 'What's this all about?'

Bluey invited her to sit as he clicked on the recorder. Anthony raised a drowsy head from his arms, took in Bluey and slowly lowered his head again, as if the grown-ups were going to discuss pensions or real estate or something else that didn't interest him.

'I'm going to be interviewing Anthony in relation to the death of Tahlia Moore. I'm going to give three options, and I'll leave the room while you decide. Option one: you stay, Ms Peters, as Anthony's mother. But you cannot interrupt at any point – he's an adult and you won't be there as a guardian, just as a courtesy from me. Option two: you arrange a lawyer for Anthony and we wait for however long it takes for the lawyer to arrive. Bearing in mind your son's a witness at this stage. Option three: I interview Anthony alone.'

Stella frowned at the third option. She clearly wanted to stay, not just for Anthony's protection but her own. Anthony sat up gradually, as though trying to appear unconcerned.

'I'll wait outside while you decide.' Bluey rose, then paused. 'But I'll tell you this for nothing, Anthony – I'll be talking to you about your online behaviour.'

Anthony started, then shook his head, as if trying to access the memory. Bluey made sure that they saw him pause the recording, then he left the room and closed the door. He walked quickly into the adjoining room, where the three of them could watch the body language through the glass, even if they couldn't hear what was said.

The moment the latch clicked, Stella started on her son. Arms wide, then pointing, then shaking her hands as if washing them of the whole thing. Anthony's body language remained buttoned down. Whatever he said by way of reply was cool and dispassionate but brutally effective. Stella seemed to change her mind on a dime, now imploring her son and making Italian-esque prayer motions for forgiveness and repentance. Anthony was unmoved.

He shook his head slowly and resumed his head-on-arms pseudo-sleep. Stella moved to the far wall and slumped, reaching for a tissue and dabbing her eyes theatrically.

The whole mimed discussion had taken thirty seconds. Lachie hadn't seen Stella so animated and wondered if this was how they behaved at home. Bluey raised an eyebrow at Lachie, the informal bet won: Anthony wanted to fly solo. Bluey went back to the room and opened the door. Stella came out, head bowed, and stood in the corridor, awaiting instruction.

'You can sit there, Ms Peters. Tyson's bringing you some water.'

Bluey arranged his file on the desk and tapped the recorder to restart it. He did the formals and lightly nudged Anthony with his foot to get him to sit up and confirm his name and address.

'You've indicated that you're happy to conduct this interview without either a lawyer or your mother present, is that correct?'

Anthony was deep inside himself, so his nod seemed zombified.

'Verbally, Anthony,' admonished Bluey.

'Yes, Detective.'

'At this stage I'm not interviewing you as a suspect but as a witness. That's why I haven't read your rights. If I think you are *definitely* a suspect, I will read you those rights and there's no way I'll continue until you have a lawyer with you. Is that clear?'

Another disconnected nod. The air in the room was one of defeat, when Bluey wanted Anthony to feel it was a blessed release. He had work to do, getting this teenager onside.

'Again, verbally.'

'Yes, Detective.'

Bluey sat back. Chatty mode.

'You chose well, sending your mum out and refusing a lawyer. It was the best of the three choices: you knew what you were doing. It makes sense to keep her out of this loop if you can.'

He looked for a flicker but couldn't discern one. Anthony was still somewhere only he knew about: a kingdom where he was deciding something momentous.

'Anthony, I've been a detective for twenty-six years. That's around six thousand working days, give or take. Let's assume I average two interviews a day – it's at least that with all those witnesses, suspects, convicted criminals, technical specialists, lawyers, families. I've done about twelve thousand interviews, in that case. Do you know how many people have successfully lied to me?'

Anthony faked indolence but he'd moved forward slightly, tilted his head a little. His focal point had retreated from a corner of the room to Bluey himself. He shook his head.

'It's three. Just three. I can remember their names, faces, every bit of them and what they did. Two of them were absolute experts, con artists who'd spent a lifetime grifting and cheating and got away with it every time. They had it honed *just so*, they had brilliant but amoral reflexes, they were tremendously quick thinkers. Would have made excellent psychiatrists if they hadn't had an ethical vacuum. The third was an out-and-out psychopath – the genuine article. Thank God they're dead now. Someone who lied so well because they totally, fervently believed in their lies and in the necessity for them; the ones they told me and the others that clogged up and propped up their entire life. They were pushed along by their total conviction.' He stared at Anthony and slowed down. 'So, that's three people out of twelve thousand.'

If Anthony was impressed, he hid it behind a pacific face that would have maddened Bluey if he'd let it. That huge decision – whatever it was – remained incomplete.

'Probably a thousand of those twelve thousand tried to lie. Sometimes deliberately, sometimes failing to mention what they knew should be said. People hiding secrets, protecting other people, making themselves look good or others look bad; shielding business or family or mates, secret affairs or their own shame. Some of them were pretty good, but only three got right past me.'

Anthony leaned forward on his elbows, closing the space between them.

He tried to make it look nonchalant, but he was too deliberate with the placing of his limbs. It allowed Bluey to drop the volume a little more, to become a touch more conspiratorial. Bluey liked the closing gap between them.

'I'm telling you all this because we've gone back over your records – school, medical, online behaviour, all of it – and it seems to me that you've been pushing this scam for around four years. Up until about year eight you were a regular, quiet, bullied kid who got decent grades without wowing anyone, hated sport, didn't get into trouble. People ignored you or pushed you around – those were your options. You were desperate for a way out from all that. Your mum felt the same; plus, she wanted some extra mayo. But we'll come to that.'

Anthony had dark chocolate eyes that sucked in the light; they flickered, as if he were about to reveal, then closed. Bluey's voice was low, secretive, intimate.

'When you changed schools: that was the moment. New school, fresh faces; no one knew you from the old place. You'd been bullied relentlessly – we've seen the reports, mate. I'm sorry that happened to you: adults of all varieties should have done better. You were convinced the same would happen at this new place, and you, with your mother, were determined to find a way out of that. I'm guessing she saw a doco, or something – there had to be some kind of catalyst. Maybe she just researched online, made notes, made you practise in the mirror. You started your little ruse and the short-term aim was to be left alone, but long-term the goal was always to be home-schooled, wasn't it? You wanted out, but you wanted to be left alone no matter where you were. She wanted you *diagnosed*: the golden egg of NDIS diagnosis for life. You both wanted the same end result, but *you* wanted it by just being quiet, *she* wanted it by you pretending.'

Bluey leaned in.

'She coached you to fake autism, didn't she?'

Anthony's gestures were on the move. Fingers crabbed in both hands but tapping together at the tips; feet scooted back under the chair instead of splayed out. More coiled, more ready. Something about to burst out of him, but not yet.

'You're not autistic, Anthony, you're just acting out clichés. No doctor has given you that diagnosis. We count seven attempts to get the magic title – those that have an official report – but there were probably more. You might have lost count yourself. You're not on the spectrum, or anything like. No one blames you, mate. Until a couple of weeks ago you were a child and she was legally in charge. We get it. But it has to stop now, yeah? You're eighteen – you can make your own choices. You've already made one, having this interview on your own. Time to come clean, move on, break the shackles. Talk to me about that, Anthony.'

Bluey could hear the teenager's breathing starting to build. Once the adrenaline started to flow it was difficult to keep any semblance of it from becoming visible. Anthony was good at hiding it, but not perfect; in an otherwise blank room it was easier to detect.

'I . . . I can't. No. She'd be in trouble, wouldn't she? If I say. And even if she isn't, she's going to know I told you. She'd know. I have to live there. You see that, don't you? I have to live there after this. So I can't.'

It was a fair point. He was barely an adult and there was no sign of somewhere else eager to take him in – no kindly aunt and uncle who'd be more than happy. Just him and Stella and an apartment overlooking a murder. He needed more coaxing; Bluey might be the father figure who could get it done.

'It's illegal, Anthony. It's against the law. It's fraud. Even though you've been a part of this, we don't blame you, like I say. But we can't have it continue, can we? It's not right. Your role becomes more active, more serious, once you're an adult who knows this is wrong, eh?'

Anthony turned slightly, as though Bluey's words were scorching. It was a fine line – Bluey wanted him edgy enough to give up his mother's behaviour, but not pushed into fearful silence. Bluey and Lachie had read the medical reports, almost incredulous. Anthony had been fourteen when the first push for diagnosis came. Initially, it was shoddy and amateurish attempts to put words in a doctor's mouth – obvious, fatuous. But in the last year or so, more sophisticated: seeking out agencies doing diagnosis by phone or tele-medicine, better coaching and more nuanced acting, less overt about getting financial payments and more subtle displays around emotion.

Anthony shuddered, beginning to crumble.

'It started like a game,' he whispered. 'Her game. Do this, act like that, let me see. She told me there was a way of behaving that would put off the bullies, that would make the teachers pay attention. *Schools ignore bullying,* she told me. *But bullying autistic kids? They don't ignore that. It can be your shield. So we have to make them see that – they have to see an autistic boy when they see you. Then they'll protect you.* She promised.'

Anthony took his first look away from Bluey. He flicked a glance around the room: at the mirror, the door. Wondering who was behind each of them, what they might do. Twelve hours ago he was cosy and it was all so containable: just his mother's obsession to negotiate. Now it was all airborne, crashing to the ground and shattering.

'So what did you do?'

'I tried to please her. Tried to do it. Wasn't very good at first – I was just extra quiet and pretended I didn't understand when people got angry, or laughed. It took about six months before the teachers started using the word. Mum said they all went on courses these days, to look out for things like that. We could make that work in our favour. If I was good enough.'

And there it was, thought Bluey. *Good enough.* That was how the leverage began – do this to please me, do it better, you're not good enough, try harder, do more. Coercive control of adults could be worked in that way – the same human clay, the same gradual corkscrew of expectations and the victim wanting to please.

Easier with kids, he understood. The clay was softer.

'Go on,' he encouraged softly.

Anthony swallowed hard.

'It became a habit. She didn't want me to stop when I got home from school: *any time we're outside,* she told me. She said practice was everything – it needed to be like a natural state to be really convincing. She had some specialists lined up. Each time a specialist said no, she got angrier. I wasn't being good enough, I wasn't helping. There was only me and her and we had to help each other and she was doing everything she could but I wasn't helping because I wasn't really trying and if I cared I'd try extra hard and –'

He shuddered to a halt. Bluey quietly gave him a moment.

'And whatever you did, it wasn't good enough for her? Never would be?'

He blew his nose as an excuse to dry his eyes. Bluey opened him a little more.

'That was all for her, Anthony, not for you. Look, I know it kept you off school for a couple of years and that probably felt like a blessing at the time. But you've missed out, mate. Education, socialisation, all the subtle things you learn from simply being there and don't realise it. You need to play catch-up now, don't you? You can get help with that, now you're an adult. Proper learning, no bullying. You're a bright spark, Anthony, you can do that, you can catch up. But before you can get on with that, we have to come clean with the other stuff.'

'Which other stuff? I've told you – she made me pretend. She wanted the diagnosis and she kept pushing me until I could fool an expert.'

Bluey nodded. 'I get it. She wanted the money from an NDIS diagnosis of autism because that's money for life: you don't get un-diagnosed later on. But we need a completely clean slate for you. Right now, I'm looking at a murder in the courtyard of your apartment block and I think you can help me. That's the next step – your cooperation in my investigation.'

'I don't – I haven't got anything to do with that.'

'See, that could well be the case, but you have information we need and we've got to tie up the loose ends involving you. That's you and your drone, specifically. Can we do that, Anthony?'

A nod as the rest of the blood drained from Anthony's face.

Bluey calmly reached into the file and pulled a photo. They'd blown it up from Anthony's blog. He'd called himself TonyPPer.

A figure, half dressed, emerging from the bathroom. Anthony blanched and, as Bluey had anticipated, tried to bristle his way out of a corner.

'Nothing showin', is there? I pixellated it out.'

'She's fifteen, though. You took video of her without her consent, posted it online. They define that in the legal system quite clearly. You don't want to go there, Anthony.'

A flicker around the eye. A quick flex of one arm.

'Fifteen? I didn't – I mean . . . but . . . but she leaves the blinds open. All the time. Some of her other neighbours can see. I'm not stupid, I can tell when the lights are on in the apartments around me. They see. So it's . . . it's public, really. And I blocked out the – I looked up the law online.'

Bluey sighed. Good dads – even the figurative ones – knew when to be tougher.

'Then blame Wikipedia for your current predicament. It's illegal is what it is. Here's another, from last week: they call that a *pattern of behaviour*. She's sixteen. Don't worry yourself about the legal age of sexual consent: this is about being *an adult* and granting permission. They aren't and they haven't.'

Anthony had thought he'd been smart: he'd thought the VPN shielded him and he couldn't be traced. He'd bet the farm on that, as it turned out. And here he was.

'How do we make this go away?'

Now Bluey had him where he wanted him; on the back foot, anxious to cooperate and unguarded in what he admitted.

'We don't. The behaviour doesn't go away and neither do the consequences. You're asking the wrong question. Think like an adult, Anthony – take that step. What you should be asking is this: how can I limit the damage? How can I keep the worst of those consequences from happening?'

Anthony was impatient now, impetuous.

'Yeah, yeah, whatever. Tell me. What can we do?'

'What *you* can do, Anthony, is several things. Firstly, you can give us the passwords so that we can download everything on the cloud, your computer and the camera you used on the drone. We want it all. You don't know what might be useful for our murder investigation, but we sure do. Second, you can cooperate when we ask you questions about last night. Full cooperation, full disclosure.'

'Yeah, yeah, and what if I do that? What do I get?'

'What you *avoid*, Anthony, is the very worst outcomes for what you've done. I put in a good word with the prosecutor; she takes it into account when she makes her own *independent* decision about you. It'll be a separate investigation to this one; I won't be on it so I can't give you any guarantees. But failure to cooperate? Will undoubtedly make it worse. So . . . what'll it be?'

Bluey slid a pen and paper across to Anthony. The teenager frowned, then slowly wrote the user names and passwords. Bluey glanced at the mirror, and it signalled Lachie's entrance with a form allowing forensic investigation of Anthony's room, myriad electronic devices and online accounts. Tyson was already heading to the apartment with the master key, waiting for the word. Anthony signed without even beginning to read the small print. Lachie grabbed the form and withdrew.

Bluey took a minute. He let Anthony stew on the situation, feel the enormity sink in. Bluey had no doubt there was some footage in the cloud a lot more serious and explicit than he'd already seen: Anthony wouldn't have caved so quickly if this was all there was. Anthony had conned himself that there was never a real downside to what he did with the drone. He'd just learned something new.

'Before you went to What's Brewin' yesterday morning, had you ever met Tahlia Moore?'

Anthony blinked too much and looked down to the left; classic signs that made Bluey take deeper notice.

'Off and on. Round and about the apartment building. I don't go out much, see? If I bumped into her I was in, uh, spectrum mode. Copped a few looks at her; she didn't seem to mind. Used to it, I guess; if you look like that then it's always gonna happen, isn't it?'

Yeah, thought Bluey. *Doesn't make it okay, though. Women must get so sick of it, and so sick of getting sick of it.* He reminded himself that Anthony was a young eighteen.

'What did you say to her when you did meet?'

'Nothing. I was supposed to be emotionally awkward, wasn't I? And Mum was with me some of the time. So it wasn't really on to chat to her or anything. I, uh, *observed.*'

'And what did you observe?'

'She was a cow, wasn't she? Totally up herself.' Anthony scooted forward and warmed to the task when it involved insulting someone else. 'She thought she was all that and a bag of chips 'cos she was good-looking. Some people do, don't they? Since I'm not actually autistic then I can tell that sort of thing, can't I?'

He allowed himself a little smirk before continuing.

'Put it this way. We had Caretaker Sally in the apartment a few weeks ago, repairing some dodgy door handles. She's everyone's go-to if anything goes wrong, because she can usually fix it and she just takes fifty bucks cash. Pretty much everyone in the building has saved heaps because of her. But she takes nothing if they're old or sick or doin' it tough; just fixes it and says 'bye. She's a good person. Tahlia would never do anything like that, even if she had the skills. She isn't that kind of person: a kind person.'

'So you started spying on Tahlia with the drone?'

'Didn't get the drone until a few months ago. Nah, just started by looking through my curtains. With my lights out, there's no way she could know. Some people leave their lights on and the curtains open and don't really care. She was one of those.'

One of those people who didn't expect their neighbour to be a perve, mused Bluey.

'What did you see?'

'Most of it was boring except for the fact that she was in her underwear when she did it. Was more interesting when she had that other girl living with her.'

'Reagan?'

'Was it? Never met her. They worked together, I think; saw her working in What's Brewin' a few times when we drove past.'

'They were sisters. But go on; what was interesting?'

'The rows. The fights. The hissy fits. Always seemed one way to me. Tahlia was older; she was the one getting mad and the other girl was trying to calm it all down. I kept wondering why they carried on living together. But if they're sisters, I guess that answers that.'

'What happened when you got the drone?'

'Took me a few weeks to sort it out. Learning to fly it, what it could do; setting up the TonyPPer blog. All the security.'

Bluey allowed himself a little jab, to keep Anthony on track.

'The security we cracked, the security that let you down.'

'Yeah, yeah, anyway. I had other fish to fry for a while, but a couple of days ago I was bored and everyone was asleep, so I dropped by Tahlia's place. She had the bedroom curtains closed, but not well enough. I could hover at the right angle. I saw.'

Anthony sat back like he had killer information and was glad of the audience.

'You saw what?'

'She injected herself. I mean, she cooked it up first. The foil, the spoon, all that crap. Then she injected, into the top of her thigh. Like you see on the telly. I filmed it.'

Ah. So that was . . .

'That was the footage you showed to her in the café yesterday?'

'Yeah.'

No wonder Tahlia went apoplectic.

'And what was the purpose of showing her?'

Anthony shrugged. 'Ah, look, it was partly just to take her down a peg, if I'm honest. I'd seen her prancing around like she was God's gift. The look on her when she saw the footage – priceless. It was tricky for me to keep up the spectrum face then. So Her Royal Highness is all shocked, then she tries to get me to delete it. Like I ever would. She sort of hissed it because she didn't want anyone else hearing.'

Now they didn't need to get that lip-reading expert from the university, Bluey realised. Lachie was good, but they'd been expecting to need specialist, credentialled help.

'You said "partly". What other reason did you have?'

'Oh, I thought it might get me somewhere. You know. I wondered what she'd do to keep it quiet. I was guessing no one else knew and she wouldn't want it spread around the apartments, or her work. She obviously wasn't rich, or anything. But I thought she might, uh, find a way to make sure that didn't happen.'

Bluey reminded himself again that this person was able to simulate a lack of knowledge of others' emotions precisely because he didn't have much knowledge.

'We call it blackmail. Coercion.'

The mention of another crime committed didn't go down well. Anthony spat a reply.

'Yeah, well, if she hadn't turned up dead, none of this would have occurred to you, eh? It's just bad luck.'

Not copping that, thought Bluey. He sat forward suddenly and was gratified that Anthony immediately moved backwards, his toes scrabbling for grip on the vinyl flooring.

'Jesus, Anthony. It's bad luck *for her*, isn't it? *Being dead?* It's just a few chooks coming home to roost for you. Get some perspective. So she accosted you yesterday when your mum was there, while you were bringing the shopping in: that was what she was yelling about?'

'Yeah. She didn't really have a game plan, eh? No negotiation.' Anthony was flustered and mistook what was common ground with Bluey. 'She could have bought me off with a blowie, to be honest, I'm not greedy. But nah, just started pushing and shoving and making stupid threats she couldn't back up.'

'And you were still working the autism con, so you couldn't react.'

'Totally. Had to give it the full idiot, didn't I?'

Bluey rolled smoothly into the ultimate reason for the interview.

'That must have annoyed you, though. I mean, you have this hold on her with those images, but *she's* taking the active role, being the aggressor. You have to suck it up. Annoying.'

Anthony frowned as he attempted to process. Bluey let him have the dead air to do so. Gradually, the implication dawned.

'Oh. Oh, I see what you're doing. Nah. Nah. I'd never –'

'Wouldn't you? It's something we've got to consider, mate, you can see that. The prosecutor – she's kinda my boss. She'd say that we've established that you'd spy on underage girls and try to blackmail a woman into having unwanted sex with you. Plus, we've established that Tahlia's reaction to all that made you angry. The rest of it's hardly a leap, is it?'

'Nah, I wouldn't do anything like *that*. You got no evidence, have ya?'

'Maybe we have. Goes easier for you, though, if you have a rock-solid alibi for the time in question. That would make any hint of involvement go away.'

'Last night? I was asleep.'

'Asleep? Or flying the drone? Think carefully, Anthony. We're downloading the metadata from that thing – dates, times, geolocation to a few metres. Don't make a bad situation worse.'

Anthony drew on some defiance.

'Go ahead. I was asleep. No drone last night. Me and Mum at home all night.'

'Well, *she* wouldn't actually know, would she? I bet she doesn't know you fly the drone around at night, eh? I'm also betting she takes a *mummy's little helper* each night to make her sleep. She's oblivious: no alibi whatsoever for you.'

'Yeah, well. I don't know how to prove it, but I wasn't awake and I wasn't flying a drone and I didn't attack Tahlia. Like you said, I had the advantage over her, eh? I didn't need to do anything like that.'

Good theory. But someone like this, thought Bluey, failed to understand what advantage they actually had, or how to press it home. Blackmail wasn't just having the information; it was knowing how to apply the leverage.

'Unless she just flat-out refused to play. That's the trouble with this stuff, especially for a novice – it crumbles when someone calls their bluff. I've seen it happen: they go from whip-hand to useless jelly in three seconds once someone actually pushes back. Here's the worst-case scenario for Tahlia, mate: she loses a job she doesn't seem to like and walks into another one because she's hot and she can pour on the charm. She apologises to her mum for dabbling in drugs and promises to clean herself up. That might seem better than *coerced* sexual acts with a blackmailer she despises, no?'

The word *coerced* brought another swallow from Anthony, digesting the implications. His voice trailed away.

'I don't think she was going to do any of that.'

It sounded weak and unconvinced.

'Oh? Maybe you saw her out in the courtyard last night and decided to test the theory. Let's run that film for the prosecutor, so you can see how we might think. Your mum's snoring away. You slip out and confront Tahlia. You want your reward for perving on her and she openly laughs in your face. It all goes wrong real fast from there. It escalates and now she's on the ground, bleeding out. You panic, run out of the *western* exit, go around the building, come back through the *eastern* entrance and home. No one sees you – *you hope* – but you've thrown a curveball if they have. You still have time to run your clothes through the wash and take a long shower, just in case. Then you turn back into autism-boy in the morning in case the cops turn up.

'That's a realistic scenario for us, mate. It fits with all that we have and you have no actual alibi. Besides, this morning has established that you're a proven liar and you have literally no evidence to refute what we say. Yeah, maybe we go with that. If we do, then your watching underage girls and the ol' autism scam comes to light; no jury's gonna want to give you a free pass on anything.'

Bluey paused, letting the blade sink in.

'It's ironic, Anthony. We've sadly had people on the spectrum wrongly convicted in the past because they didn't understand what was going on. You'd be an autism faker who *knew exactly* what was going on, but you still get convicted.'

Anthony's lips moved, but nothing came out. He suddenly looked about ten years old. He looked to the door for his mummy.

'I didn't . . . I just didn't. I never would. I was just pissing about, really. I never meant . . . I'm sorry. I've never even hit anyone. I'd never . . . I just wanted . . . I just wanted some bloody attention. I wanted to be at the centre of things. Is that so hard to imagine?'

No, thought Bluey, it isn't. *Sounds natural and not totally unreasonable. But you had motive and opportunity. Plus, the means to stab someone was sitting in your kitchen. Wasn't it?*

Bluey decided to make Anthony rot in his own guilt for a while. The forensic team would take all the tech, but it would be a while before they had anything substantial. He could hold Anthony for a couple of hours in case he had further questions, so he left him and Stella glaring at each other over plastic cups of water. Bluey and Lachie found a quiet corner of a corridor to compare notes.

'You don't actually like him for this, do you?' asked Lachie.

Bluey turned from examining a view of the visitors' car park and a melee of bin chickens attacking a dumpster across the street.

'Not really, but maybe. You of all people know how *contrary* prosecutors can be, don't ya? I can see how they'd run, if it looked like a quick and cheap conviction. Why not? He's on familiar territory with regards to criminal conduct: he's blackmailing the victim. There's established animosity between them. She has the capacity to embarrass and humiliate him, even though she's on the back foot. He's emotionally immature and can't articulate what he feels, so might resort to the physical. He has no alibi but himself. Whatever the weapon turns out to be, there'll be at least one of them in his unit. He had time to clean himself up and dispose of the weapon. Two of our witnesses saw the western exit closing; it's entirely possible that our killer went through that door. He could do that because he panics; or he could be the smart-arse kid who lives on the eastern side but used the western exit. Misdirection, means, motive, opportunity: Lachie, that's a lot of ticked boxes.'

Lachie was leaning against the wall, flicking through his phone messages.

'Point taken. But, you know . . .'

'What? You still want it to be Reuben Pearce? Because he's Reuben Pearce? Because you nearly lost your job over the bloke?'

'He was not only close by the victim in the moment; he picked Tahlia up and he's literally covered in her blood. From most witnesses, he has a break between stopping the mouth-to-mouth and letting in the ambos. We can give him thirty seconds to puke, but what about the rest of it? Weapon disposal is achievable in that time. Plus, he's a lech, he's a moron and he's a liar.'

Bluey found it hard to argue. Anthony and Reuben each had the capacity, opportunity and holes in both timeline and behaviour. Lachie found time to worry about the legal position.

'How close did you get to interviewing Anthony as a suspect rather than a witness, back there?'

Bluey smiled. 'Oh, quite close. Fairly close. But I put it all as a hypothetical. Asking about alibis is generic, not specific to him – we asked the other witnesses. I couldn't put pressure on him without sailing close to those rocks, but I think we're okay.'

'Urgh,' muttered Lachie, tapping his telephone. 'Scotty from Coffee Pouring is downstairs.'

Chapter 17

City West station. Thursday, 1300hrs

Scott Villiers was sitting in the cheap seats: moulded plastic and bolted to the floor of Reception so they couldn't become a workplace safety issue. A listless security guard – because a building full of police officers couldn't sort out security matters – watched on. Scott had looked sallow, stressed and struggling in the coffee shop; now, he looked worse. Bluey and Lachie each put on a game face and silently directed him into one of the interview rooms. He had a lever-arch file tucked under his arm which threatened to tip with every stride.

Lachie sighed. 'For God's sake, Scott, put that on the table before you drop your lollies.'

Scott did so, nudging it with his fingers until it was exactly perpendicular to the table's edge.

'It's the data you asked for: super, wages, personnel stuff, all that.'

'We'll take it back to the office, thanks.'

Lachie stood against the wall, observing. Bluey scooted his chair closer to the table. Sometimes he felt more relaxed in interviews where the direction of travel was clear. Interviewing Anthony had been a switchback ride: sympathy about Stella's scheming and his compulsory lying, then pushing him about the drone and the clash with Tahlia. Scott was more of a straight railway track.

'Right. Now, when we were at the café, you weren't very honest with us, were you, Scott?' Bluey leaned in and raised an eyebrow.

'But I . . . I showed you the CCTV. I cooperated.'

'Yeah, you see, people often do that. They have something they want to hide, so they come over all helpful in every way that points us away from them. You give us footage that shows some kid coming into the café annoying Tahlia and you expect us to drift away from thinking about you. Even though you were her boss and you saw her four or five times a week, for hours at a time.'

Scott's head shake was theatrical. 'Well, I'm . . . like you say, I'm her boss. She sees the other girls more than me, really.'

'Does she? Hmm. We're looking at anyone who spent significant chunks of time with Tahlia, because they're most likely to have developed a motive.' He sat back. 'Lachie?'

'Thank you, Bluey.' Lachie stepped forward and pressed one hand on the table, casting Scott into shadow. 'Reagan Moore, Tahlia's sister. How long did she work for you, mate?'

'Reagan?' Scott frowned. 'Uh, not sure. She came to us after her HSC. She'd done a few shifts in the school holidays in year twelve, so she knew the ropes. She did . . . maybe six months, while she saved up for a gap year. Once she had enough money, she left.'

'Hmm. Good employee, would you say?'

Scott nodded a little too enthusiastically. 'Yeah, she was great. Got on well with everyone, hard worker. Yeah, great.'

'I thought so.' Lachie stepped back again, giving Scott a moving target to follow. 'Because she's so good that you've kept on paying her while she goes around the world.'

'I've what? No way. I'd have noticed, surely?'

'You'd think so, eh? In fact, *we do think so*. For the last few months you've been paying Reagan as if she was still here as a full-time member of the gang.'

Scott put his hand on the file, as if it were a Bible to swear on and thereafter no lie could be told about financial matters.

'Oh, Jesus. Oh, this'll be a nightmare. How am I going to claw it back? God. Payroll gets complicated, you know? Penalty rates, super,

Medicare, all the rest of it. I'm usually pretty good, but – urgh, what a mess.'

'Oh, don't worry. You won't have to contact Reagan. You've been paying it all into Tahlia's account.'

'I've what? That must be wrong. I can't . . . I wouldn't.'

Bluey waved a copy of the spreadsheet under his nose.

'You can, you did, mate. And you know you did. And you know why. C'mon, Scotty. Time for cards on the table and no more of this patronising bull. We're not dummies and you treated us like we were. First black mark against you. We know you were paying for a teenage employee even though she no longer works for you. Second black mark. We know you paid tens of thousands of dollars to an employee – *who has just been murdered* – who hadn't earned that money. Third black mark. Get explaining.'

Scott rubbed the palms of his hands deep into his eye sockets. The gesture seemed to age him ten years. Beads of sweat had evolved on his wrists and temple.

'Okay. Okay. Look, I didn't do anything wrong, *as such*, but I got into a bad situation. It wasn't my fault but . . . I couldn't see a way out of it. I thought this would kick it into the long grass but, Tahlia, she – she kept pushing it. I haven't . . . I would never do anything like that. Don't get me wrong. Nothing like *that*.'

Bluey sighed loudly. 'I said *explaining*, not gibberish. Clarify for me, Scotty.'

'When Reagan was leaving we had a little after-hours party for her, to say thanks and goodbye. We put all the blinds down after we closed and, yeah, we had a bit of alcohol and a bit of a dance and stuff. It was nice. All the girls loved Reagan and she was so excited about the trip. Nice. Anyway, I was out the back getting some more sparkling and Tahlia kinda squeezed past me to get to the bathroom. It felt like . . . like she didn't have to be that close, you know? I turned around and we both sorta giggled and I – looking back, I *misinterpreted*. I, uh, thought we were gonna kiss and . . . I did, but she didn't. She slapped me. Hard. Wow, she changed quick. All bubbly and flirty and then it was full UFC in a heartbeat.

'We didn't mention it then; didn't want to spoil Reagan's big moment. But the next shift Tahls had, she was into it. She knew people – *lawyers* – she'd read up on her rights, apparently. Everyone would look at the two of us and know that she wasn't into me, that it wasn't consensual. She poured on lots of extras about my *seniority* and how *vulnerable* she was. Yeah, right. I thought paying her for a few weeks would buy me some time. Reagan had asked for all of the wages in arrears to go direct to Tahlia, because she owed her a few weeks' rent; same with her tip jar. So . . . so it seemed smart to just carry on paying Reagan's basic wage into Tahlia's account. It probably wouldn't get the auditors up and about, either: to be suspicious of the accounts you'd have to know exactly who worked there and when. It kinda hid the payments until I could work out what to do.'

Appeasement: it never worked, in Bluey's experience. You either fessed up and dealt with the problems you'd caused, or you sank. Appeasement just made you fractionally more buoyant for a very limited time.

'Yeah, but you didn't work it all out, did you?'

'I couldn't think straight about it. Every time I tried, my stomach got all twisted. I couldn't see how to stop it without Tahlia threatening me and it all starting again. Even if I sacked her, she'd have the same hold, wouldn't she? She'd have nothing to lose and everything to gain.'

'Oh, you were in a bind all right,' agreed Bluey sympathetically. 'You're a franchisee, aren't you?' He turned briefly to Lachie. 'What's Brewin' is a Seattle company, branches all over the place. Not Scotty's original idea at all – he trades off their name.'

He looked back to Scott. Some things could be said about almost any small business: they were generic leverage. 'You're stuck with a heap of debt. It's your life; your life's work, and it's your super so it's your potential retirement, too. It's not just a place you turn up to each day: you've got emotional investment as well as financial – *sweat equity*, eh?'

Scott nodded reluctantly. Bluey prodded the lever-arch file.

'And here's this silly woman, you think; making up stuff about harass-ment, you think; milking your precious livelihood, you think; a problem without end and without solution, you think.'

Lachie loomed in. 'And then, suddenly, she's dead.'

'Ah, no. For Christ's sake, nah. Nah. I wouldn't.'

'Really?' Lachie came a little closer. 'Because your life-changing issue goes right away the moment she stops breathing. You probably figure someone as volatile as that, with her eye to the main chance: she'd have caused other problems to other people. No reason for *you* to look like a suspect, eh? You're the shocked employer, closing the café out of respect and cooperating fully. *Look, here's the CCTV of someone making her angry; go check him out.* Now you can stop paying Tahlia *and* stop paying Tahlia-as-Reagan. Problem over.'

Scott was on the point of tears. Crying impressed neither detective, no matter what the reason. If someone was genuinely upset, it wasn't on the detectives, who needed to retain some professional distance. If they weren't genuinely upset, they were insulting the detectives' intelligence. Probably the former this time, speculated Bluey, since Scott was watching his tiny empire dissolve.

'Here's what we're gonna do for now, Scott. We'll have a forensic accountant at your place in about ten minutes. They will go through *everything*: they'll be so far into you they might find polyps. You'll give every bit of help they want. Meanwhile, we'll check your alibi. Because you do have one, don't you?'

Scott's brain scrambled for grip.

'Ah, last night? Ah. Yeah. With someone. But, uh, her husband doesn't . . . you know. FIFO. Nice guy. We don't want to hurt – anyone.'

'Probably a little late for that, eh? Name, address, phone. We'll be dis-creet. For now. And stay in town, Scott. We'll be chatting again real soon, mate.'

Chapter 18

When they got back to the office it was past one thirty. Late enough for Kat to have long since decided, according to a note on Bluey's computer, that it was her *lunch-hourish*. Bluey found it hard to argue with her absence because everything in the admin section was perfectly up to date, a model of clarity and accuracy. It contrasted with their whiteboards, which were getting more and more nightmarish. They'd soon have to open up the dreaded fourth board, which Bluey was loath to do. The fourth board was always the speculation board – a brief summary of theories that were constantly struck down by new evidence, inconvenient facts, or just some clear thinking.

'So,' said Lachie, dumping the lever-arch file on the spare desk, 'thoughts on Scotty?'

'A crumbling man. We'll find he's put his life savings into this. I'm willing to bet his background is in hospitality: Kat's got some research here already. He hasn't saved up the capital, or had some tremendous stock picks. So unless he inherited bigly and felt like chucking some of it away on a failed café, then this is the summit of his life's work and he'd be desperate to keep it going. Tahlia was an active threat to that.' Bluey spread his hands. 'Ironically, she was being blackmailed by Anthony but was adept at blackmailing herself; more adept, in fact. She wasn't going to stop it or reduce the amount – no smart blackmailer does that. Nah, she was seeing a steady income there and she was spending it.'

Lachie decided the lever-arch file was still in the way and put it on the floor.

'So he has motive. But maybe an alibi?'

'*Possible* alibi,' reminded Bluey. 'We'll check it out later. Scott has loads of motive and probably has access to whatever killed Tahlia. But we have no evidence that he was anywhere near the apartments at three in the morning. Until that looks more likely, I'm inclined to think that he's a poor businessman on the skids. Probably wishes he'd hired some more like Reagan and not like Tahlia.'

'Good-lookers bring in the punters, though. Male or female, it's better if your coffee comes with a dynamite smile. If a café is full of pretty people, it attracts other pretty people as well as those that like 'em. Good for business.'

'So young, yet so cynical.'

Bluey heard the lift ping and assumed that Kat had now returned. The voice was female, but not Kat's.

'If those whiteboards are like the inside of your brain, Bluey, you're in big trouble.'

They both turned, but while Lachie scowled slightly, Bluey broke into a smile. In what passed for the doorway was a tall, long-limbed, angular young woman with frizzy hair slanted to one side, a bulbous nose and a tassled suede jacket that was halfway to Nashville.

'Bloody hell, if it isn't Mila Jelovic.' Bluey crossed the room and they hugged. 'What brings you up here? Get tired of the mozzies in Carlton?'

Mila gave a rueful grin as she hitched a sleeve and showed six bitemarks on her forearm. 'The locals are immune, but I'm not. Nah, got to have my six-month review with the big cheeses here.'

'You look different.' Bluey stepped back and mimed a film director's frame-the-shot hands. 'Not sure what it is, though.'

'My legs work and the crutches have gone?'

'Nah, not that.'

'The eyepatch is gone.'

'That's it, you have two eyes now. They suit you.'

They both laughed while Lachie stood like a third wheel.

Bluey pointed at the empty desk.

'You've just missed Killer Kat. She's our admin support on this.'

'No, I met her on the ground floor.'

Mila deliberately left it at that, knowing both the detectives would be disconcerted about what Kat may or may not have intuited or revealed. Bluey stepped into the gap by introducing Lachie.

'Mila.'

'Lachie.'

There was a small flinch from Lachie as he shook hands that suggested a history of some kind. If Bluey had to guess, he'd say that *she* dumped *him*. That was Mila's usual MO with relationships: all in for a while, then a scorched-earth retreat.

'Are you working on the drive-by murders?' she asked.

Lachie snorted. Bluey gave him a reproving look and replied, 'Nah, it's the proper detectives working on that. They own the fifth floor; hence, we're up here next to the knock-off microwaves. If we fail, we'll have to quit and start a business selling . . . well, knock-off microwaves.'

Mila narrowed her eyes. 'Aren't you part of the A-team, Bluey?'

'More like the Z-team.' He pointed at Lachie, then himself. 'We're the Prince Harry of the Homicide Unit: the spare you hope won't be needed, but constantly embarrassing in the meantime.'

Mila laughed and perched herself on the edge of the spare desk. 'So, what have you got instead?'

Bluey turned. 'Lachie?'

Lachie was usually happier with work talk than social niceties. He was still a little rattled and grateful for the half-turn to the whiteboard.

'Tahlia Moore, twenty-seven, waitress. Lived alone, no partner. Found stabbed in the courtyard of her apartment complex, which is overlooked by all fifty-six units. The death is at three in the morning. Probably killed there, by the way, not dumped there, but we're waiting on a post-mortem. No apparent motive – she was flighty and flirty if you listen to some, a bit of a cow if you listen to others. Her socials haven't appeared yet; trying to get the passwords. We do know she was blackmailing her boss and she was subject to an attempted blackmail by a neighbour – he might have filmed her shooting up. No significant arguments with family, while her friends seem to be more acquaintances than die-hard. There's nothing leaping out, to be honest.'

Mila sat implacably, waiting for the rest. When they'd worked together previously on an undercover operation Bluey had found Mila to be anxious and hardened, somewhere between admirably steadfast and foolishly overcommitted. That obsessive quality had cost her dearly, mentally as well as physically; she'd been in Carlton for some type of respite and recovery. She had an easier, more controlled air now. Bluey reckoned that might have come from working in Carlton – less pressurised, and more appreciated, than she'd been during her time at Central.

'Now,' continued Lachie, 'we have five eyewitnesses, plus a drone that was definitely flying around in the general vicinity on previous nights.'

Mila raised an eyebrow. 'Five? Lucky you, especially at that time of night. So why is it so difficult?'

'Ah, that's what everyone's saying – we've got eyewitnesses, so we should make the arrest and tie it all off with a ribbon.'

Mila smiled. 'Did Bluey give you his *the eye is not a camera* thing?'

Lachie relaxed enough to smirk. 'He did, yeah.'

'Ah, the problem being that he's quite correct in that. So what's with your witnesses?'

'One is an older lady struggling with a sudden change from bright light to darkness; her view is partly obscured. Second is an old man on his fifth or sixth trip to the bathroom that night; he came late to the scene and his view is partly obscured. Third is a caretaker who was nearby but didn't arrive until the ambos did. Fourth is a young man dosed up heavily on tranquillisers, who missed some of it while he looked for his phone to dial triple-zero; his view is partly obscured. The drone is flown by a teenager who wouldn't give us the footage, probably because he was perving into people's windows. His mum has been hiding him behind the claim he's autistic, but there's no medical evidence for that. Oh, and the fifth eyewitness is Reuben Pearce – *that* Reuben Pearce – so he's a liar who lies like a Professor of Lying.'

'Okay. I'm beginning to see your problem.'

'Everything is partial or comes with a caveat or two. We're waiting on the 3-D software to map the courtyard: that should show us who can see what, regardless of what they're saying. Plus, we know that some witnesses and some other interviewees are lying, or lying by omission. We have a lot of *testimony*, but we don't have a lot of evidence.'

'Yeah. Yeah, you wouldn't.'

Mila stared intently at the whiteboard with all its asterisks, arrows and question marks: a cartography of confusion.

'Your temporary boss, Dana: she's solved every murder she's investigated, hasn't she?' asked Bluey. 'I'm happy to learn from that. What would she do with all this?'

'Dana Russo? Probably switch off all the lights and sit in a darkened room for hours. Then come up with a breakthrough. She's a very clever introvert.'

Bluey splayed his hands. 'That's the problem with open-plan offices.'

'Hmm. I guess she'd say go back to the basics.'

'Meaning?' asked Lachie, leaning forward.

'Meaning that when you've got all these witnesses, you tend to think the answer must lie with them. There's five of them and they all saw stuff: you reason that surely the answer's within what they're telling you. But it isn't panning out that way. You can't trust that evidence: you aren't sure what weight to put on each piece and, anyway, judging by the board, it's been contradictory.'

That was painfully fair comment, thought Lachie. There were major trust issues with the evidence. He was used to criminals and suspects lying to him; used to witnesses and relatives buckling under the shock and strain. But this felt different.

Mila was on a roll.

'So, go back to what you know. I mean to what you *actually* know, for sure – what you can *prove* that you know. The very fundamentals. Then build up with what you can semi-prove but you think is true. That way, you're confronting your assumptions head on as you go. Plus . . .'

'Plus?'

'It all comes back to motive, doesn't it? For all the logistical gymnastics you're doing around sight lines or a few seconds here and there, it still comes back to motive. Killing someone, especially close up, demands a strong will to do it. Someone has that reason. Find the reason, find the killer – then the rest of it will slot together.'

'It's that easy?' Lachie couldn't help lacing it with sarcasm.

'Yeah. *Simples*, eh?' Mila deadpanned as she rose from sitting. 'I'd obviously like to help you solve it, but performance reviews wait for no man, so you're on your own.'

Bluey walked her to the lift. 'Sorry, mate, I didn't realise you and Lachie . . .'

She waved it away, literally. 'Ah, no biggie. Brief for both of us, but it put me off tequila slammers for life, that's for sure.'

They hugged: Mila liked the way that Bluey only did it when he meant it.

'Are you at the big conference on Friday?' she asked.

'Should be, if I can get this case squared away.'

'Cool.' She stepped into the lift. 'You owe me a really lousy coffee.'

'Do they serve any other kind there?'

Mila grinned as the doors closed.

Chapter 19

City West station. Thursday, 1400hrs

'These are the worst sandwiches in the history of sandwiches.'

'A history that goes back several hundred years – quite the claim, Lachie. They're what you ordered. Kat doesn't do errors.'

Lachie turned one of the offending items in his hand. 'It's at the point where solid turns into liquid.'

Bluey took a swig of Coke. 'Hmm. It's all the mayo. Like a lot of things in Australia, mate: when you can't impress with quality, just give it plenty of mayo and hope they don't notice.'

'Yeah, not hungry any more. Where d'you think Kat's eating?'

Bluey considered it for a moment. 'She'll know some little place in a laneway that looks like a biohazard from the outside but turns into a Michelin-starred bistro if you know the secret phrase that gets you through the door. The chef will treat her like a long-lost rellie. She's got that vibe, hasn't she?'

'True. I get the feeling she doesn't rate me.'

'Don't take it personally. We're all sitting on a short line that runs from hateful dickhead to tolerable. None of us have anything to crow about, there. Besides, you committed a capital offence with your choice of biccie.'

'Consider me humbled.'

Bluey laughed. 'Actually, I won't. I won't ever think that of you, Lachie.' He turned to the whiteboards. 'I reckon Mila was right, don't you? It's a bit messy, to say the least.'

'Apparently we should *focus on what we know*.'

Bluey nodded. 'To be fair, that makes sense. Right. I've finished my lovely fajitas and you don't want . . . whatever that was. As we haven't got your saintly software yet, we might as well focus on what we've been told so far. Okay; everything we can prove. Shall we star chamber?'

Facing each other, perpendicular to the boards, they began.

'Tahlia Moore is dead,' asserted Lachie.

'Check. Vanessa has finished the formal ID of her daughter and it's on the system. Tahlia Moore died between 3.10 and 3.40 this morning.'

'Check. Ambos arrived at 3.32 and it was pronounced at the scene. Tahlia Moore lived at apartment 41, Pacific Heights.'

'Check. All identification and household bills say so. Six other people who live at those apartments are Bryony, Caretaker Sally, Reuben, Jody, Martyn and Anthony.

'Check. Anthony Peters lives with his mum, Stella Peters.'

'Check. Tahlia Moore worked at What's Brewin'.'

'Check. Got her employment records here. Tahlia Moore got more tips than anyone else.'

'Check. There's records go back two years to say so; she made more than the others put together, in fact. Publicly so. Tahlia Moore's sister, Reagan, lived with her.'

'Check. Payments from Reagan for her share of the bills; Vanessa confirmed the arrangement.' Lachie flicked a glance at the boards. 'Scott Villiers was paying blackmail money to Tahlia Moore.'

'Check. Scott confessed and the bank statements support it. Four different witnesses rang for the paramedics.'

'Check. Bryony, Reuben, Jody and Martyn, in that order: ambo phone records confirm it. Jody has a kidney stone.'

'Check.' Bluey had a phone photo from the apartment. 'He had all the right medications with prescription dates from three days ago. Bryony rang her grandchildren in Spain.'

'Check. Tyson got her account details for Skype, and the times match. Tahlia had clothes she couldn't afford.'

'Check. I sent a few photos to a fashion lecturer and she said . . . yeah, pretty pricey and they aren't knock-offs, either. And probably only worn once or twice.'

They paused. They'd run out of things they could prove.

'Jeez.' Lachie ran his hands through his hair. 'We don't *know* a lot, do we? I thought Mila was being a smart-arse, as per. But the amount we actually know for sure is, uh, pretty light, eh?'

'We're only about ten hours in,' reassured Bluey. 'Besides, we have plenty of stuff we're virtually sure of but haven't proven beyond doubt. Most of that will turn out to be fact.'

'Well, let's run through those, then.'

Bluey turned a page in his notebook. 'All right. Things we think are almost certainly true but we can't quite prove it yet. Go.'

Lachie played the first card. 'Tahlia Moore was stabbed.'

'Probably. Waiting on the post-mortem, but that was the paramedic's view and the ME's initial take. No weapon found yet, no autopsy yet. Anthony Peters was set to blackmail Tahlia Moore.'

'Probably. He had the material to do it – Tech have just confirmed the drone footage includes Tahlia shooting up in her bedroom. Anthony confessed to it, but no third-party corroboration that we've actually seen yet. Reuben Pearce upchucked into the drain by his terrace.'

Bluey smiled as he nodded. 'Probably. Awaiting DNA confirmation from the lab, but that'll take days. Blood-type match might be today. No one else was seen near the drain and the puke was fresh. Oh, Forensics say there's nothing under the vomit but some used gum, a couple of cockies and some mud. We're not very popular with them, for some reason. Okay. Reagan Moore was in Boston, USA, at the time of Tahlia's death.'

'Ha. Probably. Vanessa believes so. Kat's trying to track some form of proof. Unlikely to be untrue but not confirmed yet. Scott Villiers has an alibi for the time of death.'

'Probably. He was forthcoming with details, but we'll need to verify. He wasn't seen at the apartment building by anyone. Reuben Pearce was drunk.'

'Probably. He confessed to being so. Actually, I don't think he specified just how pissed he was, did he? Might have been relaxed or catatonic.' Lachie paused to consider his options. 'Tahlia Moore knew *Josh* Harris.'

'Probably. Caretaker Sally said so and Cassie thought so, but I haven't seen any other real corroboration. Something to get from Vanessa later, I reckon. Tahlia Moore knew her killer.'

'Ah, good one. Probably. There's no indication of any new third party, like a mugger or burglar. Waiting on the autopsy for signs of a struggle – skin under the fingernails, someone else's blood. If not, then she almost certainly knew the killer well enough to let them get close. The killer left by the western exit.'

'Probably.' Bluey indicated the boards with an angled pen. 'Two witnesses say they saw that door closing when they looked out at what was going on; two others might have. Kat asked Tyson to recheck it and he said from a full swing to entirely shut was twelve seconds – it's heavily damped. Try this one: none of the witnesses had a clear view.'

'Probably. If we take them at their word and based on where they say they were standing, none of them could see the whole of the scene. Each view is compromised in some way. Aggregating all their views simply gives lots of half-views, not a complete picture: they don't fill in each other's gaps. We should have 3-D images to play with later today or tomorrow morning. Anthony didn't fly his drone on that night.'

'Probably. He says not and he was sufficiently rattled to be telling the truth. Tech are currently finalizing the metadata but, given that he knew we would do that, it's unlikely he's lied about it.' Bluey puffed his cheeks. 'Yeah, this one bugs me: no one has an alibi but themselves.'

That brought Lachie up short. 'Jeez. Except maybe Scotty, then yeah, probably. All of them except Anthony live alone and at 3 a.m. they *were* alone. And, even then; Stella was probably dead to the world and can't alibi Anthony in any meaningful way. Yeah, Jeez. Okay. Three people have a motive to kill Tahlia Moore.'

'Ooh. Probably a minimum: early days, remember. Scott Villiers saw his life's work going under while Tahlia milked him dry over an accusation he could never disprove. Anthony might be humiliated if Tahlia refuses to play ball over his extortion. He'd be completely busted if she rats him out to the wider world about the autism fake – he dropped the mask when he started the blackmail talk. Reuben might have tried it on with Tahlia and been rebuffed, or she might have wound him up about his little court drama. I've gotta say, Reuben's is more possible than probable at this point. Let's add in Jody as someone with a potential motive, just because he lied about knowing her. And if we believe you about the travel, Reagan's not out of the woods either.'

'Fair enough. Is it also fair to say that each apartment has a view of the crime scene, but not always a good view?'

Bluey sat back a bit. 'Yes, that's fair.'

'Aaanndd . . . is it also fair to say that everyone involved knows each other?'

'Oh. Oh, hang on.' Bluey flicked back through his notes. 'Take Scott Villiers out of the equation, because as far as I can tell he knows Tahlia but not anyone else in the building since Reagan left. Caretaker Sally knows everyone, I think – nature of the job. All four of the others knew Tahlia to speak to: Jody lied about it. All four of the others know Reuben and dislike him. Anthony knows Tahlia and Sally, but I'm not sure about the rest. Bryony and Martyn clearly know each other and also know Tahlia and Sally. Yeah. Yeah, they pretty much do know each other, but I've no idea how well. For example, some of them "know" Reuben because they've heard of him and they've seen him around, but I wouldn't say they were mates or mortal enemies. We haven't bottomed out how much contact, really. Something for the second round of interviews?'

Lachie nodded. 'Definitely. Oh, here's one. Reagan Moore knew some of her sister's neighbours.'

'Yup, probably. She lived there for months and by all accounts she was more likeable than Tahlia. So yeah, probably knew a few of them. We need to speak to Reagan, wherever she is.'

Kat returned with, as Bluey had anticipated, absolutely no chat about where she'd been or what her lunch was like. The absence of anecdote, of even a hint about life beyond these walls, was a thing to behold.

'Did you find any confirmation of Reagan's whereabouts, Kat?' he asked.

She slid her handbag under her desk.

'Ah, yes, the nice sister. She looked to be in Boston, Massachusetts, last week. There's video footage of a Red Sox game and I've checked the score against the time stamp. A week before that she was blogging from New York. However . . .'

She stopped totally and shuffled some files from one tray to another.

'Yeah, however?' prompted Lachie.

A slight smile. 'I knew you'd crack first, Lachie. Bluey here plays the long game. *However*, Reagan Moore was somewhere in this country the day before yesterday. Phone and cash machine records. After that? I don't know yet – I'm waiting on Forensics and I'm about to pay them a visit.'

Bluey puffed his cheeks.

'Well, then. Vanessa didn't seem to know about that: I don't really see why she'd lie about knowing. That suggests that Reagan hasn't shown up yet at Vanessa's, even though her sister has just been murdered. Maybe Reagan's pretending to do the mercy dash across the globe to be with her grieving mother, when she's actually just popping down the freeway at her own convenience.'

'Why the subterfuge?' asked Lachie.

'Yeah, why that?' mused Bluey. 'There might be a prosaic reason – she ran out of cash overseas and was too embarrassed to admit that her much-vaunted year away has only lasted a few months. Perhaps she was just desperate to get away from Tahlia? Or there could be a reason that's more relevant. Kat, anything on Tahlia's phone from Reagan?'

Kat tapped the keyboard and leaned into the screen.

'I'm just checking that now. Nothing on the number we have for her. But she could have bought a separate phone in the US. I need to dig deeper. Tahlia didn't get any phone calls after midnight last night, but she got calls earlier in the evening.'

'She *got* calls that evening; did she make any?'

Kat shook her head. 'No. All incoming. And all from one number.'

'Do we know who?'

Kat held for a beat. 'Pay-as-you-go burner. From either inside Pacific Heights or within about a hundred metres, though.'

'Jesus.' Lachie threw his pen at the monitor. 'Did she answer?'

'Not that Tech could tell, no. All calls, too, not texts.'

Bluey nodded. 'All right. I'll add it to the list of things we try to tease out of people. Kat, this note says that Tech cracked open Tahlia's social media?'

Kat's world-weary smirk forewarned them this would be a dead end.

'I know detectives like to get excited about socials, thinking it's the mother lode. But you're going to be disappointed. I've sent you the *highlights*, believe it or not. Insta photos of her, Insta photos of clothes she'd like, more Insta photos of her. Facebook details about clubs, events, vouchers off, et cetera. Nothing on Twitter or TikTok. The girl's a vacuum: clothes fall into it, nothing worthwhile clambers out.'

Bluey smiled. 'I'll put you down as a "maybe" for now, shall I? And we're sure she doesn't have any other chatter lying around, any online aliases?'

'Unless she's going to an internet café, no. Which sounds very cloak-and-dagger for a girl who proclaims she'd *die for this dress* about once a week.'

Bluey glanced at Lachie, who eye-rolled. Kat had been right: they always invested extra hope in the social media and phone data of a victim, especially when they hadn't received it yet. Tahlia's life appeared to float; ephemeral and superficial even when she knew it to be so. There seemed to be no moment when she reflected and took more than a brief interest in something else.

So who, faced with someone drifting through their existence, would want to end that life?

Chapter 20

Bluey sat back and doodled on a spare page while Lachie went to the bathroom. Kat got herself some more tea from wherever she hid the fancy tea set. His phone buzzed with a message from Laxton: *Done it yet? Update at the end of the day. Expecting a solution, mate.* The *mate* didn't fool anyone: Bluey could almost see the shadow of the axe over his head. Laxton thought it was skilled motivational management, but Bluey couldn't avoid a sense that the bloke was a dickhead.

All Bluey could think of, when considering the evidence so far, was slamming doors. He had five eyewitnesses, but none of them saw more than a partial view. He had five eyewitnesses, but no one seemed to have seen the killer. If they had, they weren't saying. He had almost no forensics worth a shake: no CCTV, no fingerprints, no fibres or hairs yet, no DNA analysis to point the way, no proof about who was there besides the people already known to be there. The answer, as Mila had intuited, surely nestled within motive.

Sometimes, if he wasn't getting far with what he knew, he simply expanded what he knew until something clicked. It was time to fill in some general gaps and hope that the depth of knowledge this created would move the dial.

Back to a team of three, they went through what they held about each witness. Kat had been collating background since dawn.

'Bryony Price, what do we know about her?'

'Interesting you should ask.' Kat shuffled Bryony's file to the top. 'I looked into her work history and I found . . . nothing.'

'Nothing?' Lachie shook his head. 'She's a millionaire and she's never worked?'

'Not quite. It's difficult to trace: things that should be there, aren't. Of course I trawled tax records, super fund, driver details, major purchases like property, LinkedIn, membership of some professional bodies – she's a human jigsaw. She went to ANU and studied International Politics, that much we know. Then her entire career consists only of the words *public service*. Nothing about which jobs, which employers, length of service, location – all a zero, all the time.'

'Which tells you . . .' prompted Bluey.

'ASIO,' replied Kat. 'Even the military give some clues about where and when. I'd say she was a spook.'

Bluey couldn't help agreeing. 'Fair shout. If not actually in ASIO, in something similar. The Signals Directorate, maybe, or up at Pine Gap.'

'Yes; something specialised, secret and highly paid.'

'Requiring,' offered Lachie, 'a high degree of intelligence, organisation and discretion.'

'Oh, yeah.' Bluey nodded. 'To be fair, she seemed an impressive person and everyone in the building appears to rate her. She spoke a lot without telling us much. Bryony would know how to tailor her evidence to fit what she thought we wanted, wouldn't she?'

Lachie had to concede that. 'Can't see her stabbing Tahlia, all the same.'

'Hmm, maybe. *Physically* it's probably a bit tricky at her age, though not impossible. But I've seen an octogenarian stab someone to death: like I said, mate, my generation built this country, including the unsavoury bits. It might depend on the sharpness of the weapon and, besides, she'd probably have an element of surprise for several reasons. Tough to rule her out for sure before the autopsy.' He turned back towards Kat. 'So we don't even know where she lived before Pacific Heights?'

'Somewhere in the world: I can't narrow it down beyond that,' replied

Kat. 'She moved to Pacific Heights in 2011, that bit's certain. Any clues in the apartment?'

'Nothing overt. A couple of books on South America. The table was onyx, I think, which is African, but you can buy it in any Nick Scali. Other than that? Sadly, no Moscow tea-towel and no snow cone from Pyongyang.'

'Shame, eh?' lamented Lachie. 'So she's been somewhat spooky in her somewhat misty past. What does she do now, that we know?'

Kat tapped her notes. 'Sings in a choir at the cathedral, does welfare visits in hospitals and she's a prison visitor. She used to be a magistrate until a couple of years ago, when she hit mandatory retirement age. There's normally plenty of background with a magistrate, for obvious reasons, but it's been professionally cleaned.'

'Anything else? Politics? Sport? Online?'

'Her online is heftily encrypted. I'm not talking about ordinary VPNs or somesuch; this is heavy-duty. That's another clue there; she has access to the strong stuff, doesn't she? But no politics. Low profile, under the radar.'

'As you would, I suppose. She's used to it.'

Kat signalled there was more.

'I looked into her finances and family, too. Because while Pacific Heights isn't cheap, being Windoo, she must be able to afford better. So there's no husband any more: lung cancer. She has a daughter in London, a commercial lawyer; the two grandchildren live there, too. There's also a sister who lives in the UK, a former academic with Alzheimer's. The care home she's in is breathtakingly expensive so I think Bryony's sacrificed waterfront property over here for that. Plus, she gives about a quarter of her income to charity, according to her tax records.'

Bluey nodded. 'That all fits with her hospital- and prison-visiting, yeah. Okay. What about Caretaker Sal?'

Kat shifted files.

'Single mum to Josh, who died of a drug overdose. Sally used to work in engineering for Raven Industries, out near the airport. It's a specialist firm doing some of the interiors of passenger jets – mainly to do with air conditioning, by the looks. Grew up in Perth, went to uni there. Married Luke in 2000, divorced when Josh was two.'

'The caretaker job is a comedown, then. She's a qualified engineer?'

'Yup. Got her Masters in 2004.'

Bluey prodded. 'Hobbies, et cetera?'

'Collecting parking tickets, it seems to me. Seven still outstanding. Not appearing on any other radar; I can't see any volunteering going on. Financials are modest but solid – no significant debt, lives within her means.'

A voice from left field. 'Didn't Bryony say they were in the same book club?'

Kat raised an eyebrow. 'An unexpected insight, Lachie. Yes, they are. It meets the first Tuesday of every month, if you want to go along. Currently doing Donna Tartt's *The Goldfinch*, according to their Facebook.'

Bluey rolled his eyes. 'That would drive anyone to murder; the only book where cutting the second and third quarters makes it better. Nothing else linking her to Tahlia except the same apartment building and some on–off relationship with her son?'

'Nothing, I'm afraid.'

'Great. Anthony we've just seen, so unless you have anything more . . .' Kat shook her head '. . . then we'll try Jody Marks.'

Kat flipped a new file.

'Ah, now. Jody has quite a long history. Rattled around the justice system in the Northern Territory for a while: burglary, car crime, then an assault that seems to have been a pub fight. Then three more assaults before he moved interstate. They all seem to be in pubs, nightclubs, and so on, so it doesn't look like he goes around looking for random people to thump, but he doesn't back away, either. But his last conviction – four years ago – included carrying a knife and threatening a guy in a crowded bar. Nice.'

'So,' interjected Lachie, 'he has a short fuse and he's used to waving a sharp weapon around?'

'But you don't know what the weapon is, here,' countered Kat.

'All the same. We only have one person with a history of carrying a knife and it's him.'

Bluey played referee. 'Ookkaayy. Family?'

'He has a daughter from a marriage that's long over. The ex and kid are in Darwin. He's fine on the child support payments – as far as I can tell – and the divorce didn't mention domestic violence or anything related. He married at eighteen, so I guess he found out it was too young, eh?'

Bluey watched for a hint that any of this reflected Kat's life. She gave it a poker face and then smiled, her expression saying *I know what you tried, there*. Bluey smiled back, then threw his pen on to the desk.

'Worth a try.' He ran his hands across his face. 'Bloody hell. I feel like the more I know these people, the less likely they get. No one has a motive, no one has a trajectory that says this would become part of it. No one's in desperate financial straits except Scotty, no one had a close relationship with Tahlia except Reagan, no one's complained about her to any agency; there's just no foundation to build a murder.'

'Who else?' asked Lachie, hoping to give Bluey some sense of optimism. 'Martyn?'

'Yeah,' replied Bluey. 'Tell me the old guy is a trained assassin or something, Kat.'

'Regrettably not. Married Rosie; she died a few years ago. He suggested in his interview that he was a desk jockey in the ADF, and that's spot on. He spent most of his military career in logistics: clipboards, biros in the top pocket and doling out bits of uniform and suchlike. After he retired from that he had a few years looking after warehouses – didn't stray far from his metier, did he? – and then retired. I haven't tracked down all his medical side yet, but yes, he's certainly made a lot of claims in the past two years on his health insurance: psychologist, counsellor, psychiatrist. Not a man on the way up. Has a daughter living in Amsterdam but no other family.'

Bluey nodded despondently at the floor.

'What else do we know about Reuben?' asked Lachie. They both looked at him. 'What? I agree – I'm not his best mate. But he's the only one with blood on his hands and we can't exactly put our faith in whatever he tells us, can we? What else do we know?'

Bluey roused himself, conscious that he should be setting a better example at this point. His performance reviews always said that: at some stage he dipped and looked like a whinger.

'Yeah, fair enough. Kat?'

'Okay. Leaving aside his dodgy dealings, Reuben is a fairly successful behind-the-scenes musician. Has his own production company for tax reasons, but they've just filed for last year and he turned over half a million. I can't imagine his overheads are huge – though he's claimed a chunk of deductions – so he's making a tidy profit. He's from a family of six; his bank records show Mum gets gifted about a fifth of his income. Two sisters are still school age, so maybe that's part of it. Reuben was involved in a scam over spare parts for Holdens when he was twenty; other than that his only transgression was his famous one.'

'Online activity?'

'He used to be active on social media to push his singing career, but he obviously canned all that when he became infamous. Most of his stuff is gaming – very boring chitchat about Minecraft – and he flicks through Tinder, but I can't see any evidence that he goes on dates.'

'Huh. Tyre-kicker,' mused Lachie.

'Tell us what that's like, Lachie,' offered Bluey.

'Wouldn't go within a time zone of those websites. They work if you're a hot woman, a Chad, or a scam merchant, but otherwise they're a waste of time.'

'Hmm. Did Tahlia –'

Kat shook her head. 'It was one of the first things I looked for. No, I think she could conjure up someone whenever she wanted, but there's not much indication that she did. Hook-ups at clubs, judging by her Insta: that was more the go.'

'Bugger,' said Bluey. 'Despite Reuben being a pain in the arse, we can no more find a reason for him to want to kill than we can for anyone else. Right. I think we hit the road and try a second round of interviews. Autopsy's not until morning, forensics will be overnight; let's line up some chats for the rest of the day and see if we can squeeze blood from a stone.'

Chapter 21

Jody Marks had made an effort to tidy up.

At least, he gave the impression that he had. He'd seemed surprised to find Lachie back at his door, even though he'd agreed to it on the phone. His hair was still wet from the shower and he had a different hoodie but the same trackies. It was around twelve hours since they'd last spoken. The sink was clear of plates and the kitchen smell was now minestrone soup and not toast, the doona was semi-folded on a corner table and the pill Manhattan they'd seen on the first visit was now more Los Angeles: lower slung and spread out across the counter.

'Kidney stone any better?' asked Lachie as he leaned against a kitchen stool.

Jody was slung against the windowsill. Lachie noted that he had a perfect view of Bryony's place and Anthony's bedroom. Lachie pictured yet more imaginary laser beams firing across the courtyard; up, down, left, right, through. He couldn't stop himself: all day he'd been calculating angles and lines of sight automatically. The 3-D software would be usable tomorrow morning, apparently; Bluey wasn't that fussed, but Lachie couldn't wait.

'Nah. Still crazy painful. Your mate thought it didn't get better at all until it suddenly stops totally. That's what everyone online says. Hopefully tonight, or tomorrow. Runnin' out of painkillers.'

Lachie nodded absent-mindedly. Now he was back here he had a sixth sense that there was something he'd missed the first time around. A jigsaw piece he'd been close to, without realising the significance.

'I want to run over everything you said this morning, Jody. When we do this the second time around, people almost always remember differently – might be a trivial thing, might be important. Don't worry if you contradict yourself from earlier – it happens all the time and we don't read anything into that. We just want what you saw, what you know, okay?'

Jody swallowed another gulp of water. He still held his arm to his left side. Lachie wondered if he'd continue with that after the kidney stone passed – it seemed ingrained body language now.

'Talk me through it again, please.'

'Okay. I'm on the couch. I'm half watching baseball just 'cos it's on all night and it goes on for ever. Probably drifting in and out of sleep but it doesn't feel like it. There's some sort of noise down below. I'm not sure I give it full attention because, well, partly I'm in bloody agony and dosed up, and partly there's often something down there but it isn't very interesting.'

He looked to Lachie for affirmation but Lachie deadpanned it.

'Yeah, so, on the couch, and there's a noise. Then, there's a scream of some kind. I can't ignore that, eh? I get up, but there's trees in the way and I can really only see feet and legs.'

'Stop.' Lachie raised a hand and Jody complied immediately. *Jody now claimed one scream; before, he'd claimed two.* 'Think back, now. What shoes were these people wearing?'

Jody screwed up his face. 'Christ, mate, how would I know? It's three in the bloody morning, half dark. No idea about the one standing up; I think their clothes cover the shoes a bit. Uh . . . the one on the floor, their shoes reflected the light. Not, like, all of the shoe, but something on it. I dunno, buckle or something?'

The Italian boots with the gold on the heels, as Caretaker Sal had said. The inventory from the ME had confirmed it. Good, thought Lachie: he's not lying at the moment.

'Okay. Tell me about these two people.'

'One's kinda floppy, like they're drunk. The other one is standing up and they're trying to hold the other person up. Like you would if your mate was pissed and you were trying to get him home, yeah? Like that.'

'The one standing up: clothes?'

'Jeez. Uh, something dark. Couldn't say more than that. Could be jeans, could be leggings, could be any bloody thing. I was half awake and it was dark and there's trees in the way. What do you want from me?'

'What happened next?'

'The one standing up let the other one down on to the ground. Quite gentle, like. The one on the ground wasn't moving. I started to think maybe heart attack, stroke, that kind of thing. Even if they were just pissed, they were probably unconscious. Thought it was best to get the paramedics.'

'Okay. Then?'

'Yeah, so I tried to find my phone. It was all caught up in the doona and the TV went dark 'cos it goes into power-saving mode and it took me a few seconds to find the phone. I came back to the window while I was dialling. The person standing up was gone. I looked about, but they weren't there any more. But the western exit door, on the left, there? That was still swinging shut. So I guess they went thataway.'

Yeah, that really is a guess. Because you didn't actually see, thought Lachie.

'So you speak to emergency services?'

'Uh-huh. Just brief details – they're unconscious, looks serious, give the address. They say they've sent someone because they've already had a call. That would be Bryony, yeah? Her light was on so I guess it was her. I grab some water from the fridge 'cos I'm out of the bottle in my hand.'

Lachie wondered why Jody wasn't so fascinated by what was happening below that he forgot all about being thirsty. But then, Lachie had never had a kidney stone or gone four days without being able to sleep. Apparently, drinking water was Jody's fastest way out of that misery. So yeah, maybe.

'When I got back to the window, he was there.'

'Who?'

'Reuben Pearce. Like I told you this morning. He was half holding up the other one and on the phone.'

Another anomaly: they knew from the ambulance data that Reuben was the second caller, not the third.

'Think carefully, Jody. Did you see Reuben arrive?'

'Nah.' He paused. 'That was in the time between the exit door swingin' and me getting back to the window.'

'So you don't know which direction he came from?'

'Nope. I guess from his unit, 'cos he's on the ground floor over there, eh?'

'But you didn't see that?'

'Nah, I didn't.'

'All right. Go on.'

'So I don't know who he's ringing, but I guess it's the same as me. Because he speaks, then he checks her, then he speaks again, then he starts doing mouth-to-mouth.'

Lachie was on it.

'Checks *her*? You could see who it was?'

'Uh, crap. Not really. I mean, I know who it is now, don't I? Whole place does. Let me think. When Reuben picked her up he was half turned towards here; I could see the long hair and the crop-top so I figured it was a girl. That's why I said "her". I could see it was a woman, but I didn't know it was Tahls until after you'd gone. It's all over the building now, who it was. Sorry.'

'How long does Reuben do mouth-to-mouth?'

'You asked me before. I dunno. Couple of minutes? Then he disappeared towards his unit. I lose sight of him then, eh? You can see for yourself, trees are in the way in that corner. So I keep watching, but nothin's happening. She's on the ground, on her back, Reuben's gone. Oh, I can see blood then. Didn't see none before, but now I can, from her side, here.' He points to his left flank, around the ribs; ironically, the location of his own pain. 'Then he's back again, going over to the western entrance, and I can see the lights from the ambos outside, flashing blue.'

'No one else is around?'

'Nah. Lights are on at Bryony's place, like I say, but they often are. If I get up in the night her unit's quite often lit up. Then, after the ambos come in, I see Caretaker Sal. She just sits on the mushie, and Reuben – he's standing by in case the ambos need a hand – he kinda looks at her and shakes his head. I mean, it seems pretty obvious she's not going to end well. Tahls, I mean.'

'How do you work that out?'

'Ah, mate. Blood pourin' out? The mouth-to-mouth hadn't worked, had it? You can't go too long without oxygen. And the way the ambos worked – like they were doing what they were supposed to but they knew it was a bust. I'm not knockin' 'em or nothin'; just saying, it was a lost cause. Then one of your lot turns up and, just after that, out comes the tent thingie.'

'What happened when the officer knocked on your door?'

'He's a big unit, eh? Pacific Islanders, they're all huge. He asked if I'd been awake for a while. I said yeah, all night. He asked if I'd seen or heard anything in the courtyard. I said I'd seen bits and pieces and did he need me to make a statement or something? He told me to sit tight and some-one would interview me, but not to start tweeting or nothing.'

'And did you?'

'I didn't ring a soul and I didn't go on social media, nah. Wanna check?' He held out his phone. 'Makes me puke when people see someone dead and all they do is get out their phones and film it. Bloody gross, isn't it?'

'Yeah. Yeah, it is. Tahlia Moore, did you know her?'

'Vaguely. Like, to see around. Hardly talked to her, if that's what you mean.'

He'd called her Tahls earlier, Lachie recalled – evidence that she wasn't a virtual stranger. Lachie waited, knowing where Jody and Tahlia worked, waiting for more. Jody took another swig of water.

'She works next door to the print shop, but I barely know her: I don't drink coffee. She's out for smoko on the bench by the road when it's not pissing down. But she's always on her phone and dead to the world. I go in there for bottled water sometimes, but I don't think she's ever served me. That other girl, Cassie, she's usually there. Same name as my ex, that's why I remember hers.'

Jody paused, as if working up to something. Lachie had the brains to simply wait.

'Other than that? Oh, cabbed her a couple of times. I do Uber shifts some evenings, use a mate's car.'

Now then. Actual contact with the deceased. Lachie wondered if the taxi company knew about Jody's assault convictions, or whether Jody had forgotten to mention them. Maybe he was skating by – it might be future leverage for Lachie.

'Really? Tell me about those.'

'Oh, maybe three times, a while back? Only been doing it eighteen months or so. I usually do Saturday evenings, 'cos it's busy, and Lucas – the mate with the car – he doesn't like doing weekends; he keeps that as family time. If you've got a white Camry it seems stupid not to be a taxi, eh? Only reason to have one, I reckon. Yeah, so, a couple of times I've picked up Tahlia from out front. She was going into town with Joshie: Caretaker Sal's kid, Josh? Such a shame about him, poor bastard. Anyway, I just cabbed them down to Lion Street – all the pubs, clubs; whatever you want but don't need, you know? She basically yapped on about herself and where she got that top from and VIP lounges and her new favourite band. Josh just nodded: he fancied her enough to listen to endless garbage from her, seemed like. I tuned her out. She had that horrible thing in her voice – whaddya call it – something *fry*? Makes it sound like she's fourteen and chewing bubblegum and living in LA. Gives you earache. I don't think she even recognised me from here – people like that pay no attention to people serving them, do they? Bet she's the same with cleaners, shopworkers, Maccas, wherever. Anyway, that's the only time I've ever spoken to her – *fifteen bucks, thanks*. That's it. She tapped with her phone and never even looked.'

'So your impression of her?'

'Ah, look. If you're going into town to go clubbing, then I guess you're not being your intellectual best in that moment, eh? So, yeah, a bit self-absorbed, bit bossy? Didn't strike me as Joshie's type, but bloody hell, what do I know about women? Still payin' for my divorce, mate, I'm hardly an expert. Horrible voice, like I say.'

'Speaking of . . . you have several assault convictions, including one involving a knife. Want to tell me about those?'

Jody pushed himself away from the wall, shaking his head and taking a messy swig.

'Ah yeah, I bloody knew it. You do the right thing, you call it in, tryin' to save someone's life, and the bloody cops come along with a history book. That's what you get, eh? Lookin' for an easy mark, are ya?'

Lachie had anticipated the pushback. It wasn't unreasonable, but he needed to nip it in the bud, all the same.

'Okay, you need to pull your head in, Jody. Seriously. A young woman was stabbed to death and someone with a conviction for a knife assault is a witness. Think I can't cover that ground? Think the bosses would let me slide it? Do us both a favour, answer the question and we can move on.'

Jody looked at the carpet and took that in.

'All right. Yeah, fair enough, I suppose. Look, the ones in NT are just me being a young dickhead. I can't handle me drink, can I? It's obvious to me now, but it took a few fights to work it out. Two of 'em turned out to be connected to the cops and the third was the deputy mayor. I didn't start none of them, but who were they gonna stick in the wagon? So I learned my lesson: stay sober. Six years since I had a beer, mate. I pay my child support and I'm no bother.'

'Except . . . it happened again.'

'Oh, the one four years ago? Yeah, it did. So, me and a mate had been out on his boat down on the coast. I say boat . . . *tinnie*. Bit of crabbing, that's all. We're in the pub afterwards and I've still got the little gutting knife in my back pocket. Not deliberate, like, it's just a snug fit and I haven't noticed I've got it. Bloke kicks off on two women who don't want to party with him, and me, like a bloody idiot, steps in to tell him to cool it. Anyway, he smashes a bottle and starts comin' at me with the pointy end. Bloody crazy. My mate points to my back pocket, so I take out the knife and show the bloke it's a fair fight if he wants it. I just want him to back off. But the only bugger with their phone camera on is pointing at me. No one gets hurt, but the footage finds its way to the cops and all the magistrate sees is an out-of-towner waving a knife in a pub. Oh, and I've got previous for pub fights, so let's slug me again. The other bloke's a psycho and everyone's scared of him, so I cop it sweet.

'But no, I never went near Tahlia last night, never even left the apartment. Ask your mate – if you have a kidney stone, you don't feel like doing anything else. If the fire alarm went off right now, I'm not sure I'd leave.'

'Hmm. Have you ever seen a drone flying around the courtyard?'

Jody smirked. 'Rain Man's toy? Sure. He likes hovering around looking for people getting undressed, or screwing, or picking their nose, or whatever. I think Bryony's warned some of the residents about him – you know, keep your curtains closed when you're changing, that sort of thing. 'Specially those with teenage girls.'

'Why didn't she call the police? We can take action on that sort of thing.'

Jody squirmed slightly. 'Yeah, no offence. But, uh, lots of people reckon you can't be arsed with that kind of stuff. Too low grade to bother, eh? I mean, we see a dozen cars when some lowlife bikie gets shot, don't we? But anything short of a major crime for the rest of us, maybe not so much. I think Bryony thought she should get something done instead of waiting for cops, reports, and so on. She's very hands on. Besides, no one wanted to have a real go at Anthony 'cos he's a bit weird and it feels like bullying the disabled. Like, maybe he can't help it, or he doesn't understand?'

Oh, mate, thought Lachie. *If only you knew.*

Chapter 22

Sally Harris's apartment was tidier than Bluey had expected. He'd seen four other homes in the building: the overall average for Pacific Heights was not pristine, but Sally had kept the unit nice. It had the original 80s sense of decoration – those strange pastel greens for kitchen counters should never have been allowed, nor should the dado rail – but the veneer flooring was merbau and the pot plants were healthy. On the wall was a gorgeous large print of a black-and-white photo: Brooklyn Bridge under construction. One door off to the side was not only shut but had a black rubber wedge under the door; Bluey guessed it had been Josh's bedroom. Sally herself looked better in jeans and a T-shirt than she had in overalls and healthier for a few hours' rest. They sat across from each other in the living room, Sally pulling her feet up to sit cross-legged.

'Sorry if I woke you before, when I rang,' said Bluey.

Sally waved a forgiving hand. 'Ah, I only missed about half an hour, don't worry about it. When I do these water systems I'm up basically all night. Takes me about a week to work my sleep patterns back to normal human mode.'

'You rotate forward?'

'Exactly. A few hours each time, gradually forward, like you say, until I'm normal.'

'It helps, going in that direction, but it's still a bugger, eh?'

'Yeah, it is. Has compensations, though. The gym's empty when I use it and I don't get any noise from my neighbours. Plus, I've got an excuse to say no if anyone ever invites me somewhere. Should that happen.'

Bluey nodded. He'd intended to simply go over Sally's previous statement to see if there was any further information or any anomalies. But now he was here, he tried a slight tangent.

'Tell me some more about Tahlia. We've done some of her social media and phone calls, Google diary and the like: there's not heaps, but it all seems like a lot of froth to an oldie like me. She doesn't appear to have had any close friends.'

Sally gave a weak smile and looked away to the window. 'Yeah, well, label me surprised.' She turned back. 'When you were at school, was there one girl who stood out; the one everyone fancied?'

'Yeah. Simone. Simone Richmond.' Memories of teased chestnut hair and a red jumpsuit that everyone raved about at an end-of-year party. Simone was a radio producer now; he'd bumped into her in Myers last year. Still lovely.

'At mine it was Carla Rizzoni. Italian, like you'd expect. Total firecracker: olive skin, a rack at thirteen, bursts of passion and a tendency to thump idiots. Gorgeous, she was. And your Simone, was she a nice person?'

'She was, actually. That was part of her appeal. We were a very aggressive school – lots of little gangs and posses and if you like these then you hate those, that kind of thing. Simone was neutral territory, sorta floated above all that. She was Switzerland, I suppose.'

Sally smiled. 'Exactly. So, Tahlia – think of her like that, but with some nice bits surgically removed.'

Oof.

'Really?'

'I'd say so, based on what I know of her. Maybe she was lovely to her mum, or injured animals, or orphans, I dunno. What charms she had were really just tools at her disposal, it seemed to me – she would be nice, but only when there was something in it for her. The tips, for example, at the café: that's not an accident, it's a strategy outcome. Your Simone Switzerland was nice because she was, not because there was an end game, yeah? Tahlia always wanted product. *In every sense*, eh? She wanted an outcome for her nice behaviour that wasn't simply other people feeling warm and fuzzy.'

From what he'd gathered, Sally was something of a Switzerland herself. Jody said she'd saved him a heap by fixing his water system and helped him with a compo claim; she took turns with Bryony in saving Martyn from depression and isolation after he was widowed; Anthony said she was super-helpful – even Reuben didn't seem to have a bad word. The effort probably only ran one way, though: in Bluey's experience, most people took what was given but never thought to reciprocate. He wondered if that irked Sally, or if she thought it was just the way of the world.

'Your son, Josh, he knew her pretty well?'

Sally flushed slightly and ran her hand through her hair. Instantly she looked brittle, breakable, *broken*. The transformation was shudderingly quick.

'Sorry, Sally, if that's a bit too –'

'No, no. It's okay, you've got to ask. Thanks anyway. They hung out together, yeah. Met at a club somewhere. Lion Street, maybe: Joshie was never very specific about where he went. He didn't realise she lived here when he first met her – he was pretty gobsmacked to find her twenty metres away. Yeah, they . . . Christ, no one says *dated* any more, do they?'

'No one says *courting*, either.'

A rare full-on smile. 'Nah, shame that. Whatever they call it now, she and Josh did that off and on for about six or seven months.'

Bluey nodded. 'Out on a limb here, and not knowing either of them: Josh chased her and sometimes she relented?'

'Yeah, kind of. I mean, Josh was lovely to be around, so it wasn't exactly a chore for her. And he wasn't stalking her, or anything. But yeah, it was all a bit one-sided. He knew that. Accepted that.'

'When he was hanging out with Tahlia, were there any other regular friends in tow? Men or women?'

Sally gave a rueful smile.

'Not women, no. Tahls wasn't a gossip-in-the-loos kind of female friend. She had informal and frequently changing mini-entourages, I guess you'd call it. She mysteriously got into VIP lounges and got tickets for sold-out gigs and so on; you stayed in her orbit in case she could help you out or hook you up. She was quite an efficient middleman. Middlewoman. Blokes? Oh, I suppose there was Wasbar, while he was still alive.'

'Yeah?'

'Yeah, Warren Bartlett. About her age, good-looker. Tradie of some kind; I want to say plumber, but I might be a liar. He came round here occasionally – Josh was at TAFE, training to be a sparky, and I think Warren gave him a lift home sometimes. Yeah, everyone called him Wasbar all the time. So he was probably nearer to a constant friend of Tahlia than anyone.'

'Similar personality?'

Sally edged forward. 'Oh, no, complete opposite. Laid-back, big bear of a guy. Very athletic – he was a gymnast in high school and pretty bloody good, apparently. He was into this parkour thing: jumping and somersaults and stupid ways to cross an open space. Always taking crazy selfies hanging off things, you know the type. I was worried he might talk Josh into having a go, but Joshie never fancied it and I don't think Wasbar was much on pressuring people.'

'What happened to him?'

'Wasbar? He died, a few months before Josh. Got a bit drunk, walking home with Tahlia. Came to a building site and allegedly he wanted to show off his gymnast thing. Climbed some scaffolding but it gave way. He landed on his neck, poor bugger. Killed instantly. Shocking, stupid way to go. Total waste.'

'Tough on Tahlia, to witness that.'

Now she sat back again, regarding Bluey as an intelligent but naïve observer. 'You'd think so, yes.'

'She didn't show signs of it?'

'Not in front of me. Maybe she was a soggy mess some other time, but not in front of me, or Josh. Pretty, uh, *stoic*?'

Bluey took careful note and changed the angle.

'People tell me Reagan was a very different personality to Tahlia.'

'Oh yeah, totally. Reagan was lovely – easy-going, charming, no big ego. They loved her in that café, according to Reuben, and I'm not surprised. The sort of girl most mothers would label daughter-in-law material the first time they met. Yeah, by that stage I was hoping Joshie might switch his attention to her, but that was never likely.'

'Does that mean the sisters were competitive?'

'Nah, I don't think so. Reagan wouldn't let it happen: she wouldn't take part.'

Bluey glanced at the view outside. This was the apartment directly below Bryony's; not quite the same eagle perspective but a decent take on most of the courtyard. He now found himself constantly assessing visibility and knew Lachie had the same preoccupation, only more so.

'I often ask potentially insulting questions, Sally. Sort of a hobby of mine, it turns out. I looked up your quallies and experience: you're a pretty good engineer, expert at technical drawing and CAD as well. Isn't it a comedown to be caretaking a unit complex?'

Sally took a mouthful of what Bluey considered must be cold coffee by now. It didn't bother some people.

'Ha. I'm not insulted, mate, nah. As it happens, you're right. It's way below my education and my previous pay. I do worry that I'll never be able to climb back on to that engineering bandwagon, that I've cooked my goose. Employers don't like people who've stepped back at any point, seems to me. But no, back then I wanted more time with Josh and less commuting. This is the shortest commute in the world and I could flexi-work to be with Josh.'

Employers didn't like that career hiatus; neither did detectives. It was a point to consider whenever someone took a radical step off the career path: they seldom did it without a major catalyst. Anything like that – a rupture in the usual continuum – got a detective's attention.

'You know Reuben Pearce well?'

'He hasn't been here long, has he? Nothing's gone to buggery in his apartment so I've had no reason to be in his space. That's how I meet most residents – when they're in difficulty and grateful, or can't do something themselves.'

False modesty, thought Bluey: she was usually helping them. A bit of dissembling – she'd just mentioned Reuben's opinion of Reagan's popularity in the café, as well.

'We mainly know each other by sight, hadn't spoken much before today. But of course, I know what he did.'

'And what's your view on that?' asked Bluey.

Sally took a moment to put down the cup, as though she was coming off a long run for this one; possibly from the back fence.

'Ah, look, it was a dickhead move, wasn't it? Amateur hour. Partly because he was crap at it. If you're going to get people to fake beating you up, get some pros. Get some proper bruises that don't look like badly applied rouge; get some people who'll keep their mouths shut afterwards; do it somewhere that doesn't have CCTV nearby; don't leave an easy audit trail at four different Mitre 10s. I mean, the list of screw-ups goes on and on.

'I reckon if he'd just stuck to the story of being mugged, he might have got away with it. A bit of sympathy might have come his way. You know – faded pop star, down in his cups, now he catches another bad break. There wouldn't be much scrutiny, eh? It was when he threw in the racism angle, that was the biggie. Massive overreach, there. Everyone piles on with what a racist country we are, all the pollies and media start using him for their ends: now he's all in, isn't he? He's an . . . exemplar: *look what we've become* and so on. When it unravels, all those important people look like fools. Don't piss off people like that. So now he's hiding out here with his radical perm, like it's a disguise. Everyone online knows exactly what he looks like and it takes about five seconds to get his address. Crazy.'

'Plus, he had an example to learn from, before he even started.'

'Jussie Smollett, yeah. Didn't *learn* a bloody thing, did he? That was front and centre in everyone's mind as soon as they heard his full story. No wonder they started diggin', yeah. Imagine being a *discount* Jussie Smollett . . . Jeez. Reuben still thinks he's a celeb, as well.'

'Yeah, he mentioned that, surprisingly. Did he have any reason to hurt Tahlia?'

Sally openly laughed. 'You're kidding, right? Reuben? I reckon you're looking for someone a sight more dangerous, or at least more bloody organised, than that. Look what a clown show he produced when he was the victim *and* the organiser: proves he couldn't handle something with zero variables, doesn't it? Now imagine him organising an attack on anyone else. Nah, I don't see that at all. I suspect, under all the bluster and bull, he's probably an okay person. Got in over his head with some stuff, for sure. Besides, he tried to save Tahlia, didn't he? When I saw him, he had blood all down the – yeah, all down him.'

'Who would have a reason, then?'

Sally shrugged. 'Someone with a grudge, I guess. I mean, unless it was a mugging or whatnot? Nah? Well, then; grudge. Bearing in mind how she dismissed people from her orbit, I would think there are contenders: people she turned down, anyone who called out her behaviour. What about her family? Joshie thought she was semi-estranged from them. What was her aunt called?'

'Ruth?'

'Yeah, her. Josh said the family got right into it one day; on for young and old. Tahls slagged off Ruth's business and they had a proper spray at each other. But, frankly, it could be anyone. Yeah, I don't think you should underestimate Tahlia's ability to bring problems upon herself.'

Vanessa and Ruth Moore were on the interview list. Bluey went back to his original reason for coming here.

'Can I just go over a few details of your statement, Sally? As you'll understand, we have various witnesses and we're trying to connect dots.'

She shrugged. 'Sure, fire away.'

'Thank you. So your water system switched over at 3.02, is that correct?'

'Yup. It's a couple of minutes out of whack, but as it works okay I don't mess with it.'

'After that moment, did you hear or see anything outside the switch room?'

'It's pretty self-contained and I had earbuds on me. The room's designed so that the noises it generates don't reach into the courtyard so, hey, pretty hard to hear in the other direction as well.'

'So you came out of the switch room when you'd finished everything?'

'No, not exactly. I'd almost finished, admittedly. But no. At some point I saw the blue flashing lights and –'

'Wait. You saw the lights? How?'

Sally initially frowned, then sat back.

'Ah. Ah, I see what you mean. Yeah, the door to the courtyard is at one end, but at the far end of the room from the door is ventilation: it lets any fumes out on to the street side. Gas heater for the water, see? The vent's up high, near the ceiling, but the ambos parked right outside it. So, if you're sitting in there you'd see the blue lights spinning through the grille on the vent. Distracting – blue lights pulsing on the wall in front of you. It could have potentially been fireys, to be honest: we've had a couple of false alarms here in the past year.'

'And when you came out, you saw what?'

'Someone on the ground. You couldn't see that it was Tahls at that precise angle: just legs and waist from where I was standing. Two paramedics swept past me and went to her; I don't think they even saw me. Reuben was standing next to the bo—next to Tahlia. He stepped back to give the ambos room. He had blood on him. He looked at me and shook his head. But I already knew, I already knew. There's an atmosphere, isn't there? Hard to describe, but you know it when you feel it. Something final. Something finished about it.'

Bluey wondered about the circumstances of Josh's death: whether Sally was there in the moment, if she witnessed it happen, how she'd been when she was at the morgue. She came across like someone who'd seen death close up. There was the same semi-masked look he sometimes saw in first responders or experienced ED staff – a shuttering of emotions into strict compartments, because letting them bleed into each other would be overwhelming.

Beneath the bonhomie and obvious smarts, Sally Harris remained in turmoil.

Chapter 23

Pacific Heights apartment block.
Apartment 6. Thursday, 1710hrs

'Thanks for seeing me again, Reuben. Did you get much sleep?'

Reuben was slouched on the sofa, one arm off the edge. He'd showered and changed before Bluey arrived but he still had a slightly dreamy, just-surfaced look that Bluey was certain had been contrived. Half an hour in front of the mirror, styling wax in teasing fingers, turning this way and that to check his reflection, razor set for three-day stubble.

'Not a bunch, nah. It all kind of hit me later, you know? Took about an hour for your forensic blokes to finish: DNA swabs, all the clothing, lots of samples under the fingernails and on the face and the like. Very thorough, those boys.'

Yeah, thought Bluey, *they'd have to be. Because the last time Forensics were involved with you, it was because you'd completely invented a crime. Yeah, belt and braces this time and you know why, genius.*

'Then they came back and went after the drains. I think I forgot to tell you before that I puked. I mean, I wasn't real proud of that bit. I'd tried mouth-to-mouth on her, but it clearly wasn't going to do any good. That meant I was locking lips with a dead girl, wasn't I? Just a bit icky, eh? So I hurled into the drain and I was embarrassed to tell you that I couldn't handle the whole scene. That was why I was a bit of a cocky bugger with you, as well – trying to bluff through it. Sorry about that. Didn't mean to lie to the police or anything; just bloody pride, eh?'

Bluey inclined his head slightly, apparently acknowledging without actually doing so. Reuben had lied again and discarded yet another piece of trust from another human being; Bluey wasn't about to treat that like a jewel in his hand. He let him carry on because it was clear Reuben had some need to unburden himself.

'But after they'd gone, it all came through in a rush, what had happened. Someone died. Right out there, in front of all those apartments, next to a kids' playground. Might have been alive ten seconds before I got there. Yeah, it all hit home about then. Poor bugger, eh? Wasn't a fan but . . . bloody hell.'

The implied animosity between Reuben and Tahlia was, so far, just that: implied. There was nothing yet from Tahlia's history that suggested it, no witnesses to any confrontation that they could find. Just some generalised gossip and Reuben's word – which was worth *heaps* – that they'd argued. Bluey needed to press further.

'Let's talk about that, Reuben. You told me before that you barely knew Tahlia Moore: *a cute chick who brought me a coffee* was your description. Besides some vague chitchat at the table, you made it sound like you'd never spoken to her. So why would you now describe yourself as "not a fan"?'

Reuben roused himself from his slump and sat up straighter. Next to him on the lounge was a miniature Sherrin: he picked up the mini-ball and absent-mindedly spun it with one hand.

'Okay, so, we might have had the odd word sometimes. When I first moved in here, she seemed okay. She'd heard of a couple of my songs, asked me what I was recording now, that kind of thing. I get that quite a bit – you'd be surprised. I know that you and every other bugger thinks I just fell off the planet, career-wise, but you'd be wrong. People who don't know the industry think if you're not in the download charts or on the radio all the time, you're nobody.'

Bluey could feel the bristle in the air before it swept Reuben's face.

'But I make plenty, thanks – I do lots of radio jingles, music for ads, soundtracks for gaming, a few corporate pieces. Yeah, I do okay. Because

I can actually play instruments, I can sing, I can read music and I can compose. Everyone thinks I'm some dickhead bogan who failed in a TV show and crapped on the cops. I brought that on myself, I get it, and I don't blame them for that. But they're wrong.'

'And Tahlia thought that?'

'Yeah. After the first couple of chats she, uh, turned. Not sure who persuaded her, but someone did. Now she was all spiteful, taking the piss. I mean, I was just picking up my mail and she thought it was a good idea to lay into me about what I should and shouldn't be doing. Like she had any bloody idea. Called my career a train wreck, called me a no-mark, called me a race-cheat. I mean, Jeez, an entitled white chick calling *me* a race-cheat.'

Reuben's ethnic background was the matter of some conjecture. He claimed Indigenous heritage, which was fair enough, but declined to explain where that lineage presented itself. Online chatter and some TV pundits were sceptical, to say the least. It had made his court case all the more compelling.

'You know what she was referring to, Reuben.'

'Yeah. Yeah, I do, and I did my community service and I paid my fine and all. She just didn't like letting it go.'

Bluey's irony metre fizzed. 'And did *you* let it go?'

'Eventually.' Reuben looked down to the left. 'Oh, I admit, it cooked me up for a while. Kept brooding on it. Might have pounded on her door occasionally when I was in a mood. But I got the measure of all that, I moved on.'

'What prompted your change of heart?'

'I decided she was trash, to be brutal about it. She was cute, but there was nothing in her heart, you know? Some people – Bryony, Sally – they're just good people: you can see it, you can feel it. The way they help people, the way they are. Tahlia? None of those vibes whatsoever, mate. I decided she wasn't worth the bloody effort. Just blanked her.'

'But you still went to What's Brewin' for coffee?'

'Sure. Droughts, floods, bush fires, arguments about race – they don't get between an Aussie and a coffee, do they?'

Reuben raised an eyebrow and Bluey was forced to smile.

'Okay. Let's go over what you told me this morning about the chain of events. It's possible you'll have a different version now. In fact, you will, because you'll tell me all about the vomit this time. But don't feel bad if you recall different things on the second go: I'm not judging, I'm taking it all in. So, full disclosure. Start with you drinking tequila.'

'Yeah, fair enough. So I did a bit of gaming – that's online, you can double-check that. I dunno when I stopped, but it was around midnight, I reckon. Too tired to find the bed so I just zonked out here. Left the bloody patio doors open – rain got in while I was asleep. Woke up I dunno when and people were arguing outside.'

So far so good, thought Bluey. They'd already confirmed his gaming: logged on from 7.27 to 11.39 in the evening. The rain getting in tagged with him being asleep before 12.13; BOM had confirmed the heavy rain started then. Then it struck him; he'd told Reuben to start with the drinking, but he'd just skipped that part. Bluey let it ride, interested more in the reason for the omission than correcting it. For now.

'The voices, the people arguing. Talk to me about them.'

'So, one of them must have been Tahlia, mustn't it? I'd have thought so. But if I hadn't known it was her I wouldn't have recognised her. Even though they were arguing, it wasn't clear enough to make out what they were saying. I could hear when they went up in pitch, or sibilant sounds, but nothing precise.'

Maybe he did know something about singing, after all, mused Bluey.

'It went on for a few minutes. Then it went quieter and I thought, thank God, because my head was starting to hurt and I wanted to sleep some more. Then, almost out of nowhere, there was a scream.'

'Male or female?'

'Not sure. I've heard some real girlie screams from blokes in my time. Show 'em a snake or a spider and hear them freak. If I was pushed, I'd say woman. Fairly short; like, surprised or something.'

Bluey was going to assume for now that the scream was Tahlia being stabbed, but he knew he had nothing to back it.

'Then?'

'Well, I got up. You would, wouldn't you? I got to the patio door and I could see someone lying down, between the 'shrooms and the swings. A door was just closing over there' – he pointed west – 'and apart from that, everything was quiet. I waited a minute, thinking whoever it was would get up because they were just pissed. I thought she'd fallen over, tripped. But she didn't move.'

For the first time in the investigation, Bluey was beginning to get pictures. The stillness, the semi-darkness that soaked urban life – never quite black, but dark enough to take the edges off the third dimension. People became murky cartoons, depth got fuzzy.

'Definitely no one around?'

'Well, now I was waiting for someone to come and fetch her. You know, they were coming back to pick her up. Or leaning out of a window to shout if she was okay. Someone. Anyone. But, nothing. Community spirit, hey?'

Again, a careful slide into being indirect.

'Carry on.'

'So I think I should, you know, check if she's out cold or whatever. I still think it's just being drunk. But as I get nearer I can see she's in an odd position. On her back, like she's been put there. When you fall over pissed you don't always end up on your back, believe me. Been there, done that. And you're all floppy, so your limbs are all over the place. She looked . . . tidy. *Folded*. On purpose.'

That was useful info, thought Bluey. They had Jody's account of some-one putting Tahlia down carefully – this backed it up.

'So now I'm thinking medical. Like, maybe she's had a stroke or col-lapsed and the other person helped her down so she didn't hit her head. Could be they've rushed off to get a phone, or a first-aid kit, or someone who's a nurse, or something. Well, like I said to you before, I nippered when I was younger so I thought maybe I could help. Should help.'

Now Bluey was grasping for a picture – for video – of the scene unrav-elling. But moving pictures were more tenuous: he couldn't seem to grab them. Every time he reached, it was a different person's perspective – high up, ground level, through the trees, over the mushrooms, past the swings, above the barbie. Always something giving half a view and ending too quickly.

'I came out and, when I got near, I saw the blood. By her side. This side.' He patted his left flank, just below the heart. 'Now I start panicking. It's not accidental any more, is it? I look around in case *whoever* is coming back, but no one's movin'. I sort of pick her up, 'cos I need to know if she's still conscious or if she's breathing. Ambos are gonna want to know, aren't they?'

'You had your phone with you?'

'Yeah, of course. My hand just automatically picks it up. Doesn't yours?'

Bluey shook his head.

'Ah, doesn't even register when I do it. Anyway, I can't get a pulse and I can't feel any breath. I might have slapped her – I told the paramedics and your forensics dudes that I had, but I'm not sure – because if she's semi-conscious that can work, so I might have done that on autopilot. I've got all the emergency stuff and geolocation on speed dial, because everyone should. When they answer, I've stuffed a scarf into the wound because I can see she'll bleed out if we don't stop that. Operator tells me to try mouth-to-mouth and the paramedics are already on the way.'

They had the recordings from the emergency operator on all four calls. It was one of the few things no one had lied about. Possibly because everyone knew they were being recorded. Easy to have integrity when you know someone will check.

'Timings matter, Reuben. Think carefully. How long did you do mouth-to-mouth?'

'Yeah, this is where I lied again, isn't it? Not deliberate this time. Looking back, I guess you thought I kept going until the ambos were outside, but it was probably only two or three minutes. Maybe a bit less. Time goes funny when you're doing that: I've seen surf lifesavers trying for half an hour but thinking they've done four minutes. I wouldn't be a reliable clock for that, to be honest. At some point I realised it was a no-go. When I stood up I started to feel a bit funny, then I felt it rising. Just about made it to the drain and puked. There was a bottle of water on the table on my terrace, so I swigged that and cleaned up my mouth. About that time I saw the blue lights, outside the west entrance. Went over and let them in.'

'What did you do, while they were working on Tahlia?'

'Ah, I just stood to the side. They didn't need me gettin' in the way. I'd told them the status – *no pulse no breathing for at least four minutes open wound on the left flank.* I just stood back. I remember looking about, thinking everyone would be awake now. The paramedics hadn't used the siren, true. But just the lights, the commotion, you know?'

At least four minutes. But he'd just said he was an unreliable clock, hadn't he?

'Who was around?'

'Oh, Bryony was at her window. Up the top? Martyn was in his kitchen with his light on; he was on the phone. I could see Jody, but he was sorta coming and going across his window. I saw Sal, by the mushroom. She was staring at the whole thing. I shook my head – like, *she won't make it.* I went back to the entrance because I realised the cops would need to get in and out. Had to find a wedge for the door.'

'You didn't expect any of those residents to help?'

'Nah, not at that stage. I mean, Martyn's not going to get past his little terrace there, is he? Fence is, oh, seventy centimetres high.'

Bluey frowned. 'I don't get it.'

'Oh, don't you know? He has, like, an agoraphobia thing. Since his wife died. Since his dog died, actually, 'cos he could still take the mutt for a walk after his wife carked it. Nah, he won't leave the house, generally. I thought it was, like, PTSD from his army days, but apparently he did bugger-all in the ADF. Bryony or Sal drags him out for a compulsory walk, but that's about it.'

Bluey recalibrated. He'd put Martyn's reluctance to come out and help down to simple fear of the attacker.

'Did you speak to Caretaker Sal as you were going to and from?'

'Jeez. Might have mumbled a bit on the way past. Not sure she'd have taken it in, anyway: she felt the shock of the whole thing long before I did. Anyway, then your man arrived and the tentie thing went up. The first cop could see I had blood on me.'

'What did he do when he saw you?'

'To be fair, he could've read the blood any number of ways, couldn't he? I said that I tried mouth-to-mouth and he sorta understood, though he might not have believed me. Can't say I blame him. I had my hands out, so he could see I wasn't carrying.'

Reuben mimed the action: it wouldn't have convinced Bluey, either.

'He told me to stand still while he put bags on my hands, then he gave me a constable and we sat on the terrace.'

Bluey nodded and sat for a moment, in case it drew Reuben out into something further. Reuben spun the Sherrin a few more times. Bluey contemplated raising those unanswered phone calls to Tahlia – he considered Reuben a strong chance for the caller – but Reuben was still lying about facts and he didn't think he'd get anywhere without independent evidence. Likewise, with the amount of alcohol: he wasn't happy with Reuben skating past it, but Forensics would give him a stronger steer tomorrow. He didn't think Reuben was a flight risk for now.

'Is that it? 'Cos I've got a soundtra—'

'Who do you think killed Tahlia Moore?'

Reuben puffed his cheeks and dropped the mini-ball.

'Jeez. It's not a mugger, burglar, something like that? Assuming it isn't, then who knows? Someone who knew her, someone with a grudge. She pissed off a few people and didn't seem bothered; maybe one of *them* was really bothered.'

'What about drugs? She's a young woman in the city, she likes night-clubs and VIP lounges. What do you reckon?'

Reuben shuffled on the sofa, looking awkward.

'Look, we never bumped into each other on a night out, so I don't want to say too much when I don't really know. But, uh, like you say, she was there or thereabouts, wasn't she? *Someone theoretical*, with some connections, might have been connected to her. Someone who wanted party people to hook to; they might have thought she was an attraction, a bit of a drawcard. That someone might have used her as a link between buyer and seller. That someone might have paid her in product, or in drinks, or in gig tickets, or whatever. I mean, some of these guys know it's smarter to hand over free backstage passes than cash – looks more like mates helping mates and less like a transaction. Maybe one of those *someones* had a falling-out with her. But, like I say, I wouldn't know for sure.'

All that Reuben said was fair and reasonable supposition at this point.

All that Reuben said could apply, in Bluey's view, to Reuben.

Chapter 24

Lachie was at the entrance to the apartments when his phone buzzed: unknown number.

Your mate might be holding you back. If you think he's a dragging chain, let me know. I can get someone else reassigned.

Superintendent Laxton, team-building. Lachie shook his head. Management's inability to leave you alone for five minutes . . . he wondered where they learned their wondrous people skills. The State Police College was full of lectures on diversity and inclusion, not division. Was this divide-and-rule mentality, offering to prise apart a team that consisted of exactly two people, going with the grain or pushing against it? He deleted the message.

Martyn Brooks answered the door in a long cardigan that swept to his knees. It made him look like a tall basset hound; a sense that he was being dragged towards the ground by life. His tattered collar was up on one side and he needed a shave – he was the type to look haggard with silvery stubble.

'Come in, come in,' he gestured, with the hand that wasn't holding a mug of tea. 'Any progress?'

Ah yes, thought Lachie, *Martyn would be a gossip-merchant*. The type who might hang around with some older women, feigning boredom or a deep interest in the card game but actually fascinated by the half-whispered insinuations about others.

'Early days, Martyn. We're going back to the people we spoke to this morning, having another chat. Sometimes it jogs the memory.'

'Of course, of course.' Martyn indicated the sofa while he sat in what was clearly his favourite armchair. Hanging off one arm of the chair was a dog chain and collar for a companion who no longer existed; Lachie took a second glance at the metal canister next to the chair. He nudged a splayed copy of *The Australian* to one side so he could sit.

The room was clearly done out by a wife or sister – it didn't suit Martyn at all, yet he'd stuck with it. Too many floral patterns, too few sharp edges, too much attention to symmetry, some artificial flowers and . . . to the left was what Lachie had expected: a wedding photo of a young and gauche Martyn with a lovely dark-haired bride. The impolite would suggest Martyn had batted above his average: she had a sparkle-eyed intelligence whereas he merely looked delighted and fortunate. On the opposite wall was a carved and varnished wooden sculpture – a slash of timber with burnt edges.

'Huon pine?' Lachie asked.

'Yes, well spotted.' Martyn beamed at him like a proud parent. 'You're not allowed to cut them down, of course, but they can use driftwood from the river. Local bloke down there, hands like a surgeon. Sally put it up on the wall for me. Marvel, that girl.'

'It's beautiful. Now, Martyn, I'm going to ask you much the same questions as before. Don't worry if you contradict yourself or think of something you didn't recall this morning. That's fine – that's why we do this. Okay?'

Martyn nodded, sitting up like an obedient child about to recite his multiplication tables.

'You were coming back from the bathroom and you heard a noise, you said.'

'That's right. I was just about in the corridor between the bathroom and the bedroom. It's all a bit tricky there: sometimes, I hear something and think someone's breaking in, but it's just the fridge burping.'

Lachie smiled at the description but detected something behind it.

Martyn's fear of what was *out there* wasn't just prevalent when he thought there was a killer extant. Martyn continued.

'I've thought about this. The sound was a bit . . . *cut off*. I mean, if I hadn't seen anything in the courtyard I would have said possum, or something. It was that . . . random. Not a full scream or anything, just an odd noise.'

Lachie couldn't think of any acoustic reason why Martyn wouldn't hear a scream properly but others did: he was closer than they were. Perhaps his hearing was less than stellar. Lachie was finding it hard to read Martyn's lips and leaned forward.

'Okay. So then what did you see?'

'I just peeked through the blinds, you understand. That door, that was closing. Across the courtyard, I mean. Reuben Pearce was in the middle of the courtyard, holding someone up. He seemed to juggle a bit: I mean, he tried to hold the person up and use his phone, then he put her down. Quite gently.'

Another witness who started partway through proceedings, thought Lachie. It wasn't their fault they came late to the party – they were drawn by the scream, as he'd said – but oh, for just one person who'd seen it all. Lachie was going to dream of angles, perspectives, shuttered views and stark shadows.

'You say *her*. Could you definitely see it was a woman?'

'Oh. Well, now. Of course, I *know* it's a woman, don't I? So, maybe I didn't know then. Hmm. I think I could see the long hair, and she was obviously quite light – Reuben could hold her up with one arm, but it was awkward, not heavy. So maybe I just assumed. Sorry.'

Martyn blinked too much, and Lachie thought again of that phone conversation Martyn had with Bryony, before the first interview. He shouldn't be too surprised that Martyn's story lined up so readily with Bryony's.

'That's fine. What happened next?'

'Well, he spoke on his phone to someone. I couldn't tell who, obviously – I couldn't hear through the glass. Then he put the phone in his pocket and started mouth-to-mouth.'

The ambo logs already had details like this: Reuben ringing emergency services about a minute before Martyn himself picked up the phone.

'What did you think, at that point?'

'Well, it was clearly pretty serious. I suppose I thought heart attack, or something to do with the drink: I know she liked a drink. I didn't know if Reuben had called the ambulance, didn't know for sure. So I thought that was the least I could do – make sure the paramedics came.'

'Didn't the operator say they'd already been notified?'

'Oh, yes, she said a few people had rung. I found that reassuring.' Martyn thought for a moment. 'I lost sight of what was going on. I have quite an old-fashioned phone and the cord doesn't stretch that far, so I couldn't keep watching while I was talking.'

He pointed to a determinedly retro phone near the breakfast bar. The cord looked to be all of sixty centimetres: Martyn was from the era where people bought seats specifically to sit next to the phone. Lachie nodded.

'And then I came back to the window. I was hoping, I suppose, that he'd been able to revive her. But he wasn't there. I don't know where he went. She was on the ground. But I could see . . . I could see blood. Lots of blood. On the ground, by her left side.'

Lachie recalled how carefully Bluey had trodden this part of the path.

'Was there anyone around then? Any sign of a person, a light coming on, anything?'

'I was quite surprised. I thought the people who'd already rung the ambulance would be coming down to get a closer look or see if they could help. That made me wonder. That gave me pause for thought, I can tell you.'

Recalling the pause for thought turned Martyn ashen; waves swept his face and he was visibly shaken. Lachie thought that Martyn's hands were trembling, but he didn't want to draw attention to them by actually looking.

'The reason that you didn't go outside, Martyn. Do you want to share that with me?'

Martyn shuffled in his chair and rotated his glasses with one hand.

'Oh, self-preservation, in a way.'

Lachie tamped down his surprise. He'd previously assumed that Martyn's reticence was a fear of who was out there and what they might do. But this answer felt a little diagonal to that.

'*In a way?*'

Martyn blew on his glasses and rubbed at them with the hem of his cardigan.

'Yes, I . . . hmm. Obviously, there was a chance that someone had done something to Tahlia: that it was deliberate. Someone like that, if they ran into an old man? Well, they wouldn't hesitate, would they? As I said, I watch the news, so I know what's what: all that with machetes and things. All that. I couldn't cope with that. It was safer indoors. Besides . . .'

'Yes?'

'I find it difficult. Since my wife, Rosie, died, you see.' He glanced reflexively to the photo. 'It's all a bit . . . *big*, out there. I used to take the dog for a walk, but after he . . . yes, so, not any more. Don't want to go any more, and I probably wouldn't leave the house if not for the girls.'

'The girls?'

'Bryony Price and Sally Harris. They take it in turns, you see. Every Thursday afternoon, whatever the weather. Somewhere quiet. The library, the duck pond. Just so I get out. Oh, they wrap it up, to spare my feelings. Claim they need to change some books, or get some fresh air, or whatever. But every Thursday, they save me. So kind.'

'Ever since your wife died?'

'Yes. Nearly two years, now. It was getting a bit much for Bryony, I think: the regular commitment. I couldn't blame her. But then Sally got this caretaker job and that meant she was around on Thursdays. I mean, all through . . . what *she* went through. With Josh, I mean. Even in the midst of all that grief, she kept turning up for me. Because it helped *me*. You don't get many people like that, these days.'

He teared up and Lachie granted him some space by looking determinedly at his notes until he sensed Martyn was back on an even keel. He reached for a diplomatic form of words.

'So you kept yourself safe, here?'

'Yes. I . . . *awaited developments*. Then Reuben came back. From his apartment. Or at least, from that side. I can't quite see round there unless I'm on my terrace. Reuben came back and checked her, then the blue lights appeared at the western side. So he went over there to let them in.'

Lachie left the space. Martyn fiddled with his mug and swirled the contents.

'Oh, so then I saw the paramedics come in. They were jogging. They tried to revive her while Reuben stood to one side.'

'Did Reuben speak or gesture?'

'Not once they started. He did before – I suppose he was telling them what he'd done, what state she was in, I don't know. Oh, yes, he shook his head. But I think he could see that she wasn't going to . . . going to make it.'

Lachie made some notes that may or may not have been necessary.

'And no one came out of their apartments? No one around, on their balcony?'

Martyn shook his head slowly. 'No . . . not that I could see. Of course, only some of us have balconies, so . . . oh, Sally appeared at some point, over by the door. She lives right by there, of course, so she'd notice the ambulance lights.'

'And did you speak to anyone after that?'

Martyn took another swig of tea. 'Oh, yes, I rang Bryony, of course. She generally knows the score around here and she has a much better view. Much superior.'

'What did you say?'

'I asked her what was happening. She told me it was Tahlia Moore – I didn't know until then. Bryony has binoculars. She said that Reuben had tried to save Tahlia with the mouth-to-mouth but it didn't look like it had worked. She said there would be police, for a sudden death, and maybe I should break out the ol' picnic set and offer them some refreshments: it was going to be a long morning.'

'She sounds very practical.'

Martyn nodded vigorously, as if he was personally responsible for all Bryony's virtues and achievements.

'Oh, she is. Top sort is Bryony. She used to be a schoolteacher, apparently. I imagine her pupils didn't like her at first but adored her by the end, you know? Has a way about her. Would have done well in the army.'

'You're ex-military yourself?'

Martyn looked away. 'Oh, yes. I'm a bit embarrassed, really. Don't like to call myself ex-ADF; people get the wrong idea. I was admin for most of my service. No tales of derring-do or anything. Unless getting the right number of ready meals to base camp is a derring-do.'

Lachie shrugged. 'Napoleon said an army marches on its stomach; so yeah, I'd call that a good contribution, Martyn. Can you think of anyone who'd want to hurt Tahlia?'

'I don't like to imagine . . . you don't, do you? I mean, I heard she could be a bit unkind or a bit sharp. But, you know, that's nothing like a reason to . . . no. No, I can't, but I didn't know her very well. As I said this morning, she was a slightly lost soul on the swings.'

Chapter 25

Vanessa Moore lived in a sharp McMansion in what was routinely described by real-estate barracudas as an 'upcoming suburb'. This meant that Jindalup Creek once housed a range of people who were relatively happy with their lot, able to service a modest mortgage with one income, sent their kids to the local school and bought their groceries at the local supermarket. Nowadays it was rammed and crammed with harassed 'striving' families who competed over how much of their block they could consume with roofed-over al fresco dining, spent all of their time indoors and all of their money on their home loan, had their shopping delivered by an over-bronzed former Qantas pilot in daggy shorts, and fretted constantly about interest rates, tuition fees and the commute for their kids' education. An 'upcoming suburb' was supposedly aspirational – they were meant to dream of having this life.

Vanessa's home was what Bluey understood to be the 'Tuscan' option; its layout was identical to the two either side of it, but they'd both gone the Hamptons route and so Vanessa's home stood out. Kat's digging had suggested that Vanessa's PR business had recently done very well: a sudden escalation in wealth – or debt – that showed in the rented house and the leased BMW outside it. A Corolla was parked across the entrance, and Bluey guessed this was Ruth's lowest-cost rental choice: selling flowers paid less than digging an executive out of a self-induced mess.

Ruth answered the door with a thin smile and silently led him into the front room, discreetly withdrawing and closing the kitchen door behind her. Vanessa, still in the same outfit as this morning, was perched on the edge of the sofa, frantically swiping and pecking at her phone, pausing only to unsuccessfully push back her hair.

'Hello, Ms Moore,' said Bluey, standing awkwardly because he felt simply sitting would be rude.

Vanessa lifted her head in acknowledgement and waved a finger at the armchair opposite her. The body language and the lack of chat enhanced the frenetic, frantic, slightly desperate air. Bluey took an audit of the room; several half-empty coffee cups, a legal pad with various scrawl and some angry underlining. No sign of any other visitors since this morning; no sign of Reagan's arrival, either.

'Something online bothering you?' ventured Bluey.

She nodded, still silent, still pecking manically.

'Show me,' he said, simply as an attempt to get her to stop and look up.

Vanessa bit her lip and relented, chucking the phone to the other side of the sofa, where it lay face up, colourfully buzzing in a pleading tone.

'Vultures, eh?' She managed a half-smile and shoved her hair aside again. 'I should know, my line of work, how to deal with them.'

'I'm sure the best thing to do right now is ignore them.'

Vanessa looked up, as if he'd just suggested she fly around on a dragon's back.

'Ignore them? Huh. No, you take them head on. Otherwise, it escalates. Get ahead of their lies. The things they're saying, about Tahls. Horrible.'

Bluey made a mental note to ask Kat to have another sweep of socials, to see if there was anything actually usable there.

'I know you do PR for a living, but this is different: it's your life. My suggestion is to hand Ruth your phone and ask her to tell you any relevant messages from family and friends – those that need a reply. Everything else? She either deletes them or makes a note because it's something practical that needs to be done later. Protect yourself, Ms Moore.'

She pulled a face that suggested she was pretending to take his suggestion seriously. He knew she wouldn't. He'd found, in the past few years, that many people simply couldn't step away from what social media was saying, no matter how poisonous. He found it easy to do so, but he'd had decades when it didn't even exist: harder when it had always been a part of life, he conceded. He'd had to recognise that some found the temptation almost impossible unless you physically removed all communications. Even at a time when they were suffering and needed *human* contact and *human* solace, they still wanted to see what some random reckoned about something they couldn't possibly understand, still sought the approval of complete strangers. In fact, they also sought *castigation* by complete strangers, so that they could disagree with it – defining themselves by what they weren't, confirming their morality by what it opposed.

'I need to ask you some more questions about Tahlia.'

'Yup.'

She clasped her hands together and her gaze drifted. That was the word for it – *drifted* – because it floated gently away from Bluey, from the room, to the fading daylight outside.

'In the past few weeks, have you noticed anything changing in Tahlia's life? New friends, enemies, problems; a change in her usual habits?'

Vanessa shook her head.

'Like I said before, we really only caught up once a month. She regarded that as fulfilling requirements. It felt like that. If I tried to tell her about Reagan's adventures in the US she sort of tuned out. So, uh, I wouldn't necessarily know. I can't think of anything offhand, no.'

'Okay. Was she still upset about Josh Harris, perhaps?'

A blank look. 'I don't know who that is.'

'A friend of hers. She may have called him Joshie.' He raised an eyebrow as if her memory would be jogged. 'He died a while back.'

A bemused head shake. This was going nowhere. Vanessa started to look flustered at her own ignorance and seemed to be blaming Bluey for it, as though his questions were only attempts to make her feel guilty about her distance from Tahlia.

'Did she mention anyone causing her hassle? Getting on her nerves, hanging around, issues at work, maybe?'

'No, nothing. Last time we had lunch she showed me some flashy Italian boots she'd just bought. I didn't like to ask how much they cost because, to be honest, I didn't want to know how she'd got the money.'

Vanessa looked away, as though she was being disloyal.

'What do you mean?'

She sat back a little and hugged one knee.

'The last year or so, she was buying a lot of designer gear. *A lot.* Every time we had lunch, a different outfit. I'd ask enough questions about her outfit that I could google it later; it was a lot of money, believe me. She was a waitress, for Christ's sake – where was she getting that money?'

'How did she explain it to you?'

'She didn't, not really. First off, she tried to pretend her tips were covering it. But that didn't fly, not over time. A one-off? Yeah, maybe. But month after month of expensive gear? Then she said they were knock-offs; good fakes, convincing. But I have clients in the rag trade, you see; I took some covert photos and showed them, and they could tell – the stitching, the fabric quality, the way it hung or moved: all those outfits were kosher. My daughter was wearing thousands of bucks each time but she worked for minimum wage.'

Vanessa, he reminded himself, wouldn't know about Scotty's double-payment syndrome.

'What did you think? Suspect?'

'Ah, I'm not a total idiot where my daughter is concerned, whatever you may think of me. My opinion isn't as far from Ruth's as this morning might've led you to believe. Ruth caught me on the back foot a bit; I got defensive, but she wasn't wrong. Tahls was shallow, manipulative and beautiful . . . and good at wheedling things out of men. I don't believe she ever bought her own drink after she turned sixteen. I was actually thinking one of those sugar-daddy things – though that turned my stomach, to be honest – or maybe, you know, *tangentially*, something on the party-drugs side. She got into a lot of semi-celeb bashes – my clients saw her there – and VIP lounges. I thought she, you know, made a percentage in some way.'

'Did you tell her that? Put it to her?'

'I didn't, no. I feel like a coward, don't I, now she's gone? I took the easy route, the one that kept me in touch with my daughter. If I'd raised it she'd have blown up *deluxe* and I'd be completely out of the loop: seven kilometres and one world away. I chose to maintain some form of contact, even if I had to close my eyes to have it. Feel free to think of me as a crap mother. I do.'

Bluey also took the easy route; he declined to disagree with her.

He made an excuse of helping Ruth with the coffee, without even knowing if she was making some. He was glad to get out of the living room: it wasn't that it felt weighed down by sorrow, more that it was hamstrung by the failure to truly acknowledge sorrow. That gave the space an air of unreality or, perhaps, of reality delayed and denied.

Ruth was leaning against the counter, biting her fingers around the nails. He could see where she'd drawn blood and sucked it dry.

'How's she doing in there?'

Bluey puffed his cheeks. 'She's not. As in, she's not really doing anything in there. Just wading through social media to find morons that blame her.'

Ruth nodded. 'She's like that. An avoider. It worked with Reagan because the girl's quite a practical type; gets on with stuff and never needed a lot of direction. Tahls was different: needed a firm hand and got nothing. She turned out exactly the way you'd expect. She wasn't a surprise, Detective. Not in any way.'

'Vanessa thought she might be involved in drugs? Something to afford the designer gear, at any rate.'

'Yeah, but she did bugger-all about confirming that, eh? Yeah, it would be something like that. Probably more introducing buyer and seller, I would think, than sullying herself with the actual trade. Not that she didn't fill her boots when it was passed around. Reagan saw stuff when she lived there, you see. It's why she left early. She was supposed to save up for a year, but she only managed six months. Lied to everyone that she had enough and then she scarpered.'

Bluey raised an eyebrow. 'But not overseas?'

Ruth shuddered. 'What makes you say that?'

'The possibility that you'd react in exactly that way. She never went overseas, did she, Ruth?'

She flicked a glance out of the window. The backyard was terraced towards a shaded barbecue area. It was calculated to look like the kind of spot they'd all spill over to, when the sophisticated dinner party had finished. The whole house had a slight air of being contrived, of presenting a curated life that wasn't necessarily taking place.

Ruth folded the tea-towel carefully.

'Nah. She didn't have that sort of cash: wanted to do it right, but she just had to get away from Tahlia at that point, and I don't blame her. There was the drug-taking, of course. Reagan hates that stuff, and it had evolved beyond pills – snorts, needles. Plus, Tahls was getting into some bad situations in clubs and Reagan thought that would visit home sooner or later. She'd boxed herself into a corner a bit, saying she was definitely going around the world and then not having enough cash. She saw something online about faking trips and thought she could do that. She's actually travelled Oz a bit, done a few tricks with online chat and VPNs to make it seem like she'd done the UK, a trip to Norway, across to Boston. It's easier to fake than you'd think. Probably thought she could bluff through it and everyone would be sick of her going on about it once she came back.'

'Hmm. Those, uh, *situations* for Tahlia?'

'Tahls introduced one guy to another guy, in the VIP sections, apparently. Took a little bonus for it. If that transaction went south, one or the other would come looking for her. Reagan might have been a bit paranoid but the basics were definitely there, yeah.'

They'd already asked the Drugs section if Tahlia had appeared on their radar, but hadn't heard back yet. Probably worth another nudge tomorrow.

'Reagan confided in you, or you guessed?'

'Bit of both. She screwed up on her piccie of the Houses of Parliament in London: it's being reno'ed so it's currently covered in scaffolding, but her picture showed it in full splendour. I called her bluff and we chatted.'

Bluey smiled. *Undone by slow project management: unlucky.*

'Look,' continued Ruth, 'it's not a crime to pretend you had a better gap year than you did, is it? Otherwise the prisons would be full of bullshitters. She wanted to get away – her sister shooting up, mixing with people who were handy and had no conscience – but she didn't have the cash to do what she wanted to do, so she tried to bluff it. Nearly got there, if I hadn't been a bit of a nerd.'

'Where is she now?'

'Been in Port Douglas. She works on one of the yachts there; a huge f-off thing owned by a millionaire. It gets chartered out and they like having pretty crew. She's done fine, likes it. Might be tricky to explain a super-tan from Boston at this time of year, mind. She'll be here tomorrow; like she would be if she was flying through Los Angeles.'

Score one for Lachie's cynicism, thought Bluey. Though it also made Reagan slightly more suspect – if she'd faked Boston, maybe she faked Port Douglas for a couple of days and she was already here in town at the time of the murder.

'And who do *you* think would want to harm Tahlia?'

Ruth pushed the cups across the counter, buying time.

'Loads of people disliked her, put up with her; but kill her? Can't think of any—Me. Me, if I got her alone for long enough. Reagan told me heaps and it all fits. The crap Tahls has put 'Nessa through, the garbage she pulled at work, the supposedly glamorous parties where she helps dealers shift product, the lies: I'm sick of it. I wanted to slap her daft, make her wake up to herself. The casual damage she causes, the lack of respect – it had to catch up to her eventually. I guess it has. We're all sorry she's gone, we're all hollowed out in some way, but you won't find anyone who knew her who's that surprised. Sooner or later, she'd stumble into pissing someone off, big-time.'

'You sound like you think this was inevitable,' cautioned Bluey. 'Murder is very rare, Ruth. Even people who annoy other people usually come out of it alive. Tahlia was a waitress at a coffee shop who liked clothes and parties. Maybe a drugs contact. At most, she seems to have been personally annoying and casually ignored others who felt differently.'

Ruth turned and spoke to the garden. 'Yeah, well. Karma can be a bitch. Life gives you repercussions, doesn't it?'

Chapter 26

City West station. Thursday, 1830hrs

The office lights were still on when Lachie returned, but no one was at home. Kat's computer was still switched on, so he assumed she was somewhere about. In the far corner of the giant space, the microwaves had been joined by some fridges and a few small flatscreen televisions – assuming the cartons actually contained these things.

'Now we're getting somewhere,' he muttered to himself. If he needed a parachute out of being a detective, he now had enough stock for a viable online business.

He settled into updating the investigation log, downloading all the interviews he'd recorded on his phone – Kat would transcribe them tomorrow morning – and answering various messages. At the moment the whole thing still felt nebulous. They had evidence from all the witnesses but couldn't separate the diamonds from the coal; they had some forensics but nothing pointing in any direction; they had theories that needed leaps of logic and heroic assumptions just to stand up. It was hard to shake the notion that one breakthrough would bring all the camouflage down and leave the solution glistening in plain sight. But what that breakthrough might be, or how it would arrive, he couldn't say. He reminded himself that they were fourteen hours in; early days.

Kat came out of the lift and nodded to him as she approached the desk. She sat and tapped a pile of files into a perfect oblong block.

'Kat, can you make a note of something for the morning, please?'

She flickered an eye, her way of acknowledging Lachie's new-found politeness.

'Of course. Fire away.'

Lachie pointed at the whiteboards, which now had the ominous fourth board filled with esoteric question-marked titles of spurious theories. Bluey had said that when you started the fourth board it was the point of no return.

'Tahlia and all the witnesses, including Anthony and his mum: can we pursue those phone logs going back three months? I've ordered them but I'm sure a follow-up from you would, uh, work.'

'Hmm. You'll need waterproofs and a strong stomach.'

Lachie was perplexed. 'Huh? What for?'

'Your fishing expedition.'

He stifled a grin to avoid giving her the satisfaction. He watched as she put on her coat, trying to puzzle it out. The shoes had a medium heel – unlikely to walk far. On the other hand, they didn't show any classic heel-and-toe wear from driving long distances. Her coat was too warm for – ah, he had to admit it: like everyone else, he didn't have a clue how she got home or where that was. Someone he knew in Human Resources had taken a sneaky look: her only recorded address now was a mailbox. Maybe Kat wasn't even her real name . . .

'Not leaving before you've solved it for us, are you, Kat?'

Kat paused with one arm in her coat. 'Well, if I did that, it would be letting you two off the hook, wouldn't it?'

Lachie steepled his fingers piously. 'Absolutely not. It would be serving our community.'

Kat gave him a well-practised sceptical look as she shucked the coat on and flapped the lapels to straighten them. She took another glance at the spidery mess on the whiteboards.

'Okay, then. Well, you've got yourself a *Rashomon*, haven't you?'

Lachie sat forward. Whatever he'd expected, it wasn't that.

'A what, now?'

Kat gave an exasperated sigh.

'*Rashomon*? Japanese film? Kurosawa?' She shook her head sadly. 'Lordy, the things they don't teach you in school. Too busy turning you into a little advocate for some teacher's politics. So, in the film a samurai is killed. There are four witnesses, including the victim himself. They each tell a completely different tale about how he died. There are multiple versions of how he died, who killed him and who confesses to killing him. They can't all be giving us the truth: some or all of them must be lying. But who, and how, and why? That's the film.'

She picked up her bag and hitched it over one shoulder. Lachie leaned back, hands spread.

'And how do they tell who the killer is?'

Kat gave a smile.

'Seventy-year-old spoiler alert: they don't. That's the point of the film, but it's also the point you're at. Goodnight.'

Jeez, he thought as she left, *she's annoying*.

Bluey arrived, looking tired. *Poor old bloke*, thought Lachie, *past his bedtime already*. They traded summaries of the interviews each had done. Lachie gazed at the spaghetti of the whiteboards. Mila Jelovic had been right – this did in fact portray where their heads were at, and it wasn't impressive.

'Are we any closer, Bluey?'

'Ha. Yeah, we are.'

Bluey deliberately turned away from the boards.

'If you ever build a house, mate, you get about three quarters through it and you look around. Exposed wires, some corner where you can still see the waterproofing, splats of cement everywhere, power's not connected. Everything's a mess: none of it is actually finished, it doesn't look like a real house someone might live in, all the rooms seem smaller than you'd thought. You swear it'll never get done. But then, suddenly, you're bringing in your prized possessions and going for a dip in the pool. It's like that with this case: we're not as far away as you might imagine. Oh.'

'What?'

Bluey tapped his phone. 'Autopsy is seven o'clock tomorrow. If you fancy going?'

'I should leave that to the big, important boss because he's a lot smarter than me.'

'Good answer. Crawling, but good. Okay, I'll take that first thing, then come in. I told Kat not to be in until nine, anyway – she did fourteen hours today.'

'What do you make of her?'

Bluey smiled. 'Oh, I've worked with her before. Don't start trying to work out what lies behind anything Kat says: that way lies madness. She's spot on with everything she does, she's been involved in more murder investigations than you or I will ever be, she's really smart. We should focus on not pissing her off. If we can.'

'Yeah, I get the feeling that ship's permanently on the point of sailing. Like, there's one feeble rope keeping it in port.'

Bluey chuckled. 'Keeps you on your toes, eh? Forensics?'

'Yeah, there'll be more by the morning, but so far it's not much. They're running overnighters on about twenty samples of the blood that was all over Reuben: obviously, we can reckon it's definitely Tahlia's, but they'll check all the samples. They looked for a blood trail, but it fades out quickly – his shirt was pretty absorbent, so it wasn't dripping everywhere when he went to the drain to puke. There's no trail to his patio door, let alone into his apartment, let alone back to the body.'

'So nothing to say that he went indoors after the mouth-to-mouth?'

'Nah.' Lachie glanced back at the whiteboards. 'To be fair, no one says they can see him doing that. They say he disappeared from view – below Bryony's balcony, behind a tree – and then they *presume* he came from his apartment, like they *presume* his first arrival. No one states outright that he went back indoors and that might well be because it didn't happen: he came out to see what was what, did the first aid, puked in a drain, went back to the body. He had blood on his hands and clothing and little smudges on his face.'

Bluey nodded. 'Two things flow from that. One: that he was actually a good Samaritan and not the total bastard we've been assuming. Two: it would make it difficult to get rid of a weapon. The search team's finished, by the way: they've gone out the full two hundred and fifty metres from the crime scene and found nothing.'

Lachie still wasn't prepared to let Reuben go on to a back burner. He told himself it wasn't personal: it was logical. Reuben was the kind of person to get taunted about his own stupidity and career suicide once too often.

'But it's not impossible to lose the weapon. An accomplice could get rid of it for him.'

'Ah, let's not get more than one person involved in this murder until we have some evidence for that.'

Lachie shrugged. 'Just sayin'. What else? Oh, Forensics found fingerprints anywhere and everywhere. The doors in and out of the courtyard, the lifts, the stairs. They have them for processing, but there's so many: I told them to hang fire until we can narrow down what we're looking for.'

Bluey found it hard to see how those could get them very far. They already knew it was a high-traffic area.

'Yeah, good idea. I could blow my budget in one day just processing residents and UberEats. Fingerprints around and on the dead body?'

'Lifted but not yet sifted. Another job for the night crew. They're also going to give us a lowdown on how drunk Reuben was at the time Tahlia died. That might give us an insight.'

Bluey puffed his cheeks. 'He's been evasive about that. I let it go this afternoon because I want those forensics ducks in a row before I really go at him. He wouldn't be so pissed he couldn't stab her, mind. From how he was shortly after, he was definitely sober enough to be involved in that way.' He glanced up. 'That's what you're thinking, right?'

'Yeah, it is. Oh, we finally got the warrant for communications.'

'Really?' Bluey didn't hide his surprise. 'They don't usually give, not without a specific purpose backed up by other evidence.'

'I know, right? They clearly either need a specific purpose, or Kat talking to the right person. She's a magistrate-whisperer.'

'Told you she had more skills than we have.'

Lachie grinned. 'So, Kat's chasing the telephone records of all the witnesses to see if there's a pattern of interaction with Tahlia. We might get a clue about that burner ringing her all evening.'

'Yeah, maybe not. I didn't get the impression Tahlia gave much of a toss about anyone else in the building, so that might be a busted flush. It's a box we've got to tick now, though. Laxton would love to throw us in the crapper for failing to do it.'

Lachie wondered briefly if Bluey and Laxton didn't have a more substantial history than he'd thought: Laxton's offer to replace half the team, any time Lachie chose, was preying on his mind.

'Kat's also doing a reverse-directory job on all the numbers Tahlia contacted from her phone.'

'That must be a hefty number, eh?'

'You'd be surprised. She surfs a lot – clothes stores, fashion apps, music, all the usuals. But her only social media is self-referencing on Insta. There's very few one-to-one; only eleven people in her contacts. She might be the type who deletes you when she's done with you. Probably is.'

Bluey thought of Mila Jelovic for a second. Then he frowned. 'Eleven? You see now, I'm suspicious of that. If she was eighty years old or something, maybe. But a pretty twenty-seven-year-old? Nah. Does she have WhatsApp or something like that?'

'She does but, as you know, that's encrypted and a whole can of worms.'

'All the same. If she *is* a link for some dealers, which several people have suggested as another source of her unfeasible income beyond Scotty, that's the way she communicates. Ruth said that Reagan thought Tahlia was a middlewoman, and Reagan's the closest thing we have to an eyewitness for that claim. See if Forensics know any party tricks.'

'Gotcha. Yeah, if she stole from a dealer, or became a security risk for 'em . . . yeah.'

'Oh, speaking of. Ruth says that Reagan didn't go abroad. Been hiding up in Port Douglas, it seems.'

Lachie beamed triumphantly.

'Knew it. Told ya.'

Bluey raised a placatory hand. 'Yeah, yeah. Well, I want confirmation, and I want Reagan here. She'll be back tomorrow, allegedly, but in the meantime I've asked Kat to have a closer chase on where Reagan's been. She could, if we're honest, have been in town the last couple of days.'

'You're putting her in the frame?'

'I'm not discarding the idea. If she'd actually been in Boston, then of course it's impossible. Now she's some sort of liar who could have physically been around. Knows the building, knows the victim; strong enough to have stabbed, leaves by the western exit.'

Lachie had been thinking Reagan was just a more accessible witness than she'd been suggesting; he'd never really considered her a suspect.

'Day one, Bluey, I know. Are any of those theories on the fourth board actually viable?'

'Define *viable*.'

'Not crap.'

'Okay.' He turned towards the explosion of question marks on the dreaded fourth board.

'Theory one: Reuben killed her and magically got rid of the weapon. Theory two: someone else that she knows – from the building or from work – cornered her and got into a scrap, had something sharp on them. Theory three: she's actually involved in the drug trade and annoyed the wrong person – skimming money, stealing product, talking carelessly, whatever. Theory four: Reagan or Ruth was pushed over the limit by something we haven't found yet. The top two are viable because that's a pretty common cause of murder. The third one is possible because of the kind of person she is. The fourth one is out of left field, but a bit more viable than I'd thought.'

'I see.' Lachie shook his head. 'That thing about becoming wiser as you get older? Whaddya reckon, Bluey – complete urban myth?'

'Ha. I contributed three of those four theories. Feel free to magic up another two whenever you like. Represent your Gen Y bros and all that.'

Lachie grinned. They spent the next twenty minutes tidying up their emails and Bluey prepared a brief summary for Superintendent Laxton, still hoping to avoid a press conference in the morning. Lachie was putting on his jacket when Bluey looked up.

'Do you care about the victim, Lachie?'

He gave a start. 'What kind of question is that?'

'Oh, it's a serious one, mate. I'm not having a go.' Bluey leaned back in his chair. 'I mean, speaking for myself? I don't care. Not really. I almost never do.'

Lachie had been noticing Bluey's quiet, understated compassion all day – this was a bellringer.

'Okayyyy . . . got anything more on that?'

'Yeah, fair question. So, this victim, Tahlia Moore. I never met her. I never knew she existed until this morning. I won't *ever* meet her. So how can I really care? I don't mean that I'm glad she's gone, 'course not. I wish it had never happened, I wish she was still with us and unknown to me. But do I *care*, in any meaningful way? Nah.

'Look, I care about the family. They're in front of me – I can see their grief and I can understand what Tahlia's death has done to their life. I care very much about that. But I'm sympathetic *because* they're in front of me – I can see, hear, touch; it's clear what's happened to them. I can comprehend the reactions of others: they have memories of her or connections to her. They're also people who are affected by *my* concern or lack of it; *my* emotions matter to them and have an impact on them. But I can't affect Tahlia in any way, can I?

'So Tahlia's an abstract concept. She's a cipher. I can go and view the body in the morning, but that's just a husk now, a receptacle: there's no soul in there, is there? I can talk to people about what she was like, watch video, whatever – it's all a proxy for her. I don't really see how I can care about Tahlia the person, other than in a professional way. And I don't see the point of pretending that she's the thing I care about, when it can't possibly be the case.'

Lachie hadn't heard it put in such stark terms. He'd expect something as forthright as this from Mila Jelovic; those two seemed tight, so maybe her almost total lack of diplomacy had loosened Bluey somewhat.

'Hmm. I can understand that, I suppose.'

That felt non-committal, not to say hedging; Bluey probed further because he had a definite place he wanted to go.

'But you don't feel the same?'

Lachie had fallen into big trouble when he'd assumed that others were on the same page as him; he'd learned the hard way that it paid to be circumspect in this building.

'I'm not sure. Why d'you ask?'

Bluey leaned forward again. 'Because I've got the sense that you're wrestling with the idea that you don't really like Tahlia much, that she doesn't come across as very likeable. That seems to be a problem for you.'

Lachie perched on the edge of his desk. 'Yeah, that's true enough. She comes off as a shallow, mean, spiteful individual who skated on her looks and was careless of other people.'

'That's the impression we're building so far,' agreed Bluey.

'So, then, yeah, I do feel a bit guilty about that. I'm investigating her murder, but I don't like who she was. I feel like I'm not being empathetic, or sympathetic, when we're supposed to be.'

Bluey pointed at the floor. 'D'you think the boys and girls downstairs are empathetic about a bikie gang leader shot dead?'

'I'm sure they're not.'

'And yet, you understand that they'd still prefer it hadn't happened, that they have a basic respect for human life in whatever form it takes; you expect them to be professional.'

'Yeah, I do.'

'Because you think that if they're as callous as the killer, then the whole community suffers?'

'We've got to be better than the people we're chasing, yeah.'

Bluey spread his hands. 'So you can do a standout job on this case, without feeling like Tahlia would have been a great mate if you'd met?'

'I suppose.' Lachie considered his ground, before continuing. 'I'm not known for getting emotionally involved in cases anyway, except when I'm assassinating my own career. In fact, I try very hard to stay away from empathy.'

'Why?'

'I know it's unfashionable and all, but I don't think it makes for the best police work. I know we're told lots of stuff about body language and reading the room, but in a real-life situation it doesn't feel right. If you do that you lose focus, you lose perspective. Cooperation is good, but emotional connection is counter-productive, I reckon. Empathy's a nice touchy-feely thing to do in the moment, but it's not your best work. You do it for a way in when you need it, for the response, or for the virtue signal; for the sense that when they close the door, people think well of you.'

Bluey liked that Lachie had thought about this: it wasn't just a knee-jerk reaction or something he'd been told by others and regurgitated.

'But don't you go better when you feel on the same level as the person you're talking to?'

'Nah. No, I don't. You're the cop – that basic fact must remain. Being a cut-price, discount mate for a few minutes doesn't get you further than being an authority figure. It trades off respect for squidgy feels, but the end result isn't better. Nah. If I'm true to my nature, then I always see the scenario as me the police officer, them the witness/suspect/whatever.'

Bluey tilted his head slightly. 'It's a good answer, but it's not the *real* answer. Look, you don't have to tell me, but you can. You know that, don't you?'

'Tell you what?'

Bluey's voice softened. 'You know what. The thing you carry, Lachie. The burden.'

Lachie bristled. 'I'm pretty much known as a closed book. Didn't they tell you that, Bluey?'

'Didn't ask 'em. If you want to tell me, I'll listen, but I'm not pushing you about it. All I'll say is this: one day, the best police work you've ever done will be because you were empathetic, because you listened and *felt* and found a way to truly connect. Might not be on this case, might be years away; I just want you to be open to recognising that one opportunity and walking through that door when the time comes. That's all I'm saying.'

Lachie nodded slowly.

Bluey needed to break the moment now. 'And with that, the old bloke struggled off home to a cup of warm Milo and the prospect of five trips to the toilet before morning.'

Lachie laughed and pointed a finger. 'Ha. When Martyn mentioned it this morning: you understood too much about bathroom visits. I knew it.'

'Nah, actually, if I'm lucky, I can make the second half of the show. Be a good uncle for once.'

'Which show is that?'

Bluey eye-rolled. 'My niece is performing at her school; she's playing Sandy in *Grease, the Musical*.'

Lachie was impressed: he'd always been *fifth passer-by* or somesuch in school plays. 'Cool – she got the star role. Presumably she has the voice of an angel?'

Bluey pulled a disappointed face.

'Nearly. The voice of an angle . . . grinder. If she could butcher meat like she butchers songs, she'd already have a trade under her belt.'

Chapter 27

City Medical Examination Unit. Friday, 0650hrs

The medical examination unit was across the street from City West station. Bluey took the opportunity for some overpriced fare at the adjoining
Coffee Club. As usual the food was good, but hideously expensive if you
simply identified what else you could do with that money. Bluey com-
forted himself that he'd finished paying the loan on the XR8 and so this
was, magically, 'spare cash'. His bank statement would tell him it wasn't
so, but he'd cling to the idea for now.

One of the great virtues of the MEU was the glassed-in gallery – a
raised platform that allowed medical students and detectives with weak
stomachs to observe the autopsy and ask questions through a two-way
speaker system. At the very least it meant the dead body was three metres
away and you were spared any stench and some of the noises. Wiser heads
such as Bluey had learned from bitter experience not to ask more than
three or four pertinent questions in the entire operation. For Dr Lawson,
he eased that down to two. The ME of the day had a switch that could
obscure the gallery's glass instantaneously – some use of electrical current
that Bluey didn't understand – and did so if you were being a whiny pain
in the arse. If that happened, the much-needed report might be 'in
typing' a while. Diplomacy and post-mortems went hand in hand for a
variety of reasons.

Tahlia was the first autopsy of the day. As Lawson and his nurse went
about preparations, Bluey took a minute to close his eyes and pay his

respects. Despite what he'd said to Lachie last night – primarily to draw out the younger man and make a wider point to him – Bluey took the dignity of the dead very seriously. The quality or trajectory of the life up to this point was not a relevant factor in according due respect. He knew that behind the barking-curmudgeon act, Lawson felt the same.

'Female, approximately one metre fifty-seven, fifty kilos, brown hair, green eyes. Blood type AB negative. Hmm, a one-percenter: shame nothing was donated. No sign of a struggle or bruising, except for . . . here. On the scalp. Hair-pulling, I'd say. Almost as if Tahlia had been held up by the hair. No sign of punching or slapping. Fingernails have . . . no overt signs of blood or skin fragments, but we'll take samples anyway. Overall, no obvious signal that she fought her attacker.'

'Doc, any evidence of intravenous drug use?' Bluey's metallic voice rang from the speaker.

'Hmm. Not on the forearms, but . . . ah, possibly on the thigh, up here. It could just be a blemish or accident; there's only one mark. I'll check on the blood work for any signs of regular use. No trauma that might indicate sexual assault. Tahlia's young and fit, has good muscle tone especially around the stomach. Overall health seems good: her GP's notes came back almost empty.

'Now, your wound, Detective. Let's see. Not wide. Measurement says eight millimetres in diameter. Looks quite long, though. We'll know more when we get inside and see the trajectory closer up.'

The incisions. The saw. The muted sound and the rib pull-back. The organ-weighing. Bluey watched these parts robotically; it helped with the fluttering stomach.

Shouldn't have gone to Coffee Club.

'Ah, lungs show some signs of recent vaping. Such a stupid hobby; I can't fathom it. Anyway, yes, here's the incision.' A minute or so while they carried out detailed measurements and took photos. 'Yes, I'd say the blade is sixteen to eighteen centimetres in length. It's deflected off a rib on the way through, then up and into the heart. Hmm. She had no chance. There would be blood on the floor, but it would take some time to arrive because the heart's stopped beating: more gravity than being pushed out. Tahlia would have died instantly – there was nothing the responders could have done. Please let them know that, Detective. The blade came in, pierced the heart, then left at a slightly different angle.'

Another twenty minutes and it was done. Lawson came towards the observation booth and looked up, like a cricketer talking to the Spidercam.

'Your murderer was face on. Roughly the same height as Tahlia, but anything up to fifteen centimetres either side of that assessment wouldn't be a surprise. Right-handed, like ninety per cent of us. The angle was forward and up. Doesn't require a huge amount of strength, just some anger or adrenaline. It's not conclusive, but I would suggest, judging from the scene, that the assailant grabbed hold of Tahlia after the blade went in, perhaps holding her up. This would explain the exit being a different angle from the entrance. Can't give you the killer's name and address. Sorry.'

It was the nearest that Lawson got to avuncular, and Bluey's cue to leave.

Chapter 28

Forensics inhabited the side of the basement that wasn't car parking. Through the concrete walls you could hear the squeal of the tyres all day long. The section lived in a netherworld of artificial lighting that cloaked the time of day. Large supermarkets, casinos, the forensics unit – they all attempted to obliterate any connection between human and daylight so that you focused on the task in hand. Lachie could never understand why people wanted to work in such an environment. *Probably the fault of the* CSI *franchise*, he mused: each year the state produced far more Forensic Science graduates than it could actually use.

The manager of the unit gave Lachie a vague nod as he passed by the office; Lachie had the sort of face that made people think they recognised him from somewhere even if they'd never met him. It was an asset in surveillance or undercover because it screamed *everyman average*, but left him constantly concerned that he seemed a benign five out of ten in almost all circumstances.

Diane Cooper had, fortunately or unfortunately, known Lachie since he was a kid. They'd lived two doors apart back then; Diane had seemed impossibly glamorous with her Porsche Boxster and her days spent finding killer clues and bringing down murderers. It was likely that his interest in policing began back when he was ten, gently rising to the surface through teenage years. So he owed Diane his career and she behaved as if she was now personally responsible for his behaviour. She'd taken the recent prosecutor debacle badly and personally; he was still working his way back into her better books.

She looked over her glasses as he approached.

'Lachlan. I hear you're working with Carl Blewson now?'

'We're an elite team operating below the radar, yeah.'

'*Elite* meaning there are only two of you; *below the radar* meaning no one takes any interest in what you're doing.'

Lachie shrugged. 'Harsh, but fair.'

'Actually, I'm glad. Someone has to be an improving influence, and I'm busy down here all day.'

'We're getting by.'

Diane shook her head. 'Oh, it's better than that. You and Bluey, you're made for each other.'

'Yeah, nah. If I saw his photo online, I'm pretty sure I'd be swiping left.'

Diane took off her glasses: all the better to wax lyrical. 'I can imagine *your* profile, Lachlan. Die-in-a-ditch Dyson is not just a nickname. Unless you're equally willing to throw yourself on to a burning spear for some imagined principle, don't bother. If you swipe right, I will assume we are to be wed and will make legal arrangements accordingly. No pets, no time-wasters.'

Lachie could see Bradshaw's shoulders shudder with laughter at the far bench.

'You say all that like it's a bad thing, Diane. I'd call that honest and committed.'

She offered a sardonic look. 'Would you like some forensics, young man?'

'Yes, please, Diane.'

She moved across to a bench that held all the relevant material for the case.

'So, we have blood from Tahlia Moore. It's all the blood on Reuben Pearce and his clothing; there's no one else's there. The spread is consistent with him picking her up and holding her close, and performing mouth-to-mouth. We found no general spray of any kind, so she wasn't breathing at any point when the blood transferred. It's also all the blood on the scarf on the ground and it's all the blood spilled on to the concrete. There's a regular but declining drip profile over to the drain from the body site, consistent with Reuben walking there. There's no trail back to the body again, but I understand witnesses swear that he did.'

'Oh, he did. It fits with everyone's view – one of the few things they all agree on – and with all the back-and-forth from the paramedics.'

'Okay. There was no blood trail in any direction except that one, if that's useful.'

It was. It suggested, but didn't confirm, that no one except Reuben stepped away from Tahlia's body once she started bleeding. There might be a short period after the moment of death – no more than a few seconds, before any blood emerged – when someone else might have been there. But once Tahlia started bleeding, only Reuben moved away from the body and back again.

Only Reuben.

'Well, this might be more interesting,' continued Diane. 'Thank you for insisting that one of my crew looks underneath vomit: I was short of volunteers for that little task. As we've said, nothing but a cockroach or two – the rain around midnight had cleared the drain of anything else so we know nothing was added to the drain after the shower except vomit. Speaking of; while we haven't confirmed that it was Reuben's, we can confirm that it had zero alcohol.'

'Zero?'

'None. If he'd had a drink in the previous evening we'd have found traces of alcohol, but nothing.'

A weird thing for Reuben to lie about, thought Lachie. Perhaps, as a serial liar, he just couldn't help it. But it seemed unnecessary, and Lachie wondered what Reuben thought he was achieving. Maybe the vomit wasn't Reuben's. Had Martyn ventured out, against his own anxiety? Perhaps Reuben was covering for him, or even for a killer. Was Reuben that nice? Was he nice at all?

'Analysis of the vomit suggests it *could be* Reuben's – the same but common blood type – but that can't be officially confirmed until the DNA lab gets to it. Right. Fingerprints.'

Diane shifted to a blue file at the end of the desk.

'You have one hundred and seven individual marks in the foyer and elevator. We've simply logged them until Bluey tells us to look for something specific, so those will be confirmatory rather than exploratory. Your *under the radar* status also means you have a teeny-tiny budget, and I'm not in a forgiving mood.'

'Bluey said to focus on prints around and on the body.'

'Wise man. Look, I'm sure you know, but I'll tell you anyway: unless there's a very convenient surface you don't get great prints off human skin or certain types of clothing. We have Tahlia's prints on her blouse and six other prints as well. But we've eliminated any of the comparison prints you gave us. It's most likely that those other prints are from the clothing store or from social contact – friends pawing it when they meet up, that sort of thing. None of the people you told us about have identifiable prints on her clothing, except Reuben.'

Bugger. He'd been hoping the killer had grabbed at her top – to stop her running away, to get her attention, when the blade went in or to hold her up afterwards, for example. They had no means, as yet, of telling that.

'So . . . Reuben?'

'Yes, he has his prints on her front and back. All bloodstained to a greater or lesser degree. But you'd expect that: he was giving mouth-to-mouth, wasn't he? I can't differentiate any marks that wouldn't be consistent with being a first responder, to be honest.'

'And on the skin?'

'The same. Very tricky to get prints at all, so don't treat this as gospel. No one that you've told us about appears to have touched her, except Reuben, and his are all bloodstained. Of course . . .'

'Hmm?'

'This would be conjecture. I'm guessing it's too warm for gloves to be normal wear, even in the middle of the night. But if someone touched her hair, we wouldn't be able to tell. Maybe someone touched her, but only her hair?'

Lachie tried to imagine it. You might get Tahlia's attention, or unnerve her, by touching her hair. It could be intimate or intimidating, or even both. You might, as witnesses had described, let her gently to the ground and touch her hair to protect her head from the concrete. But in the act of stabbing? Seemed unlikely.

'That's it for fingerprints?'

'That's it. There's not always a magic bullet, as I constantly tell you.'

Yeah. *Magic* bullet and not *silver* bullet – they'd also had that conversation. Lachie tried to find a bit of light.

'I asked if anyone here could break Tahlia's phone and get into WhatsApp.'

'Yes, you did. And the answer is still no. It's end-to-end encryption: there's no cache of the messages stored by any third party, including the people at WhatsApp. It's one of the main selling features, so surprise, surprise: they aren't doing anything about changing that. Your best bet might be the other end. Find or guess who she was messaging: they might be foolish enough to keep those messages in another part of the phone, maybe on a screenshot. Not likely, but it's your only way in.'

Lachie nodded. Tahlia still offered no proven or obvious motive for being killed; fingerprints exposed no one; the blood told no new tale; telephone messages were either inconsequentially dull or a bust; everyone saw something, but no one saw everything. Someone had pestered her with a burner phone that evening, but they didn't know who.

Their best clue right now, appropriately, was a pile of vomit.

Chapter 29

City West station. Friday, 0840hrs

Bluey had told Kat to be in the office by nine, but of course she was early. Lachie came back with coffees for him and Bluey, then noticed Kat. Out of her vision, he nodded at her and mouthed, *does she want one?* Bluey enjoyed the barely suppressed fear on Lachie's face, then called loudly.

'Haven't you got one for Kat? Bloody hell, Lachie. Aren't we all on the same team? Only three of us, but you're playing favourites?'

He and Kat shared a smirk, while Lachie drained the blood from his face and nearly spilled the flat whites. Kat spoke without turning around.

'He's pranking you, Lachie. I don't drink coffee from anywhere in this building. It's a matter of principle and health guidance.'

Relieved, Lachie sat down, but he knew he wasn't going to enjoy his drink now. For something to fill the silence, he said, 'Bluey didn't panic when you weren't here first thing.'

'Nor should he,' replied Kat.

'Nor should I,' reiterated Bluey. 'Besides telling her to be here at nine, I know that Kat's a professional; no need for me to worry. It's all about trust.' He looked across at Lachie. 'I mean, we haven't been working together long; but you'd take a bullet for me, wouldn't you, Lachie?'

Lachie shrugged.

'I'd probably be the one firing it.'

Kat snorted; a rarity. Bluey laughed.

'Yeah, fair enough. You can't be in two places at once.'

Kat glanced at each of them in turn. 'I thought detectives never asked a question unless they knew the answer?'

Bluey shook his head ruefully. 'Yeah, broke my own golden rule, there. Never again.'

Kat set to work on the reverse-directory: tracing who Tahlia had called or texted in the past few weeks in the hope of discovering some kind of motive. She had a formidable set of noise-cancelling headphones that made her look – though Bluey would *never, ever, ever* say it – like Minnie Mouse.

Lachie grunted. 'Tyson followed up this morning on the customers in What's Brewin' when Tahlia and Anthony had their little stoush. Nothing useful – they only knew Anthony from around and they didn't hear what was said.'

Bluey nodded and surveyed the whiteboards and the hinterland beyond the dividers. The latter had seen the mysterious overnight removal of the microwaves by elves unknown. Instead, that corner was now full of shredding machines. At least fifty, by his reckoning, assuming the box labels weren't a Furphy. It was perhaps the clearest and earliest indication that the premier was about to call a state election.

The whiteboards were no less catastrophic. His suspects were barely suspected, the swooping arrows remained, the question marks were all underlined twice. Mila Jelovic continued to be disconcertingly on the money. The golden hours of the investigation – the first forty-eight when it was likely that they made the most rapid progress – were flying past. He had no solid hold on who, or why. The *how* was useful, but just background noise without those two answers.

'Woo-hoo.' Lachie raised his arms in triumph.

'Care to share, mate?' inquired Bluey.

'The lines-of-sight software is here. All ready to go.'

Bluey came round the desk and watched as Lachie fired it up. While Bluey had spent the night wrestling with motives – what was said and what had gone unsaid – Lachie had dreamed of fluorescent lines fired across the courtyard, spearing in at angles that magically divulged what had not been stated. It would be the mother lode, somehow.

The software was maddeningly slow; the rotating spool flicked and flickered as the software loaded up the measurements taken at the scene and the data from the blueprints. While the basics could be gleaned by physically standing at the windows and looking, the added value from the software was that Lachie could play with scenarios of the killer and victim moving, shuffling across, bending down, arching away. For that, he really needed the software. Besides, it potentially offered hard-data answers that would impress a jury and frustrate a defence lawyer.

Finally, it finished loading. Lachie took a deep breath and clicked for the program to run. Three-dimensional images of Pacific Heights – rudimentary but mathematically accurate – were punctuated by a series of pulsing dots. The imagery felt basic, like early video games: it covered the facades with comically simple flat surfaces and the human figures were simplistic ciphers. But everything was the right size and right angle and that was what counted.

'Each dot is a witness. So we've got . . . Bryony up top, Sally's apartment underneath her, Jody off to the side, there, Reuben and Martyn on the ground floor. If you click on one of them, you see the world from their perspective.'

'Sally wasn't in her apartment, though,' commented Bluey. 'Can you add her at the door of the switch room?'

'I think so.' Lachie felt their expectant silence while he scanned the screen. 'Ah, yeah, here.'

A further pulse by the switch-room door, at head height. He adjusted it; Sally was shorter than average.

'Who first?'

'Martyn. He was actually closest to the kill site.'

The image rotated until Martyn's eye-view was on-screen. Lachie could pan left and right, zoom in and out, slide a metre or two either side to allow for the full size of the window. When he did so, the image lurched before regaining perspective.

'And what can we see, that he hasn't told us?'

'Gimme a sec – just loading up the position of the blood spill, and then we can add Tahlia and whoever into the scene.'

Bluey closed his eyes as he waited. He wasn't convinced there was a breakthrough ready to be seen through someone's eyeline. He remained certain that the answer lay in someone's heart, not their retina. But Lachie set a lot of store by this type of thing.

'Okay.' Lachie double-clicked. 'If Tahlia is standing where she fell, then Martyn can . . . ah, bugger.'

'What?' Bluey drew nearer.

'Like he said – can't see faces. There's legs, but, until Tahlia's laid down, there's no way for him to be sure it's her. As far as seeing the killer . . . nah. It's actually possible for the killer to reach that western door without him ever seeing the face, even if the killer turns around. Line of no-sight runs from Martyn's eyeline towards the door 'cos the tree's always in the way.'

Bluey could feel his back seizing up and stretched.

'One down, four to go. See what the rest come up with.'

Lachie was visibly frustrated that it didn't all click for him straight out of the gate. The next twenty minutes, while Bluey and Kat worked quietly and waited for a whoop of success, passed slowly.

'Crapola.' Lachie threw his pen at the monitor.

'No go?' asked Bluey. A question to which he already knew the answer.

'I'll have to tick it off from their interviews, but judging by this no one can see Tahlia's upper half when she's standing up. Hence, they can't see the killing properly, either. Mainly those trees, but the roof over the barbie as well. Jeez, you couldn't pick a better spot, could you? Bryony can't really see any of it; Sally might, but she was in the switch room and not at home; the others . . . can only see legs or partials.'

'Like they said.'

Lachie nodded. 'Pretty much. Like they said.'

Bluey tried to placate him. 'But they can still see the exits?'

Lachie had added the western exit as a key location. He flicked the perspective around and watched the coloured arcs fire out from the exits into the windows of the building.

'Yeah, they can. Martyn and Reuben can't see the eastern door. But everyone can see that western exit. They weren't kidding, there.'

All three were quiet. Not the dazzling insight Lachie had expected: he'd anticipated that someone had a much clearer view than they'd been telling, better than Lachie had been able to notice from briefly being there. Assuming the killing occurred right next to the blood spill, so that Tahlia simply went to ground where she was and the blood flowed from her left flank, then the stabbing took place in a partial blind spot for everyone. Lachie clicked the mouse again and all the blind spots of the courtyard came up. There were at least nine blobs, but about eighty per cent of the courtyard could be fully seen by one of the witnesses. A one in five chance, then, that the murder would take place where no witness could see all of it. Once again, it baffled Lachie that a courtyard over-looked by so many people could have anywhere that was out of sight.

Lachie was clutching at straws. 'That doesn't mean they didn't see the killer, or some part of the killer.'

Bluey gave him the off-ramp. 'Yeah, that's true. The killer had to arrive and leave, if nothing else. Have another play with it later; there might be something in the rest of the evidence that we can use on that software.'

No one was convinced. It felt like a particularly busted flush.

Lachie unpacked his notebook and updated his partner on the forensics. It was a dispiritingly short briefing. Kat headed for the photocopier, which was in another time zone to the west.

'So we have bugger-all, don't we?' Lachie sighed.

Bluey looked for the upside.

'Some of those things we ran through yesterday as possibles and probables are now proven. We know how Tahlia Moore died, for sure. She was stabbed by a weapon with these measurements. The killer was probably known to her, since there's no sign of a struggle or defensive wounds. She let the killer get conversation-close, maybe closer. The weapon penetrated her heart: hence, she didn't stagger around leaving blood everywhere.

'We have a time of death, we have a cause of death, we have a location of death. We have fingerprints of everyone around the scene of the crime, albeit we have dozens of others as well. We have witness statements that corroborate at certain points: not unreasonable, given that we know no one had a clear view of everything. We have background on the victim that's a starting point for potential motive.'

Lachie leaned back, hands behind his head. 'Nice try, but I'm not feeling very pepped by your pep-talk.'

'Because you're a glass-half-empty bloke. Or a glass-never-filled bloke. Take your pick, but either way, you're not a peppy person. I'm calling it now: we have what we need to solve this thing in our hands, we just don't realise it.'

'Look at our suspects, though.' Lachie counted each one off on his fingers. 'Scotty from Coffee Pouring: his alibi reluctantly came through to Tyson last night – report's here. According to CCTV, Scottie's stopped at a servo when Tahlia was being attacked. And I mean stopped: sex obviously makes him want a meat pie because he's parked up by the barbie bricks and gas bottles, stuffing his face.

'Anthony the non-autistic kid: wasn't flying the drone that night. None of the five witnesses saw him anywhere near the courtyard that night – not before, during or after. He was a little brat who tried to rort his way into some NDIS money because Mummy told him to, and thought he might swing a blowie from a cute woman. And that's all.

'Reuben Pearce. Much as I dislike the bloke and all he stands for, the only evidence we have is that he saw Tahlia on the ground, called for the ambos, tried to bring her back to life, then puked in a drain when he failed. I'd love to smack him with some unassailable truth, but the reality is that he probably did the right thing that night. Oh, and he was stone-cold sober, if you believe the tale of the vomit.'

'For real? Crap.' Bluey frowned. 'That would have been nice to know yesterday afternoon, eh? But why would he lie about that?'

'Because he's Reuben Pearce, Australia's slam-dunk chance of a medal in the Liars' Olympics.' Lachie shrugged while Bluey continued frowning. 'Anyway. Everything else and every*one* else is just a finger in the air. Still no idea who the phantom caller on the burner was. Tahlia's mum didn't seem too ecstatic about her; Aunty Ruth didn't like her at all. I didn't get the impression that Cassie from What's Brewin' was a lifelong fan. Jody Marks wasn't impressed by Tahlia when he drove her; Sally was ambivalent about Tahlia's relationship with Josh. But none of them looked to have the reason, or the anger, to do anything approaching this. Other than that, we have no one within cooee. We need a piece of killer evidence in every sense: something that incontrovertibly ties someone to Tahlia in a way that says *murderer*. I still don't see it on that board.'

Bluey stuck out his bottom lip. 'Spoilsport.'

Lachie chuckled and filed his notes. 'Hey, let's ask Kat: she's probably actually worked it out. Right now it's as good an option as any.'

Bluey shook his head slowly. 'One: we're the detectives and we're supposed to solve it. Two: if she's right I could never survive the humiliation. Let's try the other end of the telescope. What is it about Tahlia that's different to any other annoying person? Because someone thought she was so bad they had to do something about it.'

'What's unusual about her?' Lachie slurped some coffee and reached for another file. 'Let's see. She unusually had two incomes for one person doing one job, didn't she?'

'Yeah, but the video proves Scotty's playing *ketchup* when he should have been stabbing someone. And I can't see Cassie either knowing about that double-dip income, or being so mad about the unfairness of it all that she attacks Tahlia. Not relevant. Next.'

'She was allegedly a drug user. Drone footage probably says so – they're sending it over this afternoon after they've verified the metadata – although a skilled lawyer could argue there's no definitive proof it was heroin. She also had some coke in her bedside drawer: that's a fact.'

Bluey nodded, as much to himself as his partner. 'Yeah, the drugs angle is still viable for me. She might have ripped someone off or played two against each other. But there's no solid sign of that so far; just Reagan and Ruth gabbing. We'll need to dig deeper into that; if Reagan's really coming home from Port Douglas, we can ask her. Meantime, we might have to kick around where Tahlia liked to hang out. Nag the Drug Squad again about the locations she's texted from in the past three months.'

'Shall do. If it *is* a drugs angle, then it makes sense: a middle-of-the-night meet, a transaction gone wrong or a sneer when an apology was needed. Stabbing feels like a you-didn't-respect-me killing, doesn't it? And the witnesses said the western exit door was still swingin'. That's the quickest route to the expressway.'

'Yup. You might be right.'

Lachie picked up the autopsy file, which only had Bluey's notes at this point – the ME's report would arrive before midday. 'Your writing's chronic, mate, you should have been a doctor. What's this *1%* mean?'

'Oh, Doc Lawson's little aside. He was pissed that someone who was AB negative wasn't donating organs and plasma: apparently only one in a hundred people are AB negative so I guess there's not much supply in the tank.'

Blood.

The thought made Bluey jolt. He wondered why it caused him to sit up suddenly. He saw blood on an almost daily basis. He'd stood while forensics suits took samples next to Tahlia's body. He'd interviewed Reuben Pearce when the bloke was still covered in the stuff, right down to the Gladwrap fingers. There was loads of it at the autopsy. Why would the word *blood* spark his interest now?

One in a hundred. Imagine that, he thought. Imagine being that person and knowing that, if you ever went into hospital, you were relying on another one percenter having come through already with the dona-tion: nothing else would do the same job. Perhaps you'd feel a little more vulnerable than average, if that were the case. Maybe Tahlia had felt the tightrope of being AB negative.

Click.

The magic moment. He scuffed through the piles on his desk manically. It was here. It was here just now. It had been here since the get-go. Where was –

There.

He grabbed it, found an evidence bag and jogged out of the office as quickly as he could, ignoring Lachie's smirk at his scuffling stride.

Bluey didn't care. He had the key.

Chapter 30

Lachie felt odd having the office to himself for a few minutes; it was like being a latchkey kid and sneaking some vodka from Dad's stash, topping it back up with water. Even then, eleven years old, he'd been savvy enough to wipe sticky finger marks from the bottle: tiny fingerprints would be a giveaway. The same deal with the bottles he moved for access and for the cupboard door. It was probably the only time any of those things were cleaned.

Kat's prodding had been the catalyst he'd predicted: they now had the phone logs of all the witnesses. Surely to God, he reflected, Tahlia would have been in contact with some of them. It didn't show up on Tahlia's phone records, but they were working on the assumption that it wasn't necessarily the only phone she had. If she was involved in the drugs scene she might have another – every man and his dog knew what a *burner* was. A recurring number on a witness phone log might lead them into Tahlia's second life through the back door. He started scanning backwards in time.

He spent an hour working through Tahlia's records, trawling for connections to anyone in particular. It stung when he saw the number of Warren Bartlett show up a dozen times a week, then disappear. Likewise, though with less of a build-up, with Josh Harris. It looked stark on the page – the digital snuffing-out of a life. Reagan's number drifted away once she'd gone off on her travels. Vanessa got a couple of messages a month but, Lachie noticed, no calls. All she had from her daughter were badly typed sentences. Other than that, he couldn't discern a pattern or a breakthrough.

After sighing loudly and taking a bathroom break, he tried reversing the process: using the phone records of the various witnesses to search for Tahlia. He wasn't expecting them to have contact with Tahlia, because her records showed she hadn't initiated contact with them. They were just people in the same physical building. As Bluey had said, it was a box that needed ticking and, if they ever got to court, prosecution and defence would expect to see that they'd covered it off.

No one in the building was on Tahlia's radar: most residents had the caretaker on speed dial for emergencies, but Tahlia didn't even have Sally in contacts. This was going to be a ball-ache; several hours of his life he wouldn't get back. He thought about asking Kat to do it for him.

He took a second sweep of the data. It hit him right away.

Only two witnesses in and he saw it. He saw it and kicked himself for not really considering it before. This was the subconscious *ping* he'd had in Jody's apartment. Now it was there in black and white, it seemed obvious. He started taking notes, sliding the highlighter pen across rows and columns, holding himself back and forcing himself to double-check.

Kat came back and he beckoned her over.

'See here? And here? Then, look at this. Please tell me if I'm wrong.'

As though she needed the permission. He watched her eyes as she scanned the data sheets in turn. She went through them twice.

'Yes. Undoubtedly. And that didn't crop up in the interviews, did it?'

Lachie sat back in his chair.

'Nah, it didn't. But then, we didn't specifically ask it, did we?'

'Ooh, Bluey's going to kick himself. Worth watching.' She glanced around theatrically. 'Where is he, by the way? He ought to be here to congratulate you on a breakthrough.'

'Not sure. He grabbed something off the desk, got an evidence bag and headed out in a hurry. Gone to Forensics, maybe?'

Kat peered at Bluey's desk, which was more chaotic than usual from his frenetic finger-searching a few minutes ago.

'Ah. Got it. Hmm.'

Lachie puffed his cheeks. 'Tell me you have a photographic memory without telling me you have a photographic memory.'

Kat gave a rare half-smile.

'Not quite photographic, but bloody close. He's got – ah, he's back. The stage is yours, Lachie.'

Bluey was slower coming back than he'd been heading out. Lachie waved a sheaf of papers.

'Got something.'

Bluey leaned by his chair, apparently exhausted by however far he'd walked.

'Solved the whole thing?'

'Not quite. But lookie here.' He pointed to the highlighted sections. 'Phone logs from all the witnesses. We know for certain when the paramedics arrived, yeah? To the minute?'

'Yeah, they have GPS trackers in the ambos and they radio in when they arrive, like we do.'

'Good. Then here's the news. Three minutes before the ambos arrive, Bryony rings Reuben.'

After Bryony had rung for the paramedics; *before* the paramedics arrived.

'She what?'

'She rings Reuben's mobile from her mobile. They talk for two minutes and seven seconds.'

'Bloody hell. Okay.'

Bluey tried to slow himself down, wary of a mistaken runaway train; Lachie's keyed-up energy was infectious. But his mind flew to part of his last interview with Reuben: the moment where Reuben confirmed he had his phone in his hand when he went to do mouth-to-mouth. So Reuben would have had that phone call with Bryony while he was standing over Tahlia's lifeless body.

Bluey pitched an explanation, hoping Lachie could shoot it down.

'If it was just finding out more, I'd expect her to do that *after* the paramedics got there, not before. Like asking if Tahlia's dead, if there's anything anyone can do, that kind of thing. But *before*?' He flailed around for a concrete answer. 'I dunno – maybe there's a defibrillator in the building and she knew where it was. Something like that?'

Lachie shrugged. 'Maybe. I think you're giving her the benefit of the doubt, mind. Yeah, she's smart, but how have those smarts been directed? She didn't mention to us that she rang Reuben, did she? Not at all. Especially not in the time between seeing Tahlia on the ground and the blue lights spinning. That's not all, either.'

Bluey frowned. 'Go on.'

'Sixty seconds after she's finished with Reuben, she rings Jody. Speaks for ninety seconds. Then, almost straight away, she rings Martyn. Two minutes with him.'

This would be while the paramedics were hustling but accepting the inevitable, thought Bluey.

'But I thought *Martyn* rang Bryony? After the paramedics were done?'

'That happened too, later on. But she'd rung him first.'

'Let's not get ahead of ourselves here. That's probably Bryony gossiping, or asking if anyone saw something she didn't. Even up on the top floor she could only see half of what was going on, as we know.'

That was true: the 3-D software had proven it. Lachie stemmed his impatience. They were all on the same page here, but the whole thing had to be constantly checked. Bluey was right to play devil's advocate.

'Okay, yeah. But then, once the ambos are packing up, Bryony rings Jody, Reuben and Martyn again. All *before* we interview them. So that's a double effort, eh? First: before the ambos arrive. Second: after Tahlia dies and before we speak to the three of them. Then Bryony does it *again*, as soon as we've finished interviewing them. So, all three witnesses, three times. She didn't mention any of it to us. But after that, nothing. She's not followed up.'

Three sets of calls to each witness – two before, one after – bookending their police interview.

'So I ask,' continued Lachie, 'if she just wants the insider skinny and she's milking them for gory or consequential details, why do her phone calls so closely follow our investigation moves? It's the same sequence as our movements. And why *precede* those interviews? If I want gossip, then I wait until the police have been, so I can get the juice on what they might have spilled. I don't pre-empt it, do I?'

'Unless . . .' Bluey nodded.

'Yeah, *unless* I'm directing what they should say. Unless I'm organising each person's response. That's why, apart from Martyn's boo-boo, they never ring her. Because they aren't *telling* her anything – they're getting their orders. This is coordination, Bluey. Bryony's the ringleader of whatever this is. She rings while all the crap's hitting the fan; calls each witness twice to prime them for interview. Then she rings again to make sure they did as they were told. Once she's assured of that, there's no need to draw attention by further contact: if she wants to, she can go and see them personally later in the day. She just had to do the first parts by phone for speed, and so she's not bumping into us while we're investigating.'

Martyn thought Bryony had been a teacher: Bluey and Lachie thought she'd been a spy. Lachie pushed on.

'I thought you said she was too old, not strong enough to stab someone to death?'

'For the murder?' Bluey finally sat down. 'Yeah, I'd stand by that. I'm not saying it's impossible, but bloody unlikely.'

All three were silent for a second. Kat had the hint of a smile around her lips, as though she was respecting their ability for the first time. Bluey lost himself in thought and Lachie understood enough to wait. Assuming Bluey was right and this crime was physically outside Bryony's wheelhouse, if Bryony was coordinating, then it wasn't on her own behalf. Eventually, Bluey looked up.

'Top work, mate. There's just one thing you missed.'

Lachie's smile was half exasperation. 'Knew there would be.'

'So, I just ran . . . okay, *toddled* down to Forensics. Did you see what I had in my hand?'

Lachie glanced at Kat, then back to Bluey. 'Nah. You're a slow runner, but before all the toddling it was a bit frenzied.'

'Fair enough. It's this: the map of the building layout that Tyson got for us yesterday morning.'

He waved the map, the evidence bag glistening in the fluorescent lights. Lachie couldn't see anything new or decisive in that.

'Right. Hidden door? Secret passageway for the killer's escape? Bit *Scooby-Doo*, isn't it?'

'Not the information on the map. The map. The map itself.' Bluey waved it again, as if this was clinching. 'See all these grub marks and smudges? One of them isn't greasy fingers. It's a blood spot. An *AB negative* blood spot.'

Lachie joined the dots quickly. Kat let out a little gasp. Bluey nodded.

'Yeah, Tahlia is a one-in-a-hundred AB negative. No one else that we know of has that. The chances of this being her blood are extremely high. It could only have dripped after she was stabbed.'

'Which must mean . . .'

'Yup,' confirmed Bluey. 'Plus, who was the only witness that Bryony never called? Never *needed* to call?'

'Caretaker Sal.'

'Game. Set. Bingo.'

Chapter 31

Pacific Heights apartment block.
Apartment 44. Friday, 1100hrs

Tyson knocked on the door. For the life of him, he still couldn't work out the numbering system for these apartments. Pacific Heights had a strange, tilted life of its own. Next to him, inadvertently blocking half the corridor, was the giant Samoan figure of Constable Willie Ofusa. His shadow covered most of the wall. Tyson knocked again: it was late morning, but it was entirely possible that this person was asleep.

He was nervous. No denying it. He'd had the call from Lachie and he'd been surprised. Lachie didn't have to give him an explanation – didn't owe him one – but he'd taken the time to lay it out for Tyson. It clearly mattered to Lachie that Tyson believed in what was being done, saw the logic in it.

After five minutes, Tyson did believe.

He'd gone over the sequence in his mind, the boxes he had to tick and the precise order. He didn't want to blow anything now because he'd forgotten himself in the moment. On the other hand, he wanted to be professionally humane: he'd seen officers treat people carelessly once they saw which way the evidence pointed and he didn't like it.

Eventually, a response. Padded footsteps to the door, the metallic clack of the latch, a slow opening. Bleary-eyed incomprehension.

'Hello. Sorry to wake you.'

'Oh, uh, okay. I was just dozing on the couch, really. No, you, uh, you did me a favour. What's this about?'

'Probably better not spouting it in the middle of the corridor?'

'Oh yeah, right, come in.'

Tyson went ahead, Willie following into the semi-darkness. The curtains were drawn in the living room, giving it an overly warm, stifling mugginess. There was something about the womb-like atmosphere that was not reassuring but off-kilter. The room felt like someone who was not themselves and, realising that, had retreated from the world.

Willie positioned himself by the front door, arms folded. Tyson got to the point as quickly as possible.

'So.' He swallowed and regathered. 'I'm asking you to come down to the station. Now. At this stage, you're not under arrest and there are no formal charges. But there may be both of those things later on. So if you want to call a lawyer and have them meet you at City West, you can make that call now. If not, we need to be on our way.'

He expected shock. Maybe a few tears of self-pity, perhaps an attempt to stall or distract. But there was nothing. A sweep of the hand across the kitchen counter gathered the house keys; another hand grasped a water bottle. A businesslike nod, and Willie led the way out of the door and down to the patrol car.

As he closed the rear door of the car, Willie gave Tyson a wink that said *easy as, bro.*

Chapter 32

City West station. Friday, 1130hrs

Lachie nodded to Tyson, who was guarding the door of the interview room. He'd given the task of bringing in the prisoner to Tyson as a thanks for all his back-and-forth and his insight as a local uniform; he had, in fact, procured the crucial piece of evidence without realising it. Once Lachie sat down, Tyson would be able to watch through the mirror and see the outcome of his efforts.

Caretaker Sal – Sally Louise Harris, he reminded himself – was already seated in Interview Q, her station-issue jumpsuit an incongruous orange in the otherwise grey palette. The signed form that waived her right to a lawyer for this interview was parked on the edge of the table. Lachie put it into his file and carefully set up the recorders, made sure the cameras were operating. *Sally Louise Harris.* Police officers often remembered their most difficult or most important cases by using the entire name of the key person. Three names meant you were either the victim, or . . .

'Can I get you anything, Sally? Hot drink? Snack?'

She shook her head.

'No, thanks. I'm lovin' this outfit you provide, by the way. I'm used to overalls, the job I do, but this is something else.' She mocked-weighed with two upturned palms. 'Boiler suit, Gitmo suit: they don't look much different, do they? Except, ironically, this one looks cheerier.'

'I'm going to ask you again if you wish to have a lawyer present.'

'And I'll politely decline again, Detective. It isn't necessary. I won't be needing a lawyer, thanks for asking.'

'Please, call me Lachie. Let's start wherever you want to start. Tell me whatever you want to tell me.'

Sally blew her nose and held the wadded tissue in the air. Lachie pointed to the bin in the corner and she made the three pointer off both walls.

'My lucky day,' she said, as they shared a wary smile.

'You ever lost anyone close?' she asked. 'A parent, kid, sibling?'

'Not quite,' he replied, his voice wavering at the end. It had been perilously close. They'd glimpsed what lay beyond.

Sally nodded sagely. Her voice was softer now.

'It has . . . it has quite amazing weight. That's what struck me about it. I was prepared for the howling, the gushing, the pain of it; or, as prepared as you can be, I suppose. I knew it was coming, at any rate: everything around me seemed floaty and useless and pointless. But grief has a physical weight. It was the mass that held my stomach down: I couldn't eat without nausea and couldn't chew without thinking I was gonna choke. It was the enormous burden that I could hardly carry yet always did. Even in sleep I was bearing it, like a kettlebell on my chest. The weight that never let up, that never decreased, never took a day off. Just lug it around in your heart, your guts: it's your job. The weight you can never put down to focus on something else, or someone else: always your full attention and every ounce of effort. Yeah, the absolute bloody weight of it.

'And the guilt. *Of course* the guilt. I've done a bit of the counselling stuff since Joshie died, even though it isn't really my thing. Every parent I've ever met who lost a kid, they have the guilt. Doesn't matter how their child died, or whether they could have done anything. Their guilt is beyond that. It's the simple hammer of having brought someone into this world, but you weren't able to keep them here. You didn't bring them the life they were entitled to have; you botched it. I'd done that *big-style*, hadn't I? Knew who was causing it, how they were causing it: failed to stop it. Now my child's just some ash underneath a silky oak, faded away into the dirt.'

'But sometimes you can't. The child you raised had free will. He made choices, no matter what you did or said. People do that.'

Lachie surprised himself with the intervention. *That moment* – the one Bluey had mentioned only last night – was on him and in him and out into the world before he'd even realised it.

Sally raised an eyebrow. 'Yeah?'

Lachie swallowed. 'When I was a teenager: my sister, Jules. Anorexia. The slowest way to kill yourself there is. Because it begins with nothing, really. It starts so slowly it's like the first droplet of glacier melt – a tiny change that you swear could never amount to anything; could never be significant, let alone fatal.

'She wanted to stop eating sugar. Ah, yeah, cut out the lollies, the ice cream: good idea. So we all did. A healthy family supporting each other – that's how it should be, eh? So now we're all a bit leaner, the dentist is pleased, all good. But . . . it isn't all good. Jules is taking smaller portions, she's "not hungry", she's got bellyache. My parents have The Talk – how they're starting to get worried. Jules is good at reassuring. She has this dimply smile that makes you think it's okay.

'She's not eating at school, not at all. She's fallen in with a crowd and it's all online chat and texts. *Don't eat. I skipped dinner, you don't need it. They con you that you need it, but you don't. I've found a way to skip break-fast. Tell me, tell me.* Not even evil crap, really – just ignorance, hysterical and immature, pushing each other that bit further. Dollar-store Salem witchcraft.

'Oh, yeah, and each time one of them falls to earth and starts eating again, the ones that remain true to The Word? They get more smug, more superior. They're *winning*, in their eyes. To everyone else, they go from thin, to gaunt, to scary. Each insult about how skinny they are, how shiny, how hollow-eyed, just embeds them further. They dig in for the long haul.

'All the online stuff. The *thinspiration* stuff. The lies, the goading, the pushing. The trolls who say they live on thin air, that the nutrients you need are in the air, that fat is poison, that you're carrying around poison and need to be free of it. The crazies celebrating that their fingers will encircle their bicep. The idiots urging them on, telling them they look more beautiful than ever as they fade to nothing. We lived all of that.

'We took her to doctors. We took her to specialists. We tried every scientific solution, every quack remedy, everything in between. It pulls you to pieces when the person you love is wilfully, deliberately, crushing their own spirit. You want to shake them, slap them, drag them out of this psycho state and on to firmer ground. They don't want to reach out and take your hand. Part of them does, but the other part rules the roost. They can't bring themselves to do it. The food's the mask, but the mind's the problem.

'In the end, we sent her to my aunt. Back of Bourke, arse end of nowhere. A huge station an hour's drive from the nearest town; no internet, no mobiles. It's all straight as a die out there, isn't it? The roads, the power lines, the ploughed fields, the jet trails in the sky: your mind follows what your eye sees. Simple shapes, clear directions: they push away the debris. One thing to do and all day to do it, but it must be done. It's what she needed. Simplicity, clarity; hope.'

Sally was mesmerised. She leaned forward. 'And she did make it? Your sister?'

Lachie's eyes were prickly. 'She did, yeah. Just. Married now, one kid. Still has her moments, still has to . . . think about where each foot goes along the way. But it's doable and she's happy. Yeah.'

'She made it,' Sally whispered.

'We were lucky. We know we were. And every time I meet someone who went through what you've been through, I realise it all over again.'

Sally rubbed a sleeve across her eyes and nodded, her forearms pressed together. Her fingers clasped air, then released.

'Yeah. It's important to me that you know about that; it matters that you get it. That . . . despair, that madness, can make you do terrible things. My Josh had two curses. Two things inside of him that he couldn't outrun. I tried to solve it for him, but I didn't know how. Kids don't come with manuals, do they? I mean, they come with a gazillion people offer-ing their advice, but not an actual manual, nothing you can take as fact. I'm a frigging engineer: I deal in facts and I know how to fix things. I *define myself* by fixing, by problem-solving. Yet there I was, totally bloody helpless. Josh's dad walked out when he was two – good bloody riddance – so I was flying solo with everything, but even so. When the troubles came I couldn't get on top of them and nothing seemed to help.

'Joshie's first problem was that he wanted to be loved. I mean, really, *really* wanted it. I know, I know, every kid wants to be loved; but with Josh it was a tangible, visible, painful thing. He bloody *ached* for it. He knew that I loved him, and that became – well, I reckon he took it for granted. Maybe not, I dunno. *My* love wasn't moving the dial. It was just *there*; not enrich-ing, not helping him to grow. No, he needed other love for that – the peer group, that sort of thing. He wanted it so badly it was unbearable to watch and, I suppose, unbearable to be him. It made him foolish, it made him open to things he should have closed off.'

She had a small piece of paper on the table and she began tearing tiny strips from it. The ceiling light hummed.

'That made the second thing worse. Because sometimes kids can have a couple of issues, but they're separate: they don't affect each other, and that means the kid can cope. But Josh's problems infected each other, multiplied them. His second difficulty, you see, was that he couldn't tell good people from bad. He was useless at it and always in the same direction. He con-stantly thought the best of people, even when there was no evidence to support that. Take the worst person in the world – you probably deal with them, eh – and Joshie would see the one glimmer of hope in them. He couldn't stop doing it. He wasn't even sappy about it: he didn't have some ridiculous idea of saving the world. No; he only had the blind spot with bad people who meant to do him harm.

'God knows, I've racked my brains about whether I could have stopped it. On my bad days, I think *yes, I could have. I should have.* I feel I ought to have spotted all the signs straight away – come up with exactly the right words, the ideal phrase, the perfect example; *something*, to turn

Joshie on to another path. I should have, because that's what parents do. That's what capable parents do.

'Except, on my better days, I know that's not true. I know this country is full of good parents, good people. They're baffled, distraught. Their beautiful kid is lost to them, one way or another, and they have no idea why. She's disowned them; he's somewhere up north but out of touch; she's with a deadbeat who hits her but she won't leave; he's into some heavy shit: some reason why their kid is out of reach and pulling away, unsavable. They have no idea how that happened – how their loving home, their emotional support, *their love*, wasn't enough. Because it wasn't even close to enough. When someone else brought the shiny object, the approval, the group to belong to? Their kid took off in pursuit, desperate to be part of something else, not even a backward glance.'

Lachie nodded. He got it, he really did. Sally sniffed back a tear and carried on.

'Those desperate, mystified people: I was one of them. Twelve months ago, almost to the day. A year ago yesterday, Josh got into a car and went to a party. A pretty young woman climbed out of the passenger seat so he could scramble into the back. They all giggled; excited and lithe and fresh and everything sunny-side up. I recognised her: the face in the complex, worked in a café up the street. The way she touched his arm as he brushed past: I hoped. I hoped.'

There was a thin smile that lacked warmth. She looked past Lachie to the top of the wall behind him.

'Stupid, stupid me – I was *glad* that evening. I was happy for him to be going out, because he didn't seem to do enough of that. I was feeling good about it because he seemed to have older friends who might look out for him. And selfish me, because I had a night to myself for once. Self-absorbed bitch that I was, I'd bought the wine and the fancy pasta dish and I was looking forward to being . . . without my son. My God.'

Her face darkened as she traced a crack in the plaster towards the floor.

'He didn't come back by midnight, like he'd promised. He didn't come back at one. Or at two. He didn't answer his phone. At three, I got a call from the hospital. He was in ED, hooked up to a drip. *Overdose*, they said. The word hit me like a hammer. I was incandescent. It was impossible; I told them so. The nurse was understanding, thank Christ: must have dealt with a lot of oblivious fools like me. He calmly told me that Josh had taken something and the paramedics found him unconscious. Anonymous caller. Josh was okay, stable, but I should come down to the hospital.

'Your son in a hospital bed. Maybe you get used to it? I dunno. Perhaps, if he has some kind of long-term problem, I suppose. But not like this, not at three in the morning. Not for me. I almost crumbled when I saw him, almost turned and ran. Except, when I did look away, there was an old lady behind me. She didn't jump in surprise, she just leaned in and told me it would be okay. Ridiculous, of course. She had no idea and she was bloody wrong as it turned out. But that reassurance from a total stranger – like a quiet word through the door when you're locked in the public lav and crying your heart out – it was enough. I put on a game face and walked to the bed.'

She paused, finger-nudging the small pile of paper strips and swallowing hard, then taking a deep breath.

'Wires. Bloody wires everywhere. I allowed this to happen on my watch. Josh depended on me, and I was bloody nowhere. I was tucked up at home with my precious three-fromage pasta and my bloody McLaren Vale and my selfish little *me time*. While he was floundering, lying in some gutter with his limbs drifting around and his eyesight shot and his coordination all to buggery and he was scared and so alone and wanted me needed me and I wasn't there and it was all –'

Lachie carefully slid the tissue box across, and Sally took one but didn't use it. She scrunched it in her hand.

'Anyway. He came home in the afternoon. He didn't want to talk about it. I tried being the cool mum, talking about harm reduction and how there's no blame and I just wanted him to feel safe and healthy and let's keep that communication going, eh? All the time, I wanted to strangle the casual, careless bloody bastard who'd given it to him. I couldn't conjure a scenario where Josh was the instigator, where he was eager to be a part of it and kept at it until they relented. I couldn't see that in my head at all. Another reason I was a fool.'

Lachie quietly made a note. Josh's first overdose had been at 3 a.m. A year before Tahlia's death. Practically to the minute.

'Until then I'd been working for an aeronautical engineering company across town – we made parts for the air exchangers and such. With Joshie . . . the way he was, I decided it was better if I was here more. And fate led me here, see? Caretaker's job would come up that next week, and even though I was drastically overqualified I got the gig. Figured I'd have fairly flexible hours and more time near Josh. I thought that would help.

'He stayed off TAFE for a few days after the overdose, while I turned stalker. I went to that café with all the rich kids ordering ten-dollar drinks they never finish and then climbing into cars where Daddy pays the rego and the petrol and the repair bills and every bloody thing. I waited until she was on her break, then I happened to sit next to her on the bench opposite the café.'

Sally drew her hands into her stomach and practically mimed the meeting, buttoned-down body language barely suppressing the rage.

'I couldn't get over her *indifference*. There was nothing. As if every-thing in the world was fine. While my son had to be watched over and wrapped in wires and linked to machines, she'd sailed on without a care in the world.

'"Are you Tahlia?"' I asked.

'She nodded. Carried on looking at her phone – people dancing on a beach.

'"I'm Josh's mum,"' I said.

'"Uh-huh."'

'"He was in ED last night. Overdose. Know anything about that?"'

'She shrugged. "He's an adult."

'"Didn't you help him, when he OD'd?"'

'She smirked. Still looking at her bloody phone. "Listen to you. *OD'd*. Watch a lot of telly, do ya?"

'I grabbed the phone off her. Oh, look, she *can* pay attention after all.

' "Don't you care that he was in hospital?" I asked.

'She still looked at her phone. While it was in my hand, while I was talking to her. "Is he home now, then?" '

'I nodded.

' "Then he's got a day off TAFE and he's fine. Jeez." '

'She snatched the phone back and went back inside. Gave me a little *piss off* wiggle at the doorway. I should have done it then, to be honest. Should have killed her then. Josh would still be alive, I know it.'

Lachie hovered his pen over the paper but he couldn't think what to write. The way Sally told it, the way she'd lived it, the whole thing seemed to have a black inevitability about it. He could see ways out for her – in the sense that he could see other options than killing – but he could understand how the momentum would have appeared unstoppable.

'All this means you misled us, when we first spoke to you?'

Sally smiled at the table.

'Not quite. I mean, I was scared and I didn't know which way was up. But I had angels on my side at that point. I believed . . . well, not sure what I believed. That I might get away with it, that maybe I *deserved* to get away with it, that I did the world a favour. So I was, you know, willing to give it a shot, but reluctant to actually lie: old habits die hard.

'I genuinely did need to recalibrate the hot-water system that night. Everything I told you, up until about three in the morning: that's all true. Exactly as it happened. Going to the gym, checking the emergency pump, typing up the quotes and the timesheets, going down to the switch room – all true. I did set up to monitor the water system. I did have ear-buds in, I did eat some cake I brought with me. Everything tallies – the records, everything. I didn't lie about that. It's what they tell you, isn't it? It's what they told me, anyway. Only lie when you have to – stick as close to the truth as you can. So, yeah, all those things were true.'

The crucial word was *they*. Bluey had been right. For all the confusion

about sight lines, seeing legs not bodies, timings of first aid, doors swinging shut, how many screams, when the blood started: for all that, the key
was how many people had lied.

'I didn't go down to that switch room intending to kill Tahlia Moore.
I didn't. But I was thinking about it. And I mean *killing her*, not causing
some harm. Because merely rupturing her life, just scratching her crab-
shell? Not enough. She'd already goaded one friend into doing something
fatal: stupid old Wasbar last year. If you don't believe me, look at *everything* the coroner had. *Misadventure* my arse. Then she'd turned on Joshie.
That was what I was brooding about, while the valves hissed and the
switches tripped and I made little marks in my book. I was turning ideas
this way and that, like I'd been doing for months. The way she floated
and all the consequences just slid away through her frictionless life. It
wasn't right, it wasn't fair, and I was reaching breaking point about it.
It was a gradual ratchet-up of the desperation. You know what *torsion* is,
Lachie?'

He nodded.

'Yeah, it was ever-increasing torsion. Until something broke. After
Josh's first OD – God, it sounds so . . . *ordinary;* a little habit he had, like
biting his nails – after that first OD, I begged Josh to stay away from her.
We talked about toxic relationships and toxic people; how the ones you're
drawn to aren't always those who are right for you. We talked and talked
and, like most parents I suppose, I thought I was getting through. It
made sense to me, my argument, so it must make sense to him, right? It felt
that way – he made the right noises, anyway. For a few weeks he swore he
was steering clear of her: not going to this club, or that hangout, or
mixing with those guys. All the right things.

'Except, he wasn't.

'When he told me he went out to the youth club, or to see a band, or
skateboarding, or whatever? He was hanging out with her and whichever
handful of people were orbiting her that week. She mesmerised him. I
was congratulating myself on my shrewd intervention, on how well I
knew my boy, on the bond we had. You do that, you see, when it's a single

mum and an only child: you confect a special relationship that might not actually be there, or might not survive contact with the enemy. All that time she was hooking him up for whatever he wanted to try next.

'The second OD. I was asleep – keeping odd shifts the previous week. I got a call from Bryony. Bryony Price, upstairs. I thought she had some new problem in her apartment; the electrics in that place are sketchy. But no. She'd been visiting in hospital – she volunteers there, chatting to people who don't get visitors; she's like that, Bryony – and she'd seen Josh rushed through on a gurney.

'By the time I got there he was stabilised. He'd taken a cocktail, it turned out from the blood work. Three different things, probably within the same hour. He'd told me he was playing indoor cricket, but he was at a party somewhere – he swore he couldn't remember where – and various people just kept passing him things. And it felt good, apparently. Up until the moment the lights faded out and he smacked the floor with his skull and people drifted in and out and the blue lights were spinning and he couldn't breathe and he thought he was going to die.

'I was frantic. I was looking around the ward, thinking someone from that party would have come with him, would have given enough of a crap to see if he was okay. Foolish me, again. No one. All the people at the party, staring as the paramedics got around it, taking photos on their phone? Not one of them even rang the hospital: the anonymous tip this time was a passer-by spotting him in a hedge. You can see why I despised them all.

'Next day I wheedled it out of him. He was surprisingly, appallingly, disgustingly loyal to them, so it took a while. *Of course* it was Tahlia. Her and this month's lifelong besties. She was taking those very same pills, so it must be okay for Joshie to try them, right? Except, of course, he never quite saw her taking them. He saw the pills in her hand, he saw her go to the bar or the loo and then she said she'd taken them, so it was okay. But if he wanted to be a baby, do what Mummy said . . . that was all right. They'd hang out some other time if he wasn't into it.

'Oh, the subtlety of it, eh? Reverse psychology from someone with emerald eyes and cover-girl skin and perfect abs and a smile like a loaded gun. She knew exactly what she was doing – it was deliberate, yet it was just done for a laugh. Because Joshie was widely regarded, it turned out later, as funny. But only when he swallowed a pill, or snorted something. He had such extreme reactions to drugs it was a constant source of amusement. *Here, give him this, he goes mental, you'll see. Make sure you get it on camera, yeah?* Like waving a cut onion under a cat's nose.

'That's what he was to them. That's *all* he was to them. A disposable clown act. A freak show that grew in reputation with every rush to ED. Entertainment. My son's degradation, his risk of death, the paramedic interventions: all just entertainment. And at the centre of that grinning, leering, goading crowd? Tahlia Moore.

'I went to her apartment. I knew she was in there. She refused to open the door, threatened to call the cops. Because people like that, they know how to work the system. She'd risked my kid's life twice, but she'd be the one who needed protection from the nutty mother who can't control her own kid, and anyway, he's a bloody adult, so nutty Mum should leave *him* alone and *her* alone and –'

Sally sat back, exasperated. She struggled to bring down her breathing. Just as Lachie was going to suggest a break, she resumed.

'Yeah. Anyway. I had the master key, didn't I? When I knew she was at work I let myself in and had a good poke around. No drugs. No, uh, paraphernalia. She presumably just took stuff when she was on a night out, assuming she took anything at all. I couldn't be sure at that stage if she was a user, a dealer, or some in-between that hooked one to the other and looked decorative while she did it. That's what I suspected: that she was a honeypot and introduced one person to another and got a little payment in kind for doing that, so everyone knew that's what she did and they were all cool with it because she was hot. That skating, skittling, freewheeling, completely oblivious life where everything was temporary and disposable and based purely on what it felt like *in that exact moment.* Everyone thinking with their feelings. Bloody idiots.'

She wiped the corner of her mouth with the scrunched tissue.

'A few weeks further down the track. Josh seems lost to me now. He's in the apartment, but he's not *there*. I try everything. I suggest a trip to his cousin in Tassie, but he doesn't want to play. His TAFE grades drop off. He just lolls around like his limbs are rubber. He can't concentrate. He doesn't want to concentrate. The world seems full of hard edges for him – he wants to escape it. I find booze. I find . . . remnants. Powder on his T-shirts, the melt from pills wiped on his jeans. He's falling away from me and my helping hand is out but he won't reach for it, can't grasp it, doesn't *want* to grab it.'

The imagery kicked Lachie in the guts.

'A few days later, Jody Marks knocks on my door. He does some evening work as an Uber, uses a mate's car. He's cabbed Josh and Tahlia a few times, but he doesn't like what he's seen, what he's heard. He describes it to me, and it's like being slowly sliced by a razor blade. The deadly combo is Josh's desperation for approval melting into Tahlia's glamorous indifference. He's living exactly like he lives in my head – my nightmares are what he's actually doing. I'm not exaggerating: he really is in that deep. She knows it, she just doesn't care. He's an amusing little pet, to be chucked away once he's no longer hilariously gullible.'

Sally massaged her scalp irritably, pushing her hair back into place as if it had helped to cause some of her problems. She blinked too much before she restarted. Her voice was lower, steadier now. *No*, Lachie thought, *scratch that*. Now it sounded emotionally drained, inert.

'Third time's a charm, eh? I know it, when the phone rings. I know. Something, some instinct, has taken over, and I realise what they'll say before I even pick up. My hand shakes, I crumble inside before they get the words out. *This is City West Hospital. You're shown as the emergency contact for Josh Harris. Is that right?*

'I don't answer straight away, because my brain's spinning. *No, I don't think it is right.* I don't think that I should be in charge of Josh, because they're ringing me to say that he's dead. Telling me that I couldn't save him, couldn't protect him. That I knew what was going on, and who was causing it, and how, but I hadn't stopped it. That he wouldn't let me stop it. That he's gone because I failed him. That his life will never be, because I was a bad parent. So, no; I don't think it is right that I'm the emergency contact, because I couldn't stop the emergency in the first place.'

She glanced up as though she needed encouragement. He nodded, and her voice regained some flimsy animation; some sense that she was still tethered to the world.

'Morgues. They try to pretty them up, don't they? As if it's a sanctuary, a place of quiet reflection. They do their best, bless 'em, and I get why they do it. But really it's full of brutal edges. Steel tables, metal instruments, harsh lights and everything wipe-down. And the sharpest point of all is that it's so, so *final*. Once you're there, it's over. The future will never happen. You've lost every bit of what it was to be human. Someone stole all that from Josh. I know who took it. I know the thief. She's living in my apartment block.'

Her look up was sharper now, clearer.

'That was the Rubicon, Lachie. Sitting in the morgue, nodding at the rigid face of my child, identifying him but not recognising him. Knowing that's the final moment of my life with him. That was the precise second when I began to think about killing Tahlia Moore.'

Lachie gave it a chance to settle in the air.

'So, Sally, let's get you some more water, get ourselves together. Then you can tell me what happened after three in the morning.'

Chapter 33

Lachie deliberately took his time. For his sake, as well as Sally's. The motive they'd been reaching for was now clear and brutally sharp. Josh hadn't even been wrenched from her. It wasn't like a car crash or a heart attack. She'd had to endure the extended agony of him being prised slowly from her and led to the precipice, by people doing it for casual, callous entertainment. Her impotent rage and her hopeless, helpless fear had just stretched and stretched. It only snapped nearly a year after he was gone.

He placed the plastic cup on the table and got a distracted smile of thanks. He indicated that he was recording again and sat back, hands in his lap.

'Three twenty a.m. Around then? Whenever you're ready, Sally.'

'She's sitting on one of the swings. Just tapping back and forth, like an innocent little girl with the world ahead of her. She looks young and gauche and it angers me that someone so immature came to be in charge of Joshie's life. She butchered it.

'I'm thinking all this from the doorway – the switch-room door. The work on the water system's done; I just have to wait twenty minutes to make sure nothing falters. That room gets a bit stifling. I wasn't entirely honest, before: I quite often have the door open because it's cooler that way. So I saw her calmly puffing away on her vape like she had nothing to worry her. I can barely drag myself out of bed each day – can't see the point, really – but she's swanning about doing whatever she likes, never a regret.

'I just want to talk. Seriously, that's what I believe in that second. On my bad days I've toyed with the idea of killing her, I freely admit it. She's taken the one good thing in my life and trashed it: I don't see how I'll ever recover. So I've played with the idea. But I would never kill her *there*, in the middle of the complex with fifty-six apartments overlooking. That would be stupid, madness. I just want to talk and maybe get some admission that she was at fault, that she pushed him into it.

'When I come out of the switch room the light catches her eye and she's startled. She gets off the swing and I can see her glance at the western exit. I just move across a touch to block her path. It's . . . a bit intimidating, I suppose. But I'm civilised. I only want to talk. She's not sure where to go now, so she sort of stays there; drifts a bit, scuffs the floor with one of those stupid, bogan-chic boots.

' "You killed Joshie."

'I didn't mean to be so direct, I don't think, but when I get close to her it's all I can think about. She rolls her eyes. Literally, rolls her eyes. I can imagine her: *oh, here's the mad old mum again, why won't she give it a rest?*

' "I did no such thing," she replies. "You have no clue. He said you didn't."

'No mother wants to hear that, do they? Especially not . . . in those circumstances. I was prepared to try being reasonable. Maybe. At least, hear her out. But this is just crap.

' "Look at you, trying to drive a wedge between me and my dead son, Tahlia. Not putting up with that."

'Oh, that smirk again; comes so naturally to her. "Then why come over to me, dickhead? You have nothing to say that isn't an insult, and nothing that says you knew your own kid."

'I try to swallow it down, I really do.

' "You were older than him; you could have been the responsible one. You could have saved him and you didn't bother: that's like killing him."

'She half turned away, like she'd just outright laugh if she looked at me full on.

' "Josh was a child," she said. She did laugh then. "Twenty-one and still a child. You've gotta blame the mum for that, haven't you? Coddled little momma's boy, desperate to know what the world was like. Joshie was too dim to look after himself – that's on you."

'I have to believe she meant that. Not just every word, but what those words would do to me. The arrogance of youth: to imagine you can say what you want and it'll never come back to haunt you. Well, this would. I was bloody sure it would, bloody sure it had to. I wasn't even conscious the screwdriver was in my hand, yet I knew it was. Because as she turned away I thrust it at her.

'I'd like to say I just wanted it to hurt. Maybe catch the skin, maybe leave a cut. Just something to show her how close to the edge I was, how she should pick her words more carefully. But I've had a day or so to think on it, haven't I? I meant it, Lachie. I meant every centimetre that went into that horrible, horrible woman. I meant it when I moved it about in her guts, when I grabbed her hair to stop her falling off the blade: all of it. I meant it after I'd pulled the screwdriver out and realised what I'd done. I meant it. There's no denying it.

'When I looked up, shit got real, eh? Tahlia was limp, finished. Reuben was standing in front of me. He'd seen me do it. He'd seen everything that meant anything. He knew. We both glanced up and there was Bryony, looking down from the penthouse with her binoculars. Now, two people were eyewitnesses. Maybe more. I put Tahlia down, really carefully. Crazy, after all that, to care about whether she bumped her head, but I did. Put my hand under her hair like she was a baby, like she was being baptised.

'And there's the two of us, in a courtyard in the dead of night. There's Reuben; liar, cheat, untrustworthy. There's me: the fallen angel. I was the nice lady who'd fix stuff for you and only charged if you could afford it. I watered your plants when you went on holiday. I ran you to the airport when your kids let you down. I was the good person.

'I'd murdered someone. All I could do was throw myself on the mercy of virtual strangers. Maybe in some weird way that's easier, d'you think?

There's no history with strangers, is there? All just fresh and clean and decisions made on a blank slate. You simply plead, and hope. And you know what? They came through. They bloody came through.

'Reuben told me to go back into the switch room and stay there. He said to put the screwdriver into the water tank. His phone pinged as I crossed the courtyard and I just knew it would be Bryony. I knew they were plotting how it would go for me, how they could save me. My heart just brimmed over, couldn't stop it. Had a little snuffle.

'I went back into the switch room and opened the valve on the water tank. I dropped in the screwdriver: the water's not a hundred degrees, but I reckoned it would get rid of any blood.'

Sally frowned. 'But you *have blood*, don't you? Some of Tahlia's blood. Connected to me. They said, when they booked me in. I don't get it.'

Lachie opened the file and lifted a plastic bag.

'The plans. The floor plans for the building that you gave to Tyson yesterday morning. Had all kinds of stains and marks on them because you held them with messy fingers. But this' – he pointed to a small Tassie-shaped blotch in one corner – 'isn't grey or black, it's dark red. Because it's Tahlia's blood. AB negative – rarest type there is. You're type O, Sally. Her blood would only be on that map if it had dripped off a murder weapon, just before you hid that weapon.'

Sally looked skyward then returned her gaze, eyes moist, to the table.

'Jesus. Look at that. Skewered because I was so bloody helpful. Look at that.'

Chapter 34

'Are you ready to talk now?'

Reuben was sitting with one leg crossed, sipping at his coffee and watching Bluey lean against the wall. He was still a witness, so no need to offer legal counsel; not quite yet. But Bluey had done so, anyway: insisted on it, in fact. Duty lawyer Frank Maples was less than enthusiastic once he knew the identity of his client, but respected the *next cab off the rank* ruling he lived by. The recorders did their thing and the corner cameras blinked down at the three of them.

Reuben affected boredom. 'Dunno what you mean, mate. By the way, I ordered a ristretto because that's my usual brew. This, my friend, is not a ristretto. If you point me to your machine I could probably make –'

'Stop it, Reuben. You know what? There's plenty of people think you're a dick, and one of the reasons they think that is this: the stupid act you put on. I've seen behind the mask, mate. I've seen the real you. I've seen that you're smarter, more together, more self-aware and, frankly, nicer than this. So drop the act. You're in a heap of trouble and this little piss-take is not helping you.'

Reuben took another sip, smirking.

'Maybe *NiceReuben* doesn't want to talk because it might affect other people. You know, people who actually *are* nice and don't fake it like I do.'

Bluey strolled to the chair and leaned on the back.

'Sally. Caretaker Sal. She's on the next floor, in a very different situation to you. She's been read her rights, Reuben, she knows the score. She's spilled beans, all of 'em. Confessed to murder. It's over.'

Reuben sharpened up quickly. He turned to Maples.

'Is he allowed to lie to me?'

Oh, the bloody irony, thought Bluey. *We've chased our tails through countless lies, now you want to talk about probity and honesty? And this question from Reuben, of all people.*

'The detective cannot deliberately deceive you, using something he knows to be untrue. He can miss things out, but not directly lie to you.'

'So when he says –'

A silent nod. Maples was deadpan and distant, as if a monotone would prevent this appearing on his track record. Defending Reuben Pearce would not be a dinner-party anecdote.

'Hmmph.' Reuben still didn't seem to be convinced.

'We need to fill in blanks now,' reiterated Bluey. 'The quicker we do that, the better it goes for the people who tried to take us for mugs. Look at you all: barely twenty-four hours and we have you here and Sally here. Bryony Price is getting a chat real soon. It's. Over. Mate.'

Bluey sat down and simply stared implacably at Reuben's face.

Reuben seemed to reach an epiphany. Bluey had suspected that this very situation would break his defences, and now it came together.

'All right. I tried to help her, but it looks like she isn't helping herself any more. She probably wouldn't, Sal: too nice for her own good, that one. That's why we're all here, really. I dunno if you can even save people like that. Because sometimes they have a subconscious little martyr complex going on, don't they? I mean, like they wanna be caught because then everyone will see how virtuous they'd been in the moment, how committed to their cause; how they followed through and it wasn't just talk with them.'

There was a lift in his voice: Reuben thought he was a shrewd analyst. He was entirely ignorant of the similarities to his own infamy. Bluey wanted all that punctured, fast: he leaned forward. Even Maples edged back.

'Whatever you thought of her, Reuben, Tahlia Moore is dead. I don't see *virtue* in someone causing that. Let's start with a proper run-through of that night. Bearing in mind this is the *third time* you've been asked and we're no longer interested in anything that isn't true. Oh, and your blood test shows you had zero alcohol in your system. Zero. You lied. I expect to know why you did that. Understand?'

'Okay. Yeah, I get it.' Reuben uncoiled his pose and sat up straighter. 'Well, so you know by now that I wasn't pissed. I'd had a mate around and he was the drinker, not me; I've been sober over a year. Spent half the afternoon pissing about on the guitar, yacking. No biggie. He went off about six, but all I did was move the bottle on to the table 'cos I thought otherwise I'd kick it over. I was going to throw it away, but that's no longer part of my philosophy: now it's *face what you must conquer.* I implied I was drunk because I thought that would cover any mistakes I made talking to ya. Thought you wouldn't test me until I would have been sober anyway. Wasn't expecting a bloody RBT on my puke, really.'

Bluey grunted. Time to play a hunch that went with the percentages, even if he wasn't certain about it.

'Tell me about your phone calls to Tahlia that evening.'

Reuben squirmed, on the back foot for the first time.

'Ah, yeah. Thought that would come up. My mate left his phone behind, didn't he? Thought it would be a freebie kind of thing to use it before I gave it back to him. He'd told me it was a burner so I thought . . . whatever. Look, if you've got the records, you'll know that Tahls didn't answer and I didn't leave a message or a text, or anything.' He glanced at his hands, contrite. 'I was being a dick. It was evening, I was a bit bored, I got it into my head that there was a hot woman in this place and maybe she wanted to hang out.'

'Hang out?' *Jeez, it's still blood out of a stone,* thought Bluey. *Lying's just so pathological with this bloke.*

'Okay. Maybe not just . . . yeah, okay. So, the thing is, the last time she spoke to me was by the mailboxes last week. She usually just nodded and buggered off. This time she stayed around.'

Bluey sighed. 'More lies, more delay. Don't drag it out, Reuben. We're not in some crappy true-crime podcast here. We won't be going to two minutes of bad synthesiser music and yet another recap. Get on with it.'

'She'd basically chewed me out again over my past behaviour. Got right into it – how I was a bad example, how I should reflect. Seriously, this little cow is standing there in designer gear – on a waitress wage, mind you, so how would that work? – and telling me to live my life better. I might have told her to piss off.'

'So, the calls?'

'Were to apologise, really. I was prepared to suck it up because my mate – the one who brought his own tequila – kindly reminded me that I didn't have many mates, certainly not outside the music industry, and I should be a bit more humble if I ever wanted any more.'

'So you twelve-stepped without doing the alcoholism first?'

'Yeah, kinda. I just thought I'd start with whoever was nearest. I was in a rare humble mood, which is, like those burger ads say, *not everywhere and not for ever.* Strike while the iron's hot, eh? But she never answered. I don't blame her.'

Bluey considered for a moment. Even when Reuben was explaining a lie, he lied. How could they ever tell which way was up with this bloke? Part of seeing through lies depended on a conscience, or shame, from the liar. The lack of those things made sociopaths so hard to decipher.

'Bullshit. You thought she'd caused Joshie's death. Thought she was careless about it. And Wasbar's, for that matter. What you actually did was ring her to threaten her. Using your mate's burner, because you're a coward. When she didn't answer, you were pissed off but too tired to actually follow through and go and find her. If you weren't so lazy it might have been you, ahead of Sally.'

For once, Reuben was bereft of an answer. He stared at the floor.

Bluey shook his head. 'All right. Let's get on with it. The evening. And no bullshit, I'm sick of it.'

'Gotcha. I did game online: you can check that, and I bet you have. And I did fall asleep on the sofa and I did leave the patio door open and the rain did get in. And I did wake up around three-ish, whenever it was. And I did hear voices.'

So far, so repetitious, thought Bluey. If you were going to lie yet again, it made total sense to repeat most of it, be honest about nearly all of it, then try to sneak in another lie among all that honesty. That was what Reuben had done already. Almost certainly, others had used the same camouflage trick.

'I went to the door and I could see Sal and Tahlia. They were arguing. Kind of hissing, like they didn't really want to wake anyone else. Extravagant hand gestures, too. I once saw two deaf people have a real humdinger on the train – they had crazy-big gestures and facial movements 'cos they were signing their own rage. This was a bit like that. Almost . . . yeah, almost theatrical, like you'd mime a fight. Anyway, I could see the lie of the land, so to speak: Sally was incandescent with Tahlia, while dear Tahls thought she was overreacting and this was a waste of her time. Like you can overreact about your son dying.

'I really didn't like Tahlia; dunno who did. She behaved like a spoilt brat with rich, absent parents who'd bought her off with baubles and taught her the value of nothing. Except she didn't have rich parents or expensive toys and her sister had turned out just peachy. Tahlia was a selfish bitch and had a habit of leaving a trail of destruction.'

It tallied with almost everyone's view, except for the vehemence. Tahlia hadn't had, it turned out, any deeper part to her personality. What you saw was what you got and, aside from the physical aesthetics, it wasn't pretty.

'Yeah, you're right; Sally was more active than me that night and that was probably the difference. Whole thing had been brewin' . . . ironically. I'd found out a bit about the bloke who died at the building site. Wasbar. Turns out the inquest had some CCTV footage that the public never saw. Ah, it's all a bit different when you see that. They're walking down the street, middle of the night. He's explaining some parkour move – all the gestures – and she points to the scaffolding. He shakes his head, but it's clear she's goading him. *Chicken, bullshitter* – it'll be stuff like that.

She pushes him into it. He gets halfway up the scaffolding, thinks better of it, starts to come down. More button-pushing from her, pointing to the top. He gives in again, makes it to the top, but the thing isn't safe and it crashes down. Thank God you can't see the impact in detail, but he's under a pile of poles and dust and crap and he's a goner, no question.

'You know what she does then? She sits down, checks herself in her phone. Then she scrolls for ten minutes. *Then* she calls the ambos. She's absolutely fine until the spinning lights show up. *Then* she's into catastrophised-girlfriend mode: running about, pointing, snotty tears. But only then. Ah, yeah. So we know about Tahlia Moore, don't we? I showed that footage to Sal. She had a right to know.'

Bluey sat back and scowled: Reuben bristled.

'Don't look at me like that. Jesus, you lot are sanctimonious, aren't you? I wonder which sort of *professional* I got that footage from, eh? Think on that. She had a right to know because that hollow little cow had her son on the hook and look what happened to him. Tahlia was a disaster zone: Sal had a right to know it.'

Bluey didn't have time to go through the ethics of that, but he knew he'd chew on it later. Reuben's view seemed, at first take, a bit *die in a ditch.*

'Anyway, I can see from the doorway that they're arguing. Sal hits her – at least, I thought she had – and Tahlia kinda squealed. Like she was surprised Sal had done it, like she thought it would never turn out that way or that Sal didn't have the guts. But then Tahlia went limp, proper limp; Sal did well to catch her. Now I think I need to intervene. I mean, I get it; you want to hit Tahlia and you want it to hurt and you want her to remember it. But now she's fainted or whatever and you need to pull your head in, eh?

'But when I get nearer, I see the screwdriver. I can't see any blood on it, but I can see Sal's fist around it. She's holding on to it tight and she's looking at me and she's terrified and I suddenly get it. She looks up, and so do I, and we can both see Bryony at her window, looking down. Sal still has Tahls in her arms, but she's shaking now: weakness, shock, whatever. She lays Tahlia down, real gentle, careful with the back of her head, and we both stand there for a moment.'

For the first time in the telling, Reuben took stock and started to appreciate the importance of what he was describing. Another slurp of the bad coffee; this time, as a crutch.

'I've got a choice there, haven't I? A choice I didn't ask for. We all have. We all get to pick what happens next. I take another look at the screwdriver, and I can't see any blood on it, can't see anything dripping. I make up my mind. I have no idea if anyone else will play along, but I have to do this. Sal's a good person and Tahlia was a crap person and right now that's all that matters. I tell her to go back into the switch room, get rid of the screwdriver in the water tank – the hot water will dissolve any blood, I reckon – and stay there until I speak to her. She just stands there, Sal, likes she expects God's instant retribution and there'll be some lightning bolt any second. Life isn't like that, though, is it? You know that. People do the worst stuff and the world keeps on turning; they keep a straight face and they get away with the entire thing. Eventually – seems like ages – she moves and disappears into the room. I guess she does what I told her with the screwdriver, but I don't know.

'I look up at Bryony. It's about ten seconds before she rings me. I've got a lot of time for Bryony, me. Never mind the age difference, she's quality. We agree this: I should call triple-zero – she already has – and say someone has collapsed but I don't know why. I should plug the wound because the smaller the spread of blood, the further it is from Sally. I should do mouth-to-mouth so that any blood is on me: they won't look for blood on Sal because why would they? I should wait for the ambos, and Sally shouldn't come out until they get there: that way, they'll be her corroborating witnesses. Bryony will take care of the others: she says she can see from up there that Jody and Martyn have witnessed some part of all this – she doesn't know how much. She'll sort them.'

Reuben can see Bluey's frown and pre-empts the question.

'Why do we do this? Because *I* knew what sort of venomous bitch Tahlia was with Wasbar; because *Bryony* had seen poor Josh on a gurney with a nurse pumping his heart; because *Jody* had witnessed how Tahls treated Josh and pushed him into things that undid him. Because *we all* know what Tahlia did to Josh and what Josh's death did to Sal. So we know what Tahlia did to Sal. We know that Sal is a good person. We know that Sal needs protection. All we have to do is lie a bit. Just a bit, each. If we all lie and Bryony coordinates it right, Sally's off the hook. Half the time we won't even have to lie directly. Just miss bits out, just let you make the mistakes. Bryony says it: *only answer exactly what you were asked, don't mention Sally until after you mention the ambos.* It's surprisingly easy. You lot must be so disappointed in yourselves, eh?'

Bluey gave it a poker face but, inside, he was churning. They'd worked out early that witnesses were confused, dissembling, maybe withholding: it had taken a while to consider that they were actively coordinating.

'Sal disappears into the switch room. I guess she puts the screwdriver into the water tank – I reckon it was a good hiding place. It needs to be cut open to get at the insides. You'd never think of it unless you specific-ally looked and, even then, all you'd find is a screwdriver. No blood. All she has to do is face-palm and say she dropped it in there a while back. Bit embarrassing, eh? A qualified engineer dropping a screwdriver into a little hole like that – unlikely she'd ever mention it. Why would she? But, apparently, she's spilled the lollies on the whole thing, so . . .

'I get on to triple-zero while Bryony calls Jody. Then he rings for the ambos as well: Jody. So now we have three concerned citizens and an unconscious woman who might only be very ill. While I try mouth-to-mouth, knowing it won't work, Bryony explains to Martyn what he needs to do. He rings triple-zero: now there's four worried but entirely innocent people. I go over to the drain and make myself puke: I figure it adds a bit of authenticity. It also makes me disappear and reappear – that muddies the waters on everyone's timings and movements so any, uh, *discrepancies* seem reasonable to you. I don't mind the finger being pointed at me for a while because it'll never amount to anything and it keeps the heat off Sal.

'Martyn rings Bryony back to say he's done as he was told. *Bloody hell.* We're supposed to keep the phone at minimum and Bryony's supposed to be the only one ringing out. She can explain her calls as an old woman ringing her neighbours to find out what happened. The more phone calls flying around, the more there is to cover up, eh? She tells Martyn how to justify his call when the cops show up. Then the ambos arrive and I let them in. Now Sal can come out of hiding, as if she saw nothing and is only copping on to the situation when she sees blue lights. I look across, and she can see from the paramedics slowing down that Tahlia's really dead. It sinks in a bit and I feel like she's about to blurt out something. But I shake my head and it seems to talk her out of it.

'Once the cops arrive, it's just about sticking to our stories. We keep them as simple as possible: we all have obstacles blocking the view so you won't be expecting us to know everything. Bryony has us coordinated: we agree on one thing we all "see" and that's the western door closing while Tahlia's on the ground and before the paramedics arrive. That way, you'll go looking for someone on the outside, someone who escaped and dumped the weapon someplace *out there*. It anchors everyone's story and makes it seem like we're all acting in good faith. Bryony reckons every lie needs a truth anchor and if we all have the same one we can't go far wrong. Like I say, smart girl, that Bryony.'

Inwardly, Bluey was forced to agree. He didn't really have time to contemplate how he and Lachie had gone wrong. Maybe it didn't really matter much, provided you solved the case in a day and a half. Most likely it wouldn't concern others, just him and Lachie. Outwardly, he had to show contempt for misleading the police and trying to get a murderer off the hook.

'You – all of you, in fact – could be facing multiple charges here, Reuben. You all knew exactly what you were doing; you all conspired, you all obstructed justice, and you, Reuben, helped a murderer to hide the murder weapon.'

Reuben shrugged. 'We'll cop it if we have to. I admit it – we lied to you, eh? But not much, when you examine it real close. *We answered your questions, Detective.* And it was for a good cause, we all agreed that. Listen, you blokes are in the absolute doghouse with the public right now.

All those shootings across town; we can't go to a restaurant without a free drive-by murder showing up. Dinner and a show, eh? So you don't need any more bad publicity than you have already. Sure, you solved it quick, but you'll look like a bunch of amateurs if we explain how we fooled ya. Sure, take us to court, and then we'll show how half the time it was you not asking the right questions.'

Bluey would deny that, but he suspected that when he looked back he'd still see a ton of opportunities they didn't take.

'Look,' Reuben continued, 'you got where you needed to go pretty fast. You got the killer. She's confessed. You know why she killed. Case closed, yeah? Family get closure, Sal gets convicted, public saves some money. Stop looking a gift horse in the mouth, mate.'

'Hmm. We'll let the prosecutor decide what to do with a bunch of liars who wasted police time and compromised a murder case. Lucky for you, really, that we saw through you within twenty-four hours. If this case had run for months, you'd be even further up the creek and still without a paddle.' Bluey leaned in. 'You'd better confer with your lawyer. *Mate.*'

Chapter 35

Bryony Price had a way of dressing that managed to be classy without being overtly expensive, and comfortable without seeming too casual. In other words, Bluey reflected as he nodded at her and the lounge-lizard lawyer she'd brought with her, the lady had style.

She seemed calm and dignified, too poised for the knowledge she held. Bluey felt that she should be more agitated.

'Bryony, we have Sally Harris and Reuben Pearce in custody. Sally has confessed to killing Tahlia Moore: retribution because she felt Tahlia caused Josh's death.'

Bryony raised an eyebrow. 'There's no *felt* about it, Detective. Tahlia was poison, toxic to those around her. Especially the besotted. Sally couldn't compete with that allure; Josh couldn't cope with it. Tahlia killed her boy so I can't say I'm altogether surprised by Sally's confession.'

'You're not shocked that she admitted the murder, or not shocked that she did it?'

'I can't say I'm altogether surprised . . . *by Sally's confession.*'

Bluey read the room. He hadn't exactly underestimated her previously, but he hadn't broadened his thinking about her when he should have done.

'Reuben has been telling us some interesting things. About a spider in the web: a spider with binoculars and a view of the act of murder. A spider who coordinated a systematic cover-up in an attempt to get Sally Harris off the hook.'

The lawyer harrumphed, but Bryony didn't bat an eyelid. She had a controlled, rhythmic cadence to her speech that spoke of total calm.

'Hmm. I think that you might find that Reuben changes his testimony overnight, once he's had a chance to think about it. Hardly surprising: he's a known liar, isn't he? An acknowledged waster of police time who plays fast and loose when it comes to giving evidence to the law. Not a real shock if he, uh, *enhances* his view one day, but retracts the next. Theatrical type, always has been. Martyn and Jody? They've been solid and consistent from the start, I'm sure. Sally? Well, I presume she'd be guessing about anything we did or didn't do, since she didn't speak a word to any of us that night and hasn't rung anyone since then. And I'm hardly in the mood for self-incrimination, am I?

'I might look like I'm the picture of health for my age, Bluey, but I'm not. I have maybe a year before I'm begging for the goodnight pills or a loaded pistol. I don't have time to mess around. Tahlia was not a nice person. She was not going *to become* a nice person. She had that insouciance that I see all too often; a bizarre expectation that others will orient their lives around you, that only you really matter and everyone is a satellite of you. It's depressingly common now, but that doesn't mean I have to enable it.

'I'm tired, Bluey. I'm old and I'm tired. I don't have patience any more with people who do horrible things. I used to, when I was young. Oh, I was Little Miss Compassionate and I looked for the best in everyone. When you're young, you look at bad people and you think how long their life still has to run. You think, *Ah, they have so many years; they'll change, they'll get it.* Well, I don't think that any more. I save my compassion for people who need it. People like Sally.'

Bluey got it, but he didn't have to like it.

'But you lied, Bryony. Continuously. You encouraged – *enabled* – others to lie. To the police, in a murder investigation. Should that just be forgiven and forgotten?'

Bryony shrugged. 'If you'd asked me thirty years ago, I would have shared your concern and your outrage. Perhaps. Not now. The rot set in when people realised that if they lied, they usually got away with it. Honesty no longer paid – it looks worthy but dull, noble but lacking savvy, callow not smart. If you were caught in a lie, you used to resign and feel shame or humiliation. Now you just brazen it out: shrug, shoot on through and sneer at someone being worried about it. You turn it back on them. They should be ashamed to be so bothered; look how foolishly they demand some integrity.

'It started with Iraq, didn't it? Whatever the other rights and wrongs, we really saw an awful lot of important people know that they were lying but push through anyway. And when they were caught in the act – because what they said was there was not – just a shrug that it was ages ago and, anyway, it all worked out and why are *you* so exercised about it? The people lying and the journalists and judges supposed to hold them to account? The same people. Went to the same universities, had the same mates, shared the same world view, dined at the same restaurants; mingled, friends in common, intermarried. The notion of being honest died around then. Now, it's much worse.

'I mean, we can all look up video of someone saying something – we can look it up on a phone in seconds and watch them do it. Yet they'll still stand there and deny ever having said it. Because there's no longer any sanction, no downside, no loss of face for being caught. So why worry about being caught? That's the world we're in, Detective, and I don't envy you the task. How do you get people to be honest, to value the truth, when they live in a world like that? It's like trying to stop the tides or the seasons.'

She glanced to her lawyer: not so much for permission as to give him fair warning of what she was about to do.

'So, yes, we could have cooked it up together in a few minutes. Theoretically, of course. It wouldn't take much – just a tweak here and there. Throw in a *truth anchor*, if you like. I could imagine a set of instructions: *don't answer a question you haven't been asked, don't mention Sally until after you mention the paramedics, and leave that detail stuff to me and Reuben.* It would be us trying to spare her, being on her side, wouldn't it? You and I can both imagine that fictional scenario, I'm sure. Perhaps you'll charge us, sue us, whatever. But unfortunately for you, Bluey, your bosses need some good PR at the moment, and sending a little old lady to prison wouldn't be that.'

Right now, Bluey couldn't say how his bosses would view it. She might well be right – politics knew when to rear its ugly head. Bryony was clear-eyed and clear-sighted.

'Do you believe you're in the truth business, Detective?'

'I think establishing truth is a job for the courts, not us. We enable their process. We're in the verification and credibility business.'

'Good answer, Detective; surprisingly self-aware.'

Bryony leaned in for the kill.

'I believe that we did the right thing. I will always believe it. Because that, as they say nowadays, is *my truth*. And these days, my truth is magically – and always – just as valid as your truth.'

Chapter 36

Lachie had circled the wagons with Tyson, making sure that he'd been fair and open with Sally, giving her every chance to have legal representation and avoiding putting words in her mouth. Her statement had been a smooth flow that fitted with the data and the evidence and – *almost* – the witnesses. Not coerced, barely even interrupted. He was happy that he'd let Sally say what she wanted and the chips had fallen where they may; but a second opinion never hurt and Tyson backed him in.

A third opinion was useful, too.

He'd rung the prosecutor – thankfully not the one he'd covered in spittle – to make sure of the next protocol. The prosecutor was predictably frosty on her colleague's behalf, but the chance to get a win on a murder within thirty-six hours began the thaw. Sally slurped at a hot chocolate in the interview room while the minutiae of her future life were decided by two strangers.

He came back into the room and Sally gave a watery smile.

'Dot the i's and cross the t's?' she asked.

'Something like that,' admitted Lachie. 'We've got the prosecutor on the way to take a formal statement, but that will just be the bare facts that you've already relayed to me. It's a formality, but it's important. In the meantime . . .'

'Yeah?'

Lachie shifted in his seat and wondered how exactly to phrase it.

'Look, I don't imagine this is a confessional or anything; I'm the cop and you're . . . well, you're you. But like I say, the statement will be very dry and formal. If there's anything you want to talk about that isn't all the nuts and bolts, that's a bit more . . . *feels*? We have a few minutes before the lawyers get here. Maybe about after you put the screwdriver into the tank?'

'Will it affect the case? The sentence?'

'Probably not. But it might . . . help you.'

Sally nodded and took another slurp. The clock ticked, somehow quieter now. Not everyone wanted people to know their inner turmoil, their inner shame, their inner dread. But sometimes, just for a few moments and in the right circumstances, the ground opened up and they let a stranger see inside. Sunlight wasn't always the best disinfectant, but at least it was warm.

'I've killed someone, Lachie. Ended a life. The grief that drove me to despair with Joshie – I've inflicted that on someone else. Her mother, her sister, whoever. But it didn't sink in at first. How could it? We must be hardwired to protect ourselves. There must be an instinct, something from caveman days, that allows us to function after killing. So I sat on that mushie while the ambos flitted about.

'I can see it unwind in their body language. At first they're all efficient speed: their fingers never miss, they communicate in short, sharp, little bursts. Everything crisp and super-accurate. Bless them. God, I wish I had their heart.

'After a couple of minutes they slow down. Because they know – they *know* it's no good. I get up, I want to come over and say something to them. Reuben shakes his head. He's right. I should be the passive, shocked observer who had no idea this was happening and can't imagine what's been going on. Good old Sal, working away in the switch room in the middle of the night so we can all have hot water. Reuben and Bryony and the others are trying to rescue me. It took me *killing someone* for them to truly see my pain. They're good people, but it's all too late.'

Sally paused and took a sip of water.

'You guys were easy to deal with.' She gave an apologetic smile. 'Sorry, but you were. I didn't like doing it – I tried not to lie and I tried to just leave stuff out, so I could say that I never actually lied. But, truly. I thought I was going to get away with it. I wasn't sure if I deserved that or if my conscience would catch up later. Like it is right now. But while you were asking me questions in the courtyard – and again, in my apartment – I could just focus on the answer and what others might say. I wanted it all to dovetail, to be neat and lined up, but Bryony said later that a bit of mess and contradiction was good – it was grit making an oyster. She was the only point of contact after you'd gone, you see: I haven't spoken to any of the others since that moment. It was all working. Be honest, it was working.'

Lachie didn't nod; it would be picked up by the cameras, a fait accompli that could come up in trial. Besides, the bosses would see it as disloyal. He simply gave a long, slow blink.

'It felt terrible to have killed someone. But to avenge Josh? It felt bloody fantastic. I wouldn't have believed you if you'd told me. Horrible thing is: I felt like a parent for once. Terrible as that is, it's what's in me right now. Killing Tahls held no doubt, no ambiguity, for me: I had righted a wrong, so I could rest easy now. Whatever happened afterwards, happened. If you came for me, I'd accept it. If you never got near me, I'd carry on. All the choices and torment this past year, those decisions that held a thousand dimensions? All just flew away. The clarity was unbelievable.

'This past year I've been totally shredded. Joshie tore my world apart even though I loved him. *Because* I loved him. The crazy thing, the *really* crazy thing: every now and then, I envied him. Because he had a place he could crawl into, an ecstasy he could access; when he came back from that place, someone who loved him would ride to his rescue. I had none of that. I was being shredded and no one was even trying to stop the fight. Envying the thing that was unravelling him: picture that. It's what that stuff does to people – flips them around and makes them something – *someone* – they're not.'

Sally's voice softened: still certain, but preternaturally calm. 'But then, after I killed Tahlia, all the shredding stopped. I've been released, I've come back together and it feels . . . *justified*. I know it's wrong, Lachie, and I take the punishment, whatever it is. But it still feels justified. She killed Josh, and she's paid. Hell, she killed Wasbar and now she's paid for that as well. The ledger . . . it feels balanced. So, you know, do what you must. I won't hold it against you.'

Lachie considered his options. He should wait for the lawyer to formally charge her. Sally's lawyer would be here within the hour: better for everyone to have the legal protection. But he remained concerned for her safety. That cool, overly tranquil combination of resignation and composure – he read it as a warning signal.

'You aren't . . . do we need to keep a careful watch, Sally?'

Another swig of the water. 'I wouldn't do that to you, Lachie. Or whoever you have down there, where the cells are. I don't want to inflict that on someone in this building. But here's the bottom line.

'Those things at the fun arcade – those machines with all the coins balanced, ready to fall but they never do? I've felt like that for these past months, since Josh. Right at the edge. I knew I was going to fall, but I didn't know when. I couldn't be sure what would tip me over.

'Like I told you, it feels . . . it feels *right* now. It feels better. Settled. Don't worry, Lachie, it won't be immediate. But I won't make everyone go through a trial, or the cost of keeping me. You won't have much paperwork off this one, I can make sure of that. I can tie it all off with a bow.'

'Are you saying –'

'Yeah. Yeah, I am. And I don't want you to worry about that, because it's okay. It'll be what I want. It all feels finished now; just one thing left to do. Don't you worry.'

She leaned forward, beneficent, like a mother would be.

'You're a good person, Lachie, despite yourself. You don't quite trust yourself to be as nice as you actually are. If I'm offering one piece of advice, and if you're taking advice from a murderer, it would be that: trust yourself.'

She sat back.

'Thanks for listening, mate. I probably do need my lawyer now, and you definitely need a coffee and a hug off someone.'

Chapter 37

The prosecutor took a brief summary from Lachie – reams of paperwork would follow in the ensuing weeks – then drifted to a corner to peck at her phone. She wouldn't go in without the accused having legal representation.

It took a while for Sally's lawyer to arrive and have a head-shaking, staggered conversation with his client. Lachie and Tyson watched through the glass. Lachie could lip-read but consciously chose not to; apart from the ethics of gleaning client–lawyer dialogue, it just felt like an invasion of privacy. Despite himself, he liked Sally. He could understand why she had done it.

Tyson muttered something.

'Sorry, mate, what?'

'I asked how you knew. Apart from the bloodstain, that is.'

'Ah, well, Bluey came back from the forensics lab with the proof that the bloodstain was AB negative. There was only a minuscule chance it wasn't Tahlia's blood. Which meant that Sally must be the murderer. That blood could only have come via her, and after the stabbing took place. Funny – when you know the finishing line and you look back over the obstacle course, it all falls into place.

'While he was down with Forensics, I'd got the phone records for our witnesses. They all got calls from Bryony before the paramedics showed up: pre-emptive command. Reuben got his call while he was in the courtyard with Tahlia's lifeless body. Only Martyn called Bryony back. The rest were passive but regular recipients of calls from her – two conversations before we got to interview them.

'When Bluey got back and we started from the Sally-is-guilty end, other things took on a different texture. Sally was the only one Bryony didn't ring: that didn't make sense. If Bryony was just a nosy old bird who wanted to know the whole business, she'd surely have rung Sally, because Sally was sitting on a mushroom ten metres from the body. Bryony must have had Sally on speed dial because residents usually do that with a caretaker. So not ringing Sally, ironically, stood out.

'At that point we realised they were colluding, rather than just being muddled or withholding for their own reasons. It was coordinated, deliberate. Now we could go back over their witness statements in that light. Now it all made sense. Everything to keep Sally separated from what was going on, from consequence. And, of course, we already understood that Sally had a potential motive. We'd just underplayed it because she hadn't seemed involved. Plus, much of our thinking was based around someone exiting through that western door and chucking the weapon away someplace in the city.'

'They were smart.'

'Yeah, well. We spent too long bemoaning the bits they couldn't see because they were obstructed, not long enough on the bits they could see. Obsessed with lines of sight. Our bad. *My bad*. Plus, yeah, Bryony was smart. We're willing to bet she was something at some point in ASIO, ASD; an acronym pit where they use that kind of brains. She's too calm and together for this to be her first rodeo.'

After charging, Sally was ensconced in a suicide-watch cell – at Lachie's insistence – and he and Tyson returned to the office. Kat had magicked up four chocolate eclairs from thin air.

Bluey took a call from Laxton.

'I see you stumbled over the winning line like Steven Bradbury, then.' Laxton was all heart, and still all-in on team-building.

'Yes, sir, exactly like that. He had a deliberate strategy in that race to hang back. Steven Bradbury was in the world's top ten for years and won multiple world championship medals before he got Olympic gold. Sir.'

Laxton sighed. 'Your career would have gone way better if you hadn't been such a smart-arse, Bluey.'

'Realising that more every day, sir. *Smart* is not the way to progress to senior management. Sir.'

'You solved a murder that had multiple eyewitnesses. Hardly makes you the Don Bradman of crime-fighting, does it? Dot every i and cross every t, Bluey.'

'Sir.'

As Bluey put the phone down, Lachie looked across.

'Delighted, is he?'

'Considers us princes among men, yeah.'

As they ate, Lachie could ignore the anticipation no longer.

'Okay, Kat, be honest. Did you get there before us?'

'Not as such. I had to wait for the same evidence as you. But yes, Sally was on my radar.'

Lachie slumped on to his forearms on the desk. Tyson gave out a low whistle, catching up fast. Bluey eased back and puffed his cheeks.

'Oh, crap.'

Lachie raised himself. 'How did you know?'

Kat eased into her chair and pushed the keyboard out of reach.

'Well, first I looked at motive. Tahlia was a flimsy, peripheral thing who never stayed long in one orbit. So to drive someone to murder, she had to have stayed in that orbit for a fair while, and that wasn't like her. Her family was a possibility, especially once we found Reagan wasn't overseas: she'd stayed longest around Tahlia. But of all the people you spoke to, the only one with a regular, ongoing, emotional overlap with Tahlia's life was Sally, through her son, Josh. That overlap also gave her motive, since we knew Josh died after multiple drug overdoses. It was perfectly possible that Sally blamed Tahlia for Josh's death: motive.'

Bluey couldn't fault the logic.

'Secondly, I looked at your witnesses. They all saw something, they all had a partial view, they all had a different explanation. So far, so *Rashomon*. But here's the thing: there were several things that they all agreed on, as you identified. That the paramedics showed up, that Reuben did mouth-to-mouth, for example. Those things are obvious, and they're backed up by other evidence. It didn't occur to me until you rushed off with the bloodstain on the map. I went back over all those whiteboards and it seemed to me that there's one thing they all agreed on, that they couldn't possibly have agreed unless they'd conspired.'

All three men leaned forward. Kat enjoyed the two-beat delay before the reveal.

'The western exit.'

Bluey's heart sank. *Jeez*, he thought, ahead of Kat's speech but way behind her thinking. Kat turned in her chair.

'Tyson, you demonstrated that the door to the western exit would close from fully open in twelve seconds. Yet four witnesses say they saw it closing. I mean, really? Reuben and Jody and Bryony and Martyn all saw the same door closing in the same twelve-second period? While they were searching for their mobile, vomiting into a drain, popping a tranquilliser and fetching water, walking to the phone, reaching for binoculars? From four different viewpoints?

'No, I wasn't buying that. They'd been coached to say that. Which meant that they'd colluded; so, now the rules of the game have changed. They would only collude on that one observation if they wanted you to think that the murderer had run off, exiting the building and taking the weapon with them. This meant that the murderer actually did neither of those things. They wanted you thinking *outside*, so that must mean the killer is *inside*. Which must mean that some of the witnesses had seen who actually killed Tahlia. That had to be someone who'd never left the building. Only two people other than Tahlia were ever in that courtyard; everyone else stayed in their apartment.'

Kat looked at each of them in turn.

'That narrowed it down to Reuben or Sally. And Sally had motive.'

Lachie shook his head. Kat wiped her hands on a napkin and stood.

'We all got there at the same time, but from different directions. And that, gentlemen, is how I got there. And now it's *lunch-hourish* again.'

After thanking Tyson again and shaking hands, Bluey and Lachie were left alone in the office.

'We did get hung up on what they could and couldn't see, eh? The lines of sight?' asked Lachie. 'Kat said it was like that Japanese film. Rashy? Rasha?'

'*Rashomon,*' Bluey replied. 'Ah yeah, that's a good shout from Kat. It's a classic, Lachie, you should watch it; edumacational and all that. But the theme of the movie, if I can remember right, is that everyone interprets what they see through the filter of their own mind: the prejudices, the perceptions, the wishes, fears, ambitions, and so on. It means that no one is actually a reliable witness; just a flawed, fallible human one.

'Yeah, we probably did get a bit obsessed with sight lines and angles and the height of trees, although I *was* sceptical, as I explained with my *the camera is not an eye* diatribe. Their view was partial because they could only see some of it. But also because they were partial about what they told us.'

'And, they coordinated,' insisted Lachie. 'They deliberately did that.'

Bluey could see *die in a ditch* rising to the surface. Lachie flowed on.

'There's enough for conspiracy charges, Bluey. We can't let this stand, surely? What does that do to future witnesses? They withheld evidence, they lied: at the very least, it's obstruction of justice, wasting police time, hindering a police investigation. I mean, we should –'

Bluey raised a placatory hand.

'Yeah, well. We should write all that up in our bestest neatest handwriting and give it all over to the prosecutor. And then *she* can decide what charges are brought. And we'll go along with her supreme professional judgement, won't we, Lachie?'

He raised an inquiring, challenging eyebrow. The clock ticked seven times. Lachie stared hard at the desk and muttered.

'Yeah, let's do exactly that. Good idea, Bluey.'

Bluey smiled.

'Let's do exactly that.' He raised his coffee cup. 'I have two good ideas a year, mate; that was one of them.'

THE END

Acknowledgements

They say that 'success has many fathers, but failure is an orphan'. On that basis, if I just thank enough people then this book will be a bestseller . . .

I'd like to firstly thank my agent, Hattie Grunewald, of The Blair Partnership. The story of my long journey to publication is now on YouTube, but (spoiler alert) it's Hattie plucking me from the slush pile that was the key. She continues to guide my career, in between the work of adding to the global population!

I'd also like to thank my editor, Toby Jones, and his colleagues at Headline and at Hachette Australia. He's given me the freedom to depart (temporarily) from my Dana Russo series, and I'm very grateful for his faith that I'll deliver. He and I are supported by the multitudes involved in cover design, marketing, distribution and all the other business-thingies that shape a career. As ever, my embarrassing mistakes never reach the reader because of the divine intervention of copy-editor Sarah Day.

Finally, I'd like to mention Graeme Bowden, one of the unsung heroes of the book world. Graeme ran, for over a decade, my local bookshop. Ever patient and generous with his time, Graeme was a staunch champion of local authors, a true gentleman and the kind of store owner every author wishes to meet. Happy retirement, Graeme.